LINCOLN'S BRIEFS

LINCOLN'S BRIEFS

Michael Wayne

Kellom Books
Toronto

Lincoln's Briefs
Michael Wayne

First published in 2009 by Kellom Books, an imprint of Canadian Scholars' Press Inc.
180 Bloor Street West, Suite 801
Toronto, Ontario
M5S 2V6

www.cspi.org

Some quotations in the book are cited from *The Moose Book* by Samuel Merrill,1916; Richard Hayklut, *Divers
Voyages Touching the Discovery of America*, 1582; and Richard Hayklut, *The Principal Navigations*, 1589.
'The Grey Squirrel' by Humbert Wolfe from *Kensington Gardens* (© Humbert Wolfe, 1924) is reproduced
by permission of PFD (www.pfd.co.uk) on behalf of The Estate of Humbert Wolfe. All other works cited are
fictitious.

Every reasonable effort has been made to identify copyright holders. Canadian Scholars' Press Inc. would be
pleased to have any errors or omissions brought to its attention.

Canadian Scholars' Press Inc. gratefully acknowledges financial support for our publishing activities from
the Ontario Arts Council, the Canada Council for the Arts, the Government of Canada through the Book
Publishing Industry Development Program (BPIDP), and the Government of Ontario through the Ontario
Book Publishing Tax Credit Program.

Library and Archives Canada Cataloguing in Publication

Wayne, Michael Stuart
Lincoln's briefs / Michael Wayne.

ISBN 978-1-55130-365-9

I. Title.

PS8645.A93L56 2009   C813'.6   C2009-903656-8

Book design: based on text design by Em Dash Designs.
Cover portraits and interior illustrations by Phil Richards.
Map by The Cartography Office, Department of Geography, University of Toronto.

09   10   11   12   13   5   4   3   2   1

Printed and bound in Canada by Marquis Book Printing Inc.

For Sandra

CANADA THROUGH THE E

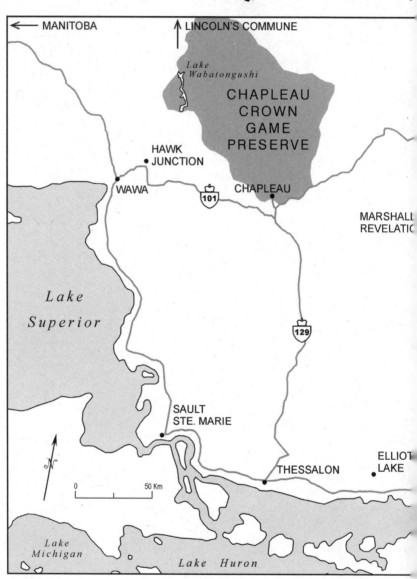

THE GREAT WHITE MOOSE

Joel was in love.

————— I —————

J oel was in love. It all went back to the introductory lecture for History 393, when he first saw Cheryl. Peroxide blonde (his favourite shade), perfect body, nails painted aquamarine to match her eyes. The sight of her had reduced him to whimpers. But when Professor Templeton handed out the syllabus and she saw the reading load, Cheryl was appalled. "Twenty pages a week! Can you believe it? What am I supposed to do? Become a monk?" And so she had dropped the course.

But then he had noticed Samantha. Dangly earrings, ruby lipstick, tattoo of a kitten peering over the top of her jeans from her perpetually exposed midriff. Even now the memory of the tattoo made his knees weak. But by the second week of class she was complaining about the lectures: "How can anyone make a course on the Civil War so *boring!*" And by the third week she had disappeared, too.

Not that it had come as a surprise to Joel that the course was boring. He had read the comments on RateMyProfessor.com: "Dry as dust." "Recommended for anyone with insomnia." "Professor Templeton should have given up lecturing when he died." It sounded exactly like the sort of course he was looking for. Peaceful. Unchallenging. No distractions. Of course, not many women were likely to be enrolled in a course on the American Civil War. But Joel needed just one more credit to graduate; his parents had threatened to cut off his allowance; and Professor Templeton hadn't failed anyone in almost twenty years of teaching. All in all, an ideal environment for the pursuit of love.

After Samantha had been Eleanor. Then Danielle. (Or was it Deirdre? He had trouble with names.) Then Jennifer. One by one they had all stopped attending class. And now there was Mona. Ah, Mona! He loved her with a breadth and depth of passion he had never imagined. She was the fulfillment of all his dreams. Well, would have been if not for her teeth, nose, complexion, and thighs. But at least she was a woman; he was pretty sure about that. And the only one left in the course, as it turned out.

In fact, by the last weeks of the term just five students were regularly showing up for class. Vince Gionfriddo, defensive tackle on the football team, always occupied a seat in the back of the hall. He was on academic probation and had been ordered by the athletic director to attend all his lectures. Which he did. And slept. In the first row, seated side by side directly in front of the lectern, were Baruch Goldbloom and Douglas Wong. They spent each class writing furiously, taking down everything Professor Templeton said. At home in the evening they would check their notes against recordings they'd made of the lecture, then type them up and run them off in duplicate, exchanging copies the following day.

Joel never wrote a thing. He just sat next to Mona, staring dreamily at her profile. Occasionally he would emit a sigh. Mona never turned toward him; she just looked ahead, smiling contentedly. Now and then she would write down a word or phrase that caught her imagination: "Shylow." "Aunt Teetum." She would use a swirling script, add little curlicues, and surround the words with flowers. Other times she would write letters to friends or jot down little reminders to herself: "Get cat food." "Party at the KAP house Friday."

Professor Templeton was oblivious to it all. He never heard Vince Gionfriddo's snoring, never noticed Joel gazing dreamily. He could not even have told you how many students were showing up for class. It could have been five, it could have been fifteen. He spent each lecture eyes fixed on his notes, reading in a monotonous drone. Not that he was bored himself. He loved the history of the Civil War. Every year he tracked down new bits of information and painstakingly added them to his lectures. He was fascinated by detail: the quantity of salt consumed in the Confederacy, the diameter of cannonballs used in naval battles, the number of cases of gangrene reported at Union military hospitals during the Wilderness campaign. Each class was an opportunity to wrap himself in the security of facts and escape for an hour into a time when outcomes seemed much more certain than they did at present.

On this particular day in March Professor Templeton was lecturing about the effect of the war on industrial development in the North. Meanwhile Joel was wondering whether he should talk to Mona. He had been sitting next to her for three weeks now, but they had never exchanged a word. Love was so much simpler that way, confined to the imagination. Still, there were only nine more lectures left in the course, he had no plans or prospects beyond this term, and he longed for someone to help him find himself.

And then his attention was momentarily distracted. Professor Templeton had uncharacteristically injected a note of urgency into his words. "Now this is important," he was saying. "Be sure to write it down." (Mona had dutifully written "important" in her notebook, dotting the *i* with a happy face.) "Pig iron production in the North increased 345 percent during the war." (Mona added a body and corkscrew tail to the happy face and turned it into a little pig.) Joel yawned. And then, as his consciousness was drifting back to concerns of a more personal nature, he heard Professor Templeton say—he *thought* he heard Professor Templeton say—"Before he was supposedly assassinated, Abraham Lincoln spoke very optimistically about the promise of industrial development after the war."

Joel started. "*Supposedly* assassinated?" He looked around. Vince Gionfriddo was still fast asleep at the back of the class. In the front row Baruch Goldbloom and Douglas Wong had their heads down and were writing furiously. Next to him Mona had drawn a tiny stovepipe hat on the pig. He couldn't help himself. "Sir," he blurted out. But Professor Templeton was now completely absorbed in an analysis of coal production in Pennsylvania. "Sir," Joel called out again, and then finally—this time shouting—"Excuse me. Professor Templeton!"

Professor Templeton looked up, startled. He didn't recognize the young man standing in the middle of the lecture hall. "It must be a student," he thought. "I wonder why he's yelling at me? Probably on drugs. I hope he isn't going to take his clothes off." Two or three years earlier a naked woman had burst into a lecture he was giving on Chickamauga, carrying a placard protesting cruelty to animals. She thought it was a lab on vivisection.

"That last point," said Joel. "Could you repeat it?"

Professor Templeton relaxed. "Most certainly," he replied, pleased to find a student who evidently shared his devotion to arcane statistics. "Pig iron production in the North increased 345 percent during the war."

"No, not that. What you said about Lincoln?"

"Lincoln?"

"His assassination."

Professor Templeton looked confused.

"I thought ... I mean ... It sounded like you were suggesting he wasn't assassinated."

"Oh," Professor Templeton said. "Yes, that's true. He was not assassinated."

"He wasn't?"

"No. He faked his own death."

"He did?!"

"He had to. Otherwise he never would have been able to take on a new identity and move to Canada."

Joel burst into laughter.

Professor Templeton looked wounded. "The evidence is quite compelling."

"He's *serious!*" Joel thought.

"He settled up near Lake Superior."

"But why in the world would Lincoln come to Canada?"

"Ah, yes. Well, that is the part that may be a little hard to believe. It seems from the time he was a teenager Lincoln had dreamed of living openly as a cross-dresser. He knew his preferred lifestyle would never be acceptable to the vast majority of Americans with their Puritan values. Canada was a logical choice because, as you know, here transvestites have not only been tolerated but regarded as a vital piece of the cultural mosaic."

Joel opened his mouth to respond, but no words came out. Next to him

Mona had drawn a dress on the pig. In the back of the class Vince Gionfriddo was snoring blissfully, while in the first row Baruch Goldbloom and Douglas Wong continued to write furiously.

Professor Templeton glanced at his watch. "Ah, will you look at that," he said. "I won't be able to complete my discussion of Northern coal production today. I guess I'll have to take it up at the beginning of the next lecture." Then he packed up his notes and was out the door.

Joel shook his head in disbelief. "Did you hear that?" he exclaimed, turning to Mona.

"Yes, it's interesting, isn't it?" she replied agreeably, giving her head a coy tilt.

"Interesting!?" Joel cried. "It's insane!"

"Oh, do you really think so?" she said, pouting. And then she brushed the hair back from her face and gave him a beguiling smile. (Well, as beguiling a smile as she could manage considering her bridgework.)

But Joel wasn't thinking about Mona or her smile. He was thinking about what had just happened. He was thinking about what had just happened and wondering how much the *National Enquirer* paid for its stories.

II

The President led the three men down a hall in the White House. He stopped outside a broom closet, then after looking around to make sure no one was watching, opened the door and hustled them all inside.

There was no light in the closet, and the men had to crush together. The Director of the CIA began to sweat profusely. Three years of hypnotherapy had not eliminated his fear of confined spaces, and the Xanax never seemed to work as well as he expected.

The Director of the FBI spoke first. "I think I'm standing in a bucket of water," he snickered.

The President sighed. "Try not to splash around too much this time, Raymond. We have a critically important matter to discuss."

"In here?!" croaked the Director of the CIA, his voice a rising falsetto.

"No, not in here, Clyde. I just need to find the—"

"Mr. President ..." The Assistant to the President for National Security Affairs discreetly cleared his throat. "Uh ... I believe you ... uh ... what I mean is, sir ... your hand ..." And he cleared his throat again.

"Oh, I'm sorry, Lloyd. I thought that was the concealed knob I'm looking for. If you can just edge over a bit." He felt along the wall. "Ah, yes, there it is." And the back of the closet swung around to reveal a hidden room.

The President stepped inside right ahead of the Assistant to the President for National Security Affairs and the Director of the FBI, his left foot dragging the bucket. The Director of the CIA followed after them, falling face first in a dead faint. "Bring him to, Raymond," the President ordered the Director of the FBI. "There must be a little water left in there."

Photographs of the President from the time he was a baby lined the walls. In each he was smiling broadly. Otherwise the room was empty, except for an American flag blowing gently in a breeze produced by a ceiling fan. To the right stood a door.

"Gentlemen," the President began gravely, "No other person knows about this room. I added it precisely for an occasion like this when ..."

"You built it yourself?" interrupted the Director of the FBI, impressed.

The President paused for a moment. "Ah, no. I see your point. No, I didn't actually build it myself. What I should have said was: No other person knows about this room besides the six workmen who constructed it." He paused and thought some more. "And the contractor who arranged for them." He paused a third time. "Oh yes, and the plumber. I had to bring the plumber in when the toilet backed up." And he indicated the door to the right.

"But aside from those eight other men, no one else knows about this room. I had it built precisely for an occasion like this, when a grave crisis threatens the nation and I have to be sure I can meet with my chief security officers in absolute secrecy."

Just at that moment they heard the sound of a toilet flushing, and into the room from the door on the right walked the Executive Assistant to the Assistant Undersecretary of Transportation. "Grave crisis? What grave crisis?" he asked, wiping his hands on his pants. "Oh, by the way, you're out of paper towels in there, and someone better call a plumber. The toilet's overflowed."

The Director of the CIA grabbed him by the collar, whipped out a Beretta, and held it to his head. "Should I kill him now, Mr. President?"

"No, no, Clyde, that won't be necessary. Lowell has been with me for more than twenty years, since I first ran for the state legislature. He has always been completely devoted to my interests and has committed a long list of indictable offenses on my behalf. It will be enough to take his children hostage."

"And my wife too, sir. You can't afford to take chances."

"Fine," said the President. "Raymond can look after it. But now let's get down to business."

He took a copy of the *National Enquirer* out of his jacket pocket. "This issue will hit the newsstands day after tomorrow," he said, holding it up so the other men could see the front page. "I don't have to tell you what a danger it poses for the country."

"Oprah Loses 40 Pounds in Three Weeks on All-Banana Diet," read the Director of the FBI. "That's astonishing!"

"No, not that. This." And the President pointed to the headline running across the top of the page: "Professor Claims Lincoln Faked Death and Moved to Canada to Live as Transvestite."

The directors of the CIA and FBI and the Assistant to the President for National Security Affairs all gasped. The Executive Assistant to the Assistant Undersecretary of Transportation looked from one face to another and back again. "What's the matter?" he said. "It's not like it's true."

"Of course it's true," exploded the President.

"Lincoln, a transvestite!?" exclaimed the Executive Assistant to the Assistant Undersecretary of Transportation.

"Half the presidents have been transvestites," the President thundered. "Coolidge was a woman, for Chrissakes!"

The directors of the FBI and CIA and the Assistant to the President for National Security Affairs all nodded knowingly.

The Executive Assistant to the Assistant Undersecretary of Transportation put his head in his hands. "I can't believe it!"

"But did Lincoln really fake his own death and move to Canada?" asked the Assistant to the President for National Security Affairs.

"Ah, well, that part I'm not so sure about," admitted the President. "I'd heard rumours about the assassination. But Canada? I don't know ..." He thought for a moment. "Of course, it makes sense. If you wanted to live openly as a transvestite, where better than Canada? It's a den of iniquity up there. Not that I think we should be too hard on the Canadians. After all, they haven't been blessed with our historic advantages. I mean, think of the legacy left us by the Pilgrims."

"Religious fanaticism?" replied the Director of the CIA.

"Smug self-righteousness?" replied the Director of the FBI.

"No! no!" shouted the President. "Decent, God-fearing family values!"

"Ah, yes," the three security officers chorused, "Decent, God-fearing family values!"

"The American people are the finest, most moral, most virtuous people who ever graced the face of the Earth," the President intoned solemnly, dabbing his eyes. "You can't expect them to understand what elevation to the White House does to a man. How it affects him knowing that with one word he can wipe out half the planet." His voice quavered. "They have no idea of the visions that haunt him. Blood-red gashes and smouldering heat. Convulsive bodies, exploding missiles, spewing fluids." His face flushed and sweat began to form on his upper lip. He took out a handkerchief and wiped his brow. "The torment is unbelievable. Who can blame a president for wanting to slip into a filmy negligee or put on lipstick and mascara?"

He stood silent for a moment, staring at a picture of himself as a grinning six-year-old boy wearing a coonskin cap and waving a cap gun as he sat proudly on a pony at Disneyland. He sighed. "American innocence is sacrosanct. We must preserve it at all costs."

"Yes, yes," chimed the directors of the FBI and the CIA and the Assistant to the President for National Security Affairs.

"So what do we do?" asked the Executive Assistant to the Assistant Undersecretary of Transportation.

"We make sure this story goes no further," replied the President grimly, and he waved the copy of the *National Enquirer* in the air.

"But how?"

"Well," said the President, "we better start with the professor who broke the story. Yale Templeton is his name. He teaches in Toronto."

"I can be up there in a couple of hours," declared the Director of the CIA, and he slapped the Beretta into the palm of his hand.

"No, that wouldn't be the way to go, Clyde. Not right now, anyway. First we have to get our hands on whatever evidence he's tracked down."

"I can take care of that, too," the Director of the CIA shrugged, and he slapped the gun into the palm of his hand again.

"No doubt, no doubt," said the President. "But in this case I think it would be better if you let your, uh, special operative handle things." And he gave the Director of the CIA a wink.

The Director of the CIA smiled. "Quite right, Mr. President. The special operative you have in mind would seem to have just the attributes needed to deal with a problem of this nature."

III

Located in the heart of the campus, the Lyceum was an imposing yellow-brick structure with Corinthian pillars, ivy-covered walls, and a domed copper roof. Internationally known for the prestigious Vincent lecture series given each spring in its two thousand–seat auditorium, it symbolized the deep and historic commitment of the university to the very highest standards of intellectual endeavour, as attested to on beer mugs, T-shirts, and bobble-head dolls sold in the lobby.

Adjoining the Lyceum, and directly across the neatly trimmed lawn of Regency Circle from the Edifice Building, where Professor Templeton gave his lectures, stood Graves Hall, staid, granite, and grey. Constructed shortly after World War I, it had served for almost fifty years as the administrative centre of the institution. However, when Felicia Butterworth left her job as head of marketing at the Frito-Lay Corporation to take over as university president and CEO, she decided to spend most of her time in the newly erected prefabricated structure at the entrance to the campus, temporary headquarters for the three-billion-dollar fundraising campaign. "So I can be close to the people who really matter around here," was the way she put it.

Flags representing two dozen of the largest corporate sponsors of the university flew in front of the headquarters, and above the entrance hung an expansive blue banner carrying a picture of the Lyceum surrounded by dollar signs and, in gilt-edged letters, the slogan "A University Education: There Can Be No Better Investment." Inside was a display case containing a scale model of what the campus would look like after plans for expansion were completed. "Your logo here!" was printed on the domed roof of the replica of the Lyceum. United Airlines and Microsoft were reported to have made preliminary bids. Disney had committed eight million dollars to the construction of an IMAX theatre and animated cartoon arcade in the Centre for Reformation Studies, while an Affordable Fashion Design Museum, funded by grants from Club Monaco, Armani Exchange, and Banana Republic, was to be built at the site on Greener Street where the campaign headquarters now stood. On the western edge of the campus the Pasteur Laboratories for Biochemical Research were to be closed and the tower housing them converted into an aluminum silo where the new Centre for the Study of Carbonation would be located. Three soft drink companies were competing for the right to have their names attached to it. Just to the north would be the Maidenform Building, which was expected to employ over forty graduate students from the School of Engineering to investigate stress and support problems. And highlighting the expansion was a new $170 million, six-story office building with state-of-the-art computer equipment that was to serve as permanent headquarters for future fundraising activities.

Felicia Butterworth had been a compromise candidate for the position of university president, between the chairman of the Philosophy department, preferred choice of the faculty, and Trustworthy Ted, the Toronto billionaire acclaimed for his liberal funding of the dramatic arts both in Canada and abroad and for the unbelievable bargains offered on toilet paper, air freshener, and other bathroom products at his discount store, located just blocks down Greener Street from the university ("prices so low you'll *flush* with excitement!!!"). Her arrival was accompanied by the announcement that Frito-Lay would be donating $25 million to the university for construction of a Snack Food Institute. And she, in turn, saw to it that the company's products were now found across the campus, from the Ruffles potato chips, Rold Gold pretzels, and Funyuns Onion-flavored Rings available at all college cafeterias, to the machines dispensing Tostitos tortilla chips in the common room of the Latin American Studies Centre, the Grandma's Homestyle Cookies provided, along with tea, to everyone attending the Gerontology Seminar in the Department of Psychology, the Sunchips multigrain snacks served in the waiting room of the Clinic for Bowel Disorders at the Medical School, and the Smartfood popcorn distributed to students in the Film Studies program. And of course, each scholarship winner now received, along with financial support and a certificate, a box of Cracker Jack, the "caramel, popcorn, and peanut snack with the prize inside."

A selection of Frito-Lay snacks was also available in the conference room at Graves Hall, where seven deans now sat waiting for President Butterworth. They had been careful to arrive a few minutes early, well aware of her views on punctuality. No one said a word. They shuffled papers, shot furtive glances back and forth at each other, and munched nervously on Doritos, Fritos, and Cheetos. Then, exactly at noon, the door flew open and she swept in, taking her place at the head of the table.

Though slender, Felicia Butterworth was an intimidating presence, over six feet tall and with hair so red you might have thought her head was on fire if you saw her at a distance. She wore an ice blue Armani Exchange dress with matching handbag. Her scarf, from Club Monaco, was winter white, embroidered with rampant black horses on a field of gold.

"Gentlemen," she said, addressing the three men and four women seated at the table, "you all know why I called you here. This morning there were three more stories in the *Globe and Mail*, two in the *Star* and *National Post*. The *Sun* has convinced some student from Templeton's Civil War class to appear as a Sunshine girl. Yesterday I had calls from *Time*, *People*, and the *Wall Street Journal*. Letterman wants me for an interview. What next? A free-for-all on Jerry Springer? It's turning into a disaster, gentlemen. I have to give my quarterly report to the Governing Council next Thursday. We're here today to assess the damage." Then nodding to a man in his forties dressed in an immaculately tailored, brown Banana Republic suit, she said, "Tom, let's start with you."

The Dean Responsible for Relations with Manufacturers of Breakfast

Food Products briefly consulted his notes, then stood to speak. "General Mills has elected to continue with its sponsorship of Professor Forenza's research into the development of a chocolate-flavoured cereal that does not adhere to braces or retainers, but Kellogg's has withdrawn its offer of eight additional Tony the Tiger fellowships. That will be particularly harmful for our affirmative action program, since three were earmarked for First Nations students. Eggo is waffling— "

"This isn't the time, Tom."

"... while Post and Quaker Oats faxed me letters yesterday afternoon withdrawing from the Breakfast Foods Consortium. The other companies say they're reserving judgment, but if Schneider Foods drops out, I think we can kiss the Pork Sausage Wing of the new Biological Sciences Complex goodbye."

President Butterworth sighed. "Jessica?"

A young woman dressed in an immaculately tailored, green Club Monaco suit rose to speak. "We won't know the full impact on our relations with the major studios for some time. But yesterday *Variety* reported that a number of actors will protest use of their voices in the Martin Luther cartoon if you continue to bar Templeton from speaking to the media. Since Disney planned on previewing the cartoon at the opening of the arcade, that could be a public relations nightmare. I hear Angelina Jolie's agent has already told Disney executives she won't do the voice for Greta, the sultry nun who haunts Luther's dreams. I think the arcade will likely still go ahead—Spielberg hinted to me he'll step in if Disney drops out—but the IMAX centre is almost certainly gone. On the other hand—although I don't know how you'll feel about this—the Coen brothers have offered us $20 million for the rights to the Templeton story, provided we let them use the campus for location shots. The word is George Clooney would star with Susan Sarandon in the role of the diabolical university president."

Felicia Butterworth grimaced. "That's enough. It's even worse than I realized. The rest of you, have your reports on my desk by the morning." Then she punched a button on the intercom in front of her. "Dolores," she said, "send in Penney."

A moment later a short, stout, balding man with wire-rimmed glasses, wearing a charcoal Armani Exchange suit and carrying a black attaché case, walked into the room.

"Those of you who were here under my predecessor know Harris Penney," Felicia Butterworth remarked, directing him to take a seat at the end of the table. "His law firm has represented us in negotiations with the Faculty Union for more than twenty years." Then, turning to him, she said, "You know the problem, Harris. What I want to know now is how do you propose we deal with it? I might add, speed is of the essence."

"Of course," Penney replied. "I've already drafted a letter to Professor Templeton outlining the substance of your concerns. I thought it best not to be too specific at this point, just in case we run into a lawsuit down the road. He has three months to submit a formal reply, after which—"

"No! No! We don't have three months. We don't have three days. I want to terminate him immediately!"

Penney stared at her in disbelief. "Absolutely out of the question. He has tenure."

"But he's made us a laughing stock all across North America!"

Penney shrugged. "Section 6, Paragraph 3 of the collective agreement, and I quote: 'Behaviour deemed by the administration to bring the university into disrepute will *not* be regarded as just cause for dismissal.'"

"But ..."

"The union insisted. Otherwise they would never have agreed to the clause requiring professors to do two-minute advertising spots for Nike before each lecture."

"Can we suspend him?"

"Yes ... if you don't mind a bloodbath over the freedom-of-speech issue. The union would hold an emergency meeting, organize a protest. They might even try to call a strike under Section 11 of the collective agreement. Then you'd have pickets in front of Graves Hall, television cameras—"

"All right, all right."

"What about getting him to take a leave of absence?" suggested the Dean Responsible for Relations with Manufacturers of Feminine Hygiene Products.

"That would be fine," replied Penney. "But only if he agrees, and then you'd have to pay him his full salary."

"Ridiculous!" snorted Felicia Butterworth. "It would be like rewarding him for his lunacy."

"Not to mention claims by the union that you were setting some sort of precedent," said Penney. "And that would open up the Pandora's box of sabbaticals all over again."

"If only he'd committed a felony," cracked the Dean Responsible for Relations with Manufacturers of Breakfast Food Products.

"You mean when he was supposed to be lecturing?" asked Penney.

"What?"

"Well, say, for example, he hijacked a Brink's truck."

"I wasn't being seri—"

"Because if he did it when he was supposed to be lecturing *and* you can prove that it was premeditated—that is, that he *intentionally* skipped his lecture—then you'd have a case against him."

"*Then* we could fire him," commented Felicia Butterworth dryly.

"No, then you could put a letter of reprimand in his file."

"A letter of reprimand?"

"For neglect of duty, under Section 9, Paragraph 7 of the collective agreement. Three reprimands and he'd have to appear before a disciplinary panel comprised of one representative from the administration, one from the union, and one mutually agreed upon by the two parties."

"And *then* we could fire him."

"And then, if at least two of the representatives deem his behaviour contrary to the standards set out in Section 17 of the collective agreement, you could send a letter to the chair of the History department requesting he take the finding into account when awarding merit pay for the following year."

Felicia Butterworth stared at him. "So what you're saying is, *if* he knocks over a Brink's truck, and *if* it can be shown he did it when he was supposed to be lecturing ...

"Providing you can establish he made up his mind to skip the lecture before he decided to hijack the truck."

"... then he *might* not get a raise the following year."

"Oh, he'd get a raise. The collective agreement mandates a 3 percent cost of living increase for all faculty. But his merit pay would undoubtedly be below average ... Unless, of course, he'd published a book during the previous year, in which case, History department guidelines dictate he must receive the maximum increase allowable."

"Then," said Felicia Butterworth, her fury rising like lava in a volcano, "how do you ever get incompetents out of the classroom here?"

"Oh, that's no problem," replied Penney cheerfully. "We just move them into the administration." And the four deans at the table who had not been hired by Felicia Butterworth all smiled and nodded their heads in agreement.

Felicia Butterworth rose from her chair and leaned forward on the table. "Now let's be clear about this," she declared in stiletto tones. "I was hired by the university for one reason. To implement a management strategy based on sound marketing principles. Animated cartoon arcades, centres for the study of carbonation, endowed chairs in the chemistry of adhesive tape do not fall from heaven. Mahogany like this," and she slammed her palm down on the burnished finish of the table, "does not grow on trees. Corporate sponsors are the lifeblood of this university, the key to our very existence. Without them we're no better than Berkeley or any other provincial backwater in the United States or Canada."

Then she addressed Harris Penney. "Notify Templeton at once that he's suspended without pay."

"But the collective ag—"

"Damn the collective agreement. The union has to deal with *me* now." Then leaning forward once more she slowly took in all the people around the table, stabbing them one after the other with her eyes. "Let me be perfectly clear about this. At the end of the day I *will* get what I want. I always do. Those of you who were with me at Frito-Lay know what I mean." And two women and one man at the table shuddered perceptibly.

It all began with the moose,
I suppose.

IV

It all began with the moose, I suppose. First, however, you will need some background information.

Eight generations of Templeton men had gone to Yale, which is how he came to be named after the Ivy League university. Not that his mother had been at all happy with the choice. Born in the very proper neighbourhood of Rosedale just before World War I, the sixth and youngest daughter of a judge whose lineage traced back to the Family Compact, her reverence had been for Tudor England, not twentieth-century America. But the family fortune—and her own prospects—had slowly been washed away by her father's thirst for Hiram Walker. Small, wilful, and painfully unattractive, she had long given up any thought of marriage on the day in 1953 when Forster Templeton arrived for dinner.

He was in Toronto to receive an award from an international bankers' association. "You must look up an old chum of mine from Upper Canada College," a fellow member on the board at the country club had told him. And so he had. He was charmed by the old Victorian house on Dunbar Road and, over the course of the evening, fell in love with the genteel refinement of Rosedale life. He fell in love with her, too, although here the encroaching Alzheimer's might have had something to do with it. They were married a few weeks later in Grace Church on-the-Hill, and after a honeymoon on his yacht in Long Island Sound, returned to his mansion in Greenwich to live. It can hardly be said she was taken by surprise when he died just a year later, several weeks before Yale was born. After all he was eighty-nine at the time of their wedding. Still, she had never imagined he would be shot in a mugging. But then neither she nor anyone else who knew him had been aware he was down in Harlem mugging welfare recipients on those days he forgot to take his medication. None of which mattered in the end, because by the time of his death, she realized she had never much cared for him. She also thought Greenwich was gaudy, New Englanders vulgar, and not to put too fine a point on it, hated everything about the United States with an intensity impossible to put into words. And so she took her son back to Rosedale, staying just long enough to finish the paperwork related to her husband's estate. Then, when her substantial inheritance had safely been transferred to Barclays Bank, she did what she had always dreamed of doing and moved to England.

They settled in the old market town of Saffron Walden, named for the crocus cultivated locally during the late Middle Ages for use in dyestuffs and medicinal products. Quaint, untouched by industrial development, and dotted with Tudor cottages, the town had an obvious attraction for a woman who since childhood had immersed herself in the literature and music of the sixteenth century and liked to dress up as Elizabeth I. And based on an argument she had overheard between her parents when she was young, she was convinced that her ancestry traced back, through her mother's grandfather, to the powerful house of de Mandeville, which had built a castle and abbey in the vicinity during the twelfth century. Years of research in genealogical records had failed to establish the family connection, however, or indeed to disprove her father's Hiram Walker–induced assurances that her maternal great-grandfather was actually a Talmudic scholar from Lemberg who fled to Canada after being caught in bed with the rabbi's wife.

All of which I mention only to explain why Yale Templeton, descended on one side from a line of wealthy American bankers and on the other from a line of distinguished Canadian jurists, grew up on a quiet lane in a small town in England. Indeed, aside from a brief trip back to Rosedale to attend the funeral of his grandfather, he spent his entire childhood within twenty-five kilometres of Saffron Walden.

It was a cloistered existence. His mother refused to have a telephone or television in the house and did not read the newspapers. They owned a radio, but she only turned it on for BBC concerts and only when the program included English choral music, especially Elizabethan madrigals.

But then, there were so many things to be avoided in contemporary society, she warned her son. For years afterward he would remember her cautionary lectures with great clarity. About London. ("A sink of iniquity. Drunks in the gutters. Pickpockets in the alleys.") Immigrants. ("Oily-skinned cutthroats just waiting to get their hands on unsuspecting little boys.") The "lower classes." ("Immoral, slow-witted, dirty.") But mainly about sex. Not that she ever used the term. Instead she filled his mind with images obviously meant to disgust: overripe female bodies awash in sickly sweet scents, lacquered lips, flesh dripping with perspiration. "They'll promise you pleasure," she confided in hushed tones, glancing around as if she thought someone might be listening, "but give in to temptation and you'll end up in disgrace." He was horrified. "Who were *they*?" he wondered. Women, it seemed. But how to reconcile the images with the matronly ladies who came to tea or the young girls he occasionally saw on the streets or in the park down the road from his house?

Nor did his confusion about sex end once he entered school. His mother enrolled him at the prestigious Robinson-Fallis Academy for Boys, just a short walk from their home. Although he had several sexual encounters during the years he was there, he never identified them as such. And because he lived at home, he was spared the ritual initiation into puberty inflicted on those other small, bookish students who boarded at the school.

But then, school was bewildering in so many ways. "After you hit the ball, run to the wicket over there," the games master shouted at him, "then run back again." "Run back again? Whatever for?" he wanted to ask. And in one game you carried the ball. In another, touching the ball with your hand was a penalty. Then there was the music the boarders liked to listen to. Loud, raucous, discordant. Nothing like the lilting melodies of William Byrd and

Thomas Morley. When he was in third form, two of his classmates were expelled for sneaking off to Newcastle to see some band called the Animals. "The Animals! What will mother say!" he wondered. He was only glad she hadn't heard the rumour that one of the boys had been caught with marijuana.

Games, music, sex. Why bother with particulars? Just about every aspect of modern existence was baffling to Yale Templeton. If his personality had been different he might have sought refuge in a fantasy world. But, unlike his mother, he had such little imagination. So instead he escaped into the past. Even as a small boy he could often be found wandering around the historic monuments of Saffron Walden: the Roman and Saxon graves; the remnants of the de Mandeville castle; vestiges of a medieval maze cut into the earth. Later, when he was school age, his mother would take him to the town museum, with its famous necklace dating back to the ninth century, and to historic Audley End, the mansion built in the early seventeenth century by the Earl of Suffolk, Lord Treasurer to James I. And there would be trips to Cambridge, less than an hour away, to visit the Fitzwilliam Museum, where he would roam the lower galleries, with their artifacts from ancient Syria and Phoenicia, Greece and Rome. The Egyptian mummies captivated him, and for weeks after seeing them for the first time he had disturbing dreams in which his mother was embalmed and wrapped in linen.

More than anything else, however, he developed an interest in the history of war. It would be difficult to say why. Maybe it was that he needed no understanding of women to talk about weapons and battles and strategy. Or maybe it was that wars allowed him to concentrate his mind on specifics: the deployment of soldiers, the quantity of armaments, statistics on casualties. Even then he was developing that fascination with detail that would so bore a later generation of students. Or more likely he was attracted to wars simply because he knew their outcome in advance. They had a definitive quality, a certainty, lacking in contemporary life.

By the time he was ten, books on war spilled out of his shelf and across the floor of his bedroom. Two years later his mother reluctantly allowed him to turn the den into his own personal library. He read about ancient wars and modern wars, border wars and continental wars. He read about the Wars of the Roses and the War of Jenkins' Ear, the Hundred Years' War, the Thirty Years' War, the Seven Years' War, and the War of 1812. And then for Christmas when he was eleven, he received a present from a distant relative in the United States who must have heard about his interest. It was a picture book of the American Civil War. And although it can scarcely be said he recognized it at the time, from that moment the future course of his life was set.

There is no obvious reason why the photographs by Mathew Brady and the coloured illustrations of Union and Confederate soldiers should have taken possession of him as they did. By this time he had seen thousands upon thousands of pictures of other soldiers in other wars. But compulsive disorders are invariably mystifying to those not similarly afflicted, and it is a sad truth that many otherwise normal people—not to suggest Yale Templeton was otherwise normal—have found themselves similarly obsessed with the American Civil War. His mother was appalled, of course, having never lost her antipathy to the United States. She would have much preferred to see him learning about the English Civil War and the triumphs of those Cavaliers she had managed to convince herself were her ancestors. So he did his best to keep his reading a secret from her, reserving his contemplation of Lee and Jackson, Grant and Sherman, and the battles of Antietam, Shiloh, and Gettysburg for the hours he spent alone at the town library in the old Corn Exchange on Market Square. And by the age of fifteen, he knew as much on the subject as anyone in the British Isles, except perhaps for a handful of scholars.

Not that he exhibited any sort of gift for original thought. His was a singularly pedestrian mind. But he had an extraordinary memory. By fourth form he was including quotations from Thucydides, Mahan, and other legendary military historians in the examination answers he wrote at Robinson-Fallis. Although quiet and timid, he was easily elected president of the Junior History Society, his wealth of accumulated knowledge discouraging other candidates for the office. He increased the meetings from once a month to twice a week, with members discussing such topics as "Confederate Cavalry in the Shenandoah Valley," "Union Strategy at Missionary Ridge," and "Who Was to Blame for Picket's Charge?" When the master responsible expressed reservations about the narrow range of topics, he replied that it "reflected the interests of the membership," which by the third week of term included just himself, two foreign exchange students from Greece (neither of whom could speak English), and the son of a Civil War specialist from Vanderbilt University on leave for the year at Cambridge. At the annual banquet held by the Society during Easter term, the Vanderbilt historian gave a talk on Confederate tactics at the Battle of Chancellorsville, which left Yale Templeton so impressed he neglected to point out the three errors of fact and one misquoted passage he had noticed.

It was a foregone conclusion that he would go on to Cambridge. Otherwise, as his mother explained, he would be unable to continue living at home. Caius College was the obvious choice, having become, under Joseph Needham, the renowned authority on the development of Chinese science, the preeminent centre for the training of historians at the university. At his interview, he dazzled the examiners with the broad sweep of his learning and not only was granted admission but became only the third student from Robinson-Fallis to win a scholarship.

His next three years were almost entirely given over to researching and writing essays. Naturally, he concentrated on American history. He attended all the lectures offered by Jonathan Steinberg, Hugh Brogan, and R.J. Post. In Part I of the Tripos, he sat "American History from 1689 to the Present Day"; in Part II, he enrolled in the seminar Post offered on "Race Relations in the United States from 1863 to 1896." And because Cambridge had recently introduced the option of the undergraduate thesis, he was able to indulge his passion for the Civil War by writing a paper of ten thousand words (his petition to triple the prescribed maximum length having been rejected) on the battle of Chancellorsville. "So I can correct the errors of the talk I heard at Robinson-Fallis," he explained to his entirely disapproving mother. The thesis was subsequently published, in expanded form, in the *Annals of the Cheshire Round Table* on the American Civil War.

The hours he spent in the university library (not to mention on the bus travelling back and forth between Saffron Walden and Cambridge) left him little time for addressing the problem of his arrested social development.

However, at meetings of the Caius History Society, he did manage to meet some students who shared his devotion to obscure detail. They would all get together in the Junior Common Room after dinner to exchange arcane bits of information or debate the proper form for citing anomalous primary sources in footnotes. On rare occasions he accompanied a friend to The Red Lion, although his mother repeatedly warned him about the dangers of pubs. He would discreetly sip tea, look around nervously, and never, absolutely never, enter into conversation with a woman.

Indeed, his bewilderment about women and sex only deepened during his years at Caius. The college did not open its doors to female students until several years after he had graduated, so there was never a chance he would find himself sitting next to a woman in the dining hall or encounter one in the Common Room. In the privacy of his own room, at night with the lights out, the images of female bodies conjured up by his mother sometimes intruded into his thoughts. He found release in the conventional way. But since her lectures on sexual activity had warned about public humiliation, not damnation, these episodes did not leave him with a sense of guilt, only additional bewilderment.

With one exception the examinations in history at Cambridge tested memory not originality. The exception was the compulsory general historical essay, which asked students to comment on a quotation by some notable figure. The year he sat Part II of the Tripos the quotation came from Lord Namier and had something to do with the role of psychology in historical interpretation. Much to his astonishment, he had never encountered the quoted passage before. At a complete loss, he filled his answer booklets with as many facts as he could scribble in three hours, only a handful of which were even remotely connected to the issue Namier had sought to raise. However, because he was able to provide footnotes documenting the source for each fact (including the author, title, edition, and place and date of publication for every book cited, as well as the relevant page number), the examiner interpreted his confusion as brilliance and awarded him a first. Since all the other examinations merely tested his ability to recall facts and statistics, he recorded firsts in them as well. He graduated with distinction, never once, it must be acknowledged, having given expression to anything approaching an original thought about history or anything else.

His grades were certainly high enough to secure him a doctoral fellowship at a prestigious university in the United States, the logical place to pursue graduate studies for someone with his interests. At Yale, perhaps, where he might have had the eminent historian of the American South C. Vann Woodward as a supervisor. But of course, his mother never would have permitted such a thing. So he remained at Cambridge, moving to Churchill College, where he could continue to study under R.J. Post, who had the advantage of being a very respected and respectable Englishman. His dissertation would deal with the Civil War; there had never been any question about that. But which specific topic? Or rather, which topic that would not require research in archives or libraries in the United States, since that was out of the question? After consulting with his mother he decided to write about attitudes toward the Civil War in the British press. There would have to be several trips to London, he explained to her. She reluctantly agreed, though only under certain conditions: He could not stay in the city overnight. He could not go to pubs. He could not speak to "strange women." (Not that he knew what a "strange" woman looked like.) And he must stay out of those neighbourhoods where immigrants or members of the lower class lived.

Three years later the dissertation was finished. "A Survey of Facts, Statistics, Editorial Opinions, and Related Material Regarding the American Civil War as Published in the British Press between April 9, 1861 and April 12, 1865" was the size of the Manchester telephone book. "And about as interesting," one of the readers commented. Yale Templeton had painstakingly examined 97 newspapers dated from the firing on Fort Sumter to Lee's surrender at Appomattox—large papers and small papers; papers from cities and papers from villages; papers from the North and papers from the South; papers from Liberal strongholds and papers from Tory strongholds. He had looked at news reports and editorials, cartoons and notices of public subscriptions. And the central conclusion he had reached? "No broad patterns can be discovered." But then, broad patterns had never really mattered to Yale Templeton. It was detail that excited him—to be able to report that on March 23, 1863, on the same day it informed its readers about the Emancipation Proclamation, the *Sheffield Register* ran a story regarding a drunken Union soldier who had shot a cow at the recent battle of Murfreesboro in the mistaken impression that it was General P.G.T. Beauregard. Now that, to Yale Templeton, was history.

"It's a monumental achievement," commented one of the readers when they all sat down to evaluate the dissertation. "Truly it is," agreed R.J. Post. "To say so much and have so little to say." And everyone nodded. Then, as anticipated, they awarded him a passing grade. No one wished to make him write another draft. Not when they would have to read it.

On a pleasant Saturday in June at two in the afternoon, Yale Templeton joined several hundred other students at the Senate House. He was dressed in a new black suit and, as prescribed by university regulations, wore a white tie and the hood and gown of someone about to receive the degree of doctor of philosophy. The senior proctor read the supplicants and then, at the appropriate moment, the praelector of Churchill College took him, right hand by right hand as was the custom, and led him to the vice chancellor to announce that he was of respectable character and had reached the level of academic attainment required to receive his degree. Then Yale Templeton knelt down and placed his hands together between those of the vice chancellor, who, with all the dignity appropriate to such occasions, pronounced the formal statement of admission to the doctorate.

Ten minutes later he was outside on King's Parade with his mother. He rented a punt and took her down the Cam to Grantchester, where they celebrated over scones and tea. Then it was back to Saffron Walden to begin preparing for his future. He had a great deal to do in only a short time. There were lectures to write, reading lists and handouts to put together. The first year of university teaching is always the most demanding. And in his case there would be additional stresses. He would be leaving the security of home for the first time. Not incidentally, he would be leaving his mother as well.

V

There had been five candidates for the position in American history at Toronto: Yale Templeton, a high school history teacher from Buffalo, a professor of Armenian history at the University of Toledo who had misread the job advertisement, a middle-aged caterer from San Francisco who was just getting over a failed relationship and wrote that he *desperately* needed a change of scenery, and a recent graduate from Harvard, described by her supervisor, the renowned historian David H. Donald, as "without question the finest student I have had in more than thirty years of teaching." Her dissertation, an investigation of the effect of the Civil War on family structure and gender relations in the Midwest, had been published by Oxford University Press. Quickly recognized as a landmark work in women's history—"vastly extending the boundaries of the subject," according to the admiring review in the *New York Review of Books*—it had been awarded the prestigious Bancroft Prize. Under the circumstances, the four men who made up the search committee had little difficulty coming up with a shortlist. They chose the caterer, the professor of Armenian history, and Yale Templeton.

A recent external review of the History department had noted a "lack of diversity" in the faculty. Accordingly the Dean of Arts and Sciences sent a memo to the department chairman requesting the search committee explain its reasons for leaving the graduate of Harvard off its list of candidates. The committee produced a detailed report outlining her numerous shortcomings, including her susceptibility to PMS, the likelihood that she would agitate for access to the men's bathroom, and the probability that one day she would decide to get married and have children, being "more attractive than most woman historians of our acquaintance." Privately the chairman complained that the commitment to "affirmative action" was sacrificing "standards" for "political correctness."

At his interview Yale Templeton presented a paper entitled "Some Rather Interesting Facts and Statistics on the Second Battle of Bull Run as Reported in the Lincolnshire *Sunday Post*." The professor of Armenian history gave a talk, in Armenian, documenting atrocities against Armenians throughout history, especially Armenian professors living in Toledo. As for the caterer, he presented a critical analysis of the menus chosen for all the inaugural balls from the first administration of Dwight Eisenhower to the second administration of Ronald Reagan, including suggestions about how they could be adapted for departmental receptions. He concluded his presentation by having one of his assistants wheel in a Lady Baltimore Cake in the shape of the Star-Spangled Banner, while a Dixieland band played "America the Beautiful" in ragtime.

When the faculty met to consider who would best serve the interests of the department, sentiment was divided about equally between Yale Templeton and the caterer. The debate had gone on for over two hours, with every prospect of a deadlock, when St. Clair Russell Hill, elder statesman among the historians and universally respected, rose to address his colleagues. He was a commanding presence, standing almost six feet, four inches tall, with a sweep of white hair.

"Gentlemen," he began solemnly, "when I first arrived here from Oxford forty years ago, this department had a distinguished reputation. Sir Graham Wright was chairman then, and Deacon Meredith was here, and Chesterton-Smythe. Fortescue had just completed the first volume of his magnificent work on the exchequer under Walpole, and Gray was well into the research that would lead to his brilliant refutation of Gibbon. Nor need I remind you of Ingersoll's seminal essay on the role of the poultry trade in the formation of Canadian national identity. These men were giants in the profession, gifted teachers, incomparable scholars." He paused to catch his breath. "But we all know what has happened since then. I think I can best express it in the immortal poetic phrases of Humbert Wolfe:

> Like a tall gray coffee pot
> Sits the squirrel.
> He is not all he should be,
> Eats by dozens trees
> And kills his red brown cousins.
> The keeper, on the other hand, who shot him
> Is a Christian
> And Loves his enemies.
> Which shows
> The squirrel is not one of those."

"Ah, I see what you mean," said the chairman. "The decline of Christianity has led to a moral relativism in the university that threatens our values, our intellectual standards—dare I say it, even the very survival of Western civilization."

"Decline of Christianity?" said Hill. "Western civilization? I'm talking about squirrels, man! Look around you! We're overrun by squirrels!" Everyone looked around.

"Don't you see them," he shrieked. "Squirrels on the tables, squirrels on the chairs, squirrels hanging from the chandeliers! Yesterday I found three squirrels in my file cabinet. They were stealing my lecture notes again. I suspect it was the same squirrels who abducted my wife and children. Possibly the same squirrels responsible for the Korean War. This is no time for Armenian caterers, no matter how expert in producing a serviceable raspberry coulis. We're under siege. We need a man of courage and fortitude. We need a man of military bearing and aristocratic breeding. We need a man versed in the historic arts of warfare." And so they unanimously voted to offer Yale Templeton the position of assistant professor, giving him special responsibility for defence of the Edifice Building perimeter.

Of course, Yale Templeton would have much preferred to remain at Cambridge. However, he lacked the wit and charm necessary to keep a roomful of students rapt for hours while saying absolutely nothing of consequence, a requisite of every Cambridge don. The only job in England available to him was at Birmingham, which to his mother meant factories, immigrants, and the working class. "Think of the people you'd have to associate with!" At least Toronto had Rosedale. And one of his aunts, now an elderly widow, still lived in the old family home.

So he rented an apartment not far from Dunbar Road, just a half hour walk from his office and the university library. Two years later Louisiana State University Press published his dissertation, in greatly expanded form, under the title *The View from Fleet Street and Beyond: English Observations on the American Civil War.* "The final word on the subject!" read a quotation on the dust jacket, taken from a review in the *Journal of Southern History* by the distinguished historian Bruce Catton. (The full quotation actually read: "We can only fervently pray that this is the final word on the subject!") A year later Yale Templeton received tenure.

Publication of his book brought invitations to participate at the annual conferences of the major historical associations. He had promised his mother he would never travel to the United States. However, without letting her know, he agreed to serve on a panel entitled "The Role of the Press in the Civil War" at the Organization of American Historians meeting to be held in Chicago. The prospect of sharing his findings with colleagues was exciting, taking him back to those happy days when he had debated proper footnoting techniques with friends in the Caius College Historical Society. "I'll give the talk I prepared for my interview at the university," he decided, "maybe just adding a few more details."

He arrived in Chicago full of expectation. However, the militant black nationalist cab driver who picked him up at the airport harangued him all the way to the hotel about "honky imperialists," then stole his watch for "reparations." At the hotel the bellboy who carried his bags kicked him in the shins for failing to come up with an adequate tip. Then, when in alarmed response, he gave the maid fifty dollars, she attacked him with a mop, thinking he was offering her money for sex.

He spent the next three days secluded in his room, using the time to go over and over the paper he would present. He paid special attention to punctuation, since colleagues had warned him that American scholars were especially crude and objectionable when they felt someone fell short of their high academic standards. By the time of the panel, he knew the talk by memory and presented it in the monotone he understood to be appropriate to such occasions. It went quite well, he thought as he sat down, although he was sorry that the chairman had cut him off after fifty-five minutes, since he had only just begun to recount the height of all the officers at the Second Battle of Bull Run mentioned by name in the Lincolnshire *Sunday Post*.

To his disappointment, the commentator on the panel, eminent Princeton historian James M. McPherson, addressed most of his remarks to the other two papers at the session, noting only that "Professor Templeton has obviously tracked down a wealth of detail about the Second Battle of Bull Run, and now I'm sure we'll all wait with interest to see what use he is able to make of it." "Now, what in the world does he mean by that?" Yale Templeton wondered.

But then came the questions from the floor. "What about Chomsky's new ideas on manufacturing consent?" demanded a graduate student from Penn. "No," interjected a graduate student from Johns Hopkins, "he needs to talk about Marx." "Not Marx himself but Gramsci," called out a third student. "Durkheim!" "Foucault!" Startled, Yale Templeton blurted out the quotation by Lord Namier he had been asked to discuss on his examination at Cambridge. This produced puzzled looks and momentary silence, until a feminist from Smith shouted out, "You don't discuss how women were kept out of the newspaper industry in England." "And out of the military in the United States," cried another from Oberlin. "And why don't you admit that the press lords were honky racist imperialists just like the Union soldiers," shouted a man who looked uncannily like the cab driver who had picked him up at the airport.

But the most humiliating moment came at the very end of the question period when a man wearing a Confederate cap and speaking in a long Southern drawl commented politely, "I'm afraid you got it wrong about Captain Bagley of the Fourth Virginia Regiment, Professor. He was five foot eight and three-quarters, not five foot six and a half."

Yale Templeton returned to his room, packed his bags, and asked for a cab. The driver turned out to be the same black nationalist who had driven him to the hotel. He harangued him once again about "honky imperialists" then stole his new watch. Yale Templeton boarded the plane for Toronto, returned to his room, and spent the next seven years going back and forth between his apartment and the university. And that is surely how he would have spent the rest of his days, had it not been for a conversation he had with the wife of the chairman of the History department.

VI

A s she always did, the chairman's wife got drunk as soon as she arrived at the end-of-term reception. And, as was always the case when she got drunk at the end-of-term reception, she looked around for Yale Templeton to torment. He was standing by himself in a corner, trying not to catch her attention. But as always, his attempts to avoid her were hopeless. She jacked up her considerable bulk, carted it over toward him, and bounced him up against the wall. She moved in so close the scotch on her breath misted his vision.

"And you've been in Canada how long now?" she slurred.

He cleared his throat while trying to make himself smaller. "Nine years come August tenth," he replied in as amiable a tone as he could manage under the circumstances.

"And in all that time you mean to tell me you've never seen a moose?"

Since moose, let it be said, are rarely found wandering south of St. Clair Avenue in Toronto, and *absolutely never* on the streets of Rosedale, he could only repeat what he'd already told her several times. Yes, it was true, he had never seen a moose.

"And you call yourself a Canadian?"

"No. I would never do that. I'm English."

"I know, I know. That crazy mother of yours. But you're descended from distinguished Canadian stock. Your ancestors were among the founders of this country. They belonged to the Family Compact. You're a historian. Have you no interest in your own personal history?"

"Well, to tell you the tr—"

"Forget England. England is nothing but pretence now. It was never anything more than that, really. But, Canada. Ah, Canada. Canada is honest simplicity. Canada is the yet-to-be-realized promise of human goodness and generosity. Canada is the North, true, strong, and free. Nothing symbolizes the North better than moose. Make your ancestors proud. Go north and find a moose." And with that, she passed out at his feet, as she invariably did at the end-of-term reception.

Over the years he had trained himself not to take her words to heart. On this occasion, however, they struck some unplayed chord deep within him. "I've been here a decade," he reflected. "Mother was born and raised here. I really should know more about Canada. If knowing more about Canada means going north and finding a moose, then I'll go north and find a moose." Being the sort of person he was, however, he began with a trip to the university library.

The card catalogue contained a considerable number of entries for moose. He settled on a work called *The Moose Book*, published by the New York firm of E.P. Dutton & Co. in 1916. Actually it was the subtitle that caught his attention: *Facts and Stories from the Northern Forests*. "Facts and stories," he read delightedly, nodding his head. "Just what I need. And with luck there will be statistics, too."

He went to the stacks, located the book, swept off the dust and cobwebs that had collected over the years, and started flipping through the pages. There were fewer footnotes than he would have liked. However, those that the author—one Samuel Merrill—had chosen to include appeared to be properly annotated. That was reassuring. He turned to the first chapter and started to read:

In a plea for the preservation of the moose Professor Henry Fairfield Osborn, president of the New York Zoological Society, has said, 'Nature has been a million years in developing that wonderful animal, and man should not ruthlessly destroy it!'

A million years! The imagination is helpless in attempting to grasp the idea of such a period of time, and the events which have taken place in it.

Yale Templeton paused. "A million years!" he murmured. And at that moment—quite uncharacteristically—he experienced a dawning of insight. Not the sort of grand insight that might have come to someone of a truly expansive mind. Not a recognition that the proper understanding of history requires contemplation of life in all its many and varied guises, life across the millennia. No, his insight was more parochial. "Moose," he concluded, "must be interesting."

He read on:

> The ancestral home of the moose (*Cervus alces*) in prehistoric times was probably Asia. Professor Osborn quotes Sir Victor Brooke as maintaining that the *Cervidae* originated in Asia, and thence spread east and west. But at just what stage in this little matter of a million years the first moose wandered into America over the land which then connected the two continents at Bering Strait, we shall never know. According to Professor William Berryman Scott of Princeton University the moose, the caribou, and the wapiti came from the Old World to the New not earlier than the Pleistocene ...

Well, who would not be stirred by such prose? He checked the book out and read through the night, and on into the early hours of the morning. And as he read his interest grew. And grew.

Every Friday evening, almost without exception, Yale Templeton had dinner with his aunt at the old family home on Dunbar Road. On the first such occasion, back when he had just taken his position at the university, she had made the mistake of asking him about his work. Several Fridays later, as he launched into a yet another discussion of statistics on pig iron production during the Civil War, she had shut off her hearing aid in desperation. The result had been entirely satisfactory from her point of view, and so after that she had taken to turning off her hearing aid whenever he came to the house. As a result he had been regaling her with stories about moose for over a month before she finally realized he was no longer talking about the Civil War.

"Moose? Did you say *moose*? With antlers?" And for a moment a light long believed extinguished was rekindled in her eyes.

"Yes," he replied. "I thought I would take a trip up north to see if I could—"

"Bag a moose! Bag a moose! Good for you!" she squealed, smiling for the first time he could remember. "You know, to tell you the truth, I always took you for a Mama's boy. Not that I blamed you, really, growing up in England, and without a father. And everyone knows the strings in my sister's lute snapped long before you were born. But now, moose hunting! Yes, moose hunting! That's an activity for real men!"

"Well, I wasn't exactly ..."

"Why, your great-grandfather used to go north every fall. Take a couple of weeks up on the French River. Hired Native guides, of course. When I was your age there was a moose head in every room of this house. I never understood why Father took them all down after Grandfather died. The one over the fireplace in the study, that one had antlers over six feet across. They noted it in the entry for Grandfather in the *Cavendish Social Register for 1911*. Here, I'll show you."

And she wrestled her tiny frame from the chair and hobbled upstairs. He remained at the table, unsettled by her sudden and entirely unfamiliar enthusiasm. She finally reappeared twenty minutes later with a large scrapbook. There was the entry from the *Cavendish Social Register* she had mentioned, as well as scores of photographs taken over the course of many summers, all of which showed his great-grandfather standing proud, patrician, erect, his right hand gripping the barrel of a rifle, the stock planted firmly in the ground, and the boot of his right foot resting upon the flank of some dead moose. Next to him invariably stood an Ojibwa guide, grinning broadly.

Yale Templeton had seen countless pictures of dead soldiers. His shelves were filled with books on the Civil War that contained image after gruesome image of battlefield scenes. But for some reason he found the sight of the dead moose far more disturbing than any photograph of mutilated human beings. And he was immediately reminded of the quotation by the paleontologist Henry Fairfield Osborn: "Nature has been a million years in developing that wonderful animal, and man should not ruthlessly destroy it!"

While he was contemplating the scrapbook, his aunt had hobbled off once more, this time to retrieve the .303 Lee-Enfield rifle his great-grandfather had used for hunting. The barrel gleamed, a tribute to her nostalgia. "It will make me so proud for you to have this," she said, placing it with loving tenderness in his hands as a tear rolled down her cheek. He stood there bewildered and more than a little distressed. At the same time, however, he was genuinely touched. And as a way of acknowledging the newly formed bond between them, he took her hand and started to tell her about moose migration patterns during the Pleistocene era. At which point she reached up and shut off her hearing aid.

VII

As it happened the cherished heirloom his aunt had given him was not in his possession long. When Mrs. Cordelia Devonshire-Hoskins saw a man walking past her stately mansion with a rifle slung over his shoulder, she did what she always did when the sanctity of Rosedale was threatened. By the time she had hung up the phone, Yale Templeton found himself pinned face first to the sidewalk by a team of police officers, a cocked revolver at his head and handcuffs severing the circulation to his wrists. The experience was one of the most harrowing in his life, he later wrote to his mother (almost as harrowing, he acknowledged to himself with a shudder, as his weekend in Chicago).

The night he spent in the Don Jail provided a fateful if entirely unanticipated compensation, however. Among his cellmates was an Ojibwa from Espanola named Charlie Lookalike, in custody for the third time in a month for impersonating the restaurant critic of the *Globe and Mail*. When he roused himself from his Grand Vin de Château Latour–induced stupor, he started railing at the police for racism and censorship of the press and shouting that he was going back north where at least the moose gave a man respect. (He interspersed his rant with perceptive observations about how hard it had become to find decent boiled leek dumplings in Toronto now that Ta-Sun

Mandarin Garden had closed.) Intimidated but mindful of the high regard shown by his colleagues in the History department for the restaurant reviews in the *Globe and Mail*, Yale Templeton stepped toward him and extended his hand in fellowship. Ten minutes later, after the guards had pulled him free and treated his wounds, and after he had made the customary propitiatory offering of fifty dollars to the Moose Manitou, he found himself deep in conversation with Charlie Lookalike.

Yes, it was true, Charlie told him—his childhood had been spent running and swimming with the moose in Northern Ontario. And, yes, he would be more than happy to take Yale Templeton to the moose grounds near Espanola. "But"—and here he paused, reflecting—"But a man of your background really needs more sage instruction than a mere restaurant critic can provide. As it happens, my great-uncle Joseph Brant Lookalike devoted ten years of his life to tracking moose and studying their habits. No one, white or Native, knows their movements better." True, hiring the services of a tribal elder would be expensive. But it would be an investment well worth making "for someone of your intellectual standards." And Charlie even offered to throw in an autographed copy of *The Globe and Mail's Guide to Fine Dining in Espanola* at only a slight additional cost.

It was settled, then. In early July Yale Templeton would travel to Espanola and book a room in the Campo de los Alces Motel, just on the edge of town. He would step outside at the break of dawn each morning and listen for a moose call. "You will know it," Charlie advised, "by its remarkable similarity to the sound of a kazoo. Follow the call until you come to a clearing." Joseph Brant Lookalike would be waiting for him there.

"And now," said Charlie solemnly, "we must seal the agreement." And so in keeping with sacred Ojibwa tradition, they exchanged clothes.

VIII

*The hair of moose is coarse and brittle, the color assuming various shades
of brown, brownish black, and gray. Albino moose are unknown.*

SAMUEL MERRILL, *THE MOOSE BOOK*

F or the first two hours of the bus ride from Toronto, Yale Templeton spent
his time alternately flipping back and forth through the pages of *The Moose
Book* revisiting those passages he found particularly interesting, and musing
about the appropriate demeanour to adopt when face to face with a moose. Once
the bus passed over the Severn River, however, and he caught sight of the rocky
outcroppings of the Canadian Shield for the first time, he experienced what can
only be described as an awakening. He had seen very little natural landscape in
his life. Just Wicken Fen in Cambridgeshire, which he had visited several times
with his science class at Robinson-Fallis Academy, and which he found spare
and forbidding. But the grandeur of the Shield, its more than three-billion-year
history, filled him with reverence. And it was at that moment, unconscious as it
may have been, that he first began to imagine himself a Canadian.

He watched with increasing enchantment as the forests, lakes, and waterfalls slipped past his window. He had heard about "cottage country" from colleagues, but now, seeing the odd assortment of structures for which it was named, he delighted in the contrary images they projected. He wondered about the people who flocked to the region on summer weekends. He saw some of them, driving their station wagons and vans, congregating at stores along the highway, packing supplies into boats at marinas. As the bus pressed north, he silently mouthed the names he saw on exit signs: Go Home Lake. Moon River. Handley Hawkins. Killbear Provincial Park. Pointe au Baril. Shawanaga. Magnetawan.

Outside Sudbury, in the shadow of the nickel mines, the old man in the seat next to him tapped him on the shoulder. "You see over there?" he chuckled, pointing to a barren ridge rising above the stripped, pockmarked landscape. "That's the very spot." Yale Templeton looked at him blankly.

"You know. Where they staged the moon landing."

Bewilderment.

"With Neil Armstrong? 'One giant leap for mankind'?"

"I'm afraid I don't understand."

"Oh, I see," snorted the man. "*You* think it really happened." And he blew dismissively through his lips and snapped his newspaper in front of his face.

The bus reached Espanola, about sixty kilometres west of Sudbury, just before sunset. From a tourist guidebook to Ontario, Yale Templeton knew that the town had a population of five thousand. The book also told him that it got its name from the days when the Spanish claimed title to much of the land in central North America. But that, Charlie Lookalike had informed him, was a common white misconception. "Espanola is really an Ojibwa word meaning 'where the moose gather.'"

As instructed, Yale Templeton checked into the Loon Lake Motel a few kilometres north of town. ("That's just the name the whites use," Charlie had confided. "We call it Campo de los Alces Motel, which has no exact translation in English but roughly speaking means 'A good place to hang around waiting for moose to come by.'") The next morning he stepped outside into a northern dawn for the first time. He had slept little and was simmering with anticipation.

The first thing that struck him was the cacophony of unfamiliar sounds: the chirks, tweeps, zzimmms, yodels. The second to strike him was a blackfly. So was the third, fourth, and fifth. The sixth would have been a blackfly as well, but before it could attack he escaped into his room and slammed the door behind him. Vigorously rubbing his arms and legs he considered his alternatives. The eight-page *Globe and Mail Comprehensive Guide to Survival in the North*, which Charlie had sold him at only slightly above cost, had inexplicably failed to mention blackflies. It had, however, led to his purchase of a number of items (again from Charlie, again at only slightly above cost) that could, he determined with uncharacteristic resourcefulness, be adapted to the situation at hand.

And so a few minutes later he emerged from his room once again, this time encased in mukluks, ski pants, a parka, and an orange balaclava. He walked to the edge of the parking lot and listened for the call Charlie had told him to expect. "It's much warmer up north than I realized," he mused, shifting the balaclava so he could breathe more easily. Just at that moment the air was shattered by a loud guttural *r-r-r-a-a-ah*. The kind of roar *The Moose Book* identified as the call of a moose in distress. Another common misconception of whites, Charlie had noted. "Just listen for a sound like a kazoo."

He heard it quite distinctly only seconds later. A high-pitched burr, but not at all unpleasant. Ironically, given the time of day, it momentarily had him humming "Eine Kleine Nachtmusik." He pushed his way into the woods, tracking the melody. A few minutes of fighting through brambles and branches led him to the edge of a clearing. There, as Charlie had promised, sat Joseph Brant Lookalike. He immediately noticed the family resemblance. Indeed, he said to himself, were it not for the grey hair, he would have thought he was looking at Charlie.

Yale Templeton adopted a rather formal pose, in keeping with the dignity he attached to the occasion. Joseph Brant Lookalike hailed him warmly, however. "I am told by my grandnephew that you are respected as a man of great learning among your people. I also understand that you have travelled all these many miles because you wish to know the ways of the moose. That is a most worthy undertaking." Then he clasped Yale Templeton by the shoulders and looked him over closely from head to foot. "I greet you as I would a family member. And for that reason I think we can dispense with the traditional exchanging of clothes." Buried deep inside his parka, Yale Templeton gave a sigh of relief.

"Our journey will be long and our way difficult," warned Joseph Brant Lookalike. "Remain close to me at all times. Your safety depends on it." And at that he set off purposefully, leaving Yale Templeton, in his mukluks, to struggle along behind.

After a few minutes they found themselves on a dirt path. "An ancient Ojibwa trail," Joseph Brant Lookalike disclosed. "It follows the course of the moose migration." Moments later a middle-aged man in jogging shorts and a Chicago Bulls T-shirt loped into view. He momentarily stumbled when he caught sight of Yale Templeton, then regained his balance and gave a friendly wave. "The village healer," Joseph Brant Lookalike explained. "He must be on his rounds."

They plunged back into the woods, periodically emerging to join the trail again. Their direction seemed impossibly confusing. The fallen logs, the rocky creeks, the abandoned blue Oldsmobiles: All appeared identical from one stretch of the journey to the next. "It just shows how hard it is to read the signs of nature," Yale Templeton thought.

At one point Joseph Brant Lookalike pointed to some marks trailing down to a pond. "Moose tracks," he noted. They got down on their haunches to examine them more closely. The depressions made by the front hooves looked like small hands, each with five extended fingers; those for the back hooves were twice as large, with webbing between the digits. Not at all what Yale Templeton had expected, considering that *The Moose Book* said a print of the animal resembled "two large toes." "Ah," Joseph Brant Lookalike commented with a knowing nod, "most of the time, yes. But moose in this part of the country have learned to disguise their tracks during the hunting season." "How remarkable!" thought Yale Templeton, only now fully beginning to appreciate the ingenuity of the species.

When they had been travelling for perhaps two hours and had arrived at a place that Yale Templeton was unable to distinguish from a dozen other places they had passed, Joseph Brant Lookalike stopped and announced with great solemnity, "We are now approaching our destination. Just beyond this stand of firs is the sacred Campo de los Alces." He then lay flat on his stomach and placed his right ear to the ground. He remained in that position for five minutes, at intervals tapping the dirt with his index finger, raising his head and sniffing, then placing his ear to the ground and tapping once again. Finally he stood up, brushed himself off, lifted his hand to his mouth, and gave the same call he had used earlier to announce his presence to Yale Templeton. From beyond the firs, they heard the sound of something stamping, as if in response. "You're in luck," Joseph Brant Lookalike said. "It seems there's a bull moose on the lek. I will take you to see him. But remain behind me at all times. And be very quiet. When angered, moose become man-eaters." Another fact not mentioned in *The Moose Book*.

Joseph Brant Lookalike dropped to his knees and began to creep. Yale Templeton dropped to his knees and began to creep, too. They breached the forest slowly and cautiously. Then suddenly, he saw it. A magnificent bull moose, and not fifteen metres away. Yale Templeton gave a start. The moose, on seeing Yale Templeton, gave a start, too, then snapped back as if yanked by some supernatural force. "A characteristic gesture of friendship," Joseph Brant Lookalike noted, patting him on the shoulder. "He likes you."

The animal was a deep brown colour, almost black, over six-and-a-half feet high at the shoulders. Like the numerous moose whose photographs Yale Templeton had studied so closely in *The Moose Book*, it had an enormous head, broad muzzle, dewlap, pointed ears, thick neck, and short body, high at the shoulders and low in the quarters. Its massive, palmate antlers were almost five feet across. The external edge of the left antler had ten points, reaching out like tapered fingers; the right antler had eleven points. "Surely the moose can lay little claim to beauty," Samuel Merrill had written in *The Moose Book*. But to Yale Templeton the moose was the most magnificent creature he had ever seen, a statement that, admittedly, would have carried more weight had he not spent his entire life in East Anglia and downtown Toronto.

As he was reflecting on the drama of the moment, Joseph Brant Lookalike commented, "You know, our people have a legend about how the moose got its appearance. The great god Manitou created men and all the animals. He made the moose as tall as the tallest trees. Then he asked the moose, 'What would you do if you saw a man coming?' And the moose replied, 'Why, I would tear down the trees on him.' Then Manitou saw that the moose was too strong and made him smaller, so that man could kill him. The short body, humped back, and bulging nose of the moose are due to the awful squeeze he received when Manitou reduced him to his present size." It was just the sort of anecdote that made history come alive for Yale Templeton. And he wondered if he might be able to work it into his next paper on the Civil War, maybe in a footnote.

The two men stood there staring at the moose for perhaps twenty minutes, the moose staring back impassively. Then Joseph Brant Lookalike touched Yale Templeton on the shoulder and indicated it was time to leave. "Even mild-mannered moose are notoriously changeable in temperament," he explained. "We don't want to strain his patience."

The way back seemed much shorter than the journey out, a matter of mere minutes, in fact. "Time and direction have such an elusive quality in the North," Yale Templeton sighed. When they reached the Campo de los Alces Motel, he pulled out his wallet, intending to pay Joseph Brant Lookalike the customary fee for his services.

"No, no," Joseph Brant Lookalike objected. "We will deal with that later. Tomorrow I will take you by canoe to the sacred Campo de los Peces. We will catch bass and pike, and I will prepare for you a traditional Ojibwa meal of fish and potatoes fried in a pail of lard." But Yale Templeton politely declined, having had a pronounced distaste for fish ever since his days at the Robinson-Fallis Academy, where lunch every second Wednesday had been kippers.

"Well then, birds," said Joseph Brant Lookalike. "We're in the last weeks of the migration now. Warblers, thrushes, penguins. I can take you to the sacred Campo de las Aves. We will bring some chicken, and I will prepare you a traditional Ojibwa meal of chicken and potatoes fried in a pail of lard." But the birdwatchers Yale Templeton had occasionally encountered growing up in England were lower class and notoriously ill-mannered, or so his mother had cautioned him. Another reason why he had viewed school trips to Wicken Fen with alarm.

They stood there for a moment in silence, Yale Templeton smiling amiably inside his balaclava. Joseph Brant Lookalike closed his eyes, placed his hands over his ears, and dropped his chin on his chest. His lips moved in some silent incantation. He continued in that way for several minutes. Finally he looked at Yale Templeton and spoke: "You are obviously a man of extraordinary honour, courage, and purity. Indeed, you have all the qualities of a great Ojibwa warrior. The spirits of my ancestors have instructed me to extend to you, at only slightly above the normal daily rate for my services, one of the greatest privileges known to my people. I am to take you to see the Great White Moose."

"The Great White Moose?" said Yale Templeton.

"Yes, the most proud, the most fierce, yet also the most venerated creature in all the North."

"But I thought all moose were brown."

"All moose known to the white man, yes. You will be the first of your people to bear witness to the majesty of the Great White Moose."

Yale Templeton was rendered speechless. Which prompted Joseph Brant Lookalike to offer to throw in, at no additional cost, a dream catcher, and miniature birchbark canoe and teepee, all made by his niece's youngest daughter at summer camp.

The expedition would take place, he told Yale Templeton, "on the morning when the sun has risen on the wings of the raven. Or, as your people would put it, the day after tomorrow. That will allow me time to make the necessary ritual preparations."

"Oh, and be sure to wear your balaclava," he added. "I don't know how the Great White Moose will react to the sight of a white man."

IX

A moose is easily tamed. If captured as a calf he shows little fear of man ... But deer of all species, including the moose, are more dangerous when domesticated than when wild, for the fear of man, which is man's safeguard in the woods, is then lost.

SAMUEL MERRILL, *THE MOOSE BOOK*

T he man sat on a stool. He had never tried something like this before, painting a moose. There were so many difficult decisions to make. What sort of paint to use? Watercolour was out of the question. It might rain. But acrylic or oil-based? And what sort of finish? Gloss, semigloss, satin, flat? And how to apply it? With a roller, spray gun, or brush? A spray gun for the first coat, surely. But a brush would be needed to get at the more hidden places. And finally, what colour? There were so many different shades of white: Ivory White, Almond, Cream, Sand White, Pearl. The choices at the Canadian Tire outlet seemed endless. His first choice was Ice White; the name had such a chill, pure ring to it. But in the end he decided that Winter

White was more appropriate. A Glidden Cold Weather Exterior Latex Flat Winter White, specially formulated for temperatures as low as forty degrees below zero Celsius and with a mildew-resistant coating.

As he had anticipated, the moose barely reacted when he started to spray. Still, he felt a touch of relief. While he was applying the first coat, there were moments when he questioned his decision not to use a primer. But now, with just a little bit of brushwork left to do, he was pleased with the result. Nice and even. No patches. He had debated about whether to paint the antlers but in the end decided that, for aesthetic purposes, he should leave them their natural tan. They would provide a stark contrast to the ghostliness of the face.

Indeed, everything had gone very well, better than he had expected. Until. Unaware of the tender sensibilities of moose—or at least of this particular moose—he reached between the animal's hind legs to finish the job. Suddenly, and without warning, the moose—the Great White Moose—gave a loud guttural *r-r-r-a-a-ah* (the very cry of distress described so precisely in *The Moose Book*) and kicked out its hind legs with all the savage force it could muster. It bucked and twisted furiously until it had yanked the tether out of the ground, crashed through the row of firs, surged out onto the ancient Ojibwa jogging trail looking frantically from left to right and back again, then tore off on its way to no predetermined destination. Face down on the ground, entirely still, Joseph Brant Lookalike would never have the opportunity to explain to the young children on the reserve why there would be no moose ride at this year's Canada Day celebration.

$$\overline{\qquad} \quad X \quad \overline{\qquad}$$

Moose Steak in Chafing Dish—Take steak for three. Melt a piece of butter the size of an egg in a chafing dish. Put in the steak, and season it; when it is seared on the outside turn it over. Cook ten minutes, keeping the dish covered. Add a tablespoonful of port or sherry for each person, and a little currant jelly. Serve hot.

SAMUEL MERRILL, *THE MOOSE BOOK*

Each morning for a week Yale Templeton climbed into his mukluks, ski pants, parka, and balaclava and waited outside the Campo de los Alces Motel. But when it finally became apparent that the expected signal was not going to come, he packed his bags and took the bus back to Toronto. He was filled with disappointment. Nonetheless in that disappointment we may see the beginning of the grand new mission in his life.

Granted, his quest to find the Great White Moose did not have the driving intensity of Ahab thundering across the seas in search of Moby Dick. But Yale Templeton had a yearning to see the Great White Moose—you might even say he had a sense, dimly perceived, that the moose was in some important measure linked to his own destiny—and he returned to the Campo de los Alces Motel in July of the following year, and stood each morning at dawn waiting for a call from Joseph Brant Lookalike. By now he had read extensively about conditions of life in the North, and so no longer packed mukluks, ski pants, and a parka. Just a beekeeper's hat, bug shirt, hiking boots, and copious quantities of Muskol, Off, and assorted other insect repellents. And his balaclava. He always brought along his orange balaclava.

He returned the next summer as well, and the summer after, until finally he reluctantly acknowledged to himself that the call he was awaiting would never come. The following summer he rented a cottage on a small lake just a few kilometres north of the motel. He had purchased a birchen horn for calling moose at Mountain Equipment Co-op in Toronto, but threw it away when the only sound he could coax out of it was a low quavering *mwar*. In the end he resorted to a kazoo, unable to identify any instrument that would reproduce the call Joseph Brant Lookalike had used to summon him. The exact tone of the call had faded somewhat from his memory, but he did remember that it had set him to humming "Eine Kleine Nachtmusik." And so, each morning at dawn, he took a chair out to the end of the dock and blew "Eine Kleine Nachtmusik" on his kazoo, switching occasionally to "Cradle Song," the beautiful madrigal by William Byrd, when he became bored. But no moose, white or otherwise, responded to the call.

He enjoyed himself at the cottage all the same. During the hours he was not sitting on the dock scanning the shoreline for moose, he devoted himself to reading. Mostly favourite passages from *The Moose Book*, of course. But otherwise a selection of books debating the wisdom of Grant's decision to implement a war of attrition in 1864. It never seemed to occur to him that there might be something preposterous about devoting hours upon hours to poring over stark depictions of horrifying battlefield carnage while lying in a deck chair next to the peace and serenity of a northern lake, sipping tea. But then, he was an academic, after all.

He found the experience so relaxing and satisfying that he determined to rent the cottage again the following summer. But just as he was about to make his arrangements, he came across an article in one of the Toronto newspapers saying that a group of hikers in Algonquin Park had reported seeing a white moose. "If the claim can be verified," the article went on, quoting a noted authority on moose at Lake Superior State University, "it would be of immense significance to biologists. Although white moose hold a prominent place in Native mythology, there has been no confirmed sighting of an albino moose anywhere in North America."

Yale Templeton immediately changed his plans and left for Algonquin Park. A colleague gave him the name of an exclusive resort where, for only seven hundred and fifty dollars a night, he could stay in a cabin named after the Jewish comedian who famously rejected job offers in the United States so that he could remain in Canada. He did not see any moose during his four days in the park, but in the internationally acclaimed dining room at the resort he did have moose steak for the first time. He found it strongly flavoured but, when eaten with a little currant jelly, more than palatable. He also sampled chocolate mousse for the first time, and noted to himself with some satisfaction that it was not at all difficult to distinguish between the two dishes.

Two years later, more reported sightings drew him to Cochrane, Kapuskasing, and Hearst. It appeared the white moose was tracking the route of the Trans-Canada Highway. But then an investigative report on *The Fifth Estate* revealed that some overly zealous bureaucrat at the Ministry for Northern Affairs had been planting stories in the newspapers to help attract tourists to the region. "Proof yet again," noted an authority from the Fraser Institute, "that we have far too much government in this country."

Yale Templeton abandoned his search, retraced his steps to Cochrane, then took the Polar Bear Express up to Moosonee. He rode in a freighter canoe out to the limestone deposits on Fossil Island, ate Cree bannock bread, took part in a hike through the Great Muskeg, and joined seventy other sightseers on a trip to Moose Factory Island, where he explored the former administrative centre of the Hudson's Bay Company. He wandered through the blacksmith shop, carefully examined the fur press, and met some members of the Moose Cree First Nations. He was disappointed that they had never heard of Joseph Brant Lookalike, but supposed that, living on the shore of James Bay, they were isolated from others of their culture. What impressed him most on his journey were the alter cloth and liturgical vestments in moosehide at St. Thomas' Anglican Church. They reminded him of his visit to the town museum in Saffron Walden when he saw the historic ninth-century necklace for the first time.

No more stories about white moose appeared in the press for several years. Editors were quick to dismiss reported sightings, mindful of the earlier hoax. Indeed, "to write a white moose story" now became journalist slang for being taken in by a government leak. But each summer Yale Templeton headed north to continue his own search, exploring farther and farther into the distant reaches of Ontario. One year he skirted the shores of Lake Superior, passing through Marathon, Schreiber, Halpern Mills, Red Rock, and on to Atikokan and Rainy River. Another he spent two weeks at a lodge in Quetico Provincial Park, then a month at a rented cottage on an island in the Lake of the Woods, where he wrote the definitive article on boot sizes among Union cavalrymen and learned the rudiments of paddling a canoe. He travelled as far west as the Manitoba border and as far north as Sioux Lookout.

And he saw moose. Young moose and old moose. Large moose and small moose. Bulls, cows, and calves. The healthy and the fit. The halt and the lame. Moose that broke for cover the moment they spotted him, and moose that regarded him with seemingly the utmost indifference. Moose that at a distance appeared black as the tar used to repair northern roads and moose that up close looked as soft and brown as the little stuffed moose sold at local souvenir shops. But no white moose. He did not see the Great White Moose.

And then one day, he came across a report of a new sighting. Not in a Toronto newspaper this time, but in the quarterly bulletin of the Federation of Ontario Naturalists. A white moose, the article said, had been spotted by a Native guide on Lake Wabatongushi, about eighty kilometres northeast of Wawa. The sighting was more than a month old by the time Yale Templeton learned about it, but he immediately bought a bus ticket north.

Lake Wabatongushi lies within the Chapleau Crown Game Preserve, the largest wildlife sanctuary in the world. The lake itself extends over forty square kilometres and has seventy uninhabited islands. "There are 2500 moose in the Chapleau Crown Game Preserve!" boasts a brochure from the resort on the lake. "Come and see one grazing on lily pads while you graze on a four-course picnic lunch prepared by our Viennese-trained kitchen staff!!!"

There are no roads to the lake. To get there you take the Algoma Central Railway from the small town of Hawk Junction just outside Wawa or, if you prefer, the scenic route through the Agawa Canyon, from Sault Ste. Marie. Yale Templeton chose the scenic route, reasoning that it would offer more opportunity to see moose. It was late August when he headed north, and the leaves on the trees were just beginning to change colour, a suggestion of the spectacular show that each year drew thousands of tourists to the canyon. And the ride did take him past several moose, although not the particular moose he was looking for.

When he arrived at the resort he learned to his disappointment that the story in the Federation of Ontario Naturalists' bulletin had been somewhat misleading. Actually it was two used car salesmen from Evansville, Indiana, who had seen the white moose. The Native guide had merely passed on what they reported to the owner of the resort, and he in turn had contacted the representative of the Federation in Sault Ste. Marie.

"Oh, yeah," a retired oral surgeon from Ottawa spending the summer on the lake told Yale Templeton over dinner the day he arrived, "it was two Americans. They said they saw a white moose over around the point there, when they were out fishing. But they were going through the vodka pretty fast by then. A couple of days later they were telling everyone they'd seen a pink eagle."

"And don't forget the blue hippopotamus," his wife added. "They said they saw a furry blue hippopotamus."

"Aw, they were just kidding that time."

"You think so? I don't know."

Undeterred, Yale Templeton made arrangements the next morning to go out with the Native guide—Samuel Beartooth Lookalike. As he was introduced by the resort owner, Samuel Beartooth Lookalike raised an eyebrow at the mention of his name. He was much more taciturn than Joseph Brant Lookalike, and kept his comments to simple declarations. "We go there," he said, laying flat a map of the lake and pointing to a little picture of a moose next to an inlet some distance north of the resort. But Yale Templeton indicated that he preferred to be taken to the spot where the fishermen had seen the white moose. Samuel Beartooth Lookalike just shrugged. They paddled south from the main lodge, passed around the bend, and then headed toward a patch of reeds where the men would have been fishing when they made their sighting. As they neared shore Yale Templeton dutifully put on his balaclava, pulled the kazoo from his shirt pocket, and started playing "Eine Kleine Nachtmusik." Samuel Beartooth Lookalike observed him with no discernible change of expression.

They repeated this exercise for three days. When, on the third day, Yale Templeton switched to Byrd's "Cradle Song," a tear trickled down Samuel Beartooth Lookalike's otherwise impassive face. A sign, Yale Templeton decided, that the melody had evoked tender memories in the Native guide, perhaps of his mother. But the calls were to no avail, and in the end, out of a sense of resignation more than hope, Yale Templeton agreed to go to the inlet marked with a moose on the map. There he saw a cow and young calf, which momentarily put him in mind of his own mother. Feeling a surge of filial devotion, he pulled out his kazoo and started playing Byrd's "Cradle Song" once again. This drew another tear to the eye of Samuel Beartooth Lookalike and sent the cow and calf stampeding into the woods in appreciation.

Despite his disappointment about the white moose, Yale Templeton found the week he spent at the resort rewarding. Touched by the emotional bond he had formed with Samuel Beartooth Lookalike, he finally suppressed his memory of kippers long enough to try the traditional Native meal of fish and potatoes fried in a bucket of lard. It turned out to be much more appetizing than he had imagined, and he resolved to introduce the dish to his aunt once he returned to Toronto. And at the end of his stay, when he went to check out, the resort owner gave him a Polar Bear badge, awarded to those guests who took a swim in the lake each morning before breakfast, as well as a key chain with a moose on it, his winnings from the weekly minnow races. He noted with gratitude that someone had painted the moose white.

XI

For his return trip to Toronto Yale Templeton decided to take the bus from Wawa down the eastern shore of Lake Superior. "Perhaps I'll even stop at one of the beaches for a swim," he said to himself, proudly fingering the Polar Bear badge in his pocket. It would mean spending a night in Hawk Junction, but he had grown accustomed to hotels in small northern communities. All he needed was the companionship of *The Moose Book* and some scholarly works on the Civil War.

He ate at the only restaurant in town, a diner that somehow had escaped the notice of the restaurant critic for the *Globe and Mail*. He ordered the signature dish of the region—frozen simulated ground beef patties, thawed and incinerated, accompanied by frozen crinkled French fries, partially thawed—then opened his book and began to read.

"Whatchya got there?" the waitress asked, sliding her pencil behind her ear.

"It's a new study of manufacturing in the North during the American Civil War," he replied. And then, just to make sure she hadn't misunderstood: "I mean in the *American* North."

"That so?" she said. "Is it interesting?"

"Oh, yes, very," he replied. "For example, did you know that pig iron production in the Union increased 345 percent during the war?"

"Can't say that I did," she answered, blowing a large bubble from the wad of gum in her mouth and popping it loudly.

"Hey, Marcel!" she shouted to the man at the grill behind the counter. "Didjya know that pig iron production increased 345 percent in the Union during the American Civil War?"

"No kidding," Marcel shouted back, exhaling a ring of smoke and crushing out his cigarette on a plate next to the sink. "How 'bout that."

These expressions of enthusiasm for his work pleased Yale Templeton immensely, and when he retired to his room in the hotel he looked forward to getting back to his reading with even more excitement than usual. But just as he sat down at the desk, he heard a knocking sound. He opened his door to find a short, stocky man in a knitted black toque, red checked shirt with fraying cuffs and collar, faded jeans, black suspenders, and heavy boots. Over his shoulders he carried a tattered canvas knapsack. He had a thick grey beard and the stooped appearance of someone in his seventies, perhaps even older.

"I'm Slinger, sir," the man said, extending a leathery hand after first wiping it across the front of his shirt. "Slinger the Trapper, they call me around here, although not with the kind of respect you might imagine. I overheard you at the diner talking to the waitress. You said you were reading a book about the American Civil War."

"That's true," replied Yale Templeton, brightening considerably at the prospect of meeting someone in this remote northern community who shared his scholarly interests.

"Well, may I ask you, sir? Do you know anything about Abraham Lincoln?"

"I know a great deal about Abraham Lincoln," replied Yale Templeton cheerfully. "Each year in my course on the Civil War I offer several lectures on his presidency. And on alternate years I give a graduate seminar on his relations with his generals."

Slinger gasped. "You teach about Lincoln, sir? You teach about Lincoln? It's the sign I've been looking for!"

"Sign?" asked Yale Templeton.

"My grandfather told me there'd be a sign. And here you are: a Lincoln expert come to Hawk Junction the one day of the year I'm in town. That's a sign if ever I saw one!" And Slinger removed his toque and knapsack and pulled a dirty handkerchief from his jeans to wipe his neck. His sparse grey hair lay matted to his head. "Do you mind if I sit down?" he asked.

"Not at all," replied Yale Templeton. And he pulled over the chair from the desk. Then he sat himself down on the bed, just opposite.

"Thank you most kindly, sir," said Slinger. And he removed a bottle of whiskey from his knapsack, took a long swig, wiped his mouth with the back of his hand, and offered the bottle to Yale Templeton.

"No, thank you," said Yale Templeton politely. "It is not my habit to partake of spirits."

Slinger nodded. "I understand, sir. I understand. Myself, I subscribe to the sentiments of the great Mississippi jurist 'Soggy' Sweat, delivered in the state legislature during the prohibition debate in 1953:

'If you mean whiskey, the devil's brew, the poison scourge, the bloody monster that defiles innocence, dethrones reason, destroys the home, creates misery and poverty, yea, literally takes the bread from the mouths of little children; if you mean that evil drink that topples Christian men and women from the pinnacles of righteous and gracious living into the bottomless pits of degradation, shame, despair, helplessness, and hopelessness, then, my friend, I am opposed to it with every fiber of my being.

'However, if by whiskey you mean the oil of conversation, the philosophic wine, the elixir of life, the ale that is consumed when good fellows get together, that puts a song in their hearts and the warm glow of contentment in their eyes; if you mean Christmas cheer, the stimulating sip that puts a little spring in the step of an elderly gentleman on a frosty morning; if you mean that drink that enables man to magnify his joy, and to forget life's great tragedies and heartbreaks and sorrow; if you mean that drink the sale of which pours into our treasuries untold millions of dollars each year, that provides tender care for our little crippled children, our blind, our deaf, our dumb, our pitifully aged and infirm, to build the finest highways, hospitals, universities, and community colleges in this nation, then my friend, I am absolutely, unequivocally in favour of it.

'This is my position, and as always, I refuse to be compromised on matters of principle.'"

"Oh, well done," applauded Yale Templeton. "An excellent recitation, even with the personal emendations. Almost as good as the one I heard Ernest Blanchard give before the Caius College History Society in 1974. But I believe the year of the speech was 1952 not 1953."

"Sir, you astound me!" exclaimed Slinger. "It only confirms my view that Providence has ordained our paths to cross. I have a remarkable story to tell. It's not my story, mind you, though with your kind permission, I will begin with myself." To this Yale Templeton gave a friendly nod.

"I was born many years ago—more years than I care to remember—in the town of Chapleau, about fifty miles east of where we are now. My mother died when I was only two years old. My father, a trapper, disappeared into the woods, never to be seen by me again. I had no brothers or sisters, no aunts or uncles living in Canada, and so I was raised by my grandfather, a widower. He was a widely respected lawyer, a pillar of the community, and a very kind and generous man. But mine was a restless spirit—a cursed inheritance from my father, I have come to believe—and at the age of fourteen I disappeared into the woods myself. By then the land around Chapleau had been declared a wildlife sanctuary, but I was able to survive by hunting and trapping and eluded the grasp of the authorities. I've lived that way for almost sixty years now.

"When my grandfather died I was his only surviving heir. By misfortune, mine as well as his, he lived just long enough to see the Great Depression wipe out his savings. When I went to collect my inheritance, all I received from the lawyers was a check for one hundred and thirty-seven dollars, three large boxes containing legal documents, and a sealed letter with my name on it. I managed to lose the letter to a campfire a few years ago—one of those occasions when whiskey did not serve me well, I'm afraid. Still, I read it enough times to know it almost verbatim."

And with that he took another swig from the bottle of whiskey as Yale Templeton waited with interest.

XII

The letter left to Slinger the Trapper by his grandfather:

My dear grandson,

Time and circumstances have wiped out the legacy I had intended
for you. While I always believed that you left home when you were
much too young, I came to accept your decision and—although I did
not admit it to myself at the time—even admired your independence.
You are a man, I know, with great courage and pride. You are also a
man with the strength of character necessary to carry out the heavy
responsibility I am about to place on your shoulders.

I must begin by going back to the years immediately following
Confederation, when I first came to the Algoma District. Hardly
twenty, but very ambitious, I settled in Thessalon, imagining that
the frontier would provide me with a quick road to wealth and
prominence. I had prepared for a career in the law but soon came to
learn how difficult it is to find clients when you are young and new
to a community. I struggled to establish myself for several years until
I met a much older man, a recent immigrant from the United States
named Lincoln Abrahams. He had been a lawyer himself, in Illinois,

but had emigrated to Canada following the Civil War. He had hoped to continue his chosen profession here, but unfamiliar with our legal system, was forced to find other employment: working on a farm, splitting rails for fences, keeping a store. We formed a partnership. I educated him in the peculiar genius of British law; he provided our firm with the face of experience, respect, and trust. I must say that we both proved adept at our tasks. Within a matter of two years we had a large and growing clientele.

Now I must tell you a little about the man who was Lincoln Abrahams. He was well over six feet tall, shambled when he walked, and generally had a soulful look on his thin, heavily creased face. Although he spoke in a high-pitched drawl, he always seemed able to charm judges and juries with simple homilies and instructive tales about life on the frontier. Of course, his name invariably provoked comment, and the truth is that although clean shaven, he *did* bear a startling resemblance to the former president of the United States. One New Year's Eve, at a celebration in the town hall, he drank a good deal of whiskey, put on a false beard and stovepipe hat, and delivered the famous Gettysburg Address flawlessly and with such feeling that several American immigrants were moved to tears. Later he retired to his lodging, then returned wearing a violet-coloured taffeta skirt trimmed with lace, with a matching jacket, ruffled at the neckline and sleeves. In his hair he had pink ribbons. He was quite the sight, especially since he had forgotten to remove his beard.

It was just a few days after this event that he informed me he intended to move farther north, to the new town of Chapleau. I was reluctant to leave Thessalon since we had established such an excellent reputation in the community. However, I did not yet feel confident enough in my own abilities to carry on without his sage advice, and so I packed my belongings and went to Chapleau with him.

As it turned out the change of address proved advantageous to both of us. I became involved in local politics, eventually securing election as an alderman. He continued on in practice for a few more years, then gradually reduced his work load in preparation for retirement. He took up the harp, did embroidery and needlepoint, and gave lectures at the library. He also involved himself in the local theatrical society, becoming especially known for his work in female roles, women being in decidedly small numbers in our frontier community.

Then one day, without having previously given me any hint of his intentions, he announced that he would be leaving Chapleau. I expressed doubts about the prudence of his making yet another move at such an advanced age. However, he had one remaining goal in life, he told me, although what that goal was he declined to say. All he would reveal was that he would be heading north again, this time into unsettled territory, and that he would be accompanied by friends who would provide for him. He asked only one thing of me: that I pack up all his old legal briefs and store them in a secure place.

I did not hear from him for some years. Then one spring afternoon a man unknown to me, a Negro, appeared at the door of my office to say that Lincoln Abrahams was dying. "He has expressed a wish to see you one last time," he told me. I immediately cancelled my appointments and hastily prepared for a journey into the wilderness.

We travelled, the Negro and I, for more than two weeks, first along scarcely trodden paths, then by canoe across silent lakes, and finally, on foot once again, through forests so dense I could scarce imagine how any man could find his way. My companion, however, born a slave near Natchez, Mississippi, seemed to have little difficulty. So it was that at last we arrived at our destination, a clearing with perhaps ten log cabins, all colourfully decorated. "Our city on a hill," the Negro said, although in fact it lay by a secluded lake at the bottom of a rocky prominence.

I was taken by surprise when I first saw the inhabitants of the settlement. They seemed to represent all the races of humanity, but that was not the most remarkable thing about them. Among the women was one dressed in armour and several wearing trousers;

they had hair cut so close to their heads they reminded me of shorn sheep. Meanwhile two of the men were in calico skirts and white blouses, while a third had on a dirndl. Many of the men had long, flowing locks, which they kept in place by bright kerchiefs of the kind Alpine peasant women wear.

The Negro led me to one of the cabins. Here I found Lincoln Abrahams sitting in a rocking chair, a shawl covering his lap. He was dressed in a simple woman's frock and wore a blue bonnet embroidered with butterflies. "I did the stitching myself," he later told me with some pride.

The cabin was suffocating from books. They squeezed into shelves, weighted down the desk, and spilled across the floor. I recognized some of the titles: *Works and Days* by Hesiod, Plato's *Republic*, More's *Utopia*, the plays and sonnets of Shakespeare. However, there were also many volumes by authors unfamiliar to me: Euhemerus, Anton Francesco Doni, Tommaso Campanella, Theodor Hertzka, Henri de Saint-Simon. To my shock I saw a considerable quantity of seditious literature, including Proudhon's *Qu'est-ce que la proprieté?* and the *Manifesto of the Communist Party*. On the lampstand next to the bed sat a dog-eared copy of Shakespeare's *As You Like It*. Scattered among the books were pages and pages of notes, most written in my former partner's distinctive hand.

"It's good to see you, Seth," he said in a voice that was so weak and quavering it near moved me to tears. I placed a hand on top of his and he smiled warmly. "Had it not been for you," he continued, "I might have spent the end of my days as a rail splitter in Thessalon."

"It's good to see you too, Lincoln," I said with great feeling, struggling to conceal my distress at finding him so frail.

"Ah, yes," he said. "Well, I suppose that should be where we begin. You see, my name is not really Lincoln Abrahams. It is Abraham Lincoln."

"Like the former president of the United States?" I said, startled. The Negro laughed.

"Please forgive Clement," he said. "But you see, I *am* the former president of the United States."

I was relieved to see that he had retained his sense of humour. "But ..." and here I put on the appearance of someone searching his memory, "I seem to recall that Abraham Lincoln was assassinated at the end of the Civil War."

"We staged that."

"And John Wilkes Booth?" I asked, carrying out what I took to be my part in the charade.

"An old friend from my amateur theatrical days. He acted the aggrieved rebel very well, don't you think? That leap on the stage. Such agility! And the cry: 'Sic semper tyrannis!' What a wonderful touch. It was improvised, you know. But then, Johnny always had a flair for the dramatic. Not that he was much good at comedy. Be thankful you missed him as Bottom in *A Midsummer Night's Dream*."

I peered into his eyes. In the old days it was easy to tell when he was pulling my leg, he could scarcely contain himself. Now, to all appearances, he was in earnest.

"But what about Mary Surratt, Powell, the others?" I said. "They all were *hanged*."

"Well, yes, we made it *look* as if they were hanged. William Herndon handled the arrangements. He was still loyal to me back then, Herndon. We paid them all well for their services and provided them with new identities. Mary and John Surratt actually moved to Thessalon just about the time I did. You remember James and Margaret Stuart, the mother and son who ran that inn down by the docks?"

"Yes."

"That was the Surratts."

"No!"

"It was, indeed. Unfortunately, John foolishly revealed his true identity on a trip abroad. He was captured and returned to the United States. It cost a lot of money, but in the end we were able to secure a deadlocked jury at his trial."

"But this is all beyond belief!" I exclaimed.

"Ah, yes, so it must seem. But as the poet once wrote, 'Truth is always strange, stranger than fiction.'"

We both fell silent.

"But," I said finally, "why not just wait until your term was over? And why come to Canada?"

"Spoken like a lawyer," he replied. "Once Lee surrendered, I felt I had fulfilled all my obligations to the land of my birth. Canada offered the promise of anonymity. In any case I could not bear the thought of living one minute longer in a country where there was so little respect for the rights of minorities."

"Ah, yes, the Negroes," I said.

"Well," he replied, and gave a sad smile to Clement. "I'm afraid my concerns were of a more selfish nature in 1865."

I gave him a blank look.

"You see I had come to the recognition that I was a woman born in a man's body."

"No!" I cried.

"You're shocked. But history provides many examples of individuals who have experienced life as I do. Hippocrates tells us of Scythian men who, and I quote, 'show feminine inclinations and behave as women.' From Philo, the Jewish philosopher of ancient Alexandria, we learn of males who, and I quote again, 'are not ashamed even to employ every device to change artificially their nature.' And it has been well documented by historians that Henri III of France appeared at court wearing a long pearl necklace and low-cut dress."

His words were halting, and his voice had started to trail off. Clement brought him a cup of water. He took a sip, paused to catch his breath, then continued.

"You yourself, I'm sure, have heard the story of the Chevalier d'Eon. And early explorers in North America found many Indian men who dressed and behaved as women. Nor, presumably, need I mention the countless stories in fact and fiction of women who acted out male roles. I imagine you have already caught sight of our own Jeanne d'Arc."

"But you were married!"

He shrugged. "It was a marriage of convenience. Or inconvenience, as it turned out. It was during my marriage that I discovered the truth about myself."

"And Mary Todd?"

"Ah, yes. Mary. A ferret born in a woman's body. I discovered that during my marriage, too." Clement muffled a laugh.

"I'm sorry. That was exceedingly unkind. I seriously doubt the result would have been any different if I had married Ann Rutledge. Let's just say I came to Canada to find peace."

"And did you?"

"As it happens, I found a great deal more. Do you recall the public lectures I used to give at the Chapleau library?"

I said I did.

"Well, do you remember one entitled 'The Slavery That Was and the Slavery That Is?'"

I shook my head.

"I spoke about the failure of the Civil War to bring true liberty to Americans. Yes, emancipation had ended slavery in the South, I said. But oppression continued, though in other forms. Men and women who wished to embrace a manner of living different from their neighbours were denied the opportunity to do so, condemned to live their lives wearing masks of conformity."

He gave Clement a wry smile: "I even quoted myself. I said," and here he cleared his throat and made a vain attempt to recapture his old speaking voice, "'Remember the words of the late President Abraham Lincoln: Those who deny freedom to others deserve it not for themselves.'" Clement applauded.

"I then told a parable about a peasant girl who dreamed of—"

"occupying the throne," I interrupted. "Now I remember. When the reigning king died, the council of electors proposed a series of tests to determine who had the heart and wisdom to succeed him. With the help of a sympathetic uncle, the girl disguised herself in men's clothing and entered the competition. The tests were extremely demanding and she faced many worthy adversaries. However, in the end, the council ranked her above all others and awarded her the crown. Almost immediately, jealous warlords rose up in rebellion. By skilful deployment of troops and judicious management of her generals, she was able to put down the uprising. However, during the victory celebration, when she chose to reveal her true identity, an assassin took her life."

"Yes, that's it exactly," he said, smiling.

"But I assumed you were just speaking in favour of rights for women."

"So did most people. Not Clement, though. He came to me some time later to say he understood my suffering, that he himself had also struggled to find his true identity, and he hoped that I would agree to join a study group that he and some others were forming. I was delighted to accept his offer.

"Over the next few years we met regularly, at first just to share our feelings and experiences, but later to discuss the origins of intolerance and debate how to build a society that would promote and protect the rich diversity of human self-expression. We read many works to help us in our search for understanding: works of history, philosophy, and political economy mainly, although occasionally fiction. As you can see," and he made a feeble sweeping gesture toward the books, "little of what we read was written by Americans. With the help of Clement and the others, I came to see that the insatiable lust for private possessions in the United States was, and remains, anathema to the cause of human freedom. It ensures that many people will have to devote their lives simply to securing a marginal material existence. However, more than that, it destroys the most fundamental of all human rights: the right of each individual to imagine himself, or to imagine herself, in whatever form he or she finds personally satisfying."

On giving voice to these sentiments he seemed to collapse within himself, his arms dropping beside the chair and his eyes rolling back into his head, which now lolled to one side. I leaned down toward him with alarm, but Clement touched my shoulder and said gently, "No, his time has not yet come. He just needs rest." So we lifted him from his chair and placed him on the bed. Clement removed his bonnet and made sure that his frock was neatly arranged. "He's a little vain about his appearance," he whispered to me as we were leaving. "But we can forgive him that. He has learned, and taught us, so much."

I stayed at the settlement for five days. Most of my time was spent simply observing the inhabitants. Every morning two or three would go off to hunt or fish, with the rest working in small gardens scattered among the cabins. It appeared that private property did not exist. Individuals shared tools, even clothes. Labour was not apportioned on the basis of sex, and I was unable to identify anyone who served as leader. Not everyone arose at the same hour or went to work for the same length of time, but so far as I could tell, no one raised a voice in protest. "Each makes the contribution he or she feels is required," Clement told me. Food was distributed communally, although not necessarily equally. However, again, there were no complaints. "We trust that each person will take only what she or he truly needs," was a statement I heard on several occasions.

When not at work individuals could be found engaged in any number of activities: reading and writing, drawing, carving, playing instruments, singing and dancing. Often in the evening small groups would form to talk about subjects as diverse as the medicinal properties of native plants and the nature of human obligation. I was told that some number among them formed a company of actors and performed Shakespeare from time to time, although there were no rehearsals or plays while I was there.

Strangely, or so I thought at the time, there was no Bible among the many books in the settlement. Nor did I witness any form of

Christian worship. Judging from remarks I overheard, the inhabitants subscribed to no recognizable faith and regarded traditional religious rituals as meaningless, if not perverse. All the same, it seemed to me that there was a great sense of human worth about the place, an impression that was reinforced every time I was able to speak with my old friend and former partner.

Each of our meetings was briefer than the one before as a consequence of his rapidly deteriorating condition. Even so, he shared many interesting observations with me. I discovered, for example, that he had little regard for most of the men who had followed him in office. His immediate successor, Andrew Johnson, he described as "a village idiot who squandered the moral capital of emancipation." Ulysses Grant was "a better historian than president and, frankly, a third-rate historian." Curiously, in view of his contempt for what he referred to as "the predatory rapaciousness" of American trust companies, he professed to hold the recently elected president, William McKinley, in high regard. "He has the capacity to grow in both compassion and understanding," he assured me.

By the time of our final meeting he was weakening rapidly and confined to his bed. His voice cracked frequently, and scarcely rose above a whisper. "Seth, I'm afraid I must impose on your kindness one last time," he said.

"Please," I murmured, my voice cracking itself.

"I have been privileged to witness in the forests of Northern Ontario 'a new birth of freedom,' to borrow a phrase I once used in a very different place and with a very different intended meaning. Someday it will be necessary for Americans to learn the truth about me, about the choices I have made and why. When that time comes, I want you to serve as my spokesman."

"But no one will believe me," I protested.

"No," he said. "Perhaps not. But they will believe me. Did you save my legal briefs, as I asked?"

"Yes, of course."

"In those briefs I have revealed everything I told you here and much more."

"I don't understand."

"If you arrange the briefs in chronological order and read every sixteenth word ..." ("Sixteenth because I was the sixteenth president," he added, making an effort to smile.) "... then you will find a complete description of how the assassination was staged, with directions indicating where to obtain corroborating evidence. You will also find a full account of my time in Northern Ontario up to the month I ceased practicing law, very candid reflections on the past, present, and future of the United States, and a statement of the insight I have gained into the true nature of human freedom and equality."

He began to cough softly. Clement lifted a cup of water to his lips. After a few moments he was able to go on.

"Concealing a record in the briefs ... it all began just as one of my practical jokes. A way to amuse myself. But later, after I moved to Chapleau and came to know the remarkable men and women you have met here, I realized that telling my story would be a way to help promote their cause, which, of course, is my cause as well."

"But you said I should come forward when 'the time comes.' How will I know when the time has come?"

"I'm afraid that's something beyond my powers to predict. But I am not engaging in false flattery when I say that I have complete confidence in your judgment."

We spoke no more words. I took his hand in mine and sat beside him for some minutes. Then, when he closed his eyes and Clement came and tapped me on the shoulder, I kissed him on the forehead, straightened his nightdress, and with an immense heaviness of heart left the cabin.

About the many interesting conversations I had with Clement on our sad journey back to Chapleau, I will not write. I will only say that through those conversations, I learned much about the Negroes who fled to Canada from the United States before the Civil War. It sparked an interest that led me to publish an article on the subject in a professional historical journal.

I never saw Clement again. Nor did I hear any more of Abraham Lincoln. However, as soon as I got home, I examined the legal briefs. The testimony he wished me to reveal was laid out exactly in the cryptic form he had described. I had the briefs stored in the bank, where they have remained until my death. Now they come into your hands.

During the Great War, when the revolution broke out in Russia, I thought perhaps that the moment had arrived to reveal what I knew. I even began to prepare an announcement to send to newspapers in New York and Washington. Then, however, came the violent reaction to the Bolsheviks in the United States, and I delayed. Later, during the 1920s, when I had the chance to read some of the writings of the Russian leader Lenin, I came to doubt whether he shared the truly radical vision of human imagination and possibility embraced by my former partner. I continued to wait and watch.

Now the responsibility I undertook must become yours. The three boxes the lawyers have given you contain the briefs. Store them in a secure place. One day you will see a sign indicating that the time has come to make their existence known. What that sign will be, I am unable to say. Of this much I am certain, however. Its meaning will be unmistakable. It is up to you to ensure that the world learns the message to be found in Abraham Lincoln's briefs. Do as I ask and you will not only honour the grandfather who loves you dearly; more than that, you will provide a service of untold value to all of mankind.

XIII

"And so you see," said Slinger, after draining the last swallow of whiskey from his bottle, "your arrival in town today must be the sign my grandfather foretold."

"It is difficult to think of any other explanation," Yale Templeton had to admit.

The two of them talked for some time longer. Slinger described how, after he came into possession of the legal briefs, he took them to his home, a cave deep in the Chapleau Crown Game Preserve, and stored them in a cedar chest he constructed specifically for that purpose. "They've been there for over fifty years." He lifted the bottle of whiskey to his lips, discovered it was empty, and cursed under his breath. Yale Templeton politely pretended not to hear.

"What I propose," Slinger went on, "is that you come out to my place to examine them for yourself. Then we can decide what to do next."

That made sense, Yale Templeton agreed. And they arranged to meet the following day just before noon in the hotel lobby.

"How long will the trip to your cave take?" Yale Templeton asked.

"I can usually manage it in five days," Slinger replied. "But with you along, I suppose it will be seven, maybe eight."

"And will we see any moose?"

"Bound to. You fancy a moose steak, do you?"

"No. Not necessarily. But did you happen to see a white moose on your way down here?"

"White moose? Course not. There's no such thing."

"How remarkable," Yale Templeton reflected. "Here's a man who has spent his entire adult life in the bush, yet he's never heard of the Great White Moose." Still, he resolved to pack his orange balaclava. Just in case.

In the morning he rose early and went to the diner for breakfast. There was a different waitress from the night before, but it was the same cook at the grill. "Hey, Curly," the cook shouted to a man seated right across the counter from him. "Didjya see our Mad Trapper is back in town?"

The question reverberated across the diner. "That Curly person must be very hard of hearing," Yale Templeton thought.

"No!" shouted Curly. "Old Slinger? Back so soon?"

"Yep."

"But those boy scouts only disappeared, what, four, five months ago?"

"Less."

"He couldn't have finished them off that fast, could he?"

"I dunno. They were a scrawny bunch."

"Maybe so. But there were at least ten of them, weren't there? And the scout leader. He was carrying a lot of meat on 'im."

"I hear he got away. A coupla the boys as well."

"That right?"

The cook cleared his throat and spit into the sink. "So they say."

"Hell, Slinger really *must* be slowing down. No one ever got away back in the old days."

"That's for sure."

"Who was it before the scouts?"

"Don't ya remember? That documentary producer from the National Film Board."

"Ah, our latest Robert Flaherty," Curly said. "More than an hors d'oeuvres or two there. He musta weighed three hundred pounds. How'd Slinger ever lure him out into the woods?"

"Fed him some story about a white moose, I think."

"'Fed him.' That's good. Naw. The white moose, that was those guys up on Wabatongushi. Just last month, eh."

"You sure?"

"Yeah. Used car salesmen. From somewhere in the States. C'lumbus, maybe."

"Oh, yeah, yeah."

"White moose," said Curly, shaking his head.

"Yeah, white moose," repeated the cook. They laughed.

"Oh, wait. I remember," said the cook. "Slinger told him he'd found the remains of the Hudson crew."

"That so?"

"Yeah. Showed him an arm bone. Said it belonged to Henry Hudson himself. I reckon it came off that Danish anthropologist he promised to take to the Native burial grounds."

"When was that?"

"A year and a half ago. Maybe two."

"I don't think I heard about him."

"Her."

"Really? I thought he made it a rule. Only males."

"Cut her up for bait, didn't he. Decided to try a diet of fish for a while. But he put on lots of weight with all that lard, so he had to give it up, eh."

"And he's back in town, you say?"

"Yep, had dinner here last night."

"I wonder who he's set his sights on this time."

"Don't know. But I feel sorry for the poor bugger, whoever he is." Then he cleared his throat, spit in the sink, and laughed again. Curly laughed again, too.

XIV

A t just before noon, when Slinger the Trapper arrived for their scheduled meeting in the hotel lobby, Yale Templeton was seated twenty kilometres away, on a bench at the bus depot in Wawa. He was wearing his orange balaclava, but not because he expected to see the Great White Moose.

Three hours later, by the time Slinger decided there was no sense in waiting around any longer, Yale Templeton had made his way as far as the bus depot in Sault Ste. Marie. And that night, just as Slinger struck a match to start a campfire in the woods outside Hawk Junction, Yale Templeton stepped into his apartment in Rosedale, turned on the lights, and finally removed his balaclava.

And there matters might have ended had it not been for that unflagging curiosity that had placed Yale Templeton inexorably on the path to a career in history, curiosity that in someone with more than an iron filing's width of personal magnetism would have been taken as a virtue. Over the Christmas break, by which time he had more or less stopped trembling, the thought crossed his mind that maybe, just maybe, Curly and the cook had been mistaken about the culinary preferences of the trapper. Maybe the incredible story Slinger had told him was true. Maybe Abraham Lincoln *did* come to Canada, and maybe he *did* take on the identity of a lawyer named Lincoln Abrahams.

And so, drawing on his training as a historian, he went to the university library to do some research. He began with a microfilm copy of the enumerators' schedules for the Canadian census of 1871. An index exists for household heads, but he found no listing for anyone with the last name Abrahams in the Algoma District. "He could have been living with someone else," he reasoned. And so he decided to look through the original schedules for himself. He did a thorough job—he always did a thorough job—but turned up nothing.

Still, it often happens that research leads historians down cul-de-sacs. Not the least bit discouraged, he turned to the census schedules for 1881. No index had yet been produced, so he went directly to the records for the town of Thessalon. There, to his satisfaction, he found an entry for a lawyer named L. Abrahams. The information provided was scant. L. Abrahams was listed as a male, seventy years old, but the boxes for "married" or "widowed," "country or province of birth," "place of birth of father," and "place of birth of mother" were all left blank.

And so he continued on, with heightened expectation, to the census of 1891. He found L. Abrahams again, in Chapleau, although this time with the name written in full as "Lincoln Abrahams." Yale Templeton smiled. Lincoln Abraham's age was recorded as eighty-two. Yale Templeton smiled again. Abraham Lincoln was born in 1809. The columns left blank in the 1881 schedules were now filled in. Place of birth: Kentucky. Place of birth of father: Virginia. Place of birth of mother: Also Virginia. Widower. (As Yale Templeton was well aware, Mary Todd had died July 16, 1882.) Potentially most revealing of all—or was it, perhaps, just a slip of the pen by the enumerator?—in the column for sex was written an "F" meaning female.

There was no record of Lincoln Abrahams in the census of 1901, but then, that was to be expected. According to the letter left by Slinger's grandfather, he must have died during the first administration of William McKinley.

Although that was all Yale Templeton was able to uncover in the university library, he did learn that several issues of a short-lived Chapleau newspaper from the 1880s had found their way to the National Archives in Ottawa. He placed an order for a microfilm copy through interlibrary loan. When it arrived a month later, he discovered two additional clues. The first was a riddle, included in a humour column that ran weekly in the paper:

Question: How long should a bat's legs be?
Answer: Just long enough to reach the ceiling.

The joke, the columnist noted, had been submitted by the well-known lawyer Lincoln Abrahams. The second clue was a photograph of the Chapleau Players, an amateur theatrical society, in their costumes for a production of *Macbeth*. There in the back row, in a wig and dress (russet flecked with gold, according to the caption), looking just a little bit like Ellen Terry, stood Lincoln Abrahams as Lady Macbeth. An accompanying story noted that he had been "wholeheartedly convincing in both his coldly calculating ambition and descent into madness."

A trip to the Archives of Ontario on Grenville Street in downtown Toronto provided the final piece of evidence. While rummaging through some boxes containing miscellaneous private papers and documents from the Algoma District, Yale Templeton came across a diary kept by the wife of a Presbyterian minister in Chapleau during the 1890s. There were two entries of interest:

Friday, September 16, 1892 — When John was passing Fitzgerald's Boarding House last night, he noticed several boys standing on tiptoes at one of the windows around back. He went to run them off, then happened to glance in the window himself. He saw perhaps twenty people gathered together in a sitting room. All the women were wearing men's clothing, and the men were in dresses. Among those present, in a rose-coloured gown, was Lincoln Abrahams, the elderly lawyer and one of our most respected citizens. He often appears as a woman in Shakespearian productions, but this was a meeting of some sort, not a rehearsal for a play. John plans to write to the synod for guidance.

Saturday, October 14, 1893 — Lincoln Abrahams has recently left Chapleau with a Negro man and some others. Beatrice says they have gone to live in the wilderness.

Yale Templeton devoted several more months to research, but was unable to turn up anything else. Still, he had found enough to convince him that the story Slinger had told him was true. The question he faced now was, what to do next? It would never have occurred to him to take his conclusions to the press. But he knew that the evidence he had collected was too thin to pass the approval of referees at a scholarly journal. What he really needed was the legal briefs. But how would he ever find Slinger again? And if he did find him, what about the conversation he had overheard at the diner between Curly and the cook?

And so he hesitated. Until that day when he was lecturing to his class on the Civil War and, in response to the question Joel asked, revealed that Lincoln had faked his own assassination. After which, as we have seen, the story found its way into the *National Enquirer*, and events quickly spiralled out of his control.

*She was drenched in a dress of
blue satin.*

XV

S he was drenched in a dress of blue satin. Think Marilyn Monroe only
better looking. As she glided across the floor of the Faculty Club, her
body swayed to some erotic rhythm that only she could hear. All eyes
were on her. All eyes but two.

Yale Templeton was sitting at the bar, staring into his cup of tea. He had
been there for five days now, ever since Felicia Butterworth had summoned
him to her office. He had explained everything: his search for the Great
White Moose, his meeting with Slinger the Trapper, the letter by Slinger's
grandfather, Lincoln Abrahams, the little community in the wilderness,
his own research at the archives. She had listened to it all impatiently. And
then, in tones that sent the same kind of chill down his back he felt when
listening to Curly and the cook, she informed him that his suspension would
continue indefinitely, and that if he ever—*EVER!!*—repeated to another
person what he had just told her, she would see to it that he never obtained
another university position anywhere. "Except perhaps as a subject for a
vivisection experiment!"

He had been devastated, only managing to cheer himself up with the
thought that at least now he could spend all his days in the library. But the
story of his lecture and suspension had attracted so much attention that he

was hunted down in the stacks by journalists and besieged with questions Felicia Butterworth had forbidden him to answer. And so he had retreated to the restricted privacy of the Faculty Club for refuge. Lost in his thoughts, he did not hear the woman in blue sit down next to him and purr in tones as sultry as her dress, "Hi, big boy."

When she got no response she lifted her hand to his shoulder and repeated the phrase. Startled, he glanced at her, then looked around. At five feet, five-and-three-quarters inches and 137 pounds, he had reason to assume she was speaking to someone else.

"Hey," she persisted, giving his shoulder a playful squeeze. "What does a girl have to do to get a drink around here?"

There could be little doubt. She was speaking to him. As wary as he always was around women, it was in his nature to be polite. "Well," he answered, "first you have to fill in one of the bar chits. You get them from Reg over there," and he gestured toward the bartender, who was watching them with incredulity as he wiped a glass at the end of the counter. "Make sure you tell him it's for a beverage. There are different chits for food. Now you write in your name and faculty number on top here"—he showed her his own chit—"and just below, I always put in the name of my department, just in case someone ..." Then he suddenly stopped and peered intently into her face. "Say," he said, "are you that new astrophysicist I read about in the faculty newsletter? I have to say, we chaps over in history were quite surprised when Physics finally agreed to hire a woman."

Four hours later he was lying stripped to his underwear in a motel bed. How he had gotten there he would have found difficult to reconstruct with any precision. She had asked him about his work; he had started into a discussion of the height of officers at the Battle of Bull Run; then she had nuzzled up against him and murmured, "Can't we go somewhere we can be alone?"

"You mean like my office?" he replied. "Then I could give you a reprint of my article."

"Actually I was hoping for someplace a little more intimate."

A motel near the airport, it turned out, where she had already reserved a room. "Make yourself comfortable," she'd said, then quickly stripped off his jacket, tie, shirt, pants, socks, and shoes, before disappearing into the bathroom. She was not, he had come to suspect, the newest member of the Physics department.

He looked around. On the walls of the room were northern landscapes, cheap reproductions of famous paintings by the Group of Seven. One scene reminded him of the view from the Campo de los Alces Motel, and it occurred to him that he had forgotten to tell the woman in blue about the Great White Moose. He started to hum "Eine Kleine Nachtmusik" under his breath. Then he remembered the warning from Felicia Butterworth and shuddered into silence.

He turned his thoughts to the Civil War to ease his mind. On the taxi ride to the motel he had described to her in detail an article he was now preparing on the incidence of poisonous snake bites at Confederate military hospitals. "How fascinating!" she had sighed, and lifted his arm so she could bury her head into his chest. In an instant his apprehension about women had melted away.

"Perhaps she'd like to hear about the battles next," he thought as he lay on his back, his hands behind his head. "I can start with Bull Run ... No. No. The shelling of Fort Sumter. Edmund Ruffin. I can finish with the story of how, at the end of the war, Ruffin wrapped himself in the Confederate flag, placed a rifle in his mouth, and blew off his head. That will provide a pleasing symmetry."

Just then the room went dark. He heard the door to the bathroom open. A spotlight came on, swathing the woman in blue in a shimmering pink light. Only she was no longer dressed in blue. She wore a studded black leather half-bra and thong panties, leather gauntlets, and a patent leather collar with glistening spikes. On her head was a Nazi storm trooper's hat, on her legs storm trooper boots, on her hands storm trooper gloves. Her right hand gripped a whip.

Bewildered, Yale Templeton started to tell her about the boots worn by Union cavalrymen. "They were different from the ones you have on," he observed. "For one thing ..."

"Silence," she shouted, and cracked the whip high over her head. He was so taken aback he decided not to risk telling her about the split he had noticed in her panties. "And in such an indiscreet place too," he said to himself, reddening.

She moved slowly toward him, the spotlight tracking the undulations of her body. From somewhere in the room there began the rhythm of a pulsing, driving beat. "If only it were an Elizabethan madrigal," he thought wistfully. She leaned over him, the studs on her bra denting his undershirt. "Give me your wrists," she commanded. He dutifully extended his hands, and she drew them behind his head, pulling out a pair of handcuffs from under the pillow and locking him to the brass headboard. "Now," she hissed with a sinister smile, "I'll show you how to make some *real* history." And placing one hand on his collar and the other on the elastic band of his boxer shorts, she ripped down hard, leaving him in a state of nature that would have made Thomas Hobbes squirm.

Certainly Yale Templeton squirmed as she flung the remnants of his underwear in a corner and started to remove her boots. "Lie still," she ordered, then sitting on the bed and thrusting her foot toward his face: "Suck my toes."

He gave her the look he used to get back at the Robinson-Fallis Academy when they placed the kippers in front of him at lunch on Wednesdays. "You dare to disobey me?" she cried. The whip cracked again, this time within centimetres of his nose. Momentarily he was left cross-eyed.

"Suck my toes!" she ordered again, her voice growing even louder and more insistent. He shook his head, though more fearfully than defiantly, and clamped his eyes and lips tightly shut. The whip cracked once more. He felt it graze a certain part of his anatomy where, according to his latest research, a mere 2 percent of rattlesnake bites had been recorded at Confederate military hospitals. Completely unnerved he pursed his lips. She slipped her baby toe inside. He held his breath as long as he could, then exhaled. The toe, he discovered, had a vaguely familiar taste. He touched it with the tip of his tongue, sucked on it gently. "You don't happen to have any currant jelly?" he said at last, opening his eyes in hopeful expectation.

She did, as it happened. Not to mention bowls of strawberry, raspberry, and apricot jam, a jar of honey, a considerable quantity of hot fudge, several dollops of marshmallow sauce, a canister of Reddi-wip, and a litre-sized bottle of Mazola oil, all of which eventually found its way onto the bed, ceiling, walls, floor and, not incidentally, his body. There were bananas, of course, peeled and unpeeled. And a hand-held electrical device in the shape of some exotic organic squash he had puzzled over at the gourmet food shop in Rosedale.

During the course of the next half hour she made him aware of various procedures that, had they been performed by a doctor, would have been condemned by the College of Physicians and Surgeons as unconscionably invasive. He discovered parts of a woman's body that he never knew existed. He discovered parts of his own body that he never knew existed. And then, just when she had succeeded in elevating him to heights rarely seen outside of certain back alleyways in Cuba before the revolution, the door to the room flew open and two men burst in, one carrying a camcorder, the other a Leica and flashbulb. They pirouetted around the room taking pictures as Yale Templeton watched in astonishment. Or rather attempted to watch, since all the while the woman no longer in blue—or in anything else, for that matter, besides her storm trooper cap and spiked collar—was exercising her extraordinary talent for manufacturing distractions. Until suddenly one of the men, the one with the camcorder, called out, "I think we've got enough."

To which the woman no longer in blue replied, "No, not yet. There's one other picture I'm supposed to get." And she disappeared back into the bathroom, returning with a stovepipe hat, which she stuck on Yale Templeton's head, a false beard, which she hung around his ears, and a fake mole, which she pasted onto his cheek. Then she ducked back into the bathroom only to reappear moments later in a short calico shift. She quickly tied clumps of her platinum blonde hair in pigtails with little ribbons, pulled out a bottle of shoe polish and smeared her face into charcoal blackness, then applied a wide slash of bright red lipstick to her mouth. When she had finished she called to the man with the camcorder, "All right, Milt. You can let 'er roll."

Then she turned to Yale Templeton and, in an impeccably inflected dialect, sang, "Oh, Massa Linkum, you dun 'mancipate me. Howsoever I gwinna thank you?" And pulling her shift up over her head, she descended on him with all the savage passion of Pickett leading his famous charge up Cemetery Ridge.

At that moment, with the camcorder whirring and the flashbulbs exploding, Yale Templeton suddenly turned stone cold. All the lectures his mother had given him years before, they now flooded back in on him. All the alarming stories she told him of debauched women and wanton seduction, all the warnings about degradation and public humiliation. And he said to himself, with that depth of profound disillusionment that only the sudden dawning of long suppressed understanding can bring—he said to himself, as he floundered about in the chaotic historical perversion being played out on his body, with lipstick and shoe polish thrusting their way lewdly into the Mazola oil, currant jelly, and simulated whipped cream—he said to himself, "Mother was wrong. Sex is fun!"

And he struggled to say "Cheese."

— XVI —

Her name was Bobbi Jo Jackson. "You know, like President Andrew Jackson," she pointed out. She had been born in the town of Sweet Dreams, in the Texas Panhandle. Her father was a Pentecostal preacher and coach of the high school football team. Unknown to her, he had also been a local operative for the CIA. It was unknown to the CIA as well, and the official in Washington responsible for domestic surveillance in the Southwest District wondered why letters crossed his desk every week from a Pentecostal preacher in Texas reporting on subversive activities by his neighbours. At first he regarded the letters with mild bemusement. But over the course of several years, as the communications became ever longer and more urgent—recording clandestine monthly visits from KGB spies and later, after the fall of the Soviet Union, subversive gatherings of Muslim terrorists, usually disguised as longhorn steer—he decided to send out a couple of agents to investigate.

What the agents discovered was the preacher's daughter: just turned sixteen, captain of the high school cheerleading team, president of the youth wing of the local American Legion chapter, winner of the Miss Teenage Oil Derrick pageant, who sang in the choir at her father's church and assisted in the Sunday school, who marched at the head of the July fourth parade in a red, white, and blue drum majorette uniform she had designed and sewed herself, who before classes every morning led the student body in prayers and the Pledge of Allegiance, and who bore a startling resemblance to Marilyn Monroe. "Only better looking," as one of the agents noted in his report.

They brought her back to Washington and took her to the Agency recruitment department across the river in Virginia, where the official in charge took one look at her and immediately placed her in a course of training specially designed to make best use of her most conspicuous assets. She learned about martial arts and how to operate various deadly weapons, but most particularly about how to perform those extraordinary feats of coordination and agility that Yale Templeton had been privileged to witness. Initially she had been horrified at the thought of engaging in activities that seemed so completely to contradict the fundamental tenets of her religious upbringing. But as she had realized when she first started to menstruate, God works in mysterious ways. And it did not take her long to grasp that He could ask no higher demonstration of her devotion than that she lay down (and occasionally elevate) her body in the service of the man who now served as His surrogate on Earth, the President of the United States. And so she put aside the reservations she initially felt and threw herself into her training with the same kind of joyful enthusiasm that she brought to speaking in tongues. And by the time six months had passed, she had absorbed her lessons so well that each of the senior officials in the CIA insisted on meeting with her privately to pay personal tribute to her achievements.

When she was sent to work in the field, she rapidly established herself as one of the CIA's most able operatives. Able, that is, if you define the term in a rather narrow way. She was never told the purpose of any mission, nor details about the man (or, on rare occasions, the woman) who had for one reason or another attracted the interest of the Agency. All she received from her superiors was an envelope containing a photograph of her intended target and information where he (or she) could be found. Nor did she ever ask any questions. It was enough to know that she was helping America fulfill its divinely ordained and indisputably Manifest Destiny.

She had been helping America fulfill its Manifest Destiny for almost five years when she received the envelope containing a picture of Yale Templeton. But all her training and experience had not prepared her for what happened next. Usually her victims—when they realized that they *were* her victims—would break down in tears and plead, perhaps even offer her a bribe. That or curse and hurl threats. Once in Ankara, a colonel in the security forces had broken free from the handcuffs, leaving her no choice but to slit his throat. On another occasion, in Bolivia, she had been pursued for days through the mountains by a guerrilla leader. Eventually she had stopped him with a bullet, although to the kneecap rather than head because, just as she cocked the trigger, she remembered the photograph he had shown her of two girls he claimed to be his daughters. But Yale Templeton did not plead, curse, or threaten. He simply addressed the man with the Leica politely: "You probably should take another shot. I think I blinked. It's hereditary. My mother always blinks when I take her picture."

And then, after the man with the Leica had obliged, and after he and the man with the camcorder had packed up their equipment and departed, Yale Templeton turned to Bobbi Jo Jackson and, smiling happily, started to tell her about Edmund Ruffin and Fort Sumter. She lay there listening, her elbow propped up on the pillow and her head resting on her hand. At first it was just out of curiosity. But as he rambled on (and on and on) she found herself swept up in an enthusiasm for the details of the Civil War—an enthusiasm, I might add, that in all his years of teaching he had never inspired in any student. And when he reached the Battle of Antietam—"or Sharpsburg, as it's known in the South" he said, since he regarded it as an obligation to be comprehensive—she interrupted him to exclaim, "This is *so* cool!"

"And I've only just started," he replied with delight. "The war goes on for three more years, until 1865."

"Then let's go get some coffee," she said excitedly, yanking the ribbons from her hair and raising her astonishing body from the bed. "It looks like we're going to be in for a long night!"

And now it was four a.m. They had been at the Tim Hortons donut shop for hours. Bobbi Jo Jackson was in blue once again, this time a pair of jeans and a navy blue sweatshirt with USA written across the front in large star-spangled letters. Yale Templeton was back in his suit and tie, although because of the gaping holes in his underwear he was starting to develop a rash. His narrative of the war had followed an entirely conventional course. Through Fredericksburg, Chancellorsville, Gettysburg; through Corinth, Shiloh ("or Pittsburg Landing as it's known in the South"), Vicksburg; by sea to New Orleans; around Chattanooga and up Missionary Ridge; down from the mountains into Atlanta and across Georgia to the sea; on horseback along the Shenandoah Valley; blindly into the Wilderness then on to Petersburg; and finally, inexorably, to Wilmer McLean's farmhouse at Appomattox. He had told her about military strategy and conditions on the home front, about bread riots in Southern cities and industrial development in the North. And at the very last, he ended up where he had always known he would end up, with Edmund Ruffin sitting in his chair, wrapped in the Confederate flag, a rifle in his mouth. He did not, however, describe Ruffin's ultimate act of defiance, out of respect for her obviously delicate feminine sensibilities.

"So we end up back with Edmund Ruffin, huh," she observed. "That creates kind of a pleasing symmetry, doesn't it?"

Yale Templeton beamed. He felt a sense of connectedness with another human being, something he had never truly, fully, experienced before. And he started to ramble on once again, but this time about his own history: about his mother and his childhood in Saffron Walden, about Cambridge and Caius College, about his years in Toronto and his disastrous trip to Chicago, about his passion for footnotes. And then, without stopping for even a moment to consider the possible consequences—indeed unmindful of anything at all beyond the stunningly beautiful woman who sat wide-eyed opposite him—he charged on into an account of his conversation with the chairman's wife at the departmental reception, and his trips north in search of moose, and his meeting with Joseph Brant Lookalike, and the Great White Moose, and his encounter with Slinger the Trapper.

And then suddenly he started to choke, the warning from Felicia Butterworth wrapping itself like fingers around his throat. Alarmed, Bobbi Jo Jackson reached over and touched him gently on the wrist. That gesture, simple as it may have been, produced the kind of miraculous cure that she had regularly witnessed in her father's little church. And now Yale Templeton charged off again, revealing all that he had been ordered never to reveal: about Lincoln, and the community in the wilderness, and the legal briefs, and even about the silence that Felicia Butterworth had imposed on him. And then he was done. There was nothing more to say. He sat there with his pulse racing, his face an expression of both great hope and boundless terror.

She stared at him for a long time. Hours, he might have claimed, if you had asked him about it later.

"So let me see if I've got this straight," she said at last. "You're telling me that President Abraham Lincoln faked his own death ..."

"Yes."

"... and then secretly came to Canada ..."

He nodded.

"... to live as a transvestite?"

"That's right."

"And that the whole story is revealed in a set of legal briefs he wrote, which are hidden in a cave somewhere in Northern Ontario?"

He nodded again.

She gazed searchingly into his face, then dropped her eyes and stared into her coffee, shaking her head. Again it seemed to him like hours passed.

Finally she looked up. And speaking with a confessional earnestness that she usually reserved for her personal communications with Jesus, she pronounced, "Well, I think that's *important!*"

"I think so too," he agreed.

Then she stared down into her coffee again, thought a moment longer, and added, "And the fact that pig iron production went up 345 percent during the Civil War, that's important, too."

"Yes," he said.

"Although in a different way," she continued.

"Yes," he acknowledged. "In a different way."

And she stared down into her coffee again and bit her lip. She was attempting to reason now, something never previously required or expected of her. There was a slight ache in her right temple, and the muscles in her neck began to tighten. All the same she felt exhilaration: exhilaration of a kind that a historian without the gift of metaphor might say the Pilgrims felt when they first caught sight of Plymouth Rock.

Then at last she crossed her arms on her chest, nodded to herself, and stated emphatically, "Well, you know what?"

"What?" he asked.

"I think *history* is important!"

And at that moment Yale Templeton knew the true meaning of love.

XVII

The five men met in a seedy bar only a few blocks from the Capitol. They came in disguise, as the President had instructed. The President himself was dressed very fashionably in a grass green ruched silk cocktail dress by Yves St. Laurent with matching strappy sandals. He wore small diamond stud earrings and carried a silver evening bag. A non-partisan observer might have suggested that he had used a touch too much mascara, but then he was always a bit heavy-handed with makeup.

The Assistant to the President for National Security Affairs came as Captain Hook. He wore a scarlet frock coat with gold brocade, a large tri-cornered hat with ostrich plumes, a white blouse with jabot and ruffles at the wrists, tight-fitting orange pants, and jewelled rings on his left hand. Fearful that his companions would ridicule him for appropriating, in exact detail, the costume that Cyril Ritchard had worn in the Broadway production of *Peter Pan,* he had added two original touches: a wooden peg leg and a stuffed parrot taped to his shoulder that screeched "Pieces of eight! Pieces of eight!" when its beak was squeezed.

The Director of the CIA was dressed as the Director of the FBI. He had gone to great lengths to produce the appropriate effect, having electrolysis to clear a bald spot at the back of his head, dying his hair bluish-grey, adding putty to his nose and earlobes, and wearing a false moustache, trimmed unevenly, the left side longer than the right. He also carried a bucket of water.

Not to be outdone, the Director of the FBI came as the Director of the CIA, wearing a custom-made mask from an upscale costume house in Georgetown. A sandy coloured wig, the hair matted on the sides and in front, sat slightly askew on top of his head and he had four-inch lifts in his shoes. He walked around with his hand in his pocket, tightly gripping a Beretta.

As for the Executive Assistant to the Assistant Undersecretary of Transportation, he was dressed in a conventional charcoal grey three-piece suit.

The President scowled when he saw the Executive Assistant to the Assistant Undersecretary of Transportation. "You were supposed to come in disguise," he groused, his voice grating with irritation.

"I *am* in disguise," replied the Executive Assistant to the Assistant Undersecretary of Transportation. "Normally I wear my *navy* suit on Tuesdays."

"Well, that's ridiculous," snorted the President. "Good thing I stopped at Lord & Taylor on the way over." And reaching into a shopping bag at his feet, he pulled out a pink feather boa. "Here, put this on," he ordered. And the Executive Assistant to the Assistant Undersecretary of Transportation obediently wrapped the boa around his neck.

"That's better," said the President, nodding his head in approval. "Now let's get down to business. As you know we're here to talk about the latest developments in the Templeton case."

"Why didn't we just meet in the secret room at the White House?" asked the Director of the CIA.

"The plumbing backed up again," replied the President. "Someone's been flushing Tampax down the toilet." And he stared accusingly at the Executive Assistant to the Assistant Undersecretary of Transportation, who threw up his arms in bewilderment while the other men at the table shook their heads at him in a collective rebuke.

"Just remember, Lowell," the President cautioned, "we're still holding your children as hostages."

"And my wife, too?" asked the Executive Assistant to the Assistant Undersecretary of Transportation.

The President looked at the Director of the FBI, who nodded.

"Yes," said the President. "Your wife, too."

"If you must," sighed the Executive Assistant to the Assistant Undersecretary of Transportation, who then ordered drinks for everyone in the bar, everyone at that moment consisting of the President and his four companions, a hooker fast asleep at the counter with her head resting in a bowl of assorted nuts, and two black men doing a drug deal in one of the corner booths.

"All right. Back to the reason we're here," said the President. "The little undertaking we discussed at our last meeting. It didn't work out exactly as we had hoped. I'll leave it to Clyde to fill in the details. Clyde?"

"Yes, Mr. President," responded the Director of the FBI and the Director of the CIA simultaneously.

"I said 'Clyde,'" the President snapped at the Director of the FBI.

"Yes, but we're in disguise, remember?"

"Well, I know, but ..."

"With all due respect, Mr. President. If we don't stick to our assumed identities we risk compromising the entire enterprise."

The President considered the argument for a moment and glanced around. The drug dealers were huddling in the booth, seemingly oblivious to anything but their own negotiations. The hooker was snoring gently into the assorted nuts. "You're right," whispered the President. "It has all the earmarks of a sophisticated espionage operation. We'd better stay in character." Upon which, the Director of the CIA got up from his chair and stepped into the bucket of water, while the Assistant to the President for National Security Affairs bellowed "Shiver me timbers!" He whapped the parrot on the beak with his hook until it squawked, "Pieces of eight! Pieces of eight!"

"Very good," whispered the President, and now, elevating his voice to an octave that would have allowed him to sing coloratura, he said loudly enough for the drug dealers to hear, "All right, Clyde, you go ahead now," and he gave the Director of the FBI (disguised as the Director of the CIA) a surreptitious wink.

The Director of the FBI nodded, then sat in silence.

"I said go ahead now, Clyde," the President repeated, once again giving a wink.

The Director of the FBI remained silent.

"Clyde?"

"I don't know what it says in the report," he whispered.

"Ah, yes," said the President. "I see the problem." And he pondered for a moment.

"Maybe I'd better make the presentation," whispered the Director of the CIA.

"No, no," whispered the Director of the FBI. "You're standing in a bucket of water. It would be a dead giveaway."

"I have a suggestion," interjected the Executive Assistant to the Assistant Undersecretary of Transportation.

"Go ahead," said the President.

"Why doesn't Clyde whisper his report to Raymond, and then Raymond can repeat it to the rest of us?"

The President reflected for a moment. "Why, that's very good, Lowell." Then he turned to the Director of the CIA (disguised as the Director of the FBI) and ordered, "Release one of his children after the meeting."

And so, with the Director of the CIA (disguised as the Director of the FBI) intermittently leaning over to tell him what to say, the Director of the FBI (disguised as the Director of the CIA) made the following report:

"Initially everything went as expected. The operative assigned to the case, Bobbi Jo Jackson—"

"Ah, Bobbi Jo Jackson!" sighed the Director of the CIA and the President in chorus.

"... as I was saying," continued the Director of the FBI (disguised as the Director of the CIA), "the operative assigned to the case, Bobbi Jo Jackson, made contact with the subject at the Faculty Club in Toronto and lured him to a motel out near the airport. She lured him out to the motel and arranged for our photographers to come in just at the right moment—"

"Ah," interrupted the President again, and again he sounded wistful, "I think I know that moment."

"... and the photographers took several reels of film and made a video and passed everything along to the man we assigned to approach Templeton.

Klein is his name, Mr. President. I think you know of him from his brilliant work in Africa."

The President nodded.

"So Klein met Templeton, showed him the photographs and tape, and said he was going to turn everything over to the university administration unless Templeton gave him the evidence on Lincoln. Templeton begged him not to do it ..."

"Excellent," interjected the President.

"Please let me finish, Mr. President," said the Director of the FBI (disguised as the Director of the CIA). "He begged him not to turn the material over to the administration because ..."

At this point the Director of the CIA (disguised as the Director of the FBI) slipped him a piece of paper with something scrawled on it. The Director of the FBI (disguised as the Director of the CIA) took out his glasses and read the note, then continued.

"It appears that I wrote down his exact words. Templeton said, and I quote, 'Please don't let the administration get their hands on the pictures. They can't keep track of anything over at Graves Hall.' Unquote. Then he asked for six-by-ten glossies of all the photographs as well as a duplicate of the videotape. To send to his mother."

"To his mother!" cried the Executive Assistant to the Assistant Undersecretary of Transportation.

"Well, she *was* born in Canada," muttered the President.

"And that's not necessarily the worst of it," blurted out the Director of the CIA.

"Hey, remember. You're supposed to be the Director of the FBI," warned the President under his breath.

"Oh ... um ... what I mean is ..." stammered the Director of the CIA (disguised as the Director of the FBI), looking around worriedly and rubbing his forehead. Then suddenly he brightened and announced loudly, "What I meant to say was, *as the Director of the CIA was telling me on the way over here*," and he gestured toward the Director of the FBI, "that's not necessarily the worst of it."

"That's right," agreed the Director of the FBI (disguised as the Director of the CIA), trying to be helpful. "I said, 'That's not necessarily the worst of it.' Now, uh, remind me, Clyde ..."

"Raymond."

"Remind me, Raymond. What else did I say?"

"You *said*," replied the Director of the CIA (disguised as the Director of the FBI), "there has been no further word from Bobbi Jo Jackson."

"You don't think Professor Templeton did away with her?!" exclaimed the Executive Assistant to the Assistant Undersecretary of Transportation.

"Oh, no," replied the Director of the CIA (disguised as the Director of the FBI). "On the contrary. She's moved in with him."

"Moved in with him?!" exclaimed the Director of the FBI (disguised as the Director of the CIA).

"Yes. Don't you remember? That's what *you* told *me*," said the Director of the CIA (disguised as the Director of the FBI), glaring at the Director of the FBI.

"Oh, yes. Of course."

"You *also* said that there are rumours she has been seen in the university library reading works of history."

"Good Lord!" said the President to the Director of the FBI (disguised as the Director of the CIA). "You don't suppose she was a double agent all along?!"

The Director of the FBI (disguised as the Director of the CIA) looked at the Director of the CIA (disguised as the Director of the FBI), who just shrugged. Then the Director of the FBI turned to the President and shrugged.

"So what do we do next?" asked the Executive Assistant to the Assistant Undersecretary of Transportation.

"Well, *I'd* be glad to han ... I mean, *Clyde* could handle it, Mr. President," said the Director of the CIA (disguised as the Director of the FBI), and he gave a slight nod of his head to the Director of the FBI (disguised as the Director of the CIA). The Director of the FBI was momentarily baffled, but then, with dawning understanding, added, "Yes, *I* could handle it." And he took out his Beretta and slapped the barrel against the palm of his hand.

"Thank you, Clyde. As I've indicated before, your personal intervention may well become necessary at some point. But for the time being I think there is a simpler, if admittedly more expensive, way of getting the information we want from Templeton."

"You mean a bribe, Mr. President?" asked the Executive Assistant to the Assistant Undersecretary of Transportation.

"Exactly. A bribe," replied the President.

"Uh, Mr. President," said the Director of the FBI, "I hate to have to tell you this, but I've been through the Templeton file many times, and there isn't a scrap of evidence to suggest that he cares about material possessions. I don't believe he can be bought off."

"Of course he can be bought off!" roared the President. "He's an American, isn't he?"

"Well, he was born here, that's true," replied the Director of the FBI. "But his mother took him to England before his first birthday and renounced his American citizenship. According to our files he's only made one trip to the United States since then, and that was to spend a weekend at a history convention in Chicago. Apparently it didn't turn out well for him. He was charged with sexual harassment and someone stole both his watches."

"Yes, yes. I know all that. But this is a matter of simple biology. Natural selection. Survival of the fittest. His American genes would have wiped out his Canadian genes long ago. And keep in mind, his ancestors were Templetons. Why, along with Biddle, Morgan, and Mellon, they practically invented banking in this country. Hell, look at his own father. His own father spent every sane moment of his life chasing the almighty dollar. Talk about a patriot. He even died mugging welfare recipients in Harlem. Deplorable, I grant you. But in a way curiously inspiring." And he removed a scented handkerchief from his handbag and dabbed at his eyes.

"So will Clyde handle it, then? The bribe, I mean," said the Director of the FBI (disguised as the Director of the CIA).

"You *are* Clyde," whispered the Director of the CIA (disguised as the Director of the FBI).

"Oh ... er ... right. So will *I* handle it?"

"No, no," said the President. "I have a personal acquaintance who is especially qualified to look after these sorts of financial arrangements."

"You mean the Sicilian gentleman we brought in to take care of that little misunderstanding with the manicurist back when you were governor?" said the Executive Assistant to the Assistant Undersecretary of Transportation.

The President froze him with a stare, then turned to the Director of the CIA (disguised as the Director of the FBI). "What I told you about releasing one of his children?" The Director of the CIA nodded. "Well, forget it." The President paused a moment, eyed the Executive Assistant to the Assistant Undersecretary of Transportation closely, then added, "Release his wife instead." And the Executive Assistant to the Assistant Undersecretary of Transportation slumped in his chair, his head falling forward on his chest.

"Sex didn't work, so we go after Templeton with money," mused the Director of the CIA. "I like it."

"Money makes the world go around," observed the Director of the FBI.

"Like the song says in *Cabaret*," answered the Director of the CIA.

"Oh, yes," said the President, clapping his hands gleefully. "Liza Minnelli and Joel Grey. Didn't you just *love* them." And he got up from the table, grabbed the pink feather boa off the Executive Assistant to the Assistant Undersecretary of Transportation, wrapped it around his neck, and started bumping and grinding across the floor, singing in the most convincing soprano he could manage, "Money makes the world go around, the world go around, the world go around. Money makes the world go around, of that you can be sure ..." Upon which the Director of the CIA and the Director of the FBI sprang up in tandem and, along with the President, bent over, stuck out their tongues, blew hard while making rude blattering noises, and finished the verse "... on being poor." After that all three men linked arms and started slinking around the bar chanting: "Money, money, money, money. Money, money, money, money ..."

Now, while all this had been going on, the Assistant to the President for National Security Affairs was sitting silently in his chair. Not that he was indifferent to the question of how to deal with the troublesome Professor Templeton. It was just that, with his ankle pulled back and strapped to his thigh and a wooden peg leg attached to his knee, he was in excruciating pain. But, perhaps buoyed by the singing, or maybe just because he had to do something to take his mind off his agony, he pulled himself up out of his seat and shouted loudly, "Avast ye mateys! Let's keelhaul the blackguard!" At which precise moment his wooden leg cracked and he started to topple over, slamming his hook into the table to break his fall (and almost surgically removing the right baby finger of the Executive Assistant to the Assistant Undersecretary of Transportation). His sudden wrenching movement caused the stuffed parrot taped to his shoulder to tear loose and go hurtling through the air, screeching "Pieces of Eight! Pieces of Eight! Squawk!!" until the Director of the FBI (disguised as the Director of the CIA) pulled the Beretta out of his pocket and coolly brought the bird down with one carefully directed shot to its beak.

After which the bartender made them all leave because they were disturbing the drug dealers.

——— XVIII ———

H. Avery Duck was head of the Faculty Union at the university. An authority on monasticism in late medieval Russia, he was fluent in twenty-four languages, all of which he had invented himself. While to a casual observer he might have appeared a surpassingly ordinary, even boring man, he prided himself on his adherence to the very highest of moral and intellectual standards. Principle dictated his every decision, from whether to support university policy on investment in countries with repressive regimes, to which flavour of jam to use on his toast each morning. It was his unwavering sense of integrity that so attracted his wife to him. "You are a man of great principle, H. Avery Duck," she would sigh every night as he wrestled with the ethical dilemma of which pair of pyjamas to wear to bed. They had no children but did keep a pet turtle named after the leader of an obscure heretical sect in thirteenth-century Kiev.

Next to principle what mattered most to H. Avery Duck was order. Indeed, the two went hand in hand, since he could imagine no more principled endeavour than imposing order on the frightening chaos of university existence. It was his commitment to order that had first drawn him to the study of monasticism, with its rigid rules, strict lines of authority, and clockwork regularity. It was his commitment to order that also explained why he so detested undergraduates. They had, he had long ago decided, no appreciation for logical discourse, for the finely crafted argument.

And they were careless. H. Avery Duck, to the contrary, was meticulous. Meticulous to a fault, some might say. "It is only reasonable," he observed at the first meeting of the Faculty Union over which he presided, "that we take the time to explore each and every issue that comes before us in painstaking detail. Otherwise we might inadvertently overlook some matter of great principle." He made the comment while overruling a motion that the minutes of the previous meeting be approved unanimously, without debate. When the faculty members in attendance responded by remaining silent after he presented the minutes for discussion, he took the opportunity to offer his own analysis of the document (consulting the seventy-one pages of notes he had composed for the purpose), covering such weighty matters as the typeface used and the design of the watermark on the paper.

During the first weeks of his tenure in office he came to the conclusion that his predecessors had overlooked many questions of principle in which the faculty had a hidden interest. Accordingly he increased the frequency of meetings from once a term to once a month, then once a week, and finally twice a day. The meetings themselves grew longer, as did his reports on the principles at stake. Inevitably attendance declined. By the time Felicia Butterworth took over as university president and CEO, it numbered exactly seven: H. Avery Duck himself, as well as the six other members of the union executive, all retired male professors, four of whom could think of nothing better to do with their time, while the remaining two had been banned from the library for scribbling obscene comments in books written by colleagues.

Hence the diminished relevance of the union on the date when Felicia Butterworth announced her decision to suspend Yale Templeton. H. Avery Duck immediately called an emergency meeting of the faculty. Then he dashed off a 112-page letter of protest, written in the language he had invented that most elegantly captured his outrage over her unprecedented action. "It has fallen to me," he announced to his wife with great solemnity, "to right a most grievous wrong." "Professor Templeton could not ask for a more noble champion," she replied with equal solemnity.

Alas, the emergency meeting did not turn out exactly as he had anticipated. He had scheduled it for one of the more spacious seminar rooms in the Edifice Building, expecting the usual turnout of seven but allowing for the possibility that three times that many might appear. In fact, when he arrived a half an hour before the proceedings were to begin, he found more than seven hundred faculty members lined up at the door. While you might think he would be elated by this impressive show of moral engagement, the truth is he was a man who experienced profound turmoil when forced to confront even the slightest departure from expectation. He sought guidance on this occasion, as he often did, in his dog-eared copy of *Robert's Rules of Order* (annotated with his personal emendations), where he found a regulation allowing him to convene the meeting, prorogue it immediately, and reschedule it for later the same day at another site on campus. The Lyceum, of necessity, since it was the only hall large enough to accommodate so many people.

Alas again, his equilibrium faced further challenges once the meeting got underway. When the octogenarian union secretary began to read the lengthy minutes from the previous meeting, shouts immediately went up from around the hall: "What about Templeton?" "What about the assault on our rights?" "To hell with the minutes!" When H. Avery Duck attempted to restore order he was rudely shouted down. "Have they no respect for parliamentary procedure?" he muttered to himself.

It appeared not, because as he flipped desperately through *Robert's Rules* for a regulation that would justify dispensing with the minutes, the unruliness in the hall only increased. Fearful of losing control, he put aside his book and started into the speech he had composed for the occasion (translating into English as he went on, since so few of those in attendance had familiarity with the language he had created specifically for use at union meetings). He had been talking for a mere ten minutes and was only just approaching the end of his preamble when a notoriously truculent member of the English department leaped to his feet and shouted, "C'mon, Duck, cut to the chase." And then someone else in the gallery was up yelling, "Stop monopolizing the floor. We want a chance to speak." And a chorus of "Yeah, yeah" echoed around the hall. And so microphones were quickly set up in the aisles while

H. Avery Duck threw up his arms in exasperation and sat down to make notes for a statement of principle to be printed in the next union newsletter detailing the ethical reasons for adhering to recognized protocol.

There then followed a stream of professors to the microphones, each of whom testified to the dire threat to academic freedom represented by the suspension of Yale Templeton. "Why, without the independence to pursue truth at any cost," asserted Maurice Ronald Tarryton of the Psychology department, "scholars would become nothing more than ciphers for special interests." His own recent work, a statistical analysis of biological distinctions between the races, had demonstrated conclusively that there exists a very precise inverse relationship between the intellectual ability of the individual male and the size of his reproductive organ. Those who knew him intimately, as well as officers of the Pioneer Fund, which had financed his research, agreed that his findings established him as one of the most brilliant men of his generation.

"Much as it pains me to support Professor Tarryton on any issue," observed the sociobiologist Bettina Fetterman, "I find I can only applaud his assessment of the formidable dangers we now face. Without academic freedom there can be no advancement of knowledge. Without advancement of knowledge there is nothing but personal prejudice." Her own decade-long study of fruit flies had demonstrated conclusively that all males of whatever species are genetically programmed to be sadistic, bloodthirsty killers and molesters of small children. She was accompanied to the microphone by her partner, the noted feminist literary critic Ariel McNicken, whose close textual analysis of English-language poetry and prose had demonstrated conclusively that Geoffrey Chaucer, William Shakespeare, Charles Dickens, and quite likely every other man who ever put pen to paper, had harboured a secret desire to rape and murder his mother and mutilate himself.

"We all depend on the freedom to pursue our research wherever it may lead, no matter how potentially controversial our results turn out to be," added Chester Pinkston of the Zoology department. "I am not a brave man, I readily confess it. I only decided to pursue a career as a scientist when I was able to satisfy myself that I would be allowed to speak my views openly and without fear of reprisal. Had it not been for the protection provided by my position at this university, I would never have had the courage to publish my recent article on colour variation in the undertail coverts of the subset of Connecticut warblers that passes through downtown Toronto during the fall migration."

One by one they made their way to the microphones. Men and women. Tenured, untenured. Linguists and botanists, mathematicians and political scientists. Full professors who specialized in ancient Greek philosophy and assistant professors who specialized in contemporary American pop music. Lecturers who studied the geology of the Earth's core and associate professors who studied the chemical composition of gasses found in stars millions of light years beyond the Milky Way. On it went for more than two-and-a-half hours. And then, when it appeared the discussion must be approaching exhaustion, someone raised what would have seemed the most obvious of suggestions: "Hey, why don't we hear from Yale Templeton?" And the cry went up around the Lyceum for Yale Templeton to take the podium.

Only at that moment Yale Templeton was comfortably seated in his Rosedale apartment surrounded by a stack of history books. Evidently no one in the union had bothered to get in touch with him about the meeting. Sitting next to him was Bobbi Jo Jackson, also surrounded by books on American history, although as she was just beginning her journey of intellectual inquiry, she had chosen for herself works that ranged well beyond the particulars of the Civil War. So at the very moment when people were chanting for Yale Templeton at the Lyceum, he was leaning over to her and remarking, "Say, here's an interesting fact I've never seen before. The captured plantation house used by Union officers as their temporary headquarters in Adams county, Mississippi, was designed by the brother-in-law of the first saw-mill operator in the region." To which Bobbi Jo Jackson nodded and replied, "You know, the book I'm reading says that the first labourers on the plantations of colonial Virginia were white indentured servants brought over from England. They were eventually replaced by slaves imported from Africa for the simple reason that slave labour was cheaper and produced bigger profits. However, to justify slavery, planters implemented a series of restrictive laws directed at all individuals of African descent, free as well as slave, that over time effectively turned what was really only a rather vague colour prejudice into racism. Not only that, the origins of the plantation economy trace back to expansionist imperatives inherent in the search for markets, itself the inevitable consequence of the emergence of merchant capitalism in early modern Europe. Wow! We never learned about any of this stuff at the CIA!"

So although the cry at the Lyceum reverberated back and forth across the hall for more than a minute, Yale Templeton did not respond. Which gave H. Avery Duck the opportunity he had been looking for to regain control of the meeting. He stepped up to the podium and said, "It appears that Professor Templeton is unable to be with us today. I wonder if one of his colleagues in the History department would be willing to speak on his behalf?" Then, after making a pretence of scanning the hall, he brought his eyes to rest on the figure of a tall, stately, white-haired man who had served with him on more than a half-dozen university committees over the years. "Perhaps you, St. Clair?" he said. And so, St. Clair Russell Hill, now a professor emeritus several years into retirement and unsteadily supported by a wooden cane, made his way through the crowd and up on to the stage. He shook hands with H. Avery Duck, advanced to the podium, took a sip of water, and began.

"We live in perilous times," he declared. "Perilous times. Hundreds of years ago our predecessors at Oxford and Cambridge struggled, at no small personal cost to themselves, to win the freedom to pursue truth no matter how unwelcome their findings might prove to the authorities. Through the centuries the rights they won have been essential to the very survival of the university, while the university itself has been essential to the very survival of Western civilization.

"Never has the independence of scholars been entirely secure. I need only mention the names Underhill, Hunter, Crowe, and Healy to remind you of hard-fought battles here in Canada. Granted, up to now our own revered institution has managed to escape such unseemly and debilitating conflicts. But by her outrageous action against my eminent colleague, Dr ... uh ... uh ..." ("Templeton," whispered H. Avery Frick) "... Dr. Templeton, President Butterworth has openly declared war on the very fabric of our scholarly community. Nor, I might add, is she acting alone. I am reminded of that famous poem by the distinguished English civil servant, Humbert Wolfe ..."

But before he could begin to recite "The Grey Squirrel," H. Avery Duck, who had heard him deliver the poem on more than a few occasions, took him by the arm and gently escorted him to one of the chairs on stage. "I think we all know your views on the squirrels, St. Clair," he whispered. "And I can assure you that the union executive will continue to back you 100 percent in your valiant campaign, as we always have in the past."

Then H. Avery Duck returned to the microphone and said, "I think we have a clear picture of the unparalleled dangers posed by the suspension of Professor Templeton. Now we must decide what action to take. Let me say, I am quite ready to accept the responsibility, as burdensome as it may be, for drafting a statement of principle that outlines our—"

"A rally!" shouted someone.

"On the steps of Graves Hall!" shouted another.

"Yeah, we'll show Butterworth that we mean business!"

And cries of approval went up all around the Lyceum.

H. Avery Duck opened his mouth to object. He much preferred the orderliness of the carefully crafted written communication to the spontaneity of public demonstrations. However, before he could utter a word, a young astrophysicist was on her feet, shouting, "When should it be?"

"Next week," shot a reply from across the hall.

"No, no. In two weeks," roared the truculent English professor. "We need time to get the students involved." At the mention of students, H. Avery Duck shuddered.

"We'll get thousands to show up!" someone cried.

"No. Tens of thousands!" Optimism reigned supreme, as it always does on such occasions.

There was little to be gained, H. Avery Duck cheerlessly acknowledged to himself, by pointing out the unpredictability that must attend any public protest. With profound misgivings he surrendered to the inevitable. "All right," he sighed. "A rally. Two weeks from today. And I will write a statement summarizing the principles involved in the case, which I will personally deliver to President Butterworth."

"A statement in English," someone shouted.

"I'll have one of my graduate students translate it into English, yes," H. Avery Duck allowed, "to submit along with the original. Now it would probably be useful at this point for me to go over the main arguments that I believe should be included in my statement."

And he proceeded to deliver the speech he had been denied the opportunity to present at the outset of the meeting. And by the time he was finished, almost four hours later, the eight people left in the Lyceum—H. Avery Duck himself, the six additional members of the union executive, and St. Clair Russell Hill—voted unanimously to approve his remarks as representing the sentiments of the faculty. And they passed a motion confirming that the statement of principle to be given to Felicia Butterworth would include a clause demanding that she reveal the true nature and full extent of her relationship with the squirrel population on campus.

XIX

J oel was in love again. With Heather. He fell in love with her the moment
he learned that she had once run naked through a vivisection laboratory
to protest cruelty to animals. He wished he could think of a reason to
run naked through a classroom.

He had met her on his way to breakfast one morning. She was standing at
the door of the cafeteria handing out leaflets about the protest the following
afternoon on the steps of Graves Hall. What he noticed first were her fingernails,
bitten down to a ragged edge, no nail polish. He liked that in a woman. Of
course, he liked long nails, too, and nail polish, the flashier the better. But
then, Joel never concerned himself much with contradictions. The second
thing he noticed was her eyes, one blue, one hazel. They had all the intensity
that his own eyes so conspicuously lacked.

"It's about the demonstration tomorrow afternoon," she said earnestly as
she handed him the leaflet. Everything she said, she said earnestly. He looked
at the piece of paper. "Defend Freedom of Speech!! Support Yale Templeton!!"
the headline read in bright red italics.

Joel knew about the controversy surrounding the suspension of Professor
Templeton. Vaguely. He had long ago stopped paying attention to what was
happening on campus; it seemed to have so little to do with the meaning of

life. Well, the meaning of his life. "I took a course from Professor Templeton this term," he commented matter-of-factly. "It was on the Civil War."

"You mean the course where he made the remark about Abraham Lincoln? The one that got him suspended?!" Heather cried.

"Yeah, I guess so," shrugged Joel.

"Then this is all about you, isn't it?!"

He thought for a moment. He thought about the lecture where Professor Templeton had made his ridiculous comment. He thought about how, afterward, he had phoned the *National Enquirer* and that now there was going to be a protest. "Hey. It *is* about me, isn't it?" he said, feeling a momentary surge of pride.

"I mean, he didn't even get to finish your course!"

"No, they brought in some grad student. Todd or Tom something."

"Isn't that just like Graves Hall!"

"Actually his lectures were pretty entertaining," Joel thought. "By comparison, anyway." But then he remembered the extra reading Todd or Tom had assigned, and he frowned, which Heather took as a sign of agreement.

"Why, you've just *got* to come tomorrow!" she exclaimed. And then she started telling him about her own involvement in previous causes on campus: protests against the plan to put up a sign for Trustworthy Ted's at the entrance to the university; the letter-writing campaign against drug company control over research at the Medical School; a sit-in against the decision to require professors to give commercials for Nike before each lecture; and, of course, her personal crusade to end vivisection experiments. And that's when Joel learned that she had run naked through a biology lab. And that's when he fell in love with her.

She was an anthropology student with a special interest in hunting and gathering societies. During the previous fall term she had done an independent study with one of the world's leading authorities on the Ju/'hoansi people of the Kalahari Desert. "The Ju/'hoansi lead an extraordinarily peaceful and contented existence," she informed him. "Unlike us they have a truly democratic way of life. There are no leaders, and when any two individuals have a disagreement, it is resolved through calm discussion, with everyone in the community having a chance to express an opinion."

Joel nodded. It was rare, he reminded himself, when his own opinions were given the respect they deserved.

"Not only that," she added, "they practice the equality we only preach. There is basically no private property. Everything is shared equally among members of the tribe."

Joel was very attached to his own possessions, but he was not doctrinaire and was more than willing to accept gifts from others.

"Best of all," she went on, "because the Ju/'hoansi are not driven as we are by the meaningless pursuit of material goods, they have lots of leisure time, which they spend visiting each other, singing, telling stories, and playing games."

Joel had a deep regard for leisure time.

"The highlight of community life is a healing dance. Specially trained men and women—the Ju/'hoansi do not draw our artificial distinctions between the sexes—dance in front of a communal fire until they go into a trance. This summons an awesome force—the Ju/'hoansi call it *n/um*—which can then be directed toward healing those afflicted by evil spirits."

Joel imagined that he would have made a very good healer and regretted that he had not been born to Ju/'hoansi parents in the Kalahari.

"So you'll come tomorrow?" Heather asked. Joel could hardly say no. He was in love.

XX

I t was warm and sunny the day of the rally, with just the occasional passing breeze. Surely the gods were looking with favour on the protest. All the same, attendance was short of the ten thousand someone had predicted at the faculty meeting. Even short of the one thousand someone else had predicted. There were, in fact, at most 270 people gathered in front of the steps of Graves Hall, including a scattering of faculty, but mostly graduate students and undergraduates.

You might be inclined to suppose that the turnout reflected badly on the faculty, but there were mitigating circumstances. When H. Avery Duck sat down to write the statement of principle he would present to Felicia Butterworth, he almost immediately realized that there were many more issues at stake than he had initially suspected. And so the document grew lengthier and lengthier. And when he was finally done, he knew he could not entrust the English translation to a graduate student. "I'll just have to do it myself," he acknowledged with a sigh. Which meant, as he explained to members of the union executive, it would be necessary to postpone the rally for two weeks.

Now, here was the problem: The protest was originally scheduled to take place the last week of lectures. The delay pushed it back past the end of term, into May. Not many people beyond the halls of university life seem to appreciate the full extent of professional obligations pressing down on academics. In addition to teaching (both graduate students and undergraduates), professors must carry out original research, present papers, write reviews, articles, and books, produce grant proposals, serve as referees for scholarly journals and funding institutions, attend conferences, and fill administrative positions both at the institutions where they hold appointments and in professional organizations. Many of these obligations require extensive travel. And so it was that on the day of the rally, a significant proportion of the faculty happened to be out of town.

The truculent English professor, for example, was chairing a session on Henry Miller's *Tropic of Cancer* at a conference in the south of France on literature and pornography in twentieth-century America. The young astrophysicist was in the south of France to assess whether data she had compiled on the Andromeda galaxy while working at the David Dunlap Observatory north of Toronto could be confirmed with sightings by binoculars from a beach on the Mediterranean. Chester Pinkston was in the south of France boldly searching for Connecticut warblers. The chairman of the History department was researching technological innovations in warfare during the Qing dynasty in the many fine Chinese archives located in the south of France. And Ariel McNicken and Bettina Fetterman were in the south of France on a cultural exchange. Or what would become a cultural exchange once they found two scholars from Provence who wished to spend the spring in Toronto.

Nor should we forget Yale Templeton. Yale Templeton missed the rally as well, although not, it must be admitted, because of some pressing professional commitment. Several days earlier he and Bobbi Jo Jackson had been listening to *Sunday Morning* on the CBC when they heard an interview with the mayor of a small town in northern Quebec where a controversy had erupted between English and French speakers over one of the few laws in the province dealing with language issues. Actually what seized their attention was not the interview itself but rather the barely audible fragment of a background remark picked up by Bobbi Jo Jackson.

"Wow! Did you hear that?!" she said.

"What?" Yale Templeton asked.

"'Un orignal blanc.' Someone said, 'Voyez! Un orignal blanc! Sacrebleu!'"

"I'm afraid I never learned Spanish."

"French," she corrected him. "I once had an assignment in Senegal. Orignal blanc means 'white moose.' Someone said, 'Look! A white moose!'"

"Amazing that they have a word for 'moose' in Senegal," thought Yale Templeton as he went looking for his suitcase. And within less than an hour, he and Bobbi Jo Jackson were speeding north in a rented car along Highway 400. (As she had explained when she diverted him from the bus depot to an Avis franchise across the street, she had been trained to drive cars at very high speeds while avoiding police surveillance.)

So the rally took place without the presence of the individual whose suspension had prompted it. Not that anyone seemed to care. The atmosphere was upbeat, even festive. Various participants had hoisted aloft colourful protest banners: "Freedom of Speech Is a Right Not a Privilege." "Unshackle Yale Templeton! Shackle President Butterworth!" (This particular banner showed a cartoon of Felicia Butterworth, red hair exploding out of the top of her head, and a gag over her mouth.) "Abraham Lincoln Is Alive and Well in Canada. So Why Does the University Treat Its Professors Like Slaves?" "Watch Out for the Squirrels!!!" And just as the speeches were about to begin, a large van pulled up carrying men and women dressed as Frito-Lay products. They jumped out and began to distribute free potato chips and pretzels to the protestors—a peace offering from Felicia Butterworth, someone speculated. And yes, Heather was at the rally. And Joel as well, although he held himself a little off to one side.

The agenda for the day's events had been worked out in advance. Normally H. Avery Duck found it distasteful to deal with the president of the Student Administrative Assembly (or, indeed, any undergraduate), but in this case he had seen no practical alternative. According to the deal they had reached, the SAA president would take responsibility for organizing the speakers and seeing that the afternoon's events unfolded (as Duck subsequently testified during the court proceedings) "in a dignified, orderly fashion." A half-hour after the rally began, Duck himself would arrive, say a few words to the crowd (presumably in English), and then proceed up the steps into Graves Hall to deliver his statement of principle to President Butterworth. It would not take him long, he managed to convince himself, to demonstrate the ironclad logic of his arguments. She would thank him for explaining the flaws in her reasoning, and he would then return to the protestors to announce that she had seen the error of her ways and had agreed to lift her suspension of Yale Templeton. There would follow wild celebrating, capped by a victory march around Regency Circle. "The students will probably want to carry me on their shoulders," H. Avery Duck said to himself. And he inwardly shuddered at the prospect.

And so the rally began. There were the usual calls for revolution from the militant fringe of anarchists, Trotskyites, and Presbyterians that can be found on any campus. But the threat to freedom of expression represented by the suspension of Yale Templeton had raised alarm across a broad spectrum of the university population. And so the president of the Young Conservatives gave a speech, as did the presidents of the Young Liberals, Young New Democrats, and Young Undecideds. In attendance as well was the Isadora Duncan Marching Band from the Engineering School, its seventeen men and one woman dressed in their familiar neon green hard hats and magenta overalls.

At exactly the appointed time H. Avery Duck arrived wearing his best brown suit and a new tie and with both volumes of his statement of principle in hand. He made his way up to the microphone, offered an awkward greeting to the crowd, and delivered the abbreviated remarks he had prepared for the occasion (or remarks as abbreviated as he could make them, given the gravity of the situation). An hour and a half later he took his leave of the one hundred or so people who remained and walked through the doors of Graves Hall to the accompaniment of the strains of a well-known drinking song performed by the Isadora Duncan Marching Band—which partially addressed the problem of rapidly diminishing attendance by attracting fifty or so fraternity brothers from Delta Kappa Epsilon who had been taking part in an Ultimate Frisbee tournament on the opposite side of Regency Circle.

And then the rally started up again with speeches from a spokeswoman for the United Jewish People's Organization, a minister from the Nation of Islam, and two or perhaps three indistinguishable missionaries from the Church of Latter Day Saints. Representatives of Asian-Canadian, Caribbean-Canadian, and Inuit students all warned of the dangers to minority groups if freedom of speech were to be curtailed, a sentiment echoed by several gay and lesbian speakers and two transvestites (who seemed to take a special interest in the proceedings). A campus gospel choir sang "Go Down, Moses" followed by a moving rendition of "We Shall Overcome." An Ojibwa poet delivered a verse he had written specifically for the occasion, celebrating the respect for liberty shared by First Nations peoples across Canada (then offered a collection of his poetry for sale, at a greatly reduced price).

When the list of scheduled speakers had been exhausted, the SAA president invited others to come forward and voice their concerns. Many did, not only students and faculty, but several members of the maintenance staff and even some interested passersby. For more than two hours the protest continued. But H. Avery Duck did not reappear. And now a chilling wind and threatening clouds began to move in from the west. Thunder could be heard in the distance. The protestors moved toward the shelter of the few nearby trees, then, in twos and threes, started to slip away. Unwilling to let the day's events end on such an irresolute note, Heather jumped forward and grabbed the microphone. "Before you go," she called out earnestly, "we should hear from someone uniquely qualified to talk about the heinous crime that is being perpetrated on this campus. Although, regrettably, Professor Templeton could not be here with us today, we are privileged to have one of his most brilliant and dedicated students." And rushing into the dwindling crowd, she grabbed Joel by the arm and pulled him toward the microphone.

Now there were many things Joel had never hoped to become in his lifetime. Ambassador to Kuwait. A contestant on *Survivor*. The world's leading authority on bonsai plants. But among the things he had most hoped never to become was a public speaker. He simply did not have that supreme self-confidence required of anyone who aspires to make a living by public speaking. Or maybe what I mean is he was possessed of that very human sense of self-doubt that so many public speakers seem to lack. Still, at that moment, he was in love. Madly, deeply in love. And so, with a reluctance that must have been evident to attentive observers in the crowd, he stepped forward.

Once in front of the microphone, he cleared his throat, coughed lightly, then cleared his throat again. The faculty and students looked at him expectantly.

"What a bunch of maroons!" he said to himself, quoting a favourite phrase from the Bugs Bunny cartoons he still liked to watch every Saturday morning. And then he cleared his throat a third time and began to sweat. Silence. Heather leaned over and whispered, "Tell them about your class. Tell them about Professor Templeton."

Joel coughed once more, cleared his throat yet again, then started to speak, his voice wobbling about half an octave in either direction. "Yes, I was in Professor Templeton's class on the American Civil War." The crowd cheered.

"Uh ... he was, uh ... he was, uh, very well organized." More applause.

"He gave us lots of details." Still more applause.

"Um ... and, uh, statistics." A smattering of applause.

"He told us that pig iron production in the West went up 693 percent during the Civil War." Silence.

"I think maybe he gave us too many statistics." Laughter. Joel exhaled. He was damp all over.

"Tell them about the lecture," whispered Heather.

Joel looked at her blankly.

"About Lincoln. The lecture about Lincoln."

Joel tried to swallow but his throat felt like sandpaper. "I was at the, uh, lecture where Professor Templeton told us about, uh, Lincoln ... uh, President Lincoln." Applause once again.

"About, uh ... about his, um, faking his own, uh, assassination." Louder applause.

"So he could, uh, live openly as ... as a, uh, transvestite." Still louder applause, especially from the transvestites. Enthusiastic whistling by the few remaining fraternity brothers from the DKE house.

Then he grew silent again. What else was there to say? That no sane person could believe that Abraham Lincoln had faked his own death so he could live as a cross-dresser in Canada? That obviously Yale Templeton should not be allowed at large in society, let alone entrusted to lecture at a university? That the only reason he, Joel, was standing in front of them at the moment was because barely more than twenty-four hours earlier he had met the woman of his dreams?

As the silence expanded he started to grow more agitated. And as he started to grow more agitated, he became convinced that the friendly faces in front of him were turning sinister, hostile. The casual chatter of the crowd now took on an ominous tone, and he strained to hear what people were saying. Out of the corner of his eye, he caught sight of what looked like a giant pretzel advancing menacingly toward him. The fears overtaking him were irrational, he recognized that. But he decided to surrender to them anyway, and turning to Heather he released a barely audible, plaintive moan, then blurted out, "This is all about me, you know!!"

The protestors looked at one another in confusion, but Heather shouted back at Joel, "Yes, it's all about you. And about me, too."

"And me!" shouted the Ojibwa poet. "And each one of us. About our right to be able to speak our minds freely."

"Right on, mon!" shouted a gay Rastafarian. "It's about me!" "And me!" shouted a Scientologist. "And me!" shouted the president of the Young Liberals. "And me!" shouted a dental student who had actually turned down medical school. "And me!" shouted Maurice Ronald Tarryton, who had happened by the rally on his way to the post office to send the Pioneer Fund his latest research proposal on sex organs and intelligence. "And me," shouted the Ojibwa poet again, who in a fit of exuberance offered to drop the price of his book of poetry by a dollar and throw in, at cost, a guide to fine dining in the vicinity of the campus. And soon everyone was shouting, "It's about me! It's about me!" Heather hugged Joel and threw his arm triumphantly in the air as the Isadora Duncan Marching Band broke into "Happy Days Are Here Again." Or perhaps it was "Camptown Races."

And in all the exuberance and commotion no one noticed that H. Avery Duck had finally emerged from Graves Hall. And because no one noticed that H. Avery Duck had finally emerged from Graves Hall, no one noticed that his pants were bulging obscenely where Felicia Butterworth had unceremoniously stuffed the two volumes of his statement of principle. Nor that he had a bag of Nachos Cheese Doritos over his head. Which the Dean Responsible for Relations with Manufacturers of Feminine Hygiene Products, who had escorted him out the door, was kind enough to remove, after which she placed complimentary bags of Rold Gold pretzels and Funyuns Onion-flavored Rings in his hands.

He stood there in a paralytic stupor for several moments, until the SAA president happened to turn in his direction. "Look!" the SAA president shouted at the crowd. And then, using the bullhorn to make himself heard, he repeated, "Look! Look!" The crowd looked, and catching sight of H. Avery Duck, gave a collective gasp. H. Avery Duck tried to speak but gagged on the corn chips in his mouth. At that point Heather grabbed the microphone and, pointing to him, shouted, "Well now we see what the administration really thinks about freedom of speech!"

The crowd gave an ugly roar.

"And are we going to let them get away with it?"

"No!" everyone shouted in unison.

"Are you with me?" she yelled, ripping off her clothes.

"We are!!" returned the crowd, several of whom doffed their hats.

"Then let's occupy the president's office!!!" she shouted. And as Joel silently but quickly slipped away, she raced up the stairs past H. Avery Duck.

Just at that moment, however, the men and women dressed as Frito-Lay products ripped off their own clothes—their costumes, to put it more precisely—to reveal police uniforms underneath. Two constables tackled Heather before she could get to the door, while a third grasped H. Avery Duck, who in trying to speak succeeded only in spitting corn chips into the officer's face, a transgression that earned him a club to the side of the head. Most demonstrators fled in alarm. The few that raised an outcry were dispersed by the police with little difficulty. The tepid nature of the resistance convinced the officer in charge to show forbearance. He ordered only three people taken into custody: Heather and H. Avery Duck for inciting the crowd to riot, and the Ojibwa restaurant critic for impersonating a poet.

Joel watched it all from the security of the Edifice Building. He was understandably unhappy when the police led Heather away. Still, he had learned long before that love could be fleeting. And in any case, the constable who escorted her to the van looked very striking in her uniform. He always had a weakness for women in uniforms.

There were two
Richard Hakluyts.

XXI

There were two Richard Hakluyts. Richard Hakluyt the elder, to use the name given him by historians, was born sometime during the 1530s to a prominent landowning family in Herefordshire. In 1555 he moved to London to pursue a career in law, settling in as a student at the Middle Temple. Although for much of the rest of his life he remained a practicing lawyer, he is best known for the role he played in encouraging English trade and exploration. He amassed a vast collection of original documents relating to overseas ventures and collaborated with many of England's leading figures involved in attempts to found colonies in North America.

He is significant to us, however, because of the formative influence he had on the career path of his more famous cousin of the same name. Richard Hakluyt the younger, whose family origins also traced back to Herefordshire, was born in 1552 in London. The defining moment of his life appears to have been a visit to his cousin at the Inns of Court in 1568 when he found "lying upon his board certain books of cosmography with a universal map ..." It spurred an undying interest in foreign exploration, and when he became a student at Christ Church, Oxford, he read everything he could find on the subject, including, or so he later claimed, works in Greek, Latin, Italian, Spanish, Portuguese, and French.

Although he took holy orders and eventually rose to a position of some standing in the Anglican Church, his principal passion became the advancement of English interests overseas, especially westward, across the Atlantic Ocean. Indeed, his two vocations were closely linked, since he believed that the Spanish, champions of Catholicism, were "dragons and infidells" and that Spanish settlement in the Americas represented a grave danger to the advancement and ultimate triumph of English liberty. He further believed that God had designated the English monarch as guardian of His interests and that the destiny of humankind would be determined on the shores of the New World. "The people of America," he wrote, "crye oute unto us their nexte neighboures to come and helpe them, and bringe unto them the gladd tidinges of the gospell."

Hakluyt knew and advised the celebrated English explorers of his age—Frobisher, Drake, Gilbert, Hudson—and he played a key role in the development of several ambitious schemes to establish settlements in North America. It was his writing, however, for which he was and is best known. Drawing on letters and records collected by his cousin, as well as journals from merchant companies, interviews he himself conducted with individuals involved in overseas expeditions, and official documents obtained through his connections at the royal court, he published, in 1582, Divers Voyages Touching the Discovery of America, asserting the right and necessity for Englishmen to plant the cross of St. George on American soil:

> I consider that there is a time for all men, and see the Portingales time to be out of date, and that the nakedness of the Spaniardes, and their long-hidden secretes are now at length espied, and whereby they went about to delude the worlde, I conceive greate hope, that the time approcheth and nowe is, that we of England may share and part stakes (if we will our selves) both with the Spaniarde and the Portingale in part of America, and other regions as yet undiscovered. And surely if there were in us that desire to advance the honour of our Countrie, which ought to be in every good man, we would not all this while have foreslown the possessing of those lands which of equitie and right appertain unto us ...

Divers Voyages Touching the Discovery of America secured him the patronage of the Lord Admiral, which in turn led to his appointment, in 1583, as chaplain to the English ambassador to France. While in Paris he collected extensive documentation on Portuguese, Spanish, and French exploration and began writing the work that, with justice, he came to regard as the crowning achievement of his life: The Principal Navigations, Voyages, and Discoveries of the English Nation made by sea or over land to the most remote and farthest distant quarters of the earth, at any time within the compass of these 1500 yeares. Published first in 1589 and then, in considerably expanded form, a decade later, The Principal Navigations—the "prose epic of the modern English nation," in the judgment of one distinguished scholar—was a compilation, with English translation where necessary, of a vast array of letters, travel accounts, and official records chronicling English exploration and colonization over the centuries. Hakluyt himself did not shrink from making readers aware of his devotion to the cause he sought to serve. As he explained in the preface:

> For the bringing of which into this homely and rough-hewen shape, which here thou seest; what restlesse nights, what painefull dayes, what heat, what cold I have indured; how many long & chargeable journeys I have traveiled; how many famous libraries I have searched into; what varietie of ancient and moderne writers I have perused; what a number of old records, patents, privileges, letters, & c. I have redeemed from obscuritie and perishing; into how manifold acquaintance I have entred; what expenses I have not spared; and yet what faire opportunities of private gaine, preferment, and ease I have neglected; albeit thy selfe canst hardly imagine, yet I by daily experience do finde & feele, and some of my entier friends can sufficiently testifie. Howbeit the honour and benefit of this Common weale wherein I live and breathe, hath made all difficulties seeme easie, all paines and industrie pleasant, and all expenses of light value and moment unto me.

Queen Elizabeth I read the writings of Richard Hakluyt the younger with enjoyment and greatly respected his opinions on the New World and its inhabitants. So did Yale Templeton's mother, both in the days when, as a young woman in Toronto, she liked to imagine herself as Elizabeth I surrounded by admiring courtiers, and years later, after her only son had graduated from university and left home, when she finally and completely lost the ability to distinguish between her fantasy and reality. And so when a series of pictures arrived from Canada depicting what she took to be one of her devoted subjects caught in the most extraordinary and disturbing of circumstances, she concluded that her only recourse was to summon Richard Hakluyt for advice. Unable, however, to remember his current place of abode—a sad reminder of her advancing age, she told herself—she decided to put a notice in the Help Wanted sections of the major London newspapers as well as the Hereford *Times* (taking care to reveal as little as possible about her intentions so as not to arouse the suspicion of the Spaniardes or Portingales):

> I request a meeting, at the earliest convenience, with Richard Hakluyt the younger to draw on the extensive knowledge he has accumulated over the past many years in service both to myself and to the realm.

And she signed it simply "E.R."

Responses began to arrive within days. She heard from Richard Hakluyt, "Cardiff's most trusted plumber since 1955," who heralded his "new no-dig technology" and promised twenty-four-hour service; she heard from Richard Hakluyt, DPodM, SRCh, MchS, FCPodS, a Shropshire podiatrist specializing in bunion and hammertoe surgery; she heard from Richard Hakluyt, second-story man ("free estimates and no overtime"), who alas would be unavoidably detained for the next two to four years, although he might be reached by post at Dartmoor Prison; she heard from RichardHakluyt.com who promised astonishing results from new non-surgical techniques in penis enlargement and offered Viagra, Sanoma, and Phentermine at "shockingly low" prices; and she heard from Melvin Garfinkle, a life insurance salesman from Golders Green. However, in the end she decided to place her trust in Richard Hakluyt the younger, rector of Wetheringsett, author of The Principal Navigations, Voyages, and Discoveries of the English Nation made by sea or over land to the most remote and farthest distant quarters of the earth, at any time within the compass of these 1500 yeares. "I am readie, as ever," he wrote, "to perform such deedes as Your Majestie may think best to advance the honour and benefit of this Common weale wherein I live and breathe."

XXII

He arrived on horseback, dressed, as one might expect, in the rather dismal attire of a sixteenth-century Church of England cleric. On being admitted to her presence he dropped to one knee and bowed his head, till she did bade him rise. He then made her a gift of one of his earliest pamphlets, "A particular discourse concerning western discoveries," as well as a signed copy, in which he had penned a lengthy dedication, of a recent disquisition he had written on the political philosophy of ancient Greece.

She thanked him with the graciousness for which she believed she was admired throughout the land and made known to him the great indebtedness she felt for all the many services he had performed on behalf of the realm. She then explained the circumstances that had prompted her to seek his advice and spread before him the disturbing pictures that she had received from Canada. There were a total of nine: four in which Bobbi Jo Jackson was entirely naked except for the Nazi storm trooper's cap and spiked collar, three in which she no longer had on even the cap, and two in which her face was smeared in shoe polish, her platinum hair pulled back in pigtails. In the first seven pictures Yale Templeton was attired in nothing except simulated whipped cream and a bewildered look. In the last two he had on, in addition, a stovepipe hat, a beard, and assorted jams and jellies.

"Of all my courtiers, I do believe he is my favourite," she confided. "Even more so than Essex. I have come to think of him almost as a son, and he to address me as his mother." And a tear rolled from her eye, stopping to rest on the circular layer of bright red rouge that protruded from the white chalkiness of her cheek.

He studied the images for several minutes and then asked, "And thou sayst that these were sente from Canada, Your Majestie?"

"Indeed," she replied, showing him the envelope. "It is a most fearsome beast pictured on the postmark, is it not?"

"A moos or moosh, the natives do call it. They worshipe it as a god."

"How extraordinary!"

"And was there no letter?" he asked.

"A brief note," she admitted, "although I confess, I am almost loath to show it to you, it has so sorely confounded me." But putting aside her reservations, she crossed the floor to her writing desk and retrieved a piece of paper, which she handed to him. It read:

My Dear Mother,
I thought you might adjudge these pictures to be of some interest. I trust they find you in good health.

With filial devotion,

Y.

P.S. I am the one on the bottom.

Richard Hakluyt read the note several times, turned it around and upside down, held it in front of one of the sconces on the wall to see if perhaps some secret message would reveal itself on exposure to candlelight, read it once more, and then commented, "Most curious. Written, perhaps under duress. Might I inquire how it is that thy servant Y. came to be in Canada?"

"Although I expressed deep misgivings about it at the time, he chose to cross the seas to take up a position as a teacher."

"To educate the Savages?!"

"Yes. Precisely."

"How remarkable! What a man of courage and depe conviction he must be."

"Indeed. He traces his ancestry back to the noblest and most honoured families of Cambridgeshire."

"'Tis odd that our paths have not crossed. Wouldst thou be soe kinde as to allow me to retaine the letter for the nonce. I shoulde like to showe it to severall former associates of mine at Oxford who have a genius for the deciphering of secrete scripte."

She thought for a moment, then replied, "By all means." And he slipped the note into the pocket of his jacket.

"Nowe, as to the images," he commented, "I can, I beleve, make some preliminary judgments, albeit I think twoulde be best if Your Majestie were to allow me to examine them at my lesure. I shoulde like to review some writings I collected during my yeares in Paris, in particular Voyage Au Canada by the French explorer Cartier."

"Of course."

Then setting aside the final two photographs, the ones in which Bobbi Jo Jackson appeared in shoe polish, he continued: "Here we see Y. with a typicall Savage of the Americas. Nowe, we learne from De Orbe Novo by the greate Florentine humanist Peter Martyr d'Anghiera, tutor at the court of Ferdinand and Isabella, that there are founde in the New Worlde two types of native peoples; those who are friendly, of which the Arawaks of Hispaniola may serve as an example, and those who are hostile and unlovely, such as the Cannibals. It shalbe necessary for us to determine whether the Savages who have captured Y. be friendly or unfriendly."

"Why, Cannibals, surely! The female in the image is wearing nothing save a collar."

"Sadly 'tis the way of most peoples who have not yet receved the worde of our Saviour."

She shook her head.

"Be not discouraged, Your Majestie. If the Savages are friendly, it shalbe possible for us to showe them the benefitt of gentle English governance and bringe them the healing balme of the gospell."

"A very comforting thought, indeed."

"Truly."

"And what of those other images?" she asked, pointing to the photographs Hakluyt had earlier set aside.

"Yes, very interesting. Very interesting," he replied. "The Portingales, of course, have solde Africans to the Spaniardes in Hispaniola and to the other Spanish colonies in the West Indies, although I have neither heard nor seen any reporte of Africans arriving at the shores of Canada."

"I have heard barbaric tales of the blacks," she said in a whisper. "That they are a people of beastly living, without a god, law, religion, or commonwealth. That they mutilate their own bodies with knives and take part in human sacrifice. I have even heard it said that their females ..." and here she discreetly averted her gaze "... engage in behaviour of a sort so indecent that I dare not speak its name."

"Tis true, as thou sayst, that Africans live a primitive existence, without Christe or manner of civilization. Howbeit they may yet prove to be of service to us."

"Indeed?"

"I am thinking here of the Symerones, Your Majestie."

"You mean the escaped slaves that Sir Francis Drake encountered on his last voyage to the Americas?"

"Nere the towne of Panama, yes. The Symerones are a people detesting the proude governance of the Spaniardes and shal easily be transported by Drake or others of our nation to the Northwest Passage, and there may be planted by hundreds or thousands, how many as we shal require. And placing over them good English captens, and maintayning in the bayes of the Northwest Passage a good navie, there is no doubt but that we shal gaine entrie to all the riches of Cathay."

"But surely the Africans would perish if sent to the extremities of the New World."

"The Spaniarde, bothe for his breeding in a hote region and for his delicacie in dyett and lodging, shal not be able to endure in the coldness of the North. But the Symeron, although borne in a hote region, hath been bredde as a slave, in all toyle farre from delicacie. He shalbe able to endure the climate, and think him selfe a happy man when he shal finde him selfe plentifully fed, warmly clothed, and well lodged and by our nation made free from the tyrannous Spaniarde, and quietly and courteously governed."

She sat silently contemplating the possibilities, so extraordinary one might have thought that they had been invented by a fabulist.

"But to return to the images, Your Majestie," he said, drawing her back to the purpose for which she had summoned him, "permitt me to offer some speculation."

"I would very much appreciate it."

"It doth appere that, in all probabilitie, Y. hath been taken captive by a bande of Savages in league with escaped African slaves."

"It was what I feared," she admitted.

"Nowe if the Savages are Cannibals, I think we may conclude that even as we speake, they have made of him a very tastie meale."

She moaned softly, then quickly collected herself, mindful of her responsibility to keep a brave face in the presence of her subjects.

"And, of course, shoulde the Savages and Africans be in the service of the Spaniardes ..." he continued, "Well then I woulde not wish to contemplate the hideous tortures that Y. hath endured."

She took a long, deep breath.

"Allow me but a fortnight to examine the images and seek counsell on the secrete meaning of the missive. Then I shal return and make a full report."

"Go with my blessing," she replied, her heart now very heavy.

"Your Majestie," he said, bowing, then taking his leave, after which she retired to her throne, removed her crown, and in the privacy of her thoughts, shed a single tear.

XXIII

The moose's heaviness and lack of grace have sometimes given him the reputation of being stupid. But the moose belongs to one of the oldest families in the animal kingdom, and it is by intelligence rather than by stupidity that the family has been able to survive the changes of climate, the attacks of predatory animals, and all the other vicissitudes of the countless ages since the moose first appeared on the continent.

SAMUEL MERRILL, *THE MOOSE BOOK*

When we last saw the Great White Moose, he was, like Stephen Leacock's memorable Lord Ronald, tearing "madly off in all directions." That was some years ago, and since then he has travelled many kilometres and had adventures too numerous and sometimes too unseemly to mention. The Glidden Cold Weather Exterior Latex Flat Winter White that Joseph Brant Lookalike sprayed on him has dulled to a shade of ivory and picked up mud and burrs, and there are brown patches here and there where his fur has been torn away in encounters with branches, thorns, rocks, and on one notable occasion—an example of those unseemly instances I mentioned a moment ago—a nearsighted porcupine. But on the whole, he looks remarkably similar to the way he did on the day he was resurrected (if I might use that heavily weighted term) as the Great White Moose.

At times his whiteness has put him at great risk—as, for example, when he stumbled from the woods at Lake Wabatongushi one summer afternoon and came face to face with two American fishermen who, apparently forgetting or indifferent to the fact that they had chosen to spend their vacation in the world's largest wildlife preserve, pulled handguns from their tackle box and started firing away. Being blind drunk at the time, however, they missed him wildly and, indeed, were fortunate not to eliminate each other. During the winter, on the other hand, rather than being a liability, his colouring has served as camouflage against the snow. Serendipity, one might say, or perhaps a benefaction from the Moose Manitou. And so he has been able to avoid the ravenous packs of wolves that pose a constant danger to the less exalted members of his species. And he has survived. By luck, but most of all by exercising that native intelligence possessed of all moose, he has survived.

But his soul—if we might think of moose as having souls—has been deeply tormented. For years he has been haunted by an apparition, a phantom, a spectre. Though shorter in stature than the humans who raised him, the spectre resembled them in having four limbs and walking upright. He—the spectre—was conspicuously different in one way, however. In the place where his face should have been, he had—or so it seemed to the moose, who, like all moose, was colour-blind—only a terrifying black void. He had first encountered the spectre one summer morning while he stood grazing in the clearing where he and his keeper used to pass much of their time. On seeing it he had bucked desperately, nearly yanking his tether out of the ground. But then he had noticed his keeper. And when the keeper gave his familiar reassuring smile, the moose grew calm.

After that, however, had come the frightening experience of resurrection. And when, after his initial panic had subsided, the moose—now the Great White Moose—returned to the clearing to look for the keeper, he found no one. He wandered through the woods briefly until he approached another clearing, the parking lot of the Campo de los Alces Motel. And then, peering cautiously through the trees, he saw the spectre again. But now there was no sign of his keeper, no comforting smile. And in the coldness of the moment, the moose instinctively understood that the presence of the one foretold the absence of the other. He retraced his steps the following day and the day after that. But on each occasion the outcome was the same, and each time his disquiet at the sight of the spectre grew more intense. Until finally he fled. The Great White Moose fled. Not far, just deeper into the woods. Years spent in the care of the keeper had left him familiar with the surrounding countryside and the caches of food that the local Ojibwa had stockpiled. There was no difficulty in finding refuge. And so he hid until the following summer. Then he ventured forth once again, past the familiar streams and the rusting blue Oldsmobile down to the clearing. But again there was no sign of his keeper. And again he continued on to the woods skirting the parking lot of the Campo de los Alces Motel. Again he saw the spectre. And again he fled. And the following summer, the same supernatural script was acted out once more. And the summer after that.

But the year following—we are now into the fourth summer since his keeper had disappeared—it seemed that at last his suffering must end. When he made his way to the motel and peeked fearfully through the trees, he saw, he heard, nothing. And for the first time since he had become the Great White Moose, he felt a heartbeat of peace. Until wandering through the woods beside a nearby lake he heard a tortured melody that reminded him vaguely of the call his keeper had used to summon him. And in a momentary surge of what passes for hopefulness among moose, he moved toward the sound. He reached a gap in the trees and scanned the shoreline. There, sitting on the end of a dock, was the spectre, the tortured melody emanating from the void where his face should have been. So the Great White Moose turned in horror and fled yet again. Fled this time without stopping. Fled forever from the security of the neighbourhood where he had been raised and where, up to that moment, he had spent his entire life.

Of course, all moose have an instinct for migration. But his years in captivity had surely dulled his sense of direction. And in any case, he was driven by something even more profoundly elemental than a quest for food. And so, while he encountered many moose on his travels, he charted an entirely independent course, a course of his own improvised design. First east to Algonquin Park. Then north to the woods near Cochrane and back toward Hearst, sometimes retracing his steps but in general tracking the westward route of the Trans-Canada Highway. He ranged across the full length of Northern Ontario to the Lake of the Woods and beyond. Wherever he went, however, it seemed to him that the spectre was following, tracking him, hidden in the shadows. Disturbing memories of the spectre filled his days; dreams of the spectre invaded his nights.

And then one afternoon on Lake Wabatongushi, just weeks after his escape from the drunken Americans, he heard a call that awakened distant echoes of home. It continued for some minutes, then was replaced by a refrain completely unfamiliar to him. He made his way forward, inexplicably drawn toward the sound. As he neared the shore, however, he heard a crashing just ahead. Seconds later a cow and calf careened past, ricocheting off the trees. Their hysterical retreat froze him momentarily. But then the beguiling melody started up again, beckoned him. He caught his breath, then slowly started to move, though cautiously, ever so cautiously. As he approached the water's edge, he took shelter behind a dense row of pine trees. He peered through the branches and dimly caught sight of the figure that, at some level of his unconscious, he surely must have understood he was destined to see. Only this time the spectre was not alone. He was in a canoe with a human who evoked an indistinct recollection of the keeper whose smile had so often comforted the moose. But there was no smile this time. Indeed, the human appeared to be in distress. Back into the woods the Great White Moose plunged. North. Then west. Then, suddenly reversing himself, east. Galloping. Galloping hard.

XXIV

*Some of the French explorers in Canada found there fishermen who had
come from the Basque country of southern France. Meeting the animal
now known as the moose, and never having seen the European elk,
these fisherman called the moose by the Basque word for deer—orenac.
From this is derived orignac, orignal, words used by French writers to
designate "l'élan d'Amerique." A well-known American writer on natural
history makes orignal an equivalent of original, signifying "un type," or
an animal of a newly found species. But derivations cannot be established
by guesswork. The Basques, untrained in zoology, in calling the moose
orenac or "deer," were doing as well as they could under the circumstances.*

SAMUEL MERRILL, *THE MOOSE BOOK*

S cientists have now conclusively proven that a moose raised in captivity
in Ontario will not be able to read a sign written in French. Nor, for that
matter, will he be able to read a sign written in English. And so when

the Great White Moose, in his erratic flight to escape the spectre, crossed the Ottawa River some kilometres north of Temiscaming, Quebec, and wandered into the small village of Je-me-souviens, he was quite indifferent to the language controversy that was tearing apart the local community.

It was a controversy with a long history, but the Great White Moose, never previously having set foot on the Quebec side of the river, could hardly have known that. Then again, being unable to read English, he would not have been in a position to avail himself of the opportunity, as we are now about to do, of enjoying the recounting of that history provided by the eminent historian of New France, Arlen Green, in his celebrated *The People of Quebec*:

> Nothing better exemplifies the turbulent recent past of Quebec than the history of the small village of Harmony (in French, Harmonie). Created with the arrival of the logging industry along the upper reaches of the Ottawa River during the late nineteenth century, Harmony received its name because of the unusually congenial relations existing between the English-speaking minority, who owned and ran the lumber mills, and the French-speaking majority, who performed the labour. It is easy to understand why the two groups got along so well. At wages of fourpence per family for a seven-day work week and with generous allowances of tree bark for their meals, the workers were substantially better treated than French Canadian labourers in other sections of the province. Even when the town came to be eclipsed in importance by Cochelin, Temiscaming, and Ville-Marie, and on the Ontario side of the river by New Liskeard and Cobalt, the mill operators showed considerable compassion for their employees by continuing the tree bark allowance after they cut wages in half, arranging for a Catholic priest to preach once a month on the mill floor about the importance of obedience and the rewards diligent workers could expect in the hereafter, and introducing Irish day labourers for the French Canadians to regard with contempt.
>
> Still, these halcyon days proved short-lived. Railway development to the east siphoned off economic opportunities, undermining the local

lumber industry. One by one, companies closed down their operations, forcing workers to seek employment elsewhere. By the time of the Great Depression there remained only a single family in Harmony: Jacques Montcalm, a third-generation mill worker turned farmer, his wife, the former Louise Wolfe, whose grandfather had built the original factory around which the town had formed, and their identical twin sons, James and Louis.

Jacques and Louise pledged to each other that they would never leave Harmony; they would keep it alive as a testament to their vision of a Canada in which people of French and English ancestry would live together in peace and, yes, harmony. They insisted that their sons become fluent in both languages, spoke of the Magna Carta and La déclaration des droits de l'Homme et du citoyen with equal reverence, celebrated Guy Fawkes' Night and Le jour de la Bastille, and managed to convince themselves that the Seven Years' War was nothing more than a minor squabble between otherwise steadfast friends.

During World War II, Jacques' deep sense of patriotism led him to enlist with the celebrated Van Doos, the Royal Twenty-Second, where he was given a position in the prestigious regimental marching band. Tragically his life came to an abrupt end when he made an ill-advised attempt to catch his tuba during a parachute drop. His death was shattering for Louise, and she only managed to outlive him by a matter of months. Before she died, however, she made James and Louis pledge to her that they would remain in Harmony and preserve the village as a symbol of the dream that she and Jacques had treasured.

The brothers made their commitment to her willingly because, in those days at least, they both held to the same dream as their parents. To deal with the practical issue of how to divide responsibility for running Harmony (population now two), they decided to alternate terms for mayor. And through the 1950s, harmony did indeed reign in the village. But the Quiet Revolution in Quebec politics ushered in by Jean Lesage in 1960 had a profound effect on James. When he took over the mayoralty in 1961, he adopted the slogan "Maîtres chez nous" and implemented a series of measures to promote French in public places. It is time, he said, for "une collaboration honnête" between the English and French of Harmonie.

At first Louis was sympathetic. And when he succeeded to the office of mayor in 1963, he made clear his intention to continue the reforms James had introduced. But only months later the village mailbox was destroyed by a letter bomb. Badly shaken, Louis contacted the provincial authorities for assistance. They sent in a forensic specialist who conducted an extensive examination and concluded that the bomb could only have been planted by someone with an intimate knowledge of the Harmony postal service. Since that effectively excluded everyone except the two brothers and since Louis could not believe that James would engage in such a dastardly act, his initial reaction was to dismiss the findings. But when the mailbox was blown up a second and then a third time in less than a month, and when James organized a mass demonstration in support of le Front de libération de Harmonie (FLH) on the steps of City Hall—attended, according to one report, by fully half the population of the village—Louis began to realize that all was not as harmonious in Harmony as he had imagined.

Then one night a masked man broke into his home while he was sleeping, threw him into a sack, and took him hostage. In response Louis outlawed the FLH and brought forward the controversial *Harmony War Measures Ordinance*, whose unprecedented restrictions on civil liberties would no doubt have outraged Canadians across a wide expanse of the political landscape had Louis not been confined to the trunk of his brother's car throughout the entire period when the legislation was in effect.

Three weeks later it was time for James to replace Louis as mayor. His first official act was to repeal the *Harmony War Measures Ordinance*. His second was to issue a general amnesty for all members of the FLH living in Harmonie. His third was to have Louis released from the trunk of his car. It seemed for a time that harmony had been restored, and for the next two years James confined his political activities to behind-the-scenes efforts to build up his power base. But then came one of those chance events that so often play a decisive role in the unfolding of history. During a detour through the village on his way to attend Expo 67 in Montreal, Charles de Gaulle delivered an impromptu speech in which he uttered the phrase that has forever altered the course of Canadian history: "Vive l'Harmonie!" he shouted. "Vive l'Harmonie libre!" The very next day James announced that he was changing his name to René Purelaine and forming his own political organization, La Partie Harmonie (PH), whose single defined goal would be securing independence for the village from Canada (while retaining the principle of transfer payments from Ottawa).

He then designated himself a municipal commission and convened a series of meetings in which he received various depositions from himself, exclusively in French, championing the principle of cultural autonomy for Harmonie. Subsequently he introduced *La charte de la langue Gallique,* which outlawed the use of English on commercial signs and required that all enterprises have names reflecting the brothers' Gallic ancestry. Confusing "Gallique" with "Gaélique," Louis opened up a pub named La famine Irlandaise and booked in the Irish Rovers.

Developments now proceeded rapidly. Attempting to follow through on his nationalist agenda, René made preparations for a referendum on the question of whether Harmonie should negotiate a new political association with Canada in which the sovereignty of the village would be acknowledged and there would be an equitable sharing of resources. The campaign for the referendum was extraordinarily heated. Signs saying "Oui" and "No/Non" went up all over the village. René made a series of impassioned speeches detailing the many forms of oppression historically faced by the French-speaking minority in Canada. Louis made a series of impassioned speeches reminding listeners that Sir

Wilfrid Laurier, perhaps the greatest of all Canadian prime ministers, had assured his countrymen that "the twentieth century belongs to Canada."* Polls conducted by Radio-Harmonie showed the voters in the village split fifty-fifty, a division that remained unchanged throughout the course of the campaign. (The polls were deemed to be accurate within 2.75 percentage points in nineteen cases out of twenty.) And indeed, the balloting produced a dead heat. A recount was held, but without affecting the outcome.

René had scheduled the referendum for the final days of his mayoralty, expecting to be able to cap his term in office with a declaration of independence. But the recount meant that he had to transfer power to Louis before he could bring down the enabling legislation, and Louis, once returned to City Hall, immediately declared the results a confirmation of the commitment in Harmony to "bilingualism and biculturalism." Bitterly disappointed, René charged that he had been defeated by "l'argent puis des votes ethniques," to which Louis, after hastily converting to Judaism, raised a countercharge that René was promoting anti-Semitism.

Still, Louis by nature was inclined toward policies likely to unite the village. To that end he announced an Olympic bid. "Where could one find a better place to hold the pre-eminent symbol of international cooperation than Harmony?" he asked. "C'est jeter de la poudre aux yeux," ridiculed the editor of the local PH newspaper, who kept up a drumbeat of criticism for months. Eventually, drawing on his insider knowledge of the workings of City Hall, the editor produced a National Newspaper Award–winning series of articles on the financing of the Olympic facilities, in which he exposed (or claimed to expose) "la fraude des fonds publics." Louis vehemently denied the accusation. But on the eve of the next transfer of power

---

* Unbeknownst to Louis, Laurier never actually uttered the famous remark attributed to him. His exact words, spoken at the first annual banquet of the Ottawa Canadian Club, January 18, 1904, were "The nineteenth century was the century of the United States. I think we can claim that it is Canada that shall fill the twentieth century."

he was forced to acknowledge that the six-seat stadium he had commissioned had brought the village to the edge of bankruptcy.

René took over the mayor's office on a high note. However, his exuberance proved short-lived because shortly thereafter the Supreme Court of Canada handed down a ruling invalidating the section of *La charte de la langue Gallique* prohibiting the use of English on signs. The court based its decision on the little known "Animal Farm" clause of the *Canadian Charter of Rights and Freedoms*: "All forms of freedom of expression are equal, though some forms may be more equal than others." René responded by introducing *l'Ordonnance municipale 178*, barring languages other than French from outdoor signs, but allowing some bilingual signs indoors. He then prohibited further court challenges for five years, invoking the "notwithstanding clause" of the Constitution ("notwithstanding the Constitution, provincial governments and the village of Harmony/ Harmonie may do pretty much whatever they like so long as they do not directly interfere with the ability of the prime minister to assist his friends through government contracts and patronage appointments").

In response Louis brought a complaint before the United Nations Committee on Human Rights. He and René both travelled to New York to testify at the subsequent hearings, each marshalling many precedents in both Canadian and international law and drawing on deep, if divergent, philosophical traditions on individual liberty and social obligation. In the end the committee agreed with Louis that *l'Ordonnance municipale 178* violated the principles for which the United Nations stands: "A state may choose one or more official languages, but it may not exclude, outside the private sphere, the freedom to express oneself in a language of one's choice." This ruling, carrying the heavy weight of moral authority, was later incorporated into the North American Free Trade Agreement with the following clarification: "Under no circumstances should this provision be interpreted in such a way as to impair the ability of multinational corporations to earn those profits to which they are entitled by the grace of God."

Following the actions of the UN, René finally, if grudgingly, sat down with Louis in an attempt to resolve their differences. The result of their negotiations was *l'Ordonnance municipale 86*, the English translation of which reads, "Public signs and posters and commercial advertising must be in French. They may also be in both French and another language provided that French is markedly prominent." This legislation, passed in the summer of 1993, seemingly represents the end to the turmoil of the past thirty years, and one may well imagine that it also signifies a truly harmonious end not only for Louis and René but, symbolically, for all the citizens of Quebec."

Arlen Green published *The People of Quebec* in 1994. Although widely praised by scholars, its concluding statement about the future of both the town and the province proved overly optimistic.

In September of 1994 Jacques Parizeau led the Parti Quebecois to victory in a provincial election, promising to hold a referendum on sovereignty. The specific question he presented to voters, modelled on the question originally set by René in the Harmonie referendum twenty-five years earlier, asked whether Quebec should declare independence, "after having made a formal offer to Canada for a new economic and political partnership."

On October 24, 1995, Cree Indians in northern Quebec voted 96 percent in favour of staying in Canada if Quebec voted to separate, and the following day the Inuit of the province opposed separation by an almost identical margin. The referendum itself was held on October 30, 1995. The opponents of sovereignty won, but narrowly, capturing a mere 50.6 percent of the ballots. Echoing René Purelaine, Jacques Parizeau blamed the sovereigntist defeat on "l'argent puis des votes ethniques" and declared, "nous l'aurons, notre pays." The current of xenophobia underlying his comments was quickly repudiated by many members of the PQ, and the following day Parizeau announced that he was resigning as Quebec premier and PQ leader.

Meanwhile in Harmony the provincial referendum revealed the village to be much less ambivalent than the rest of the province. The result, as reported by Louis, presiding mayor and officer in charge of election returns, indicated that 100 percent of the local residents were opposed to sovereignty-association for Quebec, with one spoiled ballot. René accused Louis of vote tampering, and upon succeeding to the mayoralty at the beginning of the new year, he changed the name of the village from Harmonie to Je-me-souviens. "Pour être certain," he proclaimed, "que le monde n'oubliera jamais les injustices qu'ont subie les québécois à travers les siècles." Outraged, Louis immediately sent off a letter to the editor of the PH newspaper (which the paper declined to publish since the communication was written in English): "And *I* will never forget the efforts of a militant fringe in this community to destroy the great Canadian experiment in harmonious coexistence that Providence has entrusted to us." Then he posted a white sign with red lettering outside his pub, containing the message, "And *I* will never forget!" (Though mindful of the terms he had negotiated for *l'Ordonnance municipale 86*, he took care to write in larger letters underneath, "Moi, je n'oublierai jamais!")

The next morning he discovered posted on his door an official notice from La commission pour protéger la langue française, bureau de Je-me-souviens indicating that the English words on his sign had been adjudged too large (or, alternatively, the French words too small). He was instructed to remove the sign or replace it with one in which the French message was at least twice the size of the English translation.

And so the next day a new sign appeared. As instructed Louis had written "Moi, je n'oublierai jamais!" twice the size of "And *I* will never forget!" However, while the English words were written in red again, the French words appeared in a cream colour barely distinguishable from the white background. Indeed, it would have been impossible for any visitor to the village to read the message in French (had there ever been a visitor to the village other than Charles de Gaulle).

The next morning Louis received another official notice from the commission, indicating that the French words on his sign had not been given sufficient prominence. There was also a new public ordinance stating that on any sign in which a language other than French was included, the shade distinction between the lettering and background must be more pronounced for the French words than for the words in the second language, and here "un coloromètre" was provided to help citizens quantify the distance between the principal tones represented along the colour spectrum. In cases where English has been used, the ordinance added, the English words and the background must be of an identical shade.

So that afternoon Louis erected yet another sign, this one with the French words in a pale yellow and the English in the same white colour as the background. However, each English letter protruded a full foot from the board. In the corner of the sign was a cartoon of René.proclaiming, "Vive le Canada!!"

This brought yet another rebuke from La commission pour protéger la langue Française, bureau de Je-me-souviens, and yet another ordinance, this one stipulating, first, that on all signs any message in a language other than French must be flush with the background and, second, that anyone who took actions deemed to bring the mayor into disrepute was subject to a substantial fine, the mayor himself having the authority to determine what constituted "disrepute." (The second provision was to lapse at the end of the current mayoral term.)

In response Louis built a metal frame from which he hung his English message and his French message. The French message was twice as large as the English, but the letters in the English words were illuminated by red and white light bulbs.

This tedious pas de deux came to a halt when Louis reclaimed the mayoralty and immediately rescinded all ordinances dealing with the public display of language on signs. However, it resumed on his brother's return to office two years later, indeed escalated until, finally, René had to add a wing to City Hall to house all the legislation. Still it was only when René attempted to regulate messages in vapour trails used by skywriters—in response, it should be pointed out, to a Canada Day greeting by Louis—that awareness of the controversy reached beyond the boundaries of the village. It happened that the greeting was noticed by a producer for CBS News who was in northern Quebec on a fishing trip. Astonished that someone would go to the trouble and expense of arranging for such an extravagant demonstration of patriotism in a corner of the province where few people lived, he went looking for the individual responsible. It took some searching, but in time he found the brothers and learned from them—with René communicating in French, a language which the producer did not understand—about their ongoing feud. Being American and therefore having a rather adolescent understanding of freedom of expression, he was unable to appreciate, as Canadians do, that public debate over the configuration of words on signs and the colour of vapour trails serves an essential function in any mature democracy. He returned to New York and some months later produced a satiric segment on Je-me-souviens for *60 Minutes*. This produced howls of protest from Ottawa (although the show received extremely favourable reviews in Alberta). And in turn, Michael Enright arranged for a phone interview with René and Louis on *Sunday Morning*.

Which brings us back to where we started this chapter. Because it just so happens that at the very moment when the interview began, with Louis responding to a question about the brothers' family history, the Great White Moose emerged from the Ottawa River on the outskirts of Je-me-souviens. Normally he—the Great White Moose—was careful to keep to the woods, especially when entering unfamiliar territory. But in this case he was a little disoriented after his swim, and perhaps for that reason, or maybe just out of curiosity, he edged toward a clearing. There was not much to see. A couple of houses, an Irish pub, City Hall, a half-finished Olympic stadium, the roof lying in sections on the ground. No people, though. None in view, anyway. And, of critical importance to the Great White Moose, no spectre. And so he advanced down the main thoroughfare, though all the while looking warily from side to side. But just as he reached City Hall, where the two brothers had come to take their call from Michael Enright, René happened to glance out the window. Catching sight of the moose, he blinked, rubbed his eyes, blinked again, then shouted, "Un orignal blanc. Voyez! Un orignal blanc! Sacrebleu!"

Now scientists have conclusively proven that a moose raised in captivity in Ontario will be unable to understand an imprecation shouted in French. And so, when the Great White Moose heard René cry out, he stopped and swung his head about anxiously. Perhaps he expected to encounter the spectre. Who can say? In any case, when he saw René emerge from City Hall, he stood still for a moment, as moose do when alarmed. Then he charged across the sections of roof lying next to the stadium, sending them clattering in all directions, stampeded past La famine Irlandaise, trampling a floral arrangement in the shape of the Canadian flag that Louis had recently planted (soon to be outlawed by municipal ordinance), then crashed through the framed "And *I* will never forget!" sign, setting off a recording of "O Canada" by the Barenaked Ladies, before finally plunging back into the Ottawa River. René chased after him, running right up to the water's edge. But then he stopped. It was a matter of principle with him that he had not set foot in Ontario for more than thirty years. As for Louis, he remained behind in City Hall, standing at attention, his hand over his heart. The national anthem always stirred such powerful emotions in him.

XXV

There is little difference between the night and the day in the routine
of a moose's life. He travels and feeds at night as well as by day;
he lies down to rest by day as well as by night. He usually browses
until an hour or two before midday, and then for two or three hours
is likely to lie down and chew the cud of idle contemplation.

SAMUEL MERRILL, *THE MOOSE BOOK*

From Je-me-souviens, Quebec, to Elk Lake, Ontario, is a mere 100 kilometres or so, as the crow flies (assuming the crow can be induced to fly in a northwesterly direction). It was a good deal farther than that for the Great White Moose, however, since he turned south following his escape from René Purelaine, tracking the descent of the Ottawa River along its western bank.

His second crossing of the river in under an hour had left him fatigued, but upon reaching the Ontario shore the residual effect of his panic attack gave him the energy to resume his gallop. After covering several kilometres, however, and satisfying himself that he had outdistanced anyone who might be on his trail, he settled into that shambling gait so characteristic of moose on their perambulations (as well as Abraham Lincoln). In the late afternoon he stopped to rest, falling into a deep and long sleep. When he awoke, at around ten o'clock at night, he felt uncommonly refreshed.

He made a meal of the leaves and smaller branches off an aspen sapling, then started south once more. After shadowing the Ottawa River for the better part of an hour, he drifted westward, following one of its minor tributaries. It was a very dark night, the moon hidden behind clouds, and the woods were thick and warm. There was no possibility to move rapidly here, but with an increasing sense that danger had passed, he was quite content to proceed at an easy pace.

A few kilometres above the small town of Balsam Creek, he arrived at a low bridge where the stream was crossed by the road between North Bay and Temiscaming. It was almost midnight now, and he stood there for some minutes deliberating (to the extent that we might call what he was doing "deliberating") whether to cross the road and continue along by the water, or turn around and retrace his steps, or strike north through the woods, or, finally, to cross the stream and start off south once again. A cooling breeze blew up, and the cloud cover began to break, exposing the edge of the summer moon. Since being reborn as the Great White Moose he had shown an instinct for the road less travelled. But there were no markers here—no hint that other members of his species had passed this way before—and so his apparent predisposition to chart an independent course was effectively rendered beside the point. He stood by the road, passively taking in the monotonous chirp of a tree cricket, punctuated somewhere far off in the distance by the deceptively mournful call of a loon. Surely the setting for an existential moment, if existential moments fall within the experiences of moose.

Not sharing that obsession humans have with the measurement of time, he could not have said how long it was before he heard the metallic drone of the car. He knew the sound a car makes, having crossed many roads during the years since he began his journey, from muddy country lanes to the asphalt rigidity of northern highways. Indeed, he had heard many thousands of cars. He had witnessed many thousands as well, although usually at some considerable distance. The car approaching him now was travelling fast, faster than would be expected on a small unlit country road after midnight. Not that I can say with certainty that the moose had expectations. But he did have experience. And in his experience, the sound of a car in the night was invariably followed, sooner or later, by the appearance of bright beams. Beams that warned him to move to cover; beams that allowed him to identify where safe harbour could be found.

But in this case, as the car grew nearer, the moose saw nothing. He had no way of knowing that the driver, who was rocketing at speeds well over 160 kilometres an hour through this particular corner of the Ontario backwoods, had decided to drive without headlights on. "To escape detection," as she had explained to her dazed, and dazzled, passenger. And so the car was practically upon him before the moose reacted. He dropped down into the middle of the stream, then tucked himself under the bridge. There he stood for maybe three, maybe five seconds, listening, concentrating, trying to take everything in. Then he heard it, rising somehow above the drone. Rising even as it dropped in pitch (malevolently, it must have seemed to the moose) in accord with the imperatives of the Doppler effect. It was the distinctive melody. The melody that so often stole into his thoughts and haunted his dreams.

He stood there under the bridge for some moments, breathing heavily, as moose, much like humans, are wont to do when they encounter phantoms in the night. And then he made—and here I admit to indulging my weakness for anthropomorphism—a bold decision. Rather than fleeing from the spectre, he would pursue it. He would pursue it, find it, confront it. So pulling himself out from under the bridge, he started off after the car, cantering down the middle of the road. He continued his chase through the night, stopping only for the purpose of eating and listening. But as time passed and he did not hear or see the spectre, his resolve began to diminish. And when, at daybreak, he found himself back on the western bank of the Ottawa River, he gave what among moose amounts to a shrug, then rambled off aimlessly toward the northwest.

A week later, after skirting the cottage community around Temagami, he found himself in the vicinity of Elk Lake. He felt an uncommon sense of relief among the red and white pines, a sense that in the heart of this old-growth forest he had found a place at least temporarily beyond the machinations of the spectre. We will take our leave of him now, comforting ourselves with the knowledge that, for the remainder of the summer at least, his life will be untroubled and he will have plenty of time for idle contemplation.

—— XXVI ——

Richard Hakluyt the younger returned to Saffron Walden, as he had promised he would, after a fortnight. He carried with him, in addition to the nine photographs of Yale Templeton and Bobbi Jo Jackson, various manuscripts, including a number of original works by French authors. As on the previous occasion he bowed on entering the cottage, and as on the previous occasion Yale Templeton's mother received him with the dignity and grace expected of a queen. He began with some remarks he had prepared especially for the occasion, dropping his eyes out of modesty:

"Your Majestie, my devotion to the task thou hath entrusted unto me has been ceaseless. What restlesse nights, what painefull dayes, what heat, what cold I have indured; how many long & chargeable journeys I have traveiled; how many famous libraries I have searched into; what varietie of ancient and moderne writers I have perused; what a number of old records, patents, privileges, letters, & c. I have redeemed from obscuritie and perishing; into how manifold acquaintance I have entred; what expenses I have not spared; and yet what faire opportunities of private gaine, preferment, and ease I have neglected; albeit thy selfe canst hardly imagine, yet I by daily experience do finde & feele, and some of my entier friends can sufficiently testifie. Howbeit the honour and benefit of this Common weale wherein I live and breathe, hath made all difficulties seeme easie, all paines and industrie pleasant, and all expenses of light value and moment unto me."

She had not, however, taken in a word, as he realized to his disappointment when he looked up. "Before you proceed with your report," she commented, "I should inform you that I have received a second communication from Canada."

Then, as he puzzled over this latest news, she went to her writing desk and retrieved a letter. He saw immediately that it was written in the same obsessively regular hand as the note she had shown him on his first visit. It read:

My Dear Mother,

I feel it is my duty to tell you that I am now sharing my apartment with a young lady. I realize that this news must perforce come as something of a shock to you. It will perhaps shock you even more when I relate that the young lady in question is an American. Please do not be alarmed. She is in no way at all like the representatives of her nation and her sex that you warned me about when I was a boy. Indeed, it is striking how much she reminds me of you.

With filial devotion,

Y.

P.S. You will already have seen the young lady to whom I am referring, as she is standing astride me in the pictures that I sent to you some weeks ago.

Richard Hakluyt took the letter, read it through very carefully three times, then nodded to himself.

"I confess, Your Majestie, this communication doth serve to confirme one of the conclusions I had heretofore reached."

"Indeed?" She was quite taken aback, although she did her best to conceal it. "And what, pray tell, may that be?"

"That there was but a single female in the pictures, not two as we did originally surmise."

"A single female? But I quite distinctly recall that in some of the images there was an American Savage, and in others an African. Perhaps one of the Symerones, you said."

"Soe I did think at the time. But on closer examination, it doth appere that the female we beleved to be an African is, in fact, the Savage, albeit in disguise."

She gave him a doubtful look.

"I would be most pleased to showe Your Majestie," he continued, removing the photographs from among the papers he had brought and placing them on the writing desk.

"By all means."

"Notice here," he said, and he pointed toward the likenesses of Bobbi Jo Jackson in the two different sets of pictures, "that the female we took to be an African is possessed of a nose every bit as straighte as that of the Savage."

Yale Templeton's mother looked from one set of pictures to the other but without changing expression.

"And here shal thou see that the eyes of the two females are identicall, the colour of sapphire. I consulted with severall reliable traders, and they did assure me that blue eyes be unknown among peoples founde on the coast of Africa."

She scrutinized the photographs carefully, although still keeping her thoughts to herself.

"And the hair," Richard Hakluyt went on. "The hair of bothe is of a truly remarkable colour, the purest of golde perhaps. Golde hair, soe the traders tell me, is as rare among the Africans as blue eyes."

"All that you say has a ring of truth to it," she conceded.

"And, finally, save for her face, the skin of the female we took to be an African is as faire as the skin of the Savage." ("More faire than thine own skin," he thought, though it was scarcely an observation to be repeated out loud.)

She studied the photographs in which Bobbi Jo Jackson had her face smeared with shoe polish. "You are quite right, of course," she agreed. "It is surpassingly strange that you did not notice about the skin colour previously."

"It is, in deede," he admitted, and his face flushed pink with embarrassment.

"But there is something I do not understand," she continued. "Why should the Savage have blackened her face?"

"Ah, yes. A riddle, truly. Howbeit, I beleve I may have founde the answer in an account by the French explorer Cartier describing the second of his three voyages to Canada." And here he placed a manuscript on the desk and turned the pages until he located a passage that he had earlier marked.

"Cartier here doth refer to the Savages in the harbour at Ste. Croix. I quote his remarks exactly; Despuis que le mari est mort, jamais les femmes ne se remarient; ainsi font le deuil de la dicte mort toute leur vie, et se taignent le visage de charbon pillé et de graisse, espetz comme l'espesseur d'un couteau, et à cela congnoiston qu'elles sont veuves.'"

"The widows colour their faces with charcoal?"

"Yes, Your Majestie, and with grease thicke as the back of a knife-blade."

"The Savage was a widow, then."

"Twoulde appere soe, yes."

"But what would cause an English subject of noble birth to take up with an American Savage, widow or otherwise?" ("And not just any peer of the realm, but one who enjoys a uniquely close relationship with the queen," she reminded herself with a mixture of perplexity and exasperation.)

"That is, in deede, a question that hath kept me awake these past severall nights. It is very troubling, to be sure. Very troubling. However, I do beleve that the experience of les truchements may offer us some guidance in this matter."

"Les truchements?"

"French traders in Brasill who have abandoned the wayes of their countrymen to live among the Indians. They marry Indian women and adopt Indian customs."

"Is it your intention to suggest that one of my loyal subjects—a man, I must remind you, whom I have known and to whom I have given my affection since he was a child—may have descended to such depths as to have fallen under the spell of a Savage?" The question was tinged with anger.

He lowered his eyes to the ground, unable to voice what he believed to be an inescapable truth.

"I did gather one item of information," he said at last, "that shoulde provide Your Majestie with a mesure of comfort."

Her look softened.

"It comes from the papers of the French cosmographer Andre Thevet. I have but recently begun translating his Cosmographie Universelle, a worke much derided but very valuable when approched with caution. Thevet writeth that the Savages founde in the northern parte of the Americas, in Canada, are assuredly not Cannibals. They do not partake of human flesh."

"They are friendly, then?"

"Yes. Or quite possibly soe, albeit Thevet doth mention that when Canadian warriors capture an enemie, they kill him, then throw his body to the animalls. They remove the skin from his face and head, which they lay in a circle on the grounde to dry, then carry it to their houses to showe to the olde men, women, children, and girls, who honour them with chanting and dance."

Upon hearing this, Yale Templeton's mother fainted dead away.

"Blessed Lorde!" Richard Hakluyt exclaimed in alarm, then raced around the cottage looking for spirits of hartshorn. Finding none, he began to fan her furiously—to salutary effect, it would seem, since she came to in a matter of seconds. "I beg thy forgiveness, Your Majestie. Let me assure thee that I do not beleve Y. hath suffered such cruele debasement. Thevet reporteth that, although the Canadian Savages are greate fighting men, they do not attack their enemies for sport alone, as forsooth do the Indians of Peru and Brasill. The Canadians only make warre to avenge a wronge. Is Y. of such a temperament that mayhaps he did commit a violent misdeede against the Savages?"

"Most assuredly not! He is an English gentlemen of the highest breeding." She was indignant.

"And for that very reason, because a true and honourable servant of Your Majestie is he, the bonds he hath formed with the Savages yet may prove of greate advantage to us."

She visibly brightened.

He continued: "Y., thou hast told me, did crosse the seas for the purpose of educating the Savages. I beleve that once he hath freed him selfe from his bewitchment, he shalbe in a position to fulfill that destynie."

"I pray that you are right."

"The blessed Apostle Paul, the converter of the Gentiles, writeth in this manner; 'Whosoever shal call on the Lorde shalbe saved.' The Spaniardes have builte above hundreds of houses of Relligion in the space of fiftie yeares or thereaboutes; Nowe if they, in their superstition, by meanes of their planting in those partes, have done soe greate thinges in soe shorte space, what may we hope for in our true and syncere Relligion, proposing unto our selves in this action not filthie lucre nor vaine ostentation as they in deede did, but principally the gayninge of the soules of millions of those wretched people, the reducinge of them from dombe Idolls to the lyvinge God, from the depe pitt of Hell to the highest Heavens."

"It is a worthy vision."

"It is not my vision, Your Majestie, but the vision of our Lorde. He hath chosen this moment to bringe the dark corners of the worlde into Lighte. And thou, Your Majestie, as all right thinking men acknowledge, have been ordained by the Lorde to see that His will shalbe done."

She gave a solemn nod.

"Y. is destined, I beleve, to serve as thine agent in Canada. He shal plant colonies where English men and women may remaine in safetie, learne the language of the Savages, by little and little acquainte them selves with their manner, and soe with discrecion and mildeness distill into their purged mindes the swete and lively liquor of the gospell."

"But do not the French also have designs on Canada?"

"Yes. Yes, in deede. But our wayes be much more enlightened than theirs. Once they finde them selves on Canadian soil, the French shal, with no less satisfaction than the Savages, come to recognize the superioritie of gentle and courteous English governance."

"I had much hope for the French," she sighed. "But it alarmed me sorely when Henri declared his allegiance to the Pope. And now he has come to terms with the Spanish."

"The conversion and peace were mere matters of convenience, Your Majestie, to allow him to protecte his borders. Remember, he did also proclaim the Edict of Nantes."

"'Tis true. The French have not yet entirely surrendered to the preachers of untruth."

"Those French men and women who traveil westward across the seas, they shal sing praises unto Your Majestie, for freeing them from the corrupting and tyrannous Spaniarde."

She reflected on his words, on the promise of glory to come: a new world on the northern frontier of the Americas where all peoples would live in harmony under the gentle governance of the benevolent monarch chosen by God to advance His cause on Earth. A worthy vision, to be sure.

"And how shall we now proceed?" she asked at length.

"Inasmuch as it is through Y. that thy dictates shalbe made known, our first task, of necessitie, must be to mount an expedition whereby he shalbe freed from his enchantment."

"Then it is well that we proceed with due haste." And she went to her desk, where she wrote out a commission granting Richard Hakluyt the younger authority to raise a company of men. He accepted the document with conspicuous pride, then after making a display of his gratitude with an extravagant, sweeping bow, left the cottage, mounted his horse, and rode off to begin his new mission.

*In May the rhythm of university
life eases to a comforting lull.*

—— XXVII ——

I n May the rhythm of university life eases to a comforting lull. While it
is true that many institutions now schedule courses during the summer
months, instructors are mostly graduate students who need money and
experience, and nomadic junior faculty who also need money and are hopeful
that an enhanced teaching portfolio will increase their chances of securing
a tenure-track appointment. Should a member of the regular faculty be
found offering a summer course, his colleagues will amuse themselves over
lunch debating whether his aberrant behaviour is due to crushing alimony
payments or his ineptness at negotiating a mortgage.

For the majority of faculty, summer is a time for forgetting. Forgetting
lectures that got sidetracked by daydreams. Forgetting undergraduates
and their indecipherable lab reports and incomprehensible book reviews.
Forgetting the essays they surely, but unprovably, purchased over the Internet.
Above all, forgetting the Sisyphean agony of grading. Summer is the time
for travel and rest and the rewards of pursuing research into some esoteric
subject that is of interest, at best, to a negligible fraction of that tiny subset
of humans who have been privileged to devote the better part of their lives
to the pursuit of knowledge for its own sake.

Not that this is my view necessarily. But it was the view of H. Avery Duck, president of the Faculty Union. He lived in anticipation of summer from the day he gave his first lecture in the early fall until the moment he turned in his final set of grades in the spring. For one thing, during the summer he was spared the unpleasantness of having to talk to undergraduates. And not being obliged to waste his time in the classroom, he had more opportunity for reading the surviving texts of obscure medieval Russian monastic orders which remained his primary academic interest, and above all, for writing those policy papers on behalf of the Faculty Union which he always managed to convince himself were so penetrating, so brilliantly argued that they could not help but win him the admiration and respect of all who read them (assuming, of course, anyone did read them).

He was not, as you might have suspected, demoralized by his humiliating confrontation with Felicia Butterworth over her suspension of Yale Templeton or by his subsequent arrest during the chaotic conclusion to the demonstration at Graves Hall. Quite the contrary. In the police van on the way to the Don Jail his spirits lifted when he discovered himself seated next to a woman who, despite the fact that she was an undergraduate and entirely naked, appeared to share his belief that the university administration was sadly lacking in principle. Then he spent the night in a holding cell, where his only companion was an Ojibwa restaurant reviewer who, as it happened, carried with him a collection of poems he had written to recite at the protest. The restaurant reviewer read aloud an ode about the wanderings of a white moose—an allegory, as he explained it, about the dearth of reason, order, and ethical behaviour in contemporary society. The two men spent the rest of the night in discussion, finding themselves to be entirely of one mind on every point. The restaurant reviewer was so affected by their conversation that he agreed to sell H. Avery Duck his poems at slightly above cost, magnanimously throwing in his last remaining copy of a guide to dining in the vicinity of the campus (for which he waived GST).

H. Avery Duck came home exhilarated. He proudly showed his wife his new set of Ojibwa clothes made of genuine imitation moosehide. He also informed her of the momentous decision he had reached during his night in jail.

"There is a cause on campus that requires my attention even more urgently than getting orthodontia for pets added to the faculty dental plan, my dear," he explained. "I am referring, of course, to freedom of speech!" By which he meant freedom of speech for the president of the Faculty Union. "I will write a statement outlining the relevant legal and philosophical issues. It may well be necessary for me to invent another language. Perhaps something using the Mongolian alphabet, since that worked well for the manifesto on squirrels."

"If only more professors shared your fearless devotion to principle, H. Avery Duck," sighed his wife.

"I quite agree," he replied, and with that went off to the kitchen to confront the weighty question of whether to have scrambled or poached eggs for breakfast.

XXVIII

T hose who made it a practice to observe the comings and goings of Felicia Butterworth knew that she, too, lived for much of the year in anticipation of the summer. From September through May she was burdened with constant meetings: meetings with the university's Governing Council, with the provost, with deans and department heads, with past and potential donors, with politicians, and (when it could no longer possibly be avoided) with the president of the Faculty Union. She had to give final approval to regulations on hiring practices and qualifications for tenure, oversee the budget, monitor the operation of the physical plant, and participate in national and international conferences on higher education—in short she had to deal with a diversity of issues from the most mundane to the truly consequential. Of course this spring there had been, in addition, the mountainous and infuriating distraction of the Templeton affair.

But during the summer months the meetings and conferences dwindled. The president of the Faculty Union was, mercifully, sequestered in his office, no doubt writing one of those interminable reports in a language only he could understand. Even the controversy surrounding her peremptory suspension of Yale Templeton could be expected to recede into the background.

And so it was with a mixture of relief and expectation that she welcomed the arrival of summer. It meant time for devoting herself unreservedly to what she called her "grand vision." The public face of that vision was seen on banners hanging from lampposts all over the downtown, each carrying the picture of a university graduate who had earned distinction in some or other walk of life. On the back of the banners was the slogan of the fundraising campaign: "A University Education: There Can Be No Better Investment." A metaphor, according to promotional literature released by the public relations department, for her efforts to turn the university into "the pre-eminent institution of higher learning on the continent." Not that everyone saw her actions in quite the same light. Critics accused her of harbouring a hidden and decidedly sinister agenda. Here, however, it would be useful to separate known facts from unsubstantiated rumours.

The known facts were these:

She had continued the profitable practice of allowing corporations to purchase the naming rights to university property. And so the historic Bell Tower erected in honour of graduates who had given their lives during the two world wars became the Bell Mobility Tower. (An earlier attempt by Hostess to have it named the Ding Dong Bell Tower was scuttled by Frito-Lay.) The new Imperial Tobacco Archives at the Medical School library secured the university a collection, unmatched outside North Carolina, of scientific papers relating to the neglected benefits of tobacco consumption for weight reduction.

She had also sought to strengthen the financial position of the university by aggressively acquiring real estate in downtown Toronto. On the northern edge of the campus was a building that had been occupied for years by a private high school at once both respected and derided across the city for its rigorous academic program and its impossibly high admission standards. She managed to induce the English headmaster to vacate the property by helping him secure title to a coveted lot in the Annex and having the Dean Responsible for Relations with Filthy Rich Parents of Appallingly Stupid Children show him how, through the drastic upward adjustment of tuition fees, he could fulfill his lifelong dream of building a facility that was an exact replica of the venerable public school in East Anglia where he had been beaten and sexually abused as a young boy.

She oversaw purchase of the Medical Affiliates Centre facing the entrance to the campus, ignoring opposition from a dozen or so dentists with offices in the building, as well as the proprietor of the neighbouring Hat Museum.

She undertook negotiations with the Anglican hierarchy to acquire a historic church just across Greener Street from the high school. "A new and suitably godly home for the School of Theology," she explained to the eminent bishop who served on the university's Governing Council.

Finally, citing the shortage of student housing, she arranged for the university to outbid the Hilton chain for a luxury hotel located just blocks from City Hall.

These, as I said, are the known facts. But the increasingly extravagant allegations levelled against her were based on rumours, not facts:

That she had commissioned an architect to redesign the Anglican church as an exclusive private club for men. It was even alleged in some quarters that she was making arrangements to have an escort service operate out of the church basement.

That she had actually acquired the Medical Affiliates Centre not as additional office space for the English department, as legal documents submitted to the city claimed, but to gain access to the laboratory of the small pharmaceutical company in the basement, her intention being—and remember here, I am just reporting rumour—to employ chemistry graduate students who had failed their comprehensive examinations in production of drugs for the black market.

That she had solicited bids from various Vietnamese and Chinese gangs in the city for operating a protection agency out of the former high school.

And, finally, that she had begun negotiations with the provincial government to get a law passed allowing her to turn the hotel into a casino, the largest in Canada.

"It would be easy to conclude," said one of her most acerbic critics, "that she is acting under orders from the Mafia."

But that, responded the Dean for Laundering Money, was "a patently absurd suggestion."

XXIX

ummer was also the favourite time of the year for Yale Templeton. It was during the summer that he hunted for those obscure bits and pieces of information that made the Civil War so much a present reality for him, and it was during the summer that he was able to return to Northern Ontario and resume his quest for the Great White Moose. Of course, summer had in effect come early this year with his suspension by Felicia Butterworth, meaning there had been nothing to keep him in Toronto on the day when Bobbi Jo Jackson reported that what had sounded to him like a bit of background static during a CBC radio interview was actually a man shouting in French, "Look! A white moose!"

The ride north to Je-me-souviens had been an educational experience for both passenger and driver. After some initial terror Yale Templeton came to marvel at his companion's ability to bring the rented Toyota Corolla to speeds technically impossible (at least according to the car manual) while deftly avoiding the bicyclists, porcupines, and gaping potholes that seem to appear out of nowhere on Ontario country roads. That she could maintain close to the same speed throughout the night with her headlights turned off was so beyond belief that he surrendered himself to the comforting suspicion that she had supernatural powers.

As they approached North Bay, she asked him what they would do when they reached the town where the white moose had been spotted. He suddenly realized that he had not made all the necessary arrangements, and so he had her pull up to a general store, where he bought her a kazoo and an orange balaclava. Then, as they continued on their way to Quebec, he pulled out his own kazoo and began to play "Eine Kleine Nachtmusik" (which in this case was quite fitting, since night had fallen). "This is the call moose use to signal friendship," he explained, and then he repeated the melody over and over again so she could commit it to memory.

When they arrived in Temiscaming—it was now approaching midnight—she suddenly cried, "Hey, I remember this place!"

"You've been here before?" he said with some surprise, although by now surprises were more or less what he expected from her.

"Uh-huh. A few years ago. On my way to James Bay."

"James Bay? Why did you go to James Bay?"

"Oh, just one of my assignments. I don't know. It was right after I got back from Senegal. I guess someone thought the French I'd picked up would be useful. The language they speak here is kind of like French."

"Really?" he asked. His colleagues in European history had assured him that there was no similarity whatsoever.

"Oh, sure," she replied. "Most people here even call it French."

She slowed down as they made their way through the town, then sped up once they were out in the countryside again.

"You know, they never did tell me why they sent me up here," she said. "In fact they never told me why they were sending me any place. It's not like I wasn't interested or anything. But they always said, 'You're doing it for the President. You're doing it for your country. You're doing it for God.' I don't know. I think they should have been more specific."

"At Fredericksburg, General Ambrose Burnside never told the soldiers in the army of the Potomac why he wanted them to charge Marye's Heights."

"No?"

"No. And by the end of the day, the Union army had suffered 12,653 or 13,353 casualties, depending on which source you believe."

"No kidding! Well I guess that proves my point."

They drove on more slowly now, and in silence. Bobbi Jo Jackson was wondering about her mission to James Bay. Yale Templeton was wondering whether, after he finished writing his article on poisonous snake bites at Confederate military hospitals, he might try to resolve the discrepancies between reported casualty figures for Fredericksburg. And maybe not just for Fredericksburg. Maybe for all deaths and injuries suffered in all the battles of the Civil War. "Now that would be a truly worthwhile project," he said to himself. "Think of all the tables I would need to include. Think of the footnotes." He had been trying for some time to come up with a topic for a second book. "This might turn out to be my magnum opus," he said to himself, and he nodded with satisfaction.

A sign on the town limits informed them when they had reached their destination:

JE-ME-SOUVIENS

La Belle Ville

Maire: René Purelaine

Population: 2

With no evidence that anyone else was up at one thirty in the morning, they lay down under the stars and went to sleep.

By the time they awoke the sun had already risen well above the horizon. "Not that much to see, is there?" commented Bobbi Jo Jackson, stretching and stifling a yawn.

"No," replied Yale Templeton, straightening his tie. "Although I imagine the Olympic stadium will be quite impressive once they put the roof on." Then he went to the car for the balaclavas and kazoos.

"I think we should get something to eat first," Bobbi Jo Jackson said. "Anyway, at my briefing—you know, before they sent me up here—they told me the best place to get information in small northern towns is the donut shop. Have you seen a Tim Hortons?"

But the only restaurant turned out to be La famine Irlandaise. Louis was just opening up when they arrived at the front door.

"Bonjour," he greeted them, smiling broadly.

"Bonjour, monsieur," replied Bobbi Jo Jackson. "Good morning," replied Yale Templeton.

Louis looked him up and down. "Let me guess. You have come from Ontario, n'est-ce pas?"

"Si," said Yale Templeton.

"Then we shall talk in English," Louis whispered, looking around to make sure that no one was listening.

He reached behind the counter and pulled out two copies of the menu. "Don't let anyone know about these," he said under his breath. "The mayor brought in an ordinance last week outlawing the sale of all potato dishes except for French fries."

"How extraordinary!" said Yale Templeton.

Louis broke into a loud laugh. "Forgive me, monsieur. I'm pulling your leg. Around here we call French fries—"

"Frites," interrupted Bobbi Jo Jackson.

"Frites, yes. Exactly, mademoiselle. Exactly. You're a lucky man, monsieur, to have a companion who is as knowledgeable as she is beautiful."

Yale Templeton coughed weakly and looked down at his feet.

Louis laughed again. "It is an unusual man who is embarrassed by his good fortune with women." To which Yale Templeton responded by turning the colour of a ripe tomato.

"But enough of this," said Louis, although his laughter continued. "You have the look of hungry travellers. Tell me, what can I get for you?"

Yale Templeton and Bobbi Jo Jackson studied the menu. There were a total of two items: boiled potatoes and French fries. Next to the listing for French fries was written "when in season."

"I think I'll have the boiled potatoes," replied Bobbi Jo Jackson.

"Eh bien. And you, monsieur?"

"I believe I will try the French fries."

"Alas, monsieur, the season for French fries ended two weeks ago." And Louis erupted in laughter once more. "No. The truth is, I thought I had an agreement with a chef from Marseilles who is a wizard with frites, but at the last minute he decided to accept a position at a new private men's club in Toronto."

"Then I suppose I shall have the boiled potatoes as well."

"A very discerning choice, monsieur. It's the house specialty. 'La spécialité de la maison.' I have the potatoes flown in directly from Prince Edward Island, part of my commitment to biculturalism."

Louis collected the menus and disappeared into the kitchen. "What a curious fellow," said Yale Templeton.

"Yes," agreed Bobbi Jo Jackson. "But very friendly, don't you think?"

"Yes, indeed. Very friendly." ("But perhaps a bit too familiar," he thought.)

Louis returned after just a few minutes with some boiled potatoes.

"You don't mind if they're cold, do you?"

"Not at all," said Bobbi Jo Jackson. "As it happens, we're in a hurry."

"Oh, yes?"

"We've come to see Le Grand Orignal Blanc, the Great White Moose."

Louis looked at her uncomprehendingly.

"We heard the interview you did on the CBC yesterday morning," she explained. "With Michael Enright. Someone in the background shouted, 'Un orignal blanc. Voyez! Un orignal blanc! Sacrebleu!' I heard it quite distinctly."

"Ah. That would have been my brother. He did shout something about a moose and went running out the door. But there are no white moose, everyone knows that. My guess is what he saw was a white-tailed deer." He paused. "Or maybe a white rabbit." And he laughed at his own joke.

"Interesting you should say that about the deer," commented Yale Templeton. "Some of the early French explorers in Canada found fishermen here from the Basque country. According to the noted authority Samuel Merrill, when the explorers saw moose for the first time, they called them by the Basque word for deer, 'orenac,' so perhaps your brother was simply confused."

"My brother is confused about a great many things, I am sad to say."

"Still, we should talk to him," said Bobbi Jo Jackson.

"That may not be possible. He has not spoken a word of English in many years. And except on extraordinary occasions, he refuses to talk to Canadians from outside Quebec."

"But I'm *not* Canadian," said Yale Templeton. "I'm from England."

"Tant pis. So much the worse," Louis shrugged. "He definitely *won't* talk to you."

"But *I'm* not English. Or Canadian, either," said Bobbi Jo Jackson. "I'm an American."

"Ah," said Louis. "An American. Now that's entirely different. For some unimaginable reason, he seems to place great trust in Americans."

"Et je parle le français comme une parisienne et le québécois presque aussi bien."

"Très bien. René se fera un plaisir de vous rencontrer, mademoiselle, ou est-ce que je dois dire madame?"

"Mademoiselle." replied Bobbi Jo Jackson. Then she looked at Yale Templeton and said, "Au moins, pour l'instant." And then she and Louis both broke into a laugh.

Yale Templeton laughed, too, although merely out of courtesy, since he had no idea what either of them were saying. Then he asked Louis, "Might I inquire as to the course of action you propose we take?"

"It's really quite simple. Your lovely companion must go to see René alone. He'll be arriving at City Hall shortly, and in keeping with local custom, will make himself available to the public for one hour. The daily meeting of La commission pour protéger la langue Française, bureau de Je-me-souviens does not convene until ten. You and I, monsieur, we will remain here. Although I acknowledge I have some limitations as a cook, no one in all the North makes a better cup of instant coffee. You will tell me all about this Great White Moose of yours and I will tell you all about this great nation of mine."

XXX

And so Bobbi Jo Jackson went off to meet with René Purelaine while Yale Templeton and Louis Montcalm sat down over coffee in La famine Irlandaise.

"I must say, this is the best instant coffee I have ever tasted," remarked Yale Templeton, who in fact had never tasted instant coffee before (and very little freshly brewed either, coffee being one of the lesser temptations his mother had warned him about). He always made it a rule to be polite, however, and in any case he found the beverage to be a suitable accompaniment for cold boiled potatoes.

"But we must not waste our time talking about something as mundane as food," said Louis. "Tell me, monsieur, what is your occupation?"

"I am a historian," replied Yale Templeton.

"Ah," said Louis, "a historian. Herodotus, Thucydides, Sima Qian, Ibn Khaldun, Gibbon, Carlyle, Ranke, Burckhardt, Bloch, Braudel. You have many distinguished predecessors. It is a noble profession. And what is your particular field of study? The history of England, I suppose."

"No," replied Yale Templeton. "American history."

"American history!" exclaimed Louis. "But the United States is too young to have a history."

"Many of the dons I knew at Cambridge seemed to think the same thing," Yale Templeton commented a bit ruefully.

Louis laughed. "Then they are fools. If anything, the Americans have experienced too much history. And of course, they have produced eminent scholars of their own: Prescott, Bancroft, Parkman, Turner, Beard, Schlesinger, Woodward ..."

"You seem to know a great deal about American history for someone from Canada."

"It is a necessity, monsieur. Living as I do in a nation whose continued existence depends on the sufferance of the United States, I must understand Americans better than they understand themselves. Which turns out to be not all that difficult. I mean, just look at the politicians they elect to office. Of course there are moments when even Americans make an inspired choice. Lincoln was truly a statesman of the highest order and a man of great compassion. I've always felt he would have made a fine Canadian. But enough of my foolishness. You're the professional historian. Tell me. What is your opinion of the United States?"

"Actually," said Yale Templeton, who had concluded long ago that opinion had no place in history, "my field of specialization is the Civil War."

"Ah, yes. What else? The Civil War. Brother against brother. The most colossal of all the many American acts of insanity."

Yale Templeton always found generalizations distasteful, generalizations expressed with great passion especially so. And in an effort to drain emotion from their conversation, he entered into a monologue about his research. He described to Louis the work he had done for his doctoral dissertation, discussing in painstaking detail what he regarded as the more interesting facts and statistics he had managed to uncover about the Civil War in the British press. He then went on to give a lengthy account of how he had realized that to be fully comprehensive, he would have to expand his investigation into ever more obscure British publications. "Louisiana State University Press wanted me to keep the book under 650 pages," he admitted, "but I explained that it was my style to be exhaustive."

"He must mean 'exhausting,'" thought Louis, who by now was struggling to keep his eyes open. But Yale Templeton plunged onward into a word-for-word recitation of his article on the boot sizes of Union cavalrymen, followed by a methodical explanation of how Mississippians used parched corn to produce a diverse array of less-than-satisfactory coffee substitutes during the Vicksburg campaign, and then an interminable summary of his investigation into the incidence of poisonous snake bites at Confederate military hospitals. He even spoke at torturous length about his plans, formulated just hours earlier, to produce a monograph on discrepancies in reported casualty figures for all the battles of the war. "Think how valuable it would be to know the precise number of soldiers who had their noses shot off during the fighting at Fair Oaks," he commented with unvarnished sincerity.

Louis, who by now had lapsed into that state of semi-consciousness where words mutate into hallucinations, instinctively reached for his own nose. Relieved to find that it remained in its customary place, he burst out. "Ah, yes! Fair Oaks! Riveting! Positively riveting! Your students must be transfixed when you lecture."

"I suppose they must," Yale Templeton said with more than a little uncertainty.

"But it is unfair of me to expect you to carry on this conversation all by yourself," said Louis. "Although I do not pretend to have your erudition or your way with words, still there is some knowledge I have accumulated over the years that might yet prove of interest to you. I take it you heard the story of our little village on the radio yesterday."

Yale Templeton nodded.

"Then now I must paint you a picture on a grander canvas, a national canvas."

And with that he launched into his own version of the history of Canada. It was not a plodding narrative made up of dreary facts and even drearier statistics. It was not, in other words, the sort of account likely to appeal to Yale Templeton. Quite the contrary. It was a rich, vividly imagined pageant filled with legendary figures and epic deeds. It was also quite unlike any interpretation of the Canadian past that Yale Templeton had heard in seminars given by his colleagues. It celebrated what Louis called "the grand partnership"—"l'association formidable"—between French and English.

He began, in restrained tones, with reference to the "amicable relations" between Scottish traders and French coureurs-du-bois, "symbolized so eloquently, I might point out, by the Beaver Club, whose memory is preserved today in the magnificent restaurant of the same name at the Queen Elizabeth Hotel in Montreal. You must go there someday and have the chateaubriand." He skipped lightly over "that minor misunderstanding that was the Seven Years' War," but did point out that in the *Quebec Act* of 1774, the British had "wisely" reintroduced French civil law "to ensure that Canadian society would be built on mutual respect for the traditions of both founding nations."

His depiction of the nineteenth century revolved around paired sets of heroes: the rebels Papineau and Mackenzie; Baldwin and LaFontaine, champions of "responsible government"; and of course, John A. Macdonald and George-Étienne Cartier, "the principal architects of that brilliant compromise we know as Confederation." And here he paused for dramatic effect.

"But," he continued, "it was only during the twentieth century that the full promise of a truly bicultural nationalism was realized." He paid tribute in turn, with increasing passion, to each of the prime ministers from Quebec. To Laurier. To St. Laurent. But above all to Trudeau. "All other politicians pale in comparison. A brilliant, brilliant man." His eyes glowed as he spoke of the repatriation of the Constitution and the enactment of the *Charter of Rights and Freedoms*. "It was with the *Charter*," he said, his voice now muting in reverence, "that Canada achieved that union of individual liberty and social responsibility that has forever eluded our myopic neighbours to the south." And he took a deep breath.

"But there remained one grave threat." His tone now grew ominous. "Within la belle province there lurked a traitorous band of conspirators, men who used misrepresentations of the past and false promises for the future to beguile the honest citizens of Quebec into forfeiting their patrimony. I am speaking, of course, of the separatists, René Lévesque and his hirelings in the Parti Quebecois."

At this point Bobbi Jo Jackson appeared in the doorway, cutting his lecture short. Yale Templeton gave a barely suppressed sigh of relief, buckling as he had been under the heavy weight of Louis' intensity.

"Ah, mademoiselle, your timing is no less exquisite than your smile," said Louis. "Sit down. I will boil up a new pot of potatoes for us this very moment. Then I will regale you with the wit of Jean Chrétien."

"I'm afraid, monsieur, we have no time," she replied.

"You mean René Purelaine *did* see the Great White Moose?" said Yale Templeton.

"Uh- huh. Or some sort of moose that looked white, anyway," she replied. "He says it swam across the river. Over to the Ontario side. Then it disappeared into the forest."

Louis chuckled. "I knew my brother was insane. It appears now he's having trouble with his eyes as well."

Bobbi Jo Jackson ignored the comment. "We'll have to drive back across the river," she said to Yale Templeton.

"Quite so," he replied. And he pulled on his balaclava and fumbled in his jacket pocket for his kazoo.

"It seems my brother is not the only insane person around here," Louis murmured to himself. Then he headed off to the kitchen to boil up some potatoes for his lunch.

XXXI

"I'm sorry I took so long with René," said Bobbi Jo Jackson as she started up the car, "but I just had to ask him about James Bay."

"James Bay?"

"You know ... So I could figure out why I was sent there."

"Oh, yes. And did you learn anything useful?"

"No. Nothing. Absolutely nothing. He says the only thing on James Bay are Cree Indians and hydroelectric plants. Now why would the American government be interested in Cree Indians?"

He had no response.

"And to top it all, then he starts off on this rant about Canada. It was pretty interesting, though. Historical stuff, mostly. About how awful the French have been treated here. Like first it was the Scots stealing their furs. And then they lost the Seven Years' War and the British took away their rights. And after that, when the different colonies came together to form Canada—from what you've told me, this would have been just around the time Abraham Lincoln moved to Ontario—the Québécois pretty much lost the ability to protect their way of life."

"And did René say anything about the separatists?"

"Who?"

"The separatists. René Lévesque—".

"Oh, yeah. René Lévesque. For sure. René Lévesque was the greatest of all politicians. 'Un homme sans égal.' The prophet of 'le Québec libre,' a free and independent Quebec."

"And Pierre Trudeau?"

"Trudeau?! Trudeau was a traitor to his own people! He invented something called the October Crisis so he could strip French Canadians of their civil liberties."

Yale Templeton shook his head. "A remarkable story," he said. "Truly remarkable. Just the opposite of what Louis told me. Louis sees the history of Canada as a spectacular achievement. The men who are villains to René, Louis calls heroes; the acts that René describes as shameful, Louis thinks of as honourable." And he shook his head again.

"How bizarre is that!" exclaimed Bobbi Jo Jackson.

"Bizarre, indeed," replied Yale Templeton.

"But I don't get it," she said. "History is history! It's not like there can be more than one true story!"

"You have to remember," Yale Templeton cautioned, "Louis and his brother are not professional historians. They assume that there is room for imagination in the writing of history. But real history is facts, statistics, carefully documented footnotes. Anything more than that is just fiction."

"Oh, I see," Bobbi Jo Jackson replied. But she didn't. Not really. After a lifetime spent in voluntary bondage to dogma, she had suddenly discovered she had a hunger for explanation, a yearning for the interpretive leaps that connect cause to effect. At some level she was already beginning to recognize that, for her, facts and statistics would never be enough.

XXXII

ach summer, when government activity in Washington would effectively grind to a halt, the President liked to retreat to his ranch in west Texas and ride bucking broncos. Well, not bucking broncos, exactly. A rocking horse. But a big rocking horse, almost the size of a Shetland pony. Not one of those toys parents buy for their children at Christmas.

The ranch, the President decided, would be the most discreet place for his meeting with the underworld figure who would serve as a go-between for the bribe to Yale Templeton. The man's name was Vito Pugliese, although the President always thought of him simply as "the Don." Vito had been the front man for the Mob when buying off the manicurist who knew that the President had a weakness for Primal Chic nail polish by Revlon. For putting it on his toes. This was back when the President was still a governor.

I said Vito was a front man for the Mob. That is something of a misrepresentation. The Governor had asked the aide responsible for scheduling his appointments with beauty care professionals to see that the manicurist "was dealt with in an appropriate way." Since the aide knew the Governor to be a great admirer of John F. Kennedy—or, to be more precise, a great admirer of John F. Kennedy's private life—he took this to mean that the Governor wanted the Mafia to handle the matter. The problem was, the aide himself had no personal contact with anyone in organized crime. However, he had seen *The Godfather* and reasoned that the bank officer who had approved his student loan, the aforementioned Vito Pugliese, probably had the necessary ancestry to pass for a member of the Mob. So he approached Vito with a proposition: Make sure the manicurist keeps her mouth shut, and I will see to it that the Governor quashes the current investigation into the bank for fraudulent issuing of student loans.

The manicurist was surprised (though not displeased) to receive an unsolicited fifteen-hundred-dollar student loan (at a favourable interest rate) from the bank. Not that she ever learned why the loan was issued. Vito was much too much of a gentleman to consider bringing up the subject of toenails in the presence of a lady. But here his silence proved fortuitous. Since the manicurist provided Primal Chic nail polish to almost half the male members of the legislature and two justices of the state Supreme Court, she had never imagined that the information might be worth anything to anybody. We're talking about Texas here, after all.

In any case, when it became clear that his reputation was safe, the Governor decided he wanted to meet with Vito. To thank him, but also, as he explained to his aide, "because a man with his connections might prove very useful to the nation somewhere down the road."

And so the aide—who we have already encountered in his later incarnation as the Executive Assistant to the Assistant Undersecretary of Transportation—contacted Vito to arrange a time for the meeting. "You'll have to act like an underworld figure," he advised him. But that presented some difficulties. Vito was no more acquainted with underworld figures than was the future Executive Assistant to the Assistant Undersecretary of Transportation. And, unlike the future Executive Assistant to the Assistant Undersecretary of Transportation, he had not seen *The Godfather*. Instead his entire knowledge of the Mafia came from the gangster movies that were popular back when he was a teenager in the 1940s. So he slicked back his hair, dressed himself up in a shiny black suit with sharp lapels, a black shirt, and a white tie with a ruby stick pin, put a toothpick in his mouth, and went off to meet with the Governor. In his pocket he carried a quarter, to flip during their conversation.

"This is truly a great honour for me, Don Pugliese," said the Governor. "I want to thank you so very much for the valuable service you have provided to this state."

"'Ey! Dat's a my pleasure, Boss," replied Vito, who had gained his knowledge of Italian dialect from watching Marx Brothers movies.

"You didn't have to hurt her, I hope?"

Vito shrugged. "Maybe I rough her up a little bit. Maybe I no rough her up." And he gave the Governor a sly smile.

The Governor was entirely satisfied. And so it was that years later, after he became President and needed someone to offer a bribe to Yale Templeton, he immediately thought of Don Pugliese.

By now Vito was living in a retirement home, just outside Phoenix. His eyesight was failing, and on those all-too-frequent days when his sciatica acted up, he needed a walker to get around. He had not been more than five miles from the retirement home for a decade, and so when he received a request from the President, relayed through the Executive Assistant to the Assistant Undersecretary of Transportation, to come to Texas on a matter of national importance, he asked his grandnephews—Hugh, an Iyengar yoga instructor in Taos, and Charles, a television producer in Los Angeles—to accompany him. "A nice touch, Vito, bringing along your 'godsons,'" said the Executive Assistant to the Assistant Undersecretary of Transportation with a wink when he met them at the Dallas-Fort Worth airport. Charles and Hugh looked at him blankly.

On the long drive west the Executive Assistant to the Assistant Undersecretary of Transportation explained to Vito why the President needed him. There was a history professor in Toronto who had information that was potentially dangerous to the nation. Perhaps Vito had read about it in the newspapers? Vito had not. No matter. His job would be to fly to Toronto and convince the professor to turn over certain incriminating documents—it was still not clear what those documents were—in return for a substantial sum of money. The President hoped two million dollars would be enough but was quite prepared to defer to Vito's judgment on the appropriate sum.

Hugh, who had chosen an asana that required him to balance on his forearms on the floor of the limousine with his feet placed on top of his head, did not take in much of the conversation. But Charles, who made weekly trips to the casinos in Las Vegas and knew that Caesars Palace was currently offering 3:1 odds that the Lincoln assassination had been faked and 13:1 that Lincoln had secretly fled to Ontario after the Civil War where he had been involved in a commune in the northern woods so he could live openly as a transvestite, paid close attention.

The President greeted them all warmly when they arrived at the ranch. "It's been a long time, Don Pugliese," he said to Vito. "Much too long. It's good to see you."

"Is a good to see you too, Boss," Vito replied.

Hugh was shocked. "Uncle Vito!" he exclaimed. "You must refer to the President as Mr. President."

Vito slapped him across the back of the head. "'Ey! Shaddup a you face!"

"That's all right, son," said the President with a smile. "Don Pugliese and I, we're old friends."

"'At's a right," said Vito. "I'm a da Don and 'e's a da Boss!" And he whacked the Executive Assistant to the Assistant Undersecretary of Transportation across the back of the head for no apparent reason.

"Why is Uncle Vito talking like that?" Hugh whispered to Charles.

"You mean like Chico Marx?"

"Yes."

"I think that's just the way he talks now."

"But he went to Amherst!"

"I know."

"Wrote his honours thesis on the meaning of the whiteness of the whale in *Moby Dick*."

"Who didn't back then?" shrugged Charles.

"Yeah. But he was elected to Phi Beta Kappa in his junior year. Was a member of the Bond Fifteen. Graduated magna cum laude."

Charles just shrugged again.

"Lowell," the President said to the Executive Assistant to the Assistant Undersecretary of Transportation, "why don't you give the boys a tour of the ranch while Don Pugliese and I sit down over a little vino to discuss our, uh, business."

"It would be my pleasure, Mr. President," said the Executive Assistant to the Assistant Undersecretary of Transportation, whose ears were still ringing from the slap Vito had given him.

─── XXXIII ───

"Now you will see," said the Executive Assistant to the Assistant Undersecretary of Transportation after he led Charles and Hugh outside, "that the President has turned his ranch into a celebration of the distinguished men who preceded him in the White House. Here, for example," and he directed their attention to the left, "is a grove of cherry trees. The President cuts one down each morning, then dutifully phones his father to confess what he's done. His father forgives him and commends him for his honesty. This allows the President to retain his sense of moral incorruptibility for the rest of the day while telling all those lies that the public expects from a chief executive."

"Ah," said Hugh.

"I see," said Charles.

Just back of the grove of cherry trees was a man-made hill. "Identical in every detail to San Juan Hill in Cuba, where Teddy Roosevelt led his famous charge during the Spanish-American War."

"Actually," said Charles, who had once produced a documentary on the war, "Roosevelt rode up the much smaller Kettle Hill, which was virtually undefended. And he had to dismount and finish the climb on foot. He fabricated the story of a charge up San Juan Hill to boost his political career."

"Precisely the reason why the President holds him in such high esteem," replied the Executive Assistant to the Assistant Undersecretary of Transportation, who had thought that the point was too obvious to make.

At the foot of the hill was an exact replica of the Union cemetery at Gettysburg. "The President likes to come out here from time to time and deliver Lincoln's famous address," he said. "It's his second favourite among all the great orations by American statesmen, right after Nixon's Checkers speech. He admires it so much, he has committed most of the first sentence to memory."

"Do you think he delivers it wearing a dress?" whispered Charles to Hugh, with a smirk.

"Only on infrequent occasions," said the Executive Assistant to the Assistant Undersecretary of Transportation, who had overheard the remark.

Off in the distance was a lake the size of San Diego Harbour. Here they could see an aircraft carrier built to the exact dimensions of the USS *Abraham Lincoln*. "Would you like to visit it?" asked the Executive Assistant to the Assistant Undersecretary of Transportation. They said they would. So he called for the limousine to drive them all to the President's private landing strip where an S-3B Viking jet flew them out to the ship. They donned flight suits and, carrying their helmets, strolled around the plane, where they were greeted with enthusiasm by the actors hired to play the part of midshipmen. Aloft flew a banner that read, "Mission Accomplished."

"During the Vietnam War, as you probably know, the President was denied his dream of taking a place in the front lines because of the Constitutional amendment prohibiting military service below the rank of major for sons of white corporate executives and politicians. However, he has consistently shown his devotion to our dedicated fighting men by putting on a neatly pressed uniform and bravely posing in carefully staged settings and by investing trillions of dollars in equipment designed to make their jobs obsolete."

Hugh and Charles clapped in acknowledgment of the President's courage while the midshipmen cheered and threw their hats in the air, as instructed by the television prompter.

When they finished their tour of the ranch and arrived back at the house, the President was just concluding his negotiations with Vito. "I'm afraid $12 million is all the money I have on hand," they heard the President say, as he handed Vito a large suitcase.

"Dat's a okay, Boss. I make sure da professore, he no a complain."

The President smiled. "You and I understand each other perfectly, Don Pugliese." Then he dropped his voice and added, "And after you have possession of the documents, feel free to take whatever measures you think necessary to see that the professor represents no further threat to the nation."

"Ey, Boss, you can count on me," said Vito, and he slammed his right fist into the palm of his left hand. This filled the President with delight. "As I said, Don Pugliese, you and I understand each other perfectly."

Then the President turned to the Executive Assistant to the Assistant Undersecretary of Transportation. "Don Pugliese is going to fly to Toronto on a commercial flight so as not to arouse suspicion. Have the limousine take him and the boys back to Dallas. Oh, and be sure to give the boys a little something to remember their visit to the ranch."

So the Executive Assistant to the Assistant Undersecretary of Transportation went to a cabinet where he removed a couple of autographed photographs of the President riding his rocking horse on top of the imitation San Juan Hill. In the picture the President was wearing thick spectacles and held a Rough Rider hat, pinned up on one side, which he was waving high over his head, just like Teddy Roosevelt.

XXXIV

fter they left Je-me-souviens, Yale Templeton and Bobbi Jo Jackson spent two weeks scouring northeastern Ontario in search of the Great White Moose. They first drove south along the Ottawa River as far as Petawawa, then retraced their steps and headed north, in the direction of Cochrane. Had they turned west at Earlton, they would have eventually come to the forest where the Great White Moose was spending his summer in idle contemplation. But instead they continued on to Englehart and Kirkland Lake, eventually arriving at the shores of the Abitibi River. At every gas station, diner, and country store, they would stop and ask if anyone had seen a white moose. But no one had. Not ever. And so the hopefulness they had brought with them from Je-me-souviens started to dissipate.

Perhaps inevitably, then, their thoughts turned elsewhere. For Yale Templeton, to the prospect of resolving the disparities in casualty figures for all the battles of the Civil War. Being very systematic in his approach to work ("plodding" as he was described by more than one colleague), he decided that first he would have to complete his article on the incidence of poisonous snake bites at Confederate military hospitals. He was satisfied that he had now collected virtually all the available evidence. Allowing himself three weeks to write the body of the paper, then another three months to get the footnotes in proper order, he could expect to send the article off—he had decided to submit it to the *Journal of American History*—by Remembrance Day. If Felicia Butterworth continued to bar him from the classroom, an early October start for the new project was not out of the question.

As for Bobbi Jo Jackson, with each passing hour she became more determined to find out why the CIA had sent her to James Bay. After several days of trying to puzzle it out for herself, she decided to ask Yale Templeton for advice. This was during one of those rare occasions when he was not playing his kazoo out the car window. "What would you do if you were me?" was the way she put it.

He thought for a moment. "I should begin by learning something about the history of northern Quebec," he replied. Then he paused, his mind going back to their recent experiences with Louis Montcalm and his brother. "Of course," he added, "I would only consult works written by respected scholars."

"Of course," she replied. And did he have any books to recommend? Indeed, he did. His colleague Arlen Green had written a work called *The People of Quebec* that he understood to be very respected by specialists in the field. "No doubt that would be a good place to begin. Or perhaps," he added on further reflection, "it might be simpler to go directly to Arlen himself. Even if, in my opinion, he would be well advised to take a little more care with his footnotes—they at times seem rather untidy, if you know what I mean—still, he is quite a gracious fellow. He spent his last sabbatical at Cambridge. Clare Hall, I believe."

So when they returned to Toronto, Bobbi Jo Jackson arranged a meeting with Arlen Green. He was, as Yale Templeton had told her, very gracious, every bit the gentleman. Although his own writing concentrated on relations (theological and otherwise) between Jesuit missionaries and Native women in New France, he shared with her what he knew about the history of James Bay and provided her with a copy of the reading list he gave to graduate students preparing for their comprehensive examinations on the history of French Canada. She immediately went to the library, checked out as many books as she could carry, and returned to the little apartment near Dunbar Road to begin her research.

Her training at the CIA had included a course in speed reading. In her first class, one of the other recruits had leaned over and whispered to her, "You know what Woody Allen said about speed reading, don't you?"

"No," she replied.

"He said, 'I took a speed reading course. Afterward I was able to read *War and Peace* in twenty minutes. It's about Russia.'"

That evening she had gone to a bookstore near her apartment and bought a copy of *War and Peace*. It took her the better part of the evening to finish it, almost three hours, leaving her quite dismayed about her inability to read as quickly as this Woody Allen character. Nonetheless she was determined and practiced hard, and by the end of her training program, she could get through the book in an hour and a half. "Still not as fast as Woody Allen," she said to herself with disappointment. But then again, with her photographic memory, she could absorb a good deal more of the narrative than he apparently did. Months later she was still able to provide a summary of each chapter in the book, including quotations by the most obscure of characters.

It did not take her long, then, to read all the works Arlen Green had recommended. She discovered that quite a few of the authors went well beyond mere facts and statistics, and slipped into the kind of speculation and imaginative interpretation that Yale Templeton had warned her against. It was hard to escape the conclusion that most historians lacked his principled devotion to craft. All the same it was precisely the speculation and imaginative interpretation that engaged her most (as she admitted to herself with some embarrassment). And while she at first was confused by the fact that the various authors produced views of the French Canadian past that were, in some cases, seemingly almost as irreconcilable as those held by Louis Montcalm and René Purelaine, in the end she found that she very much enjoyed the competitive thrust and parry of scholarly debate. She even had moments where she mused about one day producing a historical work of her own.

Here I am digressing, however (although for the perfectly legitimate literary purpose of foreshadowing). The fact is, when she was reading about the history of Quebec, Bobbi Jo Jackson only occasionally slipped into reflections on the nature of historical inquiry. Mostly she was concerned with determining what it was about James Bay that had attracted the interest of the CIA. And after getting through all the books on the list Arlen Green had given her, she decided that she had reached something of a dead end.

"I'm not sure I understand much more now than I did when I started," she told Yale Templeton over dinner one evening.

"Perhaps," he replied, "you need to broaden your research."

"Broaden my research?"

"Well, to this point you have concentrated on Quebec. Maybe now is the time to do some reading in American diplomatic history." And he went to his bookshelf and pulled down a number of books he had collected on the subject. As you might imagine, except for a handful of works on the War of 1812, they all dealt in one way or another with the Civil War. The problem was, the question she was seeking to answer really required knowledge of the more recent past. "Not my area of expertise, the twentieth century," he conceded. However, he was acquainted with an authority on diplomatic matters, a former colleague in the History department now retired, who might well be able to give her some useful guidance. "From what I hear, he is still deeply involved in scholarly pursuits and very active in the life of the campus. He received his education at Oxford but otherwise is quite respectable. A very regal looking man, in fact. Furthermore, I can assure you that his footnotes are beyond criticism." And so it was that Bobbi Jo Jackson went off to consult with St. Clair Russell Hill.

XXXV

C onspiracy theories abound in American diplomatic history. There are
those who will tell you that James Madison declared war on Britain in
1812, during the last months of his administration, because he feared
he was in danger of losing the forthcoming election and wanted to deflect
attention from his disastrous trade policies. There are those who will tell you
that James Polk provoked a boundary dispute with Mexico in 1846 simply to
create an excuse for seizing the vast territory that became California and the
American Southwest. There are those who will tell you that William McKinley
annexed the Philippines in 1899 to ensure that the American Sugar Refining
Company could acquire cane from the islands without paying a tariff. There
are those who will tell you that Lyndon Johnson misrepresented reports of
an attack on American destroyers in the Gulf of Tonkin in 1964 so that he
could justify massive American air strikes against the North Vietnamese. And
there are those who will tell you that George W. Bush purposely withheld
evidence disproving the existence of weapons of mass destruction in Iraq
so that he could mount an invasion whose main objective was ensuring
American control of Middle Eastern oil.

St. Clair Russell Hill believed in all of these conspiracies and, indeed,
had produced summaries of each and every one, which he kept locked in a

safe in his bedroom. And Bobbi Jo Jackson, being young and innocent, was prepared to believe in all of them as well. Emblazoned on the front page of one of the manuals she had received during her training at the CIA was the following aphorism attributed to Richard Nixon: "Deceit by politicians is one of the fundamental safeguards of a democratic society." It took no great leap of faith for her to accept that James Madison and James Polk had deliberately provoked wars, or that William McKinley, Lyndon Johnson, and George W. Bush had wilfully lied to justify military ventures abroad.

Not that she took everything St. Clair Russell Hill said at face value. "His allegations about the squirrels, I found those hard to swallow," she confessed to Yale Templeton. "I mean, if squirrels had control over American foreign policy, I think my instructors at the CIA would have mentioned something about it, don't you?"

"I have to agree," he responded. "It always seemed to me that St. Clair exaggerated the squirrel threat a little bit. In all my years as commander in chief for defence of the Edifice Building perimeter, the squirrels did not mount more than five or six offensives that suggested anything other than a most rudimentary understanding of military tactics." He paused, then added, "Granted they show a certain sophistication in their approach to guerrilla warfare."

But Bobbi Jo Jackson was no longer thinking about the squirrels. Something had occurred to her when she was reciting the list of conspiracies enumerated by St. Clair Russell Hill, something that she dimly perceived might be of importance.

"What about this?" she said. "If it's true that the United States invaded Iraq to get control of the oil fields, well, maybe that explains why the CIA sent me to James Bay. Maybe it didn't have anything to do with the Cree Indians."

"Is there oil in James Bay?"

"Well, no. I mean, I don't know. I guess there could be. But oil is used to create power, right? And hydroelectric plants are used to create power, too. I'm pretty sure about that. So maybe, you know, maybe the CIA sent me because of the hydroelectric plants."

Yale Templeton mulled over her suggestion. She was relying on inference here, not his strong point. Still, what she said had a certain logic to it, even he could see that. And being a trained historian, he knew what her next step must be.

"You will have to locate some primary source evidence," he said.

"Primary source evidence? What's that?"

"Original documents. Something that shows a link between the CIA and the hydroelectric facilities on James Bay."

"What exactly do you mean by 'original documents'?"

"Well in my own work I have made very good use of newspapers. Many American dailies—some weeklies, too—have been copied onto microfilm and can be found at the university library. There is even an index for the *New York Times*. Then there are the published government records. Congressional debates, for example. You can find them at the library as well. Of course, to *prove* that there was some sort of conspiracy, for that you would need to get your hands on internal CIA documents: classified memos and such."

"And where can I find those?"

"Classified memos? You can't. Those are secret, not open to the public. Eventually most of them will be destroyed. However, not to worry. In all likelihood a few will survive. Someday—a hundred years from now, maybe two—a historian will stumble upon them. Then the whole story will come out."

"A hundred years! But I can't wait a hundred years!"

Her impatience took him by surprise. "I suppose some documents might become available before then. Maybe in seventy-five years. No earlier than that, I should think, however. Not in the case of classified information."

Bobbi Jo Jackson frowned. "Well where would these records be kept now?" she asked.

"I have no idea. Some storage facility at CIA headquarters, I imagine."

She raised her eyebrows. "At CIA headquarters?"

"Yes. Probably. But no one except a handful of officials would be allowed access to them."

"Hmm ..." she murmured. And then, "Hmm ..." again.

*The growth of the antlers of the
bull moose, and the brief season
of mating, are physiologically
closely associated.*

─── XXXVI ───

The growth of the antlers of the bull moose, and the brief season of mating, are physiologically closely associated. With antlers fully grown, the bull sets out to find a mate, manifesting a variety of emotions and qualities in his encounters with moose and men which are doubtless as little understood by himself as by any hunter who may chance to observe him.

SAMUEL MERRILL, *THE MOOSE BOOK*

A male moose sheds his antlers between December and March. He will produce a new set in the spring, their growth triggered by hormones that are themselves triggered by the now advancing sunlight. They will be covered at first by a coat of linty velvet, but that will die off over the course of the summer, the moose finally and completely removing any last vestiges by rubbing the antlers against the trunks and stumps of trees. Once the entire process is complete—this will be in August or September—he will start to journey about the countryside in search of a mate.

It is the female, in fact, who initiates the mating ritual. She emits a loud beckoning cry to indicate where she can be found, the male responding with an extended series of repetitive grunts as he searches for her. The two will continue this amorous call and response until he arrives at the corner of the forest where she stands waiting, after which he will position himself sideways directly in front of her. If she for some reason decides to amble off, he will accompany her, adopting the same pose once she comes to a halt.

This bawdy behaviour may well continue for days. Eventually the pair will come upon a spot that, for moose, bespeaks romance. Here the male will urinate and, if the mood suits him, defecate. He will paw and scrape at the ground for some considerable length of time until he has created a large, odoriferous, muddy pit known to biologists as a wallow. (What term moose use when thinking about it remains unknown.) He will lie down in the muck and begin to roll around in a manner so inviting that the female is soon captured by an irresistible urge to hurl herself into the wallow alongside him. Once covered in the fetid compound of his affection, she is overtaken by passion and emits a slow, erotic moan. He responds by laying his head tenderly against her back. Love is in the air. It is time to consummate their relationship. And so they do. In five seconds (give or take a second).

By the end of August—and here I mean the particular August at which we now arrive in our story—the Great White Moose had grown a magnificent set of antlers, more than five feet across, which he had honed to a glistening sheen in the old growth forest near Elk Lake. Still, any discussion about the link between antler growth and sex drive would have to be pretty much hypothetical in his case, since the Great White Moose had been neutered at birth. Granted, he took unalloyed delight in rolling about in a wallow. But other intuitive aspects of the mating ritual were effectively unknown to him, a circumstance exacerbated by the fact that almost all of his instincts had for years been overridden by his fixation on the haunting image of the spectre.

In that regard, however, the past summer had proven therapeutic. The quiet calm near Elk Lake had reduced his obsessiveness to the point that an observer familiar with his troubled history might well have concluded that he had stumbled across a cache of Paxil. And so, as the last shreds of velvet dropped from his antlers, he felt a stirring within himself, an imperative to search. But for what? The intimations of sexual desire were so muted and unfamiliar to him that he had no means to comprehend them. All he knew was that the time for idle contemplation had come to an end. He must be on the move.

But not east. Not back across the Ottawa River, where the man speaking the strange language had seen him, chased after him. Better to turn toward the security of home. Although to suggest that he still had anything other than the vaguest perception of what home was and where it might be found would be misleading. His uncertain instincts would eventually take him west. But not too far west. As poor an understanding of geography as he had, and as unable as he was to interpret the large wooden signs with maps he occasionally puzzled over by the side of the road, the Great White Moose sensed that he must remain within a certain territory. It was purely by chance that the limits of that territory coincided precisely with the boundaries of Ontario.

Now at this point I feel obliged to anticipate an objection that some readers, whether human or moose, are bound to raise: "Here we have, in the Great White Moose, what is apparently a clumsy attempt at a metaphor for Canadian identity. Yet does the moose wander into New Brunswick and cross the Confederation Bridge to Prince Edward Island, or find his way to Cape Breton and catch the ferry to Newfoundland? Does he migrate west across the Prairies to British Columbia or north to Nunavut and the Yukon? Or, for that matter, does he even place a solitary hoof on Manitoba soil? No, most assuredly not. In fact, other than a brief and notably unsuccessful excursion into Quebec, he remains entirely within the political jurisdiction where he was born. What conceit! What typical Ontario conceit! To believe that the totality of the Canadian experience can be represented by a denizen of the most privileged, the most self-satisfied—hence the most unrepresentative—of provinces."

To which I can only reply that, in my honest opinion, the Great White Moose should not be held accountable if he has mistakenly concluded that larger truths can somehow be derived from the narrow circumstances of his own personal history. It is, after all, a mistake that humans commonly make. And it would seem rather hard to hold a moose to higher standards. Even a Great White Moose.

—— XXXVII ——

A t around the same time the Great White Moose experienced the inchoate stirrings that led him to abandon the security of Elk Lake, Richard Hakluyt the younger returned to the little cottage in Saffron Walden to report to Yale Templeton's mother on his efforts to raise a search party for the man he knew simply as Y.

"I can not tell you what restlesse nights, what painefull dayes, what heat, what cold I have indured," he began. "How many long & chargeable journeys I have traveiled; into how manifold acquaintance I have entred; what expenses I have not spared; and yet what faire opportunities of private gaine, preferment, and ease I have neglected; albeit thy selfe canst hardly imagine, yet I by daily experience do finde & feele, and some of my entier friends can sufficiently testifie."

This all had a familiar ring to it. Had she not heard it before? Perhaps not. "This Commonwealth wherein you live and breathe takes due note of your sacrifices," she responded.

"Truly that makes all my difficulties seeme easie, all paines and industrie pleasant, and all expenses of light value and moment unto me."

She nodded graciously. "But before you proceed further," she said, "I should apprise you of some new information I have received from Canada about the noble young man whose fate I have entrusted to your hands. It appears that he has lately made his way to a French settlement."

Richard Hakluyt stroked his beard in thought. "A French settlement. That is in deede interesting."

She searched his face silently.

"I would be soe bolde as to suggest, Your Majestie," he responded at length, "that Y. hath anticipated us here."

"Anticipated us? In what sense?"

"I did offer the opinion on my last visite, did I not, that the French in Canada will ere long come to recognise the benefitt of gentle English governance? In all probabilitie, Y. has sought out the settlers from France with that ende in minde."

"Do you think so? But he writes that he remained with the French less than a day. He was unable to arrange a meeting with the leader of the community, and they fed him some food fit only for the Irish."

"Ah, that is disappointing, to be sure. But we may assume, I think, that Y. hath conceived of this preliminarie contacte as a way to prepare the grounde for future negociations."

"Very promising, if true. Still, the communication I have received indicates that he continues in the company of that American Savage widow whose likeness I am loath to look upon."

"I see. Dost thou beleve he is yet under her spell?"

"It would appear so from his communication, yes."

"Then we must proceede posthaste to free the valiant Y. from his bewitchment and provyde him with the men and materials he will need to bringe to fruition Your Majestie's wishes. In that regarde I have good news to report. I beleve I have founde a leader for our expedition."

"Sir Martin, I presume?"

He dropped his eyes, dismayed that she was unaware of what he now must reveal to her. "Alas, Your Majestie, the brave Frobisher was mortally wounded by the Spaniardes off the coast of France some yeares since."

"This news does grieve me most sorely."

"A great loss for us all, truly."

She dabbed at her eyes. "Then if not Sir Martin, who? John Davis?"

"Not Davis himself, but an able member of his crewe, one Henry Hudson."

"Henry Hudson," she said to herself. "Henry Hudson. I do not believe I know that name."

"In all likelihood not, Your Majestie. He is a man yet unheralded outside the circle of adventurers, albeit I have no hesitation in saying that he is destyned to win renowne for his traveils in the New Worlde."

"Then tell me about him. Who are his people? What services has he performed for the Crown?"

"I do so gladly, Your Majestie. His grandfather was an alderman in the citie of London involved with the younger Cabot in founding the Muscovy Company. His father was a man of some substance, a member of the Skinners & Tanners with propertie in Lincolnshire. After he, by which I mean the father, died, his widow married Richard Champion, who, I am sure Your Majestie will recall, served as Lorde Mayor of London. The Hudson family coat of arms is an argent semée of fleurs-de-lis gules, a crosse engrailed sable.

"Henry Hudson first gained his passion for overseas exploration in the offices of the Muscovy Company. He did subsequently take parte in trading missions to the Mediterranean, the North Sea, and the coast of Africa. In 1587 he shipped out with John Davis in search of the Northwest Passage, returning in time to serve heroically in our triumphant battle against the king of Spaines' dreadfull Armada."

"And you are satisfied that he is the man to lead our expedition?"

"I am, Your Majestie. He not only hath studied all the logbooks of those who sailed before him, but I have procured for him the journals of the Dutch explorer Willem Barents. And he is entierly familiar with the mappes of Mercator, Ortelius, Hondius, and Petrus Plancius."

"Sir, I have always found your judgment to be impeccable. If you believe he is qualified to serve the interests of the Crown, then I have no hesitation in giving my approval. And when might I meet this estimable young man?"

"Immediately, Your Majestie, he tarries outside."

"Then by all means show him in."

"I am most pleased to do so."

XXXVIII

B ut in fact Richard Hakluyt the younger was something less than pleased to do so. He had serious misgivings about what Henry Hudson might say. That his name was Sebastian Higgs, for instance. That was how he had introduced himself when he arrived at the rectory in Wetheringsett. He had heard about the plans for an expedition and wanted to offer his services. "You see, I was Henry Hudson in a previous life," he had explained. A man of unbalanced mind, Richard Hakluyt had decided. And if others had responded to the call for volunteers, he would have summarily turned Sebastian Higgs away at the door. But there had been no others. And so he had invited the eager young man in.

The conversation that followed had been, to say the least, rather unusual. Sebastian Higgs, according to his claims, had lived many previous lives. He had been a Norman archer at the Battle of Hastings, a Benedictine monk, Geoffrey of Monmouth, a signatory to the Magna Carta, the Wife of Bath. He had been wounded at Acre during the Third Crusade. He had been wounded at Agincourt during the Hundred Years' War. He had been slain at Bosworth Field during the Wars of the Roses. But even more fantastical were his claims about what would happen in the future (what, in his representation of things, had already happened!): A rebellion in which an English monarch would lose not only this throne but his head. The emergence of a political philosophy based on the principle that all men are born with "natural rights." A "Glorious Revolution" in which Parliament would assert its authority over the Crown. He himself, under the name of Isaac Newton, would discover mathematical laws explaining the movement of the planets. He would march off in the army of Lord Wellington to fight the French, then, more than a hundred years later, march off in the army of a General Montgomery to save them. He would be a mill owner in the Midlands; a dockworker in Liverpool. And in his present life, as Sebastian Higgs, he was something called a "computer systems analyst."

Now, if these wild fantasies were all Sebastian Higgs had to offer, obviously Richard Hakluyt would never have seriously considered him as a candidate to lead the search for Yale Templeton. But the future he described included an empire for England, an empire the like of which Richard Hakluyt the younger had foretold in his writings. An empire of such grandeur that it would cast the Roman Empire into insignificance. An empire extending to all corners of the world. And an empire, it must be added, whose potentially richest possession was that vast northern expanse where the courageous Y. had chosen to cast his lot among the Savages.

And there was more. Sebastian Higgs had many innovative ideas that, on the face of them, sounded quite reasonable—ideas that Richard Hakluyt was prepared to concede were ahead of their time. About marine navigation, to cite just one example. He drew a diagram of a device he claimed to have invented in a later life (by which I mean later than his life as Henry Hudson) that allowed sailors to determine degrees of longitude. A chronometer, he called it. The design seemed entirely plausible, Richard Hakluyt had to admit.

Beyond that, Sebastian Higgs expressed a very personal reason for wanting to cross the Atlantic. He wished, he said, to recover his self-respect.

"Historians have written that I was indecisive," he complained, "that I wasted time tracking up and down the shore of the bay that has come to bear my name."

("Come to beare his name?" thought Richard Hakluyt.)

"They say that my men starved, that I drove them to mutiny. But my travels along the waters of the northern wilderness were not aimless. I saw immediately that we had arrived at a land rich beyond our dreams. Not in gold and silver, perhaps, but in trees, animals, useful metals. Many brave sailors had given their lives in the quest for a Northwest Passage. But why yearn for the silks and spices of Cathay when you can have the beaver pelts and nickel of Canada?"

("Nickel?" thought Richard Hakluyt.)

"And we did not starve, I assure you. I had the crew set up a small camp in the woods where I assigned each man a task appropriate to his station in life. Indeed, I saw it as my duty to fulfill your injunction to remake the New World in the image of our own blessed Commonwealth. But there were those among the men—the Dutch, in particular, and that scoundrel Henry Greene—who placed their personal ambitions above the advancement of our nation. One night, while I was asleep, they sailed off in the *Discovery*, never to be seen again by me in this life."

"But," objected Richard Hakluyt, "Abacuk Prickett did testifie when he returned to England that the mutineers set thee adrift in a shallop. He made no mention of an encampment."

"The traitors did not want anyone to know they had sabotaged an enterprise that promised untold glory for the Crown. Your call for volunteers came to me as an opportunity—an opportunity to replicate the voyage to Canada I made when I was Henry Hudson. But pray tell me, what prompts you to mount an expedition at this particular time?"

And so Richard Hakluyt explained to Sebastian Higgs about the courageous Y.—about his bold decision to cross the seas so that he could educate the Savages and about his subsequent bewitchment by a Native widow. He also predicted that once Y. was liberated from her spell, he would use his multitude of talents to demonstrate to both the Native population and French settlers the many advantages to be realised from English rule, and to secure the vast north of the New World for the Crown.

"It is what I myself intended to do," Sebastian Higgs said wistfully. "And does this mission go forward with the blessing of the Queen?"

"It does," replied Richard Hakluyt. "In deede, it was Her Majestie who first did bringe the plight of Y. to my attention and it was she who charged me with the responsibilitie for effecting his rescue."

"Then, sir, I must insist that you avail yourself of my services. Not only have I always been a loyal servant of the Crown, but I particularly admire the present Queen for the discretion with which she has handled the many derelictions of her children."

"Her children?!"

"Yes, her children. Especially her eldest son."

"Queen Elizabeth has no son, nor daughter neither! She took a vow never to marry!"

"Sir, you jest with me. Of course she married. She married Philip."

"Philip?! Philip?! Her greatest enemie?!"

(Now here it should be noted what you already may have guessed. While Sebastian Higgs was speaking of Queen Elizabeth II and her consort, Philip, the Duke of Edinburgh, Richard Hakluyt was speaking of Elizabeth I and Philip II of Spain, who at one time offered Elizabeth marriage but later plotted her assassination, laid a claim to the English throne, and sent the Armada on its ill-fated invasion.)

Sebastian Higgs and Richard Hakluyt continued on in this same vein for some minutes longer. Anyone familiar with the comic routines of Abbott and Costello should have little difficulty reconstructing their dialogue. I myself refrain from doing so only because I have no wish to detract from the otherwise serious nature of their conversation. It is enough to point out that, by the time they had sorted out their misunderstanding, Sebastian Higgs had concluded that the woman who had commissioned the expedition to save Y. had been Elizabeth I in a previous life. And Richard Hakluyt had concluded that the man who called himself Sebastian Higgs almost certainly belonged in Bethlem. Still, he had to admit, the fellow had a remarkable knowledge of navigation and geography. Under careful supervision—the kind of supervision Richard Hakluyt had every confidence he himself could provide—Sebastian Higgs might well be able to lead a successful rescue mission. In any case, no one else had presented himself as a candidate for the job.

The two men talked at some length about the hazards of sea travel. The bitter cold, the storms, the icebergs, the leviathans. Sebastian Higgs—but, no, it is time I start calling him Henry Hudson, since that is how he will be known to Yale Templeton's mother—Henry Hudson described in great detail his reaction on sighting a gargantuan pod of whales off Spitsbergen Island. "They were awe inspiring, truly awe inspiring. It pains me deeply to think that some refer to me as 'the grandfather of the whaling industry.'"

They talked as well about the diseases commonly faced by mariners. And here Henry Hudson had some novel solutions to offer. "It is now possible to vaccinate crew members to ensure that they do not contract typhus, to supply them with citrus fruits from the tropics to spare them the black gums and swollen limbs of scurvy, to give them antibiotics to treat dysentery."

("Vaccinate?" wondered Richard Hakluyt. "Antibiotics?")

He also had many revolutionary ideas about how to deal with problems of food preservation, dead beer, and the cramped, cold quarters found on seagoing vessels. (Richard Hakluyt did think, however, that he was too dismissive of the potential dangers posed by pirates.) In the end they formalized the terms of an agreement. Henry Hudson would take on the task of securing a suitable ship and hiring a crew. However, he would make regular reports to Richard Hakluyt, who would retain ultimate authority over all aspects of the expedition.

—— XXXIX ——

o it is evident why Richard Hakluyt the younger was filled with misgivings when he introduced Henry Hudson to Yale Templeton's mother. Indeed, he had spent many hours preparing the younger man for that very moment, providing him with a suitable set of clothes, instructing him in the proper manner and speech to adopt in the presence of Her Majesty, and doing his very best to convince him that any comments he made about alleged developments subsequent to the sixteenth century would be damaging to his prospects for winning her favour.

And by and large things turned out very well, better than Richard Hakluyt had anticipated. The one troublesome moment came shortly after the two men entered the little cottage. Henry Hudson was admiring the several tapestries hanging on the walls when his eyes fell on a painting just to the side of the throne, a portrait of Henry VIII.

"A remarkable study, Your Highness," he said.

"The likeness of Father, you mean. Yes, quite remarkable. Holbein did a fine job, I must say."

"He did, indeed. And the copy you have is almost as impressive as the original."

"As the original! Whatever can you mean? This *is* the original!"

"Surely not. I saw the original last month. In Madrid."

"What!! In Madrid! You mean that despicable Philip claims to have this very same portrait?!"

(Knowledgeable readers will know that Philip II made Madrid the location of his royal court in 1561 and that the famous Holbein painting of Henry VIII, executed around 1537, is currently in the collection of the Thyssen-Bornemisza Gallery, also in Madrid.)

Here Richard Hakluyt fell into a coughing fit, which evidently had its intended consequence, because immediately afterward Henry Hudson apologized to Yale Templeton's mother for having distressed her and acknowledged that, on reflection, not only must he have been mistaken in his identification of the painting but in fact he had never actually been to Spain. Then he added, "I do enjoy madrigals, however." And he produced a lute that he had brought with him at Richard Hakluyt's insistence.

Considering the number of centuries that had passed since he had made his living as a wandering minstrel, he performed quite competently. His selections were well chosen to appeal to Yale Templeton's mother. He began with "My Bonny Lass She Smileth" and "April Is My Mistris Face" by Morley, offered a selection of representative works by Ravenscroft and Byrd, then finished with John Hilton's "Fair Oriana, Beauty's Queen." It seemed to Yale Templeton's mother that she had never received a more pleasing tribute. Whatever doubts she initially may have felt about Henry Hudson wafted away on the cadences of his lilting melodies.

Later, as they chatted over hot spiced wine, he offered some preliminary thoughts on the expedition. "Since we are interested in speed, my recommendation is that I take a single ship. There will be time enough to send for more men later, after I have freed Y. from the clutches of the Savage woman." A visit to the docks in London, however, had convinced him that the kind of vessel he required was not currently available. He would have no choice but to build his own. "Alas, I seem to have misplaced the blueprints for the *Discovery*. However, I believe I can get my hands on the plans for my earlier ship, the *Half Moon*. I will set to work on construction presently. In many ways the *Half Moon* would be a preferable choice. It is somewhat smaller and will require no more than eighteen men to operate, even fewer if I reduce the scale of the ship, as I may well do, to save time."

"Spare no expense," said Yale Templeton's mother. "Be assured that you have the full financial resources of the Crown behind you."

"Although, of course, 'twoulde be best not to make that facte publick," cautioned Richard Hakluyt, "as we have no wish to arouse the suspicions of the Spaniardes and Portingales." To which they all agreed.

A most curious band they made, the two men and one woman who met in the little cottage in Saffron Walden. I mean, think about it for a moment. In Yale Templeton's mother we have an elderly dowager who believes that she is Queen Elizabeth I. In Sebastian Higgs, we have a computer systems analyst from Bournemouth who believes he was Henry Hudson in a previous life. And in Richard Hakluyt the younger, we have ... well, for all I know, he really *is* Richard Hakluyt the younger, author of The Principal Navigations, Voyages, and Discoveries of the English Nation made by sea or over land to the most remote and farthest distant quarters of the earth, at any time within the compass of these 1500 yeares, who had endured "restlesse nights," "painefull dayes," "heat," "cold," and so on for "the honour and benefit of this Common weale wherein I live and breathe."

And the three of them have come together for what purpose? To rescue our—how shall I call Yale Templeton? Hero? No, that implies a nobility that would seem, at least on the evidence so far, conspicuously at odds with his character. Protagonist, then? But even that carries a suggestion of engagement hardly suitable for someone more acted upon than acting. Let us just say, they have come together to save the rather nondescript person who, without at all intending to, set our plot (such as it is) in motion. Not that they are likely to come up with the most practical of plans for effecting his rescue. Still, their intentions are admirable enough. And there are moments in life when no doubt it is advisable to trust your fate to individuals unconstrained by conventional attitudes regarding the limits of the possible.

XL

The corridors at the storage facility where the CIA houses its classified documents are dimly lit, with doorways hidden in shadows. At least that was the explanation the three security guards gave as to how a person or persons unknown had been able to overpower them. Why they were naked and handcuffed to each other when the cleaning staff found them remains a mystery.

A team of agents was sent in to determine which materials had been targeted in the break-in. They began with the records on al-Qaeda and other anti-American terrorist organizations. They then moved to the files for Iraq, Iran, North Korea, Afghanistan. The files for China, Russia, Pakistan, Cuba, Haiti, the Dominican Republic, Grenada, Chile, Nicaragua, Panama, El Salvador, Guatemala, Libya, Lebanon, Syria, Egypt. The files for the former Soviet Union as well as its satellites in Eastern Europe and its client states in Asia and Africa. The files from the Vietnam War, from the undeclared war in Cambodia, from the Korean War. And—in the room reserved for records from the prehistory of the CIA—the files from World War II, from World War I, from the Spanish-American War. But they found nothing indicating that the security of the nation had been compromised. Not a single document was missing; not a single document was out of place. And according to the sophisticated forensic tests used by the Agency, no records had been photographed. It appears, reported the Director of the CIA to the President, still at his ranch, that the break-in was nothing more than an elaborate practical joke.

But then, no one had thought to examine the files on Quebec.

XLI

In table manners the moose shows little of the gentility of most of the deer. He of necessity straddles like a giraffe to reach moss or other browse which is close to the ground, and often rears on his hind legs to reach attractive morsels which cannot otherwise be nibbled from the limbs of trees. He frequently "rides down" saplings by walking over them, bringing the tender twigs within easy reach.

SAMUEL MERRILL, *THE MOOSE BOOK*

Surprisingly little has been written about the political opinions of moose, and about the views of the Great White Moose on the pressing issues of the day, we know absolutely nothing. That would have to be considered a shame, because during the years when he was trekking back and forth across the distant reaches of Northern Ontario, the government of the province was in the hands of a party determined to overturn the social contract that had existed for half a century.

The party in question had at one time been the dominant force in provincial politics, but after languishing in opposition for years had chosen a new leader dedicated to returning what he called "horse sense" to government. A bowling instructor—"bowling professional" was the term he himself preferred—born and raised in a northern town not far from the Ojibwa settlement where the Great White Moose had spent the early years of his life, he believed that everything you needed to know about how to run the province could be learned over a beer with friends in the local bowling alley. And the more beers the better.

The most important lesson he had learned was that all his problems—and he had many—as well as all the problems of his friends—and they had many, too—were the result of nefarious actions by the government. And so, prompted by the local bowling association, he entered provincial politics, winning rather handily in his first campaign for office. In the years ahead, as the fortunes of the party declined, his public profile rose. As a result, by the time he took over the leadership, he was largely able to shape the party platform according to his own beliefs. During the next election, handbills with a picture of the new leader flashing a combative smile were plastered everywhere. Running across the top of the handbill was the new party slogan in bold print: "THE BUSINESS OF THE GOVERNMENT IS TO GO OUT OF BUSINESS." One of the handbills somehow became stuck to the antlers of the Great White Moose while he was skirting the shores of Lake Nipissing, remaining with him until moulting season the following spring.

In the election, the party and its bowling instructor leader were swept to power, taking 40 percent of the vote, which, due to the logic of Canadian democracy, translated into 75 percent of the seats. "A clear mandate for change," rejoiced the new premier, drawing on the fine understanding of democratic government, not to mention statistics, he had honed in the brief year he had spent as a high school teacher.

The throne speech outlined the full measure of revolutionary change he had in mind for the province:

To quote Winston Churchill: "It has been said that democracy is the worst form of government except all those others that have been tried from time to time." Mindful of that fundamental truth, your new government promises to centralize power in the hands of unelected officials answerable only to the premier.

To ensure that the citizens of Ontario receive the quality of public services that they truly deserve, your new government promises to remove the delivery of those services from the hands of dedicated civil servants who have devoted their lives to promoting the public good and turn it over, through untendered bids, to private sector firms whose principal obligation is to secure short-term profits for their CEOs, if not, perhaps, their shareholders.

Because the vast majority of people in the province live in urban centres in the South, we will implement forms of municipal government suitable for small towns in the North. To allow us to fulfill our promise to balance the provincial budget, we will download a vast range of expensive services onto the municipalities, while denying them access to the additional tax revenues they will need to provide those services adequately.

The primary requirement of any government is to ensure fiscal responsibility. It is well established that in Ontario the greatest obstacle to a balanced budget is the vast sums of money in the hands of the poor. The homeless, in particular, are inexplicably privileged. They have no overhead (so to speak), provide no work for Portuguese cleaning ladies, and rarely employ illegal immigrant women from the Philippines as nannies, yet for some reason they continue to receive public assistance. It will be the intention of your new government to shift the resources of the province to the deserving rich, who as a result will no longer be compelled to tie up their inheritances in tax havens off shore.

In keeping with our campaign pledge to restore dignity to labour, your new government promises to eliminate the minimum wage and drastically expand the number of workers denied the right to strike.

Perhaps the greatest challenge facing any government today is to provide an education that will prepare children to compete in the global economy of the twenty-first century (or at least serve as a pliant, cheap labour force for multinational corporations based in the United States). To that end your new government makes the following promises: to appoint a high school dropout as Minister of Education; to substantially reduce the pay of school board members, while cutting back on the financial resources available for them to perform their duties; to increase the number of courses each instructor will be required to teach, while slashing the time allotted for classroom preparation; to cut programs for students with learning disabilities or for whom English is a second language; and to eliminate one year of high school.

Universal health care is regarded by Canadians as a sacred trust. Accordingly your new government will negotiate a fee schedule with doctors that will require a significant paring down of the services covered by OHIP along with massive cutbacks in the number of nurses hospitals can afford to hire. This will necessitate our licensing private facilities to attend to the medical needs of the deserving rich, allowing Ontario to produce a health care system every bit as efficient as the one currently operating in the United States, where over 40 million people find themselves without health insurance and per capita medical costs are almost 50 percent higher than in Canada.

Implementation of the agenda outlined in the throne speech created labour discord, seriously undermined the quality of health care in the province, produced chaos in the schools, and substantially increased homelessness while significantly enriching the wealthiest 2 percent of the population. In the minds of the voters who had elevated the bowling instructor to power, there could hardly be clearer evidence that, unlike any other politician in recent (or distant) memory, here was a man prepared to carry out his promises without compromise or indeed concern for (not to mention awareness of) their consequences. It came as no surprise to political commentators when, four years later, these same voters used their considerable electoral voice to return him to office.

Now, however, he faced a dilemma. Having fulfilled all the commitments he had made in his first throne speech, he was at a loss about what to do during his second term. Here, however, he came up with a solution that won over even his most severe detractors. He proposed to spend the better part of the year in California. This proved so satisfactory that he decided to remain indefinitely outside Canada while giving up the office of premier (after having first done the paperwork necessary to ensure that Ontario taxpayers would cover all his expenses).

Once he announced his intention to resign, party officials called a convention to select a new leader. Candidates included the most prominent members of his cabinet: the Minister for the Deserving Rich, the Minister for People Even More Deserving than the Deserving Rich Because They Have Even More Money, the Minister for Neglecting the Mentally Ill, and the Minister for Contradicting Himself on Energy Policy. In the end, however, the party turned to the Minister for Selling His Soul to Bay Street on the grounds that, of all the candidates, he alone had the capacity to foster the illusion that the government had a deep sense of compassion for all residents of the province, poor as well as rich.

Unfortunately, the new premier became embroiled in controversy almost from the moment he took office. He was severely taken to task for his decision to rent out the legislature to a car parts manufacturer who was looking for a more dignified setting than his factory to hold the annual shareholders' meeting. (I was going to say that he made arrangements to bring down the provincial budget in a car parts factory, but parody, to be effective, must at least carry the hint of credibility.)

But the major problem he confronted came after a Supreme Court ruling forced the legislature to address the question of same-sex marriage. The former premier, like all beer-drinking bowlers from the North, held old-fashioned views on matrimony. He was deeply committed to family values, devoted not only to his own wife, but to the wives of several of his fellow citizens as well. His successor, however, was less dogmatic on social issues. And so he directed the Minister for the Deserving Rich Who, Through No Fault of Their Own, Happen to Be Gay, to come up with legislation that would acknowledge the emerging willingness among certain privileged elements of society to tolerate homosexual relationships while showing respect for those no less worthy individuals adhering to traditional standards of morality. The resulting statute was carefully designed to chart a middle course. It gave government sanction to same-sex marriages, but only for heterosexuals. This compromise was applauded by the *Globe and Mail* as "a very Canadian solution to a divisive issue." Indeed, it proved so successful that Parliament later drafted Federal legislation for same-sex marriages modelled on the Ontario law.

Now, I know what you are wondering. What did the Great White Moose think about all these remarkable developments? Having no disposable income to speak of, no children to educate, being relatively healthy, and spending his life as a transient in the wilderness, he was little affected by many of the initiatives introduced by the government. As for sexual relations, while I feel confident in saying that the majority of moose believe that the state has no place in the wallows of the nation, since the Great White Moose had been neutered at birth, we can by no means take it for granted that he held to mainstream (moose) views.

There was, however, one area of public policy that had a direct and immediate impact on his life. I am speaking, of course, of the environment. "Being born and raised in the North," said the bowling instructor upon becoming premier, "nothing is more important to me than preserving the rich natural heritage entrusted to us by our ancestors." With that in mind, as his first official act, he granted fifty square kilometres of old growth forest to a developer. "The white pine is of the very highest quality, exceptionally well suited for the construction of bowling lanes," the premier remarked proudly when making the announcement. Critics accused him of using his office improperly to benefit a friend. But he replied testily that the only connection he had with the developer was that they had grown up together, gone to the same school, and were members of the same private clubs. "Oh yes, and he was best man at my wedding. But other than that I hardly know the fellow." His supporters always loved it when he replied testily to his critics.

Not that there is any reason to believe that the Great White Moose cared much one way or the other about bowling. But it was distressing to him when, after abandoning the comfort and quiet of Elk Lake and starting off in the general direction of North Bay, he came to a stretch of land that he remembered as a pine forest only to find nothing but tree stumps, a bulldozer, and some men in hard hats. He retreated hastily, heading north and west. Eventually he arrived at the Temagami district, over 10,000 square kilometres containing fully one-third of North America's red and white pines. It is also home to a number of important endangered species, including the aurora trout, golden eagle, and eastern cougar. Polling indicates that fully 96 percent of residents of Ontario support preserving old growth forest. And so the premier created the Ministry to Encourage Illegal Clear-Cutting to see that the interests of the remaining 4 percent of the population—deserving rich loggers and developers according to the Minister for Deserving Rich Loggers and Developers—were protected.

When the lumber crews moved into Temagami, so did the protesters. They staged sit-ins at the headquarters of the logging companies and set up roadblocks on the highway running through the forest. On one of his excursions into the Temagami woods some years earlier, the Great White Moose had come upon a camp set up by the protesters. As fortune would have it, they were off in town for the evening—their monthly beer and bowling fest—and he was able to enjoy a box of granola bars before moving on. The protesters also engaged in a massive letter-writing campaign to individuals they hoped would be sympathetic to their cause. Yale Templeton's name apparently found its way onto their mailing list, because one day he received a pamphlet containing the stunning revelation that the logging plan called for "10,042 hectares of clear-cuts—an area larger than 17,000 football fields." He was surprised to learn that there was so much demand for football fields in a section of the province that his travels told him was largely unpopulated. But then the peculiar reality of life in the North never failed to amaze him. The pamphlet also pointed out that the loss of old growth forest could have disastrous long-term consequences for wildlife, which prompted him to send the environmental group a ten-dollar donation. "On behalf of the Great White Moose," he told Bobbi Jo Jackson.

The very same Great White Moose who, in retreat from the bulldozer and men in hard hats, now found himself by the shores of Lake Lokash, one of the contested sites in Temagami. The red and white pines that had formerly covered the ground were gone, but in their place stood saplings, planted only a day earlier. Part of a compromise that had been worked out between the government and the loggers. The loggers would be permitted to cut down the red and white pines, but only if they replaced each and every tree harvested. The protesters had been unappeased when the deal was announced, but to the population at large it seemed a reasonable way around a contentious issue. Public interest in the Temagami forest began to flag, and the controversy had disappeared from the pages of all but the local newspapers by the time the Great White Moose arrived at Lake Lokash.

Generally speaking, he preferred to dine on birch, willows, and balsam trees during the summer months. But saplings of any species had an appeal, since he enjoyed riding them down to bring the tender twigs within easy reach. Which he now proceeded to do, straddling a white pine sapling and stepping forward. And it was then that the Great White Moose became the first creature not involved in the negotiations—man or moose—to discover that there had been the finest of fine print in the agreement signed between the government and the logging companies. The saplings, you see, were plastic. Cheaper than live saplings, the representative of the logging company had argued. And plastic saplings would serve as a very attractive background setting for the bowling complex developers intended for the shores of the lake.

Not that the Great White Moose realized what was causing the pain that now shot from the plastic tip of the sapling upward through his body, a pain originating in exactly the same sensitive place and carrying exactly the same intensity as the pain he had experienced on the day he was reborn as the Great White Moose. And as on the day he was reborn as the Great White Moose, he tore off on his way to no predetermined destination. An opportune occasion, one might think, for him to reflect on the perpetual difficulty the government faces in getting health care professionals to locate in the small communities of the North.

XLII

eanwhile, back at the ranch, the President had called an emergency meeting of his chief security officers. The latest attempt to solve the problem of Yale Templeton had gone awry. The Executive Assistant to the Assistant Undersecretary of Transportation filled in the details for the Director of the FBI, the Director of the CIA, and the Assistant to the President for National Security Affairs as they rode in the limousine from the President's private landing strip: "As you are aware, the President provided $12 million to a representative of a private organization long identified with the interests of the government to compensate Professor Templeton for the evidence he found about Lincoln's faked assassination and subsequent life in Canada."

"'Private organization.' I like that," interrupted the Director of the FBI with a smirk. Then he reached over and started to tickle the Director of the CIA, who was still in the Xanax-induced stupor he had needed to get him through the plane ride.

The Executive Assistant to the Assistant Undersecretary of Transportation went on: "The President instructed the party responsible to fly to Toronto, arrange a meeting with Professor Templeton, secure the documents in question, and then ..." and here he discreetly cleared his throat, "... and then take whatever further steps he believed were necessary to protect the inalienable right of every American to believe in the innocence of his country."

"And do we know what those documents are yet?" asked the Assistant to the President for National Security Affairs (who had been under the mistaken impression that the President wanted them to come in disguise and so was dressed once again as Captain Hook, although this time without a peg leg, since he had torn his ACL when his knee buckled during their meeting at the bar in Washington).

"No, not yet," admitted the Executive Assistant to the Assistant Undersecretary of Transportation. "That was one of the things the party responsible was to determine when he met with Professor Templeton. The thing is, he apparently never made it to Toronto. Instead he caught a flight to Chicago, where, I am reliably informed," and here he nodded in the direction of the Director of the FBI, "that he and his two ... uh ... godsons used the $12 million to bankroll an attempted takeover of organized crime in the city."

"With just $12 million?" exclaimed the Assistant to the President for National Security Affairs. "That's ridiculous."

"You're quite right," replied the Director of the FBI, whose agents in Chicago had been closely monitoring the situation. "Pocket change for the Mob. But it was enough for him to form a syndicate and wrest control of student loans from local banks. Since then he has begun expanding into related fields."

"That's ingenious," exclaimed the Assistant to the President for National Security Affairs.

"I quite agree," said the Director of the FBI. "This Don Pugliese—the crime boss we're talking about—is obviously an extraordinarily resourceful character. For a number of years he has been masquerading as a retired bank employee in Arizona. However, his distant past remains shrouded in mystery. My agents have had a great deal of difficulty determining where he fits into the underworld's chain of command ..." (The Executive Assistant to the Assistant Undersecretary of Transportation rolled his eyes.) "... Right now he's running his operation out of an Iyengar yoga school in Joliet, Illinois. That's about all I can tell you." And he added gravely: "I did warn the President. Organized crime marches to its own drummer." Then he snickered, grabbed the Director of the CIA by the nose, and made a beeping sound. In response the Director of the CIA, who by now had started to shake off the effects of the Xanax, snatched the Director of the FBI's hairpiece and hurled it out the window of the limousine. The Assistant to the President for National Security Affairs broke into a laugh and then squeezed the beak of the stuffed parrot on his shoulder. "Keelhaul Yale Templeton! Squawk! Make him walk the plank!" the parrot screeched. "I put together the new soundtrack myself," the Assistant to the President for National Security Affairs said proudly.

When they finally arrived at the ranch house, the men found that the President was temporarily indisposed. Apparently he had been practicing his crossover draw on the rocking horse, snagged an acrylic nail on his holster, lost balance, and pitched forward. The cap gun accidentally discharged when it hit the floor, singeing his eyebrow. While he was being attended to at the infirmary, the others took the opportunity to go outside for a look at the new monument he had commissioned in honour of the late Senator Strom Thurmond. "It will be identical in size and structure to the Jefferson Memorial in Washington," observed the Executive Assistant to the Assistant Undersecretary of Transportation. "The President very much admires the way both leaders were able, apparently in good conscience, to draw a clear distinction between their professed beliefs and personal conduct. The dedication ceremony is to take place late in the fall. I understand that Essie Mae Washington as well as several descendants of Sally Hemings are expected to attend."

After the President had received a fake eyebrow (that, to be perfectly honest, looked too much like rabbit fur to be convincing), he summoned the men back to the ranch house. "I presume Lowell has brought you up to date on the most recent developments in the Templeton affair," he said.

The men all nodded.

"Good. Then we can get right down to business. The question I have is a simple one: What the hell do we do next?"

The Director of the CIA removed the Beretta from his pocket. "Mr. President," he said, "let me repeat the offer I made at our previous meetings." And he slapped the barrel of the gun in the palm of his hand.

"Thank you, Clyde. Your eagerness to perform gratuitous violence under the guise of patriotism is duly noted and, as always, greatly appreciated. Still, I would first like to explore options less likely to land another caricature of you on the cover of *Mad Magazine*."

"What about trying a bribe again?" suggested the Executive Assistant to the Assistant Undersecretary of Transportation. "Just because the ... uh ... Sicilian gentleman absconded with our money, that doesn't mean it was a bad idea."

The President glared at him. "Let me make one thing perfectly clear. To all of you. The Don is an old and dear friend of mine. He would never ... I repeat, *never* ... betray my trust. Not for a mere $12 million, in any case." To which the Executive Assistant to the Assistant Undersecretary of Transportation rolled his eyes once again.

"We can take it for granted," the President continued, "that if Don Pugliese stopped in Chicago before going to Canada, he had perfectly good reasons for doing so. And he would regard it, justifiably, as a deep offence against his sense of honour if I were now to send someone else to offer a bribe to Professor Templeton. Still, each day that passes without getting this matter settled increases the danger to the nation, by which of course I mean to myself. I believe we have no choice but to take some alternative course of action, and immediately."

"What about the first agent we sent to deal with Templeton?" asked the Assistant to the President for National Security Affairs.

The President raised an eyebrow. The fake one, as it happened, which now became unstuck and started to tilt upward.

"The one who arranged for the compromising photographs," explained the Assistant to the President for National Security Affairs, who instinctively adjusted his eye patch when he saw that the President's fake eyebrow was shifting position. "Is there any chance she might be willing to help us now?"

"Ah, you mean Bobbi Jo Jackson!" sighed the President, his fake eyebrow settling in at a right angle to his eye.

"Out of the question," interjected the Director of the CIA. "We can no longer even be certain she remains loyal to the United States. Rumour has it she spends her days—and nights, too—carrying out research on the history of Quebec."

"The history of Quebec?" queried the Executive Assistant to the Assistant Undersecretary of Transportation. "Whatever for?"

"I have no idea," replied the Director of the CIA. "We sent a couple of agents to Toronto to try to, shall we say, reason with her, but one ended up with a fractured collarbone and the other is currently awaiting a double hernia operation. And our attempts to put her under surveillance have been a complete washout. The fact is, she knows our procedures better than I do. We placed a tap on the phone in the apartment she shares with Templeton. Less than two hours later it was picking up what I am told were the sounds of a urinal in one of the men's rooms at the Air Canada Centre. How it got there, I have no idea."

"I take it from what you say, she's still involved with Templeton," commented the Assistant to the President for National Security Affairs.

"Still involved with Templeton. And apparently blindly devoted to his interests. Anyone trying to approach him will almost certainly have to deal with her first. And that—I make no bones about it—would be a very hazardous undertaking."

The President massaged his eyebrows in thought, the fake one becoming dislodged in the process. "It seems to me," he said, trying to shake the eyebrow from his middle finger, "that the continuing involvement of Bobbi Jo Jackson in this matter limits our options significantly. Obviously whoever goes to Toronto must be someone she trusts. Either that or a person with intimate knowledge of her methods."

The Director of the CIA slapped the barrel of the Beretta in his palm again, only this time he had a broad grin on his face.

The President, who had now rubbed the eyebrow off on his pants, studied him in silence. He was trying to remember why he had appointed a man with homicidal tendencies to such a politically sensitive position. "Oh, yes," he remembered with a smile. "He fixed it so I received the endorsement of the NRA."

"Well, Clyde," he said, "I guess you finally get your wish. Remember, though: Violence only as a last resort. And *only* once you have gotten your hands on the evidence."

"Thank you, Mr. President. You won't regret this," replied the Director of the CIA. And in gratitude, he peeled off one of his own fake eyebrows and patted it onto the bare spot above the President's eye.

XLIII

Meanwhile, back at the university, Felicia Butterworth was facing a problem of her own. For the most part the summer had gone very well. The various projects she had initiated were moving rapidly ahead, both those being carried out in the open, such as acquisition of the Anglican church on Greener Street, and those that were hidden from public view, such as negotiating the terms for the protection agency operating out of the former high school.

But then the letter had arrived. It had appeared, as all previous communications from Chicago had appeared, in a plain brown envelope slipped under the door of her office. The jerky handwriting was entirely unfamiliar to her, however, and she found the message to be virtually incomprehensible:

> Give a dis money to da professore. Da Boss, he need a da evidence 'bou' Lincoln. Capeesh?

It was unsigned, but then all the communications she received from Chicago were unsigned. In the envelope along with the letter was a form approving a student loan to Yale Templeton for fifteen hundred dollars, with very favourable terms of interest and a flexible repayment schedule. There was also a gift certificate for a month of lessons at an Iyengar yoga school in Joliet, Illinois.

Felicia Butterworth reread the letter more than a dozen times, trying to decipher its message. She guessed that, on the basis of the accompanying student loan form and the references to a "professore" and Lincoln, it had something to do with Yale Templeton. But what? She passed it on to the Dean Responsible for Relations with the Mafia, but he was equally mystified. "Perhaps it's from the president of the Faculty Union," he suggested. "It could be in some new language he's invented." But Felicia Butterworth had never received anything from H. Avery Duck concise enough to be slipped into a single envelope. And there was also the gift certificate to a yoga school in Joliet. No, the letter was from Chicago, she felt quite certain about that. And to protect herself, she dispatched the Dean Responsible for Relations with the Mafia to see what he could find out.

He booked into his usual suite at the Palmer Hotel and arranged for a meeting with his most trustworthy Mob contact. The letter, he learned, had not been sent by anyone previously involved in dealings with the university. "Definitely not our work," the informant assured him. "No one around here does Chico Marx. Not anymore, anyway. The older guys, they all try to sound like Brando. The younger ones, they're Sopranos. And look at the grammatical errors. Disgraceful! No, like I said, definitely not our work. But there's a new guy down in Joliet you should probably contact. Well, an old guy, really, but he's new to the territory. Muscled his way into the student loans racket. He runs his operation out of an Iyengar yoga school. Oh, and have a look at the ad for the school in yesterday's *Tribune*. I think it mentioned something about a limited-time offer for free beginner-level lessons."

So the dean went to Joliet, received his complimentary yoga lessons, and then one evening (feeling now much more supple and relaxed), met with Vito Pugliese for dinner in a little out-of-the-way Italian place not far from the former site of the SMC Cartage Company warehouse. "I love a dis neighbourhood," Vito told him, swirling a gold toothpick in his mouth. "It bring a back such memories." His two grandnephews, or godsons as they introduced themselves—Hugh, who ran the Iyengar yoga school, and Charles, who operated a bookie joint out back—stood behind the table as bodyguards, submachine guns resting conspicuously in their arms. Over veal piccata, the dean determined that it had indeed been Vito who was responsible for the letter. He was also able to establish (more or less) what Vito's intention had been in sending it.

"Don Pugliese is interested in Yale Templeton all right," he explained to Felicia Butterworth when he got back to Toronto. They were sitting at the dining room table in her spacious Rosedale mansion, only blocks from the apartment near Dunbar Road, where, as it happens at that very moment, Yale Templeton and Bobbi Jo Jackson were wrapped up in their own entirely different conversation. But more on that shortly.

"He says," the dean continued, referring to Vito Pugliese, "that he needs to get his hands on the evidence Templeton discovered about Abraham Lincoln. About Lincoln faking his own assassination, moving to Canada. You know."

Felicia Butterworth was perplexed. "The evidence he discovered? Templeton discovered no evidence. It was a figment of his imagination."

"Are we really sure about that?" the dean replied. "Don Pugliese doesn't seem to think so. Not from what he said to me, anyway."

Felicia Butterworth pressed her hands together in front of her mouth. "How far does this lunacy extend?" she wondered.

"Not only that," the dean continued, "he led me to believe that he's working for someone higher up."

"Someone higher up?"

"Someone in the government. The Don chose his words carefully. Or at least I think he chose his words carefully. Frankly I found his dialect difficult to penetrate. But I got the impression from one of his godsons that he's taking his orders from the White House."

"The White House!" burst out Felicia Butterworth. "Are you sure?"

The dean shrugged.

"The White House! Christ Almighty!" And she shoved back her chair and went to the sideboard, where she downed a large tumbler of vodka. The Dean Responsible for Relations with the Mafia remained seated, watching her without comment.

"So what does he want from me, this Don Pugliese?" she said, returning to the table and throwing herself back into the chair.

"He wants you to pay Templeton off for the evidence. Then when you get it—the evidence, I mean—you're supposed to contact him and he'll send his godsons to pick it up."

Felicia Butterworth rose from the chair again and started pacing, her hands thrust deep in the pockets of her Armani Exchange pants. "Look," she said, "if Templeton really has tracked down some papers about Lincoln coming to Canada ... and it still sounds crazy to me, but if the White House ..." Her voice trailed off. "Anyway," she started up again, "if Templeton really has tracked down some papers about Lincoln, there are easier ways than a bribe to get them from him." And to illustrate what she meant, she picked up two unopened bags of Doritos from the sideboard and smashed them together, sending corn chips flying across the room.

"Well," rasped the dean, gagging on the shattered fragments of a corn chip, "I did explain to the Don about your preferred methods of persuasion. But he was quite insistent. No force. No intimidation. Templeton might panic and destroy whatever he found. Then there would be hell to pay. So it has to be a bribe. That's why he sent the money."

"Money? What money?" said Felicia Butterworth. "He sent no money."

"The student loan."

"The student loan! He expects us to bribe someone on the faculty with a student loan? A student loan for fifteen hundred dollars?"

"The repayment schedule is very flexible, he assured me." Although he tried to sound upbeat, the dean winced when he said it.

Felicia Butterworth threw her head back and exhaled heavily, her cheeks puffing out.

"Perhaps," offered the dean, "it would make more sense if we came up with some money ourselves."

"Perhaps it would," she agreed with a sigh, returning to her chair. "Although I'd have to use some creative bookkeeping to get it past the Governing Council."

They sat there without speaking for several minutes, Felicia Butterworth staring down at the bits and pieces of corn chips on the floor, and the dean distracted by her fingers drumming on the table. She had, at best, limited confidence in most members of her administration. However, the Dean Responsible for Relations with the Mafia had been with her in the marketing department at Frito-Lay. During their years together, she had developed great respect for his business skills and implicit trust in his judgment. For his part he could think of no more useful purpose in life than serving as her deputy, and in whatever enterprises she might propose.

It was the dean who broke the silence. "Perhaps we should try another tack. Not all forms of bribery require approval of the Governing Council."

"Go on."

"Templeton is English, right?"

"English. Yes."

"Well, it seems to me that the English value something even more than money."

She gave him a quizzical look.

"Titles," he trumpeted. "The English love titles. Kings and queens. Dukes and duchesses. Earls and ... uh ... whatever they call the wives of earls. You could offer Templeton a title."

"You think I should knight him?" she replied.

The dean groaned.

Felicia Butterworth laughed. "Relax, Bugsy. Giving him a title is a terrific idea. Absolutely inspired. Why, I could make him a dean!" And she laughed again.

The dean frowned.

"No. Quite right. Not impressive enough. I'll name him to an endowed chair."

"An endowed chair. Yes. That would be just the sort of thing."

"A university professor," Felicia Butterworth went on. "I could give him one of the university professorships. They're very prestigious."

The dean nodded.

"On the other hand," she continued, affecting a thoughtful pose, "there are currently a dozen university professors. Perhaps what we need for such a noteworthy scholar as Yale Templeton," and now her voice took on a sardonic edge, "is something that will truly set him apart."

"Like 'Distinguished Professor of American History'?" hazarded the dean.

"Like 'Distinguished Professor of American History,'" repeated Felicia Butterworth. "Or," she said, her imagination bounding exuberantly ahead of her, "'Distinguished Professor of the American Civil War.'"

She paused, a malefic smile appearing on her face. "*Or*," she continued, surging to a triumphant conclusion, "'*Abraham Lincoln* Distinguished Professor of the American Civil War.'" And she erupted in a violent, self-satisfied, demonic cackle.

XLIV

Meanwhile, back at the apartment near Dunbar Road, Yale Templeton and Bobbi Jo Jackson were sitting on the floor of the small living room surrounded by books, articles, and documents. Off against one wall stood a nondescript upright piano—a black Krakauer—that had been abandoned by the previous tenants. While a student at the Robinson-Fallis Academy for Boys, Yale Templeton had occasionally been required to play bells, cymbals, and the triangle in school concerts. That was the extent of his musical training, however. The piano in his apartment intrigued him, and from time to time he would sit down and poke away at the keys, usually producing a discordant noise. But Bobbi Jo Jackson had the ability to play piano by ear—a talent she had first discovered in her father's church—and by listening to recordings of Elizabethan madrigals, she had very rapidly built up a substantial repertoire of his favourite pieces.

At the moment, however, the two of them were hardly thinking about music. Yale Templeton was putting the finishing touches on the footnotes for his seminal article on the incidence of poisonous snake bites at Confederate military hospitals. No one in North America had a more thorough knowledge of the appropriate form of punctuation for historical citations. Still, next to him on the floor lay the *Modern Humanities Research Association Style Book:*

Notes for Authors, Editors, and Writers of Theses; *Copy-Editing: The Cambridge Handbook for Editors, Authors, and Publishers*; Kate Turabian's *A Manual for Writers of Term Papers, Theses, and Dissertations* (a rather reluctant concession on his part to American standards); and, his very favourite, because of its distinguished pedigree, *Hart's Rules for Compositors and Readers of the University Press, Oxford*. He painstakingly checked the guidelines laid down in all four texts before committing himself to each comma, semicolon, and set of quotation marks.

Bobbi Jo Jackson, on the other hand, was busily involved in making her way through an extensive set of CIA records on Quebec: memos, correspondence, field reports. Some of the material was written in code. "But it's pretty easy to figure out," she confided. He gave her a doubtful look.

"Well, it is once you realize that the code is based on football statistics," she insisted. "You know. The jersey numbers of punt returners in the NFC during the 1980s; the AP College coaches' poll rankings in years ending in an even number; Norv Turner's blocking assignments for third and long situations. I mean, like, who doesn't know that kind of stuff?"

As Yale Templeton had taught her, she was carefully copying all the information she found onto index cards. On top of each card she would write down the author and name of the source, assiduously following the rules set out in Turabian. "I think it is advisable in your case to use an American reference work," he had said. "If later you decide to produce a monograph, in all likelihood the scholars who referee it will be from the United States." (Logically, then, you might think that he would rely on Turabian in preparing his own manuscripts. But his deeply ingrained prejudice in favour of the footnoting conventions he had learned at Cambridge meant that he invariably cast his lot with English opinion when there was a choice to be made, comforting himself with the suspicion that most American editors were lax when it came to checking footnotes.) When she needed some clarification or was examining the kind of document that, for one reason or another, was not explicitly discussed in Turabian, Bobbi Jo Jackson would lean over and ask his advice. Never having had occasion to use classified documents in his own research, he often had to make judgments based on inference. Not his strong suit, as we have seen, but he did the best he could.

Her initial intention had been to scan the material as quickly as possible looking for evidence about her mission to James Bay. But he stressed to her the importance of approaching sources in a systematic—which to his way of thinking meant strictly chronological—manner, and so she had begun with the earliest document she had found, a report on American intelligence activities in Lower Canada during the War of 1812, and slowly worked her way forward. Well slowly for her. With her speed reading ability and the knowledge of shorthand she had picked up in high school, she would have been quite capable of getting through all the considerable body of material she had retrieved in little more than twenty-four hours. However, Yale Templeton was firmly of the view that anyone with aspirations to scholarly respectability should write out all notes in full to avoid the risk of error when transcribing information. As a result, it was several days before she actually came across the first CIA document—a memo—that mentioned her assignment.

"This was the man they told me to contact," she said, passing Yale Templeton a photograph that had been attached to the memo.

"What odd attire!" he replied.

"Oh, that was after he put on my dress. A local ritual or something."

"Exchanging clothes," he commented. "That's an ancient Ojibwa custom. He must have been an Ojibwa."

"Oh, really?" she replied, surprised. "I just thought it was a Canadian thing. At the CIA they told us all Canadians were transvestites."

"No, not all." But now Yale Templeton was staring at the photograph. The figure looked very familiar. "Do you happen to know his name?" he asked.

She shuffled through some papers. "Here it is," she said. "Jean-Guy Lookalike."

Yale Templeton examined the photograph. Aside from the sequined dress and toque, the man could have been Joseph Brant Lookalike, or Charlie. Or Samuel Beartooth Lookalike, for that matter.

"They seem to have collected a lot of information about him," said Bobbi Jo Jackson, and she held up a handful of documents.

"Oh, yes?" he replied. But his eyes remained fixed on the picture.

"It appears you're right," she went on, glancing at one of the memos. "He was a Native Canadian, although it says Cree, not Ojibwa. Do the Cree exchange clothes, too?"

Yale Templeton thought he remembered hearing from a Native guide at Moosonee that the Cree and Ojibwa were related. "I suppose they could," he said, turning back to her. "It's not like the CIA would ever get its information wrong." And, no, he was not being facetious. Like many historians he had inordinate faith in the competence, not to mention fundamental honesty, of the bureaucrats who prepared the records he relied on in his research.

Bobbi Jo Jackson snorted. "Don't get me started. Someday I'll tell you about my last mission to Baghdad ... Anyway," and now she was talking more to herself than to Yale Templeton, "I guess this means I was right the first time."

"The first time?"

"About my mission. It really did have to do with the Cree, not hydroelectric plants ... Although," and here she was rapidly flipping through a secret report put together for the Department of the Interior, "it looks as if somebody had the idea of bribing Canadian officials into approving a 'Grand Canal'—that's the term they use, a Grand Canal—from the southeastern corner of James Bay down through Quebec and across Ontario all the way to Lake Huron. It says the water could then be diverted into the Midwest and the Southwestern states ..."

Yale Templeton politely waited for her to finish, but now she was completely absorbed in the report, and so he turned back to the (for him) far more interesting task of ensuring uniform punctuation in his citations. Not that he was unfamiliar with the often misquoted remark of Emerson: "A foolish consistency is the hobgoblin of little minds ... With consistency, a great soul has simply nothing to do. He may as well concern himself with the shadow on the wall." But that was just proof, he told himself, that Emerson understood very little about footnotes and punctuation.

During the next two weeks he was able to make great progress on his article, satisfactorily getting through more than half of the 228 footnotes he had projected. When, some years earlier, he had submitted an article entitled

"A Day-by-Day Recounting of Weather Patterns During the Siege of Vicksburg as Reported in the British Press" to the *American Historical Review* (where it was rejected as being "rather too narrow for our purposes"), one of the scholars who served as a referee observed that "perhaps the best thing that can be said about it is that the footnotes are neatly organized." He had taken this as the highest form of compliment and since then had made it a practice to keep extensive notes outlining the logic behind each of his citations. His goal, he told Bobbi Jo Jackson, was to donate these "footnotes on footnotes" (as he happily thought of them) to the archives at Cambridge upon his retirement. "They might well prove to be the very greatest contribution I make to the advancement of knowledge," he said. It would be hard to disagree.

But we must not dwell on Yale Templeton's footnotes any longer, no matter how fascinating they must inevitably seem to most readers. It is time to turn our attention back to Bobbi Jo Jackson. Or more specifically, to the discoveries she made in the files she smuggled out of Washington. Yes, she learned the reason for her mission to James Bay. But she also found evidence of a heretofore untold story of clandestine CIA activity—a story that, in the words of one distinguished scholar with whom she shared her findings, can only be described as "truly shocking."

XLV

**THE TRULY SHOCKING YET SHOCKINGLY TRUE
STORY OF HOW THE GOVERNMENT OF THE
UNITED STATES CONSPIRED TO BRING ABOUT
QUEBEC INDEPENDENCE, AS REVEALED IN
SECRET CIA DOCUMENTS AND AS TOLD BY ST.
CLAIR RUSSELL HILL, PROFESSOR EMERITUS**

*Let every nation know, whether it wishes us well or
ill, that we shall pay any price, bear any burden, meet
any hardship, support any friends, oppose any foe to
assure the survival and the success of liberty.*

John F. Kennedy, Inaugural Address, January 20, 1961

The first action by the Kennedy administration in its purported crusade
to spread liberty across the face of the globe was the Bay of Pigs invasion.
The second was a plot to ignite separatism in Quebec. Kennedy assigned
responsibility for the Quebec portfolio to Richard Helms, chief of covert

operations at the CIA. Helms began with a pilot project along the Ottawa River in the northwest corner of the province. The small village of Harmony (today known by the name "Je-me-souviens") was home to two men, identical twins, devoted to each other and to the vision of a united Canada they had inherited from their French-Canadian father and English-Canadian mother. Helms assumed that if he could turn brother against brother, that would promise well for creating internecine warfare across Quebec. Operating on the assumption that all Canadians are transvestites, he had his agents offer one of the brothers a bribe of dresses, blouses, jewellery, hose, and high heels to embrace the cause of separatism. That and five million dollars were enough to accomplish their purpose, and soon the village was riven into two factions, one committed to independence for Harmony, the other to Canadian nationalism.

The successful outcome of the pilot project convinced Helms that conditions in the province were propitious for fulfilling the mandate given him by the President. He assigned agents to infiltrate various fringe groups dedicated to independence for Quebec, some on the right, some on the left. Most notable was the Front de libération de Québec, or FLQ, which became involved in a series of terrorist acts, including bank robberies and bombings and, in 1970, the kidnapping of a British trade representative and the murder of a provincial cabinet minister. In the end, however, Helms decided that the most expedient course would be to secure a collaborator within the government. He targeted René Lévesque, a journalist and television personality who had served as a liaison officer for the U.S. Army during World War II. Whether Lévesque was actively taking orders from the CIA when he won election as a Liberal member of the Quebec legislature in 1960 is at this moment uncertain. However, internal Agency documents confirm that Washington was delighted when he received an appointment as minister of hydroelectric resources and public works and then used his position to nationalize Quebec's private electrical companies and merge them with the Crown Corporation Hydro-Quebec. "This will significantly aid our efforts to establish control over Canadian energy policy," Secretary of State Dean Rusk wrote approvingly to John McCone, Director of the CIA.

In 1967, Lévesque abandoned the Liberals to establish the Mouvement souveraineté-association, uniting it with the Ralliement national the following year to form the Parti Quebecois. CIA payroll records indicate that by this time he was receiving weekly shipments of cigarettes from Washington. Skilled at exploiting the media, Lévesque was able to gain support from labour and from the middle class, especially civil servants, teachers, and professionals. As a consequence the PQ rose rapidly in popularity, finally capturing power in 1976.

Just four years later Lévesque took what he conceived to be the first step toward Quebec independence by calling a provincial referendum in which he sought authority to negotiate sovereignty-association with Ottawa. The initiative went down to defeat, however, winning the support of only 40 percent of the voters. CIA director Admiral Stansfield Turner saw the result as "an important first step." "I firmly believe," he wrote in his journal, "that we can achieve our objective of an independent Quebec within fifteen years." Lévesque, however, was deeply disappointed. Even worse from the point of view of the Reagan administration, he stopped agitating for separatism and began to concentrate on providing socially progressive government. The White House abandoned him, and when, after he left office in 1985, agents adjudged his personal popularity to be dangerous to American interests, CIA director William Casey arranged for him to suffer a fatal heart attack.

By then, however, Washington had adopted a new strategy for promoting Quebec separatism. Vice President George Bush, a former Director of the CIA himself, was certain that the Canadian prime minister, Brian Mulroney, could be effectively manipulated to do whatever the White House wanted. As a young man Mulroney had been infatuated with American wealth and power, and by the 1960s his name was appearing on a secret CIA list of "useful Canadian contacts." In 1977 he secured an appointment as president of the Iron Ore Company of Canada, a subsidiary of the Cleveland-based Hanna Mining Company. He demonstrated abject submissiveness to his American bosses by shutting down a profitable mine in Schefferville, Quebec, allowing Hanna to transfer its operations to Brazil. Bush took note and advised Casey to "keep a close eye on Mulroney. He could be very valuable to us down the road."

In fact, only a year later, the Republican Party helped Mulroney win the leadership of the federal Progressive Conservative Party by secretly channelling funds to him through the Mormon bishop of Virginia. Soon afterward he led the Conservatives to power with the largest majority in Canadian history. He quickly set about putting in place the program Washington had outlined for him, lifting restrictions on foreign ownership of Canadian mines, pushing through free trade with the United States, and eventually putting his signature to the NAFTA agreement. Independence for Quebec remained at the forefront of the White House agenda, however, and with that in mind, Mulroney agreed to bring his old friend Lucien Bouchard into the government, first as ambassador to France and then, in 1988, as secretary of state. Bouchard, who had actively campaigned for separatism during the 1980 referendum, placed a team of his own men in the RCMP, where they quickly took control of the Canadian drug trade. He also added 5 percent to all public contracts. The goal in both cases was to generate revenue that could be skimmed off for the Parti Quebecois. To all appearances the stage was now set for the final act of the drama Washington had been scripting since 1961.

In 1987 Mulroney had met with provincial premiers in Ottawa to hammer out a deal for amending the Constitution. The Meech Lake Accord, as it came to be known, included recognition of Quebec as a "distinct society" and the transfer of a range of federal responsibilities to the provinces. CIA intelligence indicated that such terms would never be acceptable to a majority of the Canadian people and, in fact, would help fuel the very separatism that the agreement was ostensibly designed to eliminate. However, agents had not anticipated that the premiers, driven by the promise of increased personal power, would be prepared to ratify the deal even in the face of popular indifference and, in some provinces, hostility.

Here serendipity came to the aid of Washington, however. Elijah Harper Lookalike, a Cree member of the Manitoba legislature, used parliamentary procedures to delay ratification of the accord on the grounds that it did nothing to address the historic pattern of injustice faced by First Nations peoples and would perpetuate the myth that Canada had only two founding nations, the French and English. Anxious to avoid charges that his government was insensitive to Native concerns, the premier of Manitoba responded in the traditional way, offering to build a casino on tribal lands. By then, however, opposition to the accord had spread across the country, effectively ensuring its defeat.

Bouchard was now free to carry on with the original plan the CIA had drafted. He made a public display of resigning from the government, then set up his own federal party, the Bloc Québécois, with the single declared purpose of preparing the way for Quebec independence. His calculated and conspicuous defiance of Ottawa had the desired effect of inflaming passions in his home province, and in the federal election of 1993 the Bloc won fifty-four seats, emerging as the Official Opposition. By now Mulroney had abandoned politics to take advantage of business opportunities in the United States. The Liberals were in power, led by Jean Chrétien, a perfect foil for the separatists because he was widely distrusted in French Canada for his perceived role in the patriation of the Canadian Constitution. In 1994 Jacques Parizeau and the PQ won a decisive majority in a provincial election and immediately called a second referendum on Quebec sovereignty. To help build sympathy for the separatist cause, CIA agents infected Bouchard with necrotizing fasciitis, better known as the "flesh-eating disease." When doctors amputated his leg, ostensibly to save his life, his stature as an iconic figure soared.

The referendum was held in October 1995. Parizeau proved a less than inspirational leader, and Bouchard took command of the campaign. His charisma had a catalytic effect, and separatist support pitched upward. However, at a critical moment, he made a costly error. In an unrehearsed comment intended to win favour in the United States, he referred to the Québécois as a "race blanche," a white race. The remark caused a backlash among immigrants, especially from Haiti and Africa. Although the CIA was able to rig the ballot count in most ridings through the promiscuous dispersion of bribes, in the end the separatists fell 53,000 votes short of victory.

Following the referendum, Parizeau resigned in disgrace and Bouchard left Ottawa to become leader of the PQ. However, the people of Quebec had grown weary of the sovereignty debate and Bouchard spent the next few years trying to overturn the social-democratic framework that Lévesque had worked so hard to put in place. The success of his efforts represented a consolation prize of sorts for Washington, but it was far from what the White House had anticipated or desired.

George Tenet, who became Director of the CIA under Bill Clinton and continued in that office under George W. Bush, eventually came up with a new plan designed to rescue the separatist cause. An agent in Quebec had reported that the Cree in the northern reaches of the province were angry about the rumoured construction of a canal to divert water from James Bay to the Great Lakes and then on to the United States. Tenet reasoned that if the Cree could be induced to rise against the Quebec government, provincial authorities would be compelled to send in police to restore order. Jean Chrétien would presumably respond by calling up the army under pretext of protecting the indigenous population. Fighting would then ensue, reigniting calls for Quebec independence.

In attempting to implement the plan, however, the CIA was a victim of its own careless intelligence. Agents misidentified an Ojibwa poet and restaurant critic as a local tribal leader. Attempts to blackmail him with compromising photographs proved unsuccessful, although the young female agent entrusted with the task was able to acquire, at only slightly above cost, a guide to fine dining on the coast of James Bay and a collection of limericks about moose ...

*[Ed. note: At this point the account by Professor Hill wanders off into a discussion of nefarious activities by squirrels. As his remarks on that subject are not based on any of the evidence made available to him by Bobbi Jo Jackson, the editors have chosen to omit them from the text.]

XLVI

"That truly is a shocking story," said Yale Templeton.

"Yes," agreed Bobbi Jo Jackson, "truly shocking."

"But one thing I don't understand," he admitted. "Why should the White House want Quebec to gain its independence?"

"To weaken Canada, silly. It's all part of the plan."

"Plan? What plan?"

"The plan Professor Hill told me about. Ever since ... well, ever since the American Revolution, really ... Presidents have been plotting to grab all the land in North America right up to the Arctic Ocean. Mexico too."

"Ah, St. Clair must have been referring to the concept of Manifest Destiny."

"Yes, Manifest Destiny. That's right."

"Manifest Destiny," repeated Yale Templeton. "The term was first employed by the New York editor John L. O'Sullivan in an article on the proposed annexation of Texas published in Volume 17, Issue 86 of the *United States Magazine and Democratic Review*, July, 1845." (Here readers may feel free to let their eyes glaze over just as the eyes of Yale Templeton's students glazed over whenever he read a quotation.)

"'Why, were other reasoning wanting, in favour of now elevating this question of the reception of Texas into the Union, out of the lower region of our past party dissensions, up to its proper level of a high and broad nationality, it surely is to be found, found abundantly, in the manner in which other nations have undertaken to intrude themselves into it, between us and the proper parties to the case, in a spirit of hostile interference against us, for the avowed object of thwarting our policy and hampering our power, limiting our greatness and checking the fulfilment of our manifest destiny to overspread the continent allotted by Providence for the free development of our yearly multiplying millions.' End of quotation."

"Later," Yale Templeton continued, "O'Sullivan broadened the meaning of the term in an editorial printed in the *New York Morning News* on December 27, 1845. He was, by the way, editor of both the *Morning News* and the *United States Magazine and Democratic Review*. In the editorial he claimed, and again I quote, 'the right of our manifest destiny to overspread and to possess the whole of the continent which Providence has given us for the development of the great experiment of liberty and federative self government entrusted to us. It is a right such as that of the tree to the space of air and earth suitable for the full expansion of its principle and destiny of growth—such as that of the stream to the channel required for the still accumulating volume of its flow.' End of quotation.

"However, most scholars argue that the idea of Manifest Destiny was already implicit in an essay he wrote in 1839 for Volume 6, Issue 23 of the *United States Magazine and Democratic Review*. I quote, again:

"'We must onward to the fulfilment of our mission—to the entire development of the principle of our organization—freedom of conscience, freedom of person, freedom of trade and business pursuits, universality of freedom and equality. This is our high destiny, and in nature's eternal, inevitable decree of cause and effect we must accomplish it. All this will be our future history, to establish on earth the moral dignity and salvation of man—the immutable truth and beneficence of God.' End of quotation."

"Uh-huh," said Bobbi Jo Jackson. St. Clair Russell Hill had shown her the very same passages by John L. O'Sullivan, and she knew them by heart. It was the one characteristic she and Yale Templeton had in common: a photographic memory.

"Only the thing is," she said, and now she was pouting, "it just doesn't seem right to me, the presidents plotting to take over Canada. I mean, Canadians are pretty much free already, aren't they? So what if most of them are transvestites? Abraham Lincoln was a transvestite, and he wrote the Emancipation Proclamation. *And*," and she shook her finger to give the point emphasis, "he decided to move *here*."

"Yes," said Yale Templeton, nodding his head. "He most certainly did."

"So that's why I've decided to write about it."

"Write about what?"

"About the American plot to take over Canada. It was Professor Hill's idea. I just have to get my hands on some more secret documents. He even told me where to look for them."

She went on to describe her plans for circumventing the security forces in Washington, but Yale Templeton was no longer paying attention. He was thinking about footnotes again. Not his own this time, but the ones Bobbi Jo Jackson would have to prepare. She would most certainly need his help. "Scholarly presses are especially demanding when evaluating manuscripts written by authors from outside the academic community," he reminded himself. And he looked around for his copy of Turabian.

—— XLVII ——

In his Maine Woods, Thoreau relates the circumstances of a visit which he paid in 1853 to Neptune, then, at 89 years of age, the head of the Penobscot tribe. The old Indian gave an account of the origin of the moose, as follows: "Moose was whale once ... Sea went out and left him, and he came up on land a moose."

SAMUEL MERRILL, *THE MOOSE BOOK*

When Governor Neptune Lookalike (to use his full name) made the comment "Moose was whale once" he was, of course, speaking metaphorically. Alas, being American and therefore rather credulous, Thoreau accepted what the Penobscot chief said at face value and undertook a series of anatomical investigations intended to verify the ancestral links between whales and moose. It is most fortunate for his reputation that, immediately upon his death, his heirs disposed of the unfinished manuscript he produced on the subject, *Fluke and Antler*, before its existence could become widely known. In Thoreau's defence, while his interpretation of moose fossils may have been deficient, at least he understood, as Herman Melville apparently did not, that the whale is a mammal. "Be it known," wrote Melville in *Moby Dick*, "that waiving all argument, I take the good old fashioned ground that the whale is a fish, and call upon holy Jonah to back me." But then Melville, like Governor Neptune Lookalike, was more concerned with the whale as metaphor than biological reality. Or so the literary critics inform us. Myself, I have more than a few doubts. And even if the literary critics are correct, I think a reasonable case can be made that Melville should have checked his facts a little more closely before putting pen to paper. Personally, I would not expect a reader to take my own metaphoric excursion seriously if I had begun by claiming that moose were a species of fish.

And so we arrive by a somewhat circuitous route back at that creature of legend and lore, the Great White Moose. He has finally started to recover from the painful wounds he suffered while straddling the plastic white pine sapling along the shores of Lake Lokash. A period of convalescence in a corner of the old growth forest not yet ravaged by the logger's axe has left him refreshed, his spirits lifted. He is ready to begin his perambulations once more.

First, however, I wish to introduce a new theme for your consideration: Manifest Destiny. Yes, I know. I discussed Manifest Destiny in the last chapter. Indeed, I—or rather Yale Templeton—subjected you to a series of (admittedly) tedious (and certainly in one case virtually impenetrable) excerpts from the writings of the New York editor who coined the phrase. But in the last chapter I was speaking about Manifest Destiny as a concept developed by American politicians to describe and justify their continental aspirations. Here I am referring to the Manifest Destiny of the Great White Moose. Not a subject that John L. O'Sullivan cared to comment on. Nor anyone else, so far as I can determine. In other words, in revealing to you the Manifest Destiny of the Great White Moose, I am breaking new ground in the same way Yale Templeton was breaking new ground when he published his seminal article on boot sizes among Union cavalrymen. The feeling is intoxicating, let me tell you.

Whether the Great White Moose himself fully understood his Manifest Destiny is an interesting but ultimately unanswerable question. Did the Great

White Fish understand the Imperative Force that drove him on to his final confrontation with Captain Ahab? ...

But wait. Now that I think about it, how likely is it that you would have read *Moby Dick* right through to the end if Melville had chosen to divulge the elements of his dramatic climax at some midpoint in the novel? Be honest now. Remember all those passages on cetology. (And who knows? I may yet feel prompted to regale you with more recitations by Yale Templeton.) No, prudence clearly dictates that I allow the Manifest Destiny of the Great White Moose to become evident allusively, through the gradual unfolding of events over the remaining chapters. For the time being you will have to content yourself with the following information: After recovering from his wounds, the Great White Moose did indeed start on his travels again. But his course was no longer erratic, driven by troubling, if dim, memories. His stride was now purposeful, and in his mind's eye he had a clear picture of his destination. He was on his way to that vast tract of land known as the Chapleau Crown Game Preserve. You may remember it better as the home of Slinger the Trapper.

Joel was in love again.

───── XLVIII ─────

J oel was in love again. With Maureen, the new assistant in the Office of the Registrar. He fell in love with her when she told him about the Committee on Standing.

His final course at the university—or what he had expected would be his final course—had not turned out at all as he had intended. The graduate student who had replaced Yale Templeton in History 393, Todd or Tom something, had set a very difficult and unfair examination, filled with multiple choice questions that only someone who had taken notes in lectures and actually done the assigned reading could have answered. In keeping with departmental policy, Todd or Tom had posted final grades on the Internet, with students listed by their identification numbers to ensure privacy. Not that Joel had difficulty interpreting the results. The two students who sat side by side at the front of the lecture hall—he had never bothered to learn their names—had each received an A+, and Moira (or was it Monica?)—had ended up with a C-. But even Vince Gionfriddo had apparently passed the course, scraping by with a D. "Obviously the athletic director made some deal for him," Joel told himself.

But now he faced a truly unsettling prospect. His parents would not be at all happy when they saw another F on his transcript, and he had little reason to hope they would be willing to subsidize the next stage of his search for meaning in life. At twenty-five he had already managed to extend his time at the university three years beyond what they had anticipated and increase their financial burden by thirty thousand dollars beyond the savings they had put aside for his education. He had felt confident when he assured them that he would pass the course. After all, Professor Templeton had never failed a student in over twenty years of teaching. (Possibly because he always gave the same examination with the same single essay question: "Provide a representative sample of facts, statistics, editorial opinions, and related material regarding the American Civil War as published in the British press between April 9, 1861, and April 12, 1865. Use footnotes where appropriate.") Surely the university had some policy to protect students who were innocent victims of developments beyond their control.

And so he went off to see the registrar. Joel recounted the unfortunate turn his academic career had taken: how he had signed up for a course on the American Civil War believing that it would be taught by "a well-known authority" on the subject. "A great passion of mine, the Civil War," he assured the registrar. But then, for reasons he had never entirely understood, Professor Templeton had been replaced by a mere graduate student—"a graduate student without any appreciation of the great drama and significance of the war, or of its deep complexity." It was perfectly understandable, Joel said, that he had performed poorly on the examination. He had prepared for an essay question that would challenge him intellectually, present him with the opportunity to discuss some issue of momentous historical significance. Instead he faced the mundane task of answering multiple choice questions that merely tested his ability "to dredge up trivia."

The registrar, a large, affable bear of a man, sighed. He had been listening to students explain away their failings for over twenty-five years. The excuse Joel offered ranked rather low on the scale of originality, he thought. But it was his responsibility to give helpful advice to undergraduates, and so he informed Joel about the petition process. If Joel had indeed received a grade that he believed was unfair, he could submit a petition to the Dean Responsible for All Matters Unrelated to Generating Revenue. In the event his petition was successful, he would have the option of writing a make-up examination or dropping History 393 without penalty (meaning, the registrar said, he could sign up for a new course in the coming term). However, the dean would approve a petition, the registrar also told him, only if he found the arguments and supporting evidence compelling. The fact that Professor Templeton had been suspended would not, in and of itself, be sufficient. And he picked up the copy of the *Student Handbook* on his desk and directed Joel's attention to the following provision: "In the event that an instructor finds it necessary, for whatever reason, to retire from a course before its scheduled completion, the chair of the department concerned will be responsible for securing the services of a qualified replacement."

"But Todd or Tom was not really a qualified replacement," Joel protested, though rather weakly.

"Apparently he was in the eyes of the chairman of the History department. In any case, the appropriate time to raise an objection would have been when the new instructor took over the course, not after you received your final grade." And here the registrar pointed to a paragraph in the handbook that made that very point.

"But I never looked at the handbook," Joel protested again.

The registrar rolled his eyes. He never failed to be amazed at how much value students placed in ignorance.

But Joel had few options. So he sent off a petition to the dean. He had gathered from his conversation with the registrar that there would be little point in alluding to the conspicuous shortcomings of Todd or Tom. Instead he settled for this simple statement: "The final grade that I received does not reflect my true abilities." Which, as it happens, was not only inaccurate but repeated the explanation most frequently offered by undergraduates wishing to have failing grades removed from their transcripts. "Funny," the dean once commented to the registrar, "how no student ever seems to question whether an A reflects his true abilities."

When Joel received the letter from the dean indicating that his petition had been rejected, he went to see the registrar again to find out whether he had any further recourse. The registrar was out of his office, however, since every Wednesday afternoon during the summer he relived his misspent youth by playing hockey with some faculty and graduate students from the History department. (One Wednesday Yale Templeton had appeared at the rink in response to bullying by the wife of the department chairman at the end-of-term reception. However, all he knew about hockey had come from physical education classes at the Robinson-Fallis Academy for Boys, and so he showed up in shorts and running shoes. He watched with fascination as his colleagues careened recklessly around the ice, periodically spinning out of control and colliding with each other, or falling head first into the boards or goalposts. He never returned.)

It was because the registrar was off at his weekly hockey game that Maureen was given the task of dealing with Joel. She had taken on the position of assistant to the registrar's administrative assistant only three days earlier, having just completed her bachelor of arts in English literature. She was a sensitive person. "Hypersensitive" as the professor in her Tudor Poetry and Prose course had warned the teaching assistant assigned to grade her essay examining images of love in *The Faerie Queene*. And when she learned from Joel about the unforeseen set of circumstances that had led to his failing grade in History 393, her heart went out to him. "Oh, but you must submit a petition!" she exclaimed.

He had already done that, he replied. And then he showed her the response he had received from the dean.

"That is *so* unfair!" she said. And then she proceeded to tell him about the Committee on Standing. Which is when he fell in love with her.

The Committee on Standing was responsible for hearing appeals from students whose petitions had been turned down by the dean. It was made up of a representative from the dean's office, the registrar, and five members of the faculty. "You know," Maureen told Joel, "sometimes the dean does make a mistake. You just have to find the right words in putting together your case."

"But I explained that the grade did not reflect my true abilities," Joel told her.

Maureen nodded sympathetically. It was a perfectly legitimate excuse, she believed. Indeed, it was the very same excuse she had unsuccessfully used only weeks earlier in an attempt to get the teaching assistant in her Tudor

Poetry and Prose course to raise the grade on her paper about images of love in *The Faerie Queene*.

"I think you should appeal to the Committee on Standing," she said. "But write more than one sentence this time. Spell out in detail exactly why the grade you received does not reflect your true abilities. Maybe you can talk about other courses you have taken."

"Well, I got a B- in Introduction to Semiotics," Joel pointed out. He did not mention that the class average was A. Vince Gionfriddo had received a B+. Nor did he mention that his transcript included mostly Ds and Fs, and that he had spent the better part of his life at the university on academic probation.

Maureen mused, "It really is ridiculous, you know. I mean, grades *should* reflect ability. In my Tudor Poetry and Prose course the TA gave me a C+ on a paper that was worth at least a B, so I went to the professor to complain. You know what he said? 'Were you sick when you wrote the paper? Did you have any family problems?' Like the low grade was *my* fault."

When the Committee on Standing held its meeting there were three items on the agenda, all written appeals by students whose petitions to have failing grades removed from their transcripts had been denied by the dean. Two of the students invoked the familiar "the grade does not reflect my true abilities" excuse. Their requests were rejected with barely any discussion. Joel, on the other hand, drew attention to mitigating circumstances that had "prevented him from performing at the level necessary for success in the course," circumstances that, "out of a sense of propriety," he had chosen not to mention in his petition to the dean. Said circumstances were as follows: Shortly before he took the final examination he had contracted lupus. The beloved family pet, a dachshund, had contracted lupus as well. When his mother was driving the dog to the veterinarian, her car had been sideswiped by an ambulance carrying his grandmother, who had just suffered a stroke. Both his mother, who was pregnant, and his grandmother, who was also pregnant, had been killed in the accident. Unhinged, his father had joined the French Foreign Legion and disappeared into the heart of darkest Africa. Meanwhile the beloved dachshund, who was also pregnant, had survived the accident, but run off, never to be seen again. "Oh, and I should mention one other thing. The grade I received does not reflect my true abilities."

Since the meeting of the Committee on Standing fell on a Wednesday afternoon, the registrar was unable to attend. Maureen was there, however, having volunteered to serve as his representative. She was very surprised to hear about Joel's serious illness, the tragic deaths of his mother and grandmother, and the disappearance of his father and beloved dachshund, none of which he had mentioned during their interview. But when the mathematician on the committee suggested that his letter strained credulity, Maureen spoke at great length and with great feeling about what a diligent and serious student she had found Joel to be and how impressed she had been with his truthfulness. And so, with only the mathematician dissenting, the committee voted to overturn the ruling of the dean and erase the failing grade for History 393 from Joel's record.

Joel was, of course, delighted when he received the news. His parents would be delighted as well, he managed to convince himself. And if not, at least they would probably be willing to provide him with financial support for another term so he could finally complete the one course he needed to graduate. But which course? There were so many offered at the university, covering such a wide range of subjects, and Joel was equally disinterested in each and every one of them. "It really is too bad," he reflected, "that I've already had the introduction to semiotics, whatever semiotics is."

But then one afternoon, while he was sitting on the steps of Graves Hall looking absently out across Regency Circle, Heather came running up to him. He had not seen her since the day of the protest and did not recognize her with her clothes on. "Isn't it wonderful!" she exclaimed. "We won!"

"We who? Won what?" Joel wondered.

"President Butterworth has lifted the suspension on Yale Templeton. He'll be able to return to teaching next term."

And suddenly Joel knew exactly what course he was going to take. And as he went off to register for History 393, his heart filled with love once more. For Heather. And for Professor Templeton as well.

—— XLIX ——

eather was right, of course, about Yale Templeton being allowed to
return to teaching in the fall. But she was wrong about the reason. When
Felicia Butterworth decided to lift his suspension, it was not because
of the protest in May or threats by campus activists to begin a new round of
demonstrations once classes resumed. As you have already learned, she was
responding to orders from the White House (through a self-described Mob
boss in Chicago) to get whatever evidence Yale Templeton had found that
proved Abraham Lincoln faked his own assassination and moved to Canada
so he could fulfill his dream of living as a transvestite.

But no one outside of the Dean Responsible for Relations with the Mafia
and Felicia Butterworth herself knew the true story. And once rumours
began to circulate that she had decided to lift the suspension, observers
inevitably reached the conclusion that she had caved in to pressure. Recall
what Heather said to Joel: "We won!"

Now, to understate the obvious, Felicia Butterworth was a proud woman.
The thought that anyone might suppose she was the slightest bit influenced
by the opinions of faculty members or students was infuriating to her. It
was essential from her perspective that the formal announcement lifting
the Templeton suspension be accompanied by a face-saving public relations

campaign. And for that reason she called the Dean Responsible for Relations with the Mafia and the Vice-President for Manipulating the Media to a meeting in her office.

The Vice-President for Manipulating the Media was an efficient, middle-aged woman who had joined the university administration after serving for a decade in the Central Communications Office of the Ontario government. She had all the qualities that Felicia Butterworth looked for in a female executive: She was unmarried, childless, easily intimidated, and entirely lacking in principles. She appeared at the meeting in practical pumps and glasses and wore a trim grey Armani Exchange suit. Although she had not been told, nor did she consider it her place to ask, why Felicia Butterworth had decided to lift the suspension, she understood what was expected of her. "There's no denying it," she said. "The optics here could be more than a little unfavourable. It's important that people believe you were acting from a position of strength."

"Which I always do," bristled Felicia Butterworth.

"Exactly," continued the Dean Responsible for Relations with the Mafia, addressing the Vice-President for Manipulating the Media. "We simply want to make sure that our corporate sponsors understand that."

"Well then here's a thought," suggested the Vice-President for Manipulating the Media. "In politics it's pretty standard practice to disguise partisan proposals by claiming that they have the most benevolent of intentions."

"Like when the government says cutting taxes for the rich benefits the poor," quipped the Dean Responsible for Relations with the Mafia.

"Exactly the example I was going to use," lied the Vice-President for Manipulating the Media. "In this case we would concoct some reason why suspending Professor Templeton was in his own best interests. Say, to make him see how crazy it was to go around telling people that Lincoln was a transvestite. We release a statement to the press that basically says 'He's mended his ways; he can return to teaching.'"

"Except that it would be preferable not to revisit the Lincoln issue at this point," replied Felicia Butterworth irritably.

The Vice-President for Manipulating the Media shifted uncomfortably in her chair. "Well, of course we could always come up with some other explanation for the suspension. The bottom line is, you say it served its purpose."

Felicia Butterworth put her fingers to her mouth in thought. "I don't think so," she said at last. "As soon as we acknowledge that the suspension was for disciplinary reasons, it becomes impossible to explain why I have decided to name Templeton the first Abraham Lincoln Distinguished Professor of the American Civil War."

"What!" exclaimed the Vice-President for Manipulating the Media. "You're appointing him to a chair!"

"Yes," replied Felicia Butterworth curtly. "Why? Do you have some objection?"

"No, no. Of course not," replied the Vice-President for Manipulating the Media, dropping her eyes. To borrow time she helped herself to a Tostitos tortilla chip from a bowl on the table. "Of course not," she repeated, though this time under her breath. And then she said out loud, "I suppose we could, uh, argue that the suspension was technically not really a suspension?"

"'Not really a suspension?'" said Felicia Butterworth.

"Ah, the Clinton defence," broke in the Dean Responsible for Relations with the Mafia. He was smiling when he said it.

"Oh. The Clinton defence," repeated Felicia Butterworth, who, to the relief of the Vice-President for Manipulating the Media, was smiling as well. "No. That won't do here. The suspension was consummated."

The Vice-President for Manipulating the Media dutifully forced up a laugh, and then helped herself to another Tostitos chip.

"Any other thought?" asked Felicia Butterworth. "Perhaps something a little more helpful this time." Her smile had disappeared.

"Well," coughed the Vice-President for Manipulating the Media. She was starting to regret her decision to take the Tostitos. "In the government we always assumed that as a last resort we could fall back on the respect Canadians traditionally show to authority."

"The wilful national commitment to naiveté, you mean," countered Felicia Butterworth. "Go on."

"Well perhaps you could say ..." (and here the Vice-President for

Manipulating the Media looked around for water but found none) "... you could say it was all a subterfuge. You could say ..." (and here she momentarily had to catch her breath to keep from choking) "... you could say Templeton was off on a secret mi—" (and now she *was* choking).

"A secret what?" demanded Felicia Butterworth.

"Mission?" guessed the Dean Responsible for Relations with the Mafia.

The Vice-President for Manipulating the Media, who was sinking to her knees and clutching her throat, pointed at the dean and nodded.

"What sort of mission?" asked the Dean Responsible for Relations with the Mafia.

"That's the beauty ... of it," gasped the Vice-President for Manipulating the Media, on her knees on the floor. "It's secret, confidential ... too sensitive ... for anyone except ... President ... Butterworth ... to ... know."

The Dean Responsible for Relations with the Mafia turned back to Felicia Butterworth. "I can see where that might work in government. But at a university?"

Felicia Butterworth was intrigued, however. "Certainly it would make it easier to explain why Templeton was being honoured with a chair. You know, services to the university. That sort of garbage. Still," she spoke out loud to herself, "it could be a tough sell, the idea that the suspension was a charade all along. That I sent Templeton off where? Someplace up north, I suppose. On some special assignment?"

"Some ... special ... assign ... ment ... of ... the ... ut ... most ... sensitiv—" choked out the Vice-President for Manipulating the Media before losing consciousness.

"The utmost sensitivity," mused Felicia Butterworth. The phrase appealed to her. "A secret assignment of the utmost sensitivity and vitally important for the future of the university ... No, for the future of the country."

The Dean Responsible for Relations with the Mafia was skeptical. "I don't know. Will anyone buy it? At the very least we'll have to get some of the faculty on side."

"Yes. The faculty," murmured Felicia Butterworth. Her mind was working rapidly now.

The Dean Responsible for Relations with the Mafia shook his head. "The idea of Yale Templeton being sent off on some secret mission of vital importance. Who would believe a story like that? I mean, who in his right mind?"

"Yes," murmured Felicia Butterworth. "Who, indeed?" And at that she pushed the button on the intercom in front of her and called to her secretary. "Dolores, make an appointment for me with H. Avery Duck."

L

H. Avery Duck considered wearing his bicycle helmet for his meeting with Felicia Butterworth. He did have on a variety of protective under-gear that his wife had purchased for him at Just Hockey, in the city's east end.

He was entirely in the dark as to why Felicia Butterworth had asked to see him. Her secretary had provided no explanation, and he himself had only partially completed the report he was preparing in support of free speech on campus (with special reference to free speech for the president of the Faculty Union). He had invented a new language, in the Bulgarian Cyrillic alphabet, sufficiently ponderous to convey the magnitude of the principles involved, and since he had no time to translate the 637 pages he had completed into English, he had assumed that there was little point in taking along a draft to show her. Considering what she had done to the report he had brought to their last meeting, during the demonstration in May, it was a prudent decision.

As he climbed the steps of Graves Hall, memories of that previous meeting crowded in on him. Every frail muscle in his body tightened, causing the oversized hip pads he was wearing to ride up uncomfortably. A further reminder, he reflected ruefully, of the pain, physical as well as psychological, that she had inflicted upon him on that earlier occasion.

Under the circumstances—given their past history—he found the greeting she now gave him quite disorienting. She took his hand warmly and commented, with what sounded like genuine disappointment, how sorry she was that their paths had not crossed over the summer. She was looking forward, she said, to working with him in the months ahead on the many challenges facing the university. "As always, your advice will be indispensable."

It was only then that he noticed the figure standing in the corner of the room. Although he had never actually met the Dean Responsible for Relations with the Mafia, he recognized him immediately by his dark pinstripe suit and brass knuckles. H. Avery Duck knew little of the gossip that circulated endlessly around the campus (which was odd considering that he was head of the Faculty Union). However, even he had heard of the privileged relationship that the Dean Responsible for Relations with the Mafia enjoyed with Felicia Butterworth, how she respected and at times deferred to his judgment. So it only added to his confusion when the dean came over and clapped him exuberantly on the shoulder pads. Then Felicia Butterworth took him by the arm and led him to the soft cushioned chair she normally reserved for the university's corporate sponsors.

Perhaps he would like a little snack before they began? she suggested. And as if on cue, the Dean Responsible for Relations with the Mafia went over to a cabinet and grabbed one bag of Rold Gold pretzels and another of Nacho Cheese Doritos. H. Avery Duck shrank inside his pads, remembering the unfortunate role Doritos had played in the climax to his meeting with Felicia Butterworth in May. But when he saw that the dean was smiling broadly, his anxiety began to ease. And after removing his mouth guard, he helped himself to a pretzel.

"Now to business," said Felicia Butterworth, pulling her chair directly opposite his. "It's time that I revealed to you the true reason I suspended Yale Templeton." And she proceeded to recount the following tale:

"Late one night in March, three Mounties appeared, unannounced, at my home. They informed me, under pledge of secrecy, that a band of terrorists had managed to slip across the border and establish a base at some unidentified location in the North. Terrorists in the service of a foreign nation with designs on Canada. But about that I can say no more. The Mounties had been given the task of recruiting a man on the faculty to infiltrate and destroy the terrorist cell. He was well known to the RCMP as someone trustworthy, resourceful, quick-witted, and courageous. He was, in addition, the leading authority on American military strategy and covert operations. The man they wanted, in other words, was Yale Templeton.

"And as it turned out, Yale Templeton was more than ready to volunteer his talents and expertise to his adopted country. But there was a problem. Time was of the essence. It was the middle of the school term. How was I to free him from his classroom obligations without arousing suspicion? I conferred with the Dean Responsible for Relations with the Mafia and we decided the best course was to suspend Templeton. True, it would mean violating provisions in the collective agreement. But no other option seemed available.

"That only led to another question, however: What reason could I offer for the suspension? The dean is connected with certain individuals who, in return for unspecified favours, would be willing to fabricate evidence that Professor Templeton had committed an offence against the ethical standards of the university." ("Say, something involving a saddle, a cattle prod, butterscotch pudding, and one of the defensive linemen on the football team," the dean elaborated.) "But, no. Templeton objected, concerned about the effect a scandal involving supposed lewd behaviour would have on his mother, who was famously puritanical. And in any case, he is known around campus as a man of incorruptible morals. It seemed improbable anyone would credit charges that he had engaged in an act of impropriety, sexual or otherwise.

"And so the dean proposed an alternative: have Templeton make some comment in class that would raise questions about his sanity. It was an ingenious suggestion."

"But give credit where credit is due," said the dean. "It was Professor Templeton who dreamed up the story about Lincoln and Canada."

"Quite so," replied Felicia Butterworth. "The man has an extraordinarily vivid imagination."

She continued with her tale: "Templeton set the plan in motion by telling his Civil War class that, contrary to what they had heard, Lincoln had not been assassinated. Instead he had faked his own death and disappeared into the backwoods of Ontario so that he could live as a transvestite." ("As you said," the dean interjected, "the man has an extraordinarily vivid imagination.") "His ludicrous remarks provided the excuse I needed to suspend him. Free now to get on with his assignment, he vanished into the northern wilderness. During the following weeks he faced countless dangers, and on more than one occasion only narrowly evaded death. In the end, however, his bravery, ingenuity, and sheer determination saw him through. Today the terrorists, or at least those who survived their encounter with him, are locked away. I very much hope that one day, when security concerns no longer dictate his silence, he will overcome his modesty and publish an account of his experiences." (To which the dean added, "Amen to that.")

"I feared that the glamour of undercover work might lure him away to CSIS, but his sole wish, he told me, was to return to the quiet of scholarly reflection. Although I realized that it was not yet safe to let the world know about his heroic efforts, I resolved to show my personal appreciation by naming him the first Abraham Lincoln Distinguished Professor of the American Civil War (to which the dean responded with a hearty applause).

"Of course, to suspend a professor in the middle of one term, then elevate him to a prestigious chair the next was bound to raise questions. But it is paramount that his clandestine activities remain a secret. Lives could well be at stake.

"So you see, Avery," Felicia Butterworth concluded, "for security reasons I have no choice but to keep this information from becoming public. Which is why I have called on you. You are, without a doubt, the most high-minded figure on campus. Your word, far more than mine, carries the weight of moral authority. What I hope you will agree to do—what I am begging you to do—is take on responsibility for representing me before the public, for explaining that the suspension of Yale Templeton was not an abridgment of his right to free speech but, in fact, a principled act whose higher purpose will become apparent in the fullness of time."

"Do what you do so well," said the dean. "Produce a lengthy monograph. Outline the underlying ethical issues in endless detail. Build your case methodically, brick by monotonous brick. Invent a new language worthy of the abstruse nature of your reasoning. Invent two or three if that will help."

"The point is," continued Felicia Butterworth, "you will become the public face of the administration. It will be your task to brief the press about the high principles involved. True, the reporters will quickly lose interest, as newspaper people invariably do when confronted by arguments addressed to an adult audience. However, you will be left with the satisfaction of knowing that you have made a contribution of profound importance to the university, and to your country."

H. Avery Duck had sat in silence throughout, his eyes wide open. He was dripping in sweat, partly out of anxiety, partly out of excitement, partly because it was summer and he was wrapped in a cocoon of hockey equipment. Now he spoke for the first time. "But I'm the president of the Faculty Union," he said. It was not meant as a protest. Rather his words expressed his sense of bewilderment.

"Yes, of course," Felicia Butterworth responded. "Our thinking was that you would take temporary leave from the union. I would give you a new position: Adviser to the President and CEO."

"Adviser to the President and CEO with Special Responsibility for Matters of Principle," amplified the dean, with Felicia Butterworth giving him a nod of approval.

H. Avery Duck was a tangle of emotions. Over the course of little more than an hour his feelings had gone from dread to confusion and now to joy. Imagine. Adviser to Felicia Butterworth with special responsibility for matters of principle. He ran over the title in his mind several times. It was obvious to him what he would do, what he must do. As president of the Faculty Union he had come to recognize and appreciate the value of secrecy. Indeed, it was the anarchic behaviour of faculty members at the meeting he had convened in April to discuss the Templeton suspension and of both faculty members and students at the subsequent demonstration in front of Graves Hall that had led to his incarceration in the Don Jail. Free speech, indeed!

Yes, he said. He would do what she asked. He would temporarily put aside his union responsibilities to aid her in this time of crisis. And then, lifted by feelings of joy, he recommended that they seal their agreement by adopting an old Ojibwa custom. In response to which, the Dean Responsible for Relations with the Mafia (to the enormous relief of Felicia Butterworth) rushed forward enthusiastically and embraced him. And so it was that H. Avery Duck went home in brass knuckles and a Banana Republic pinstripe suit, while the dean left in a rumpled tweed jacket over a set of sweat-soaked hockey pads.

LI

The corridors in the White House are dimly lit, with doorways hidden in shadows. That, at least, was the explanation given by the President as to how it was that a person or persons unknown had been able to overpower him. Why, when he was found by the Executive Assistant to the Assistant Undersecretary of Transportation, he was hanging naked from the chandelier in the East Room remains a mystery.

The Director of the CIA was away from Washington at the time, and the Assistant to the President for National Security Affairs was performing in *Peter Pan* at the Kennedy Center, so it was left to the Director of the FBI to organize an investigation. There was no need, however, the President assured him.

"I know what she was after," he confided.

"She?" said the Director of the FBI.

"Did I say 'she'? replied the President. "I meant some person or persons unknown. I know what she, he, or they were after."

"Mr. President?"

"The secret White House files on Canada."

"The secret files on Canada? Why would anyone want the secret files on Canada?"

"A very good question. I suspect it has to do with that professor in Toronto, the one who broke the Lincoln story."

"You mean Yale Templeton?"

"Yes. Yale Templeton. Somehow he's behind it all. Good thing I sent Raymond up there to deal with him."

"But I'm Raymond."

"You're Raymond?"

"Yes, Mr. President."

"Are you sure?"

"Pretty sure."

"Then who did I send to Toronto?"

"Clyde."

"Clyde! But he's a homicidal maniac!"

"Yes, Mr. President."

"Oh, well that's all right, then."

LII

The meeting Felicia Butterworth had with Yale Templeton was very different from her meeting with H. Avery Duck, being brief and to the point. Nor was the Dean Responsible for Relations with the Mafia present. She informed him—she informed Yale Templeton—that his suspension had now been lifted and he would be allowed to return to teaching in September. And she added, without offering congratulations (or even a Dorito), that she had decided to appoint him the first Abraham Lincoln Distinguished Professor of the American Civil War. In return he was to turn over the evidence he had uncovered indicating that Lincoln had faked his assassination and moved to Canada.

As so often in his life, Yale Templeton found himself at a loss. Titles had never meant much to him. That might seem odd, given that his mother had been obsessed with her imagined aristocratic lineage. But perhaps that was the explanation. Over the years she had traced her ancestry back to so many ancient titled houses—the de Mandevilles, the de Veres, the Lancasters, the Percys, to name just four—that it had all washed over him. Especially after his first day at the Robinson-Fallis Academy for Boys, when he announced proudly that he was descended, on his mother's side, from Thomas Radcliffe, third earl of Sussex, who had put down a rebellion during the reign of Elizabeth I, only to be soundly thrashed by six other students who promptly made the same claim. No, he had learned early on to discount the value of titles.

And as for the evidence Felicia Butterworth had demanded—well, here again he was baffled. He was sure he had told her about the legal briefs back in the spring. But suppressing a sigh, he started in once more, taking pains to spare no details. He began by reconstructing his trips north in pursuit of the Great White Moose. He then proceeded to describe his encounter with Slinger the Trapper, to recite what Slinger had told him about Lincoln Abrahams, to explain that Lincoln Abrahams was really Abraham Lincoln, to further explain how and why Abraham Lincoln had come to Canada, and to explain further still how he (Abraham Lincoln) had cryptically recorded the Canadian chapter of his life in the briefs he had written while serving as a lawyer in Northern Ontario. Yale Templeton also noted that he had made arrangements to go into the woods himself with Slinger to recover the briefs, but that, "for personal reasons," he had changed his mind and returned to Toronto.

"And so you see, I don't actually have the evidence," he concluded. "It's in a cave, somewhere in the Chapleau Crown Game Preserve."

Felicia Butterworth appeared to look right through him.

"Just make sure you have the document or documents on my desk by the end of the week," she ordered through clenched teeth, her face split by a tight smile. "Oh, and under no circumstances make any statements about any of this to the press." Then before he could say another word, she grabbed him by the collar of his jacket, yanked him out of his chair, hustled him across the floor of her office, and shoved him into the hall.

As the door slammed behind him, Yale Templeton took a deep breath and struggled to compose himself. It was all so mystifying. He had never really understood why Felicia Butterworth had suspended him in the first place, and he had no clue what had prompted her to reinstate him now. As for his appointment to a named chair ... well, how to make sense of that?

When he arrived back at his apartment, Bobbi Jo Jackson was exactly where he had left her two hours earlier, sitting in the middle of the living room floor going methodically through the boxes of papers she had only days before brought back from Washington. "What did President Butterworth want?" she asked without looking up.

"Apparently I am no longer under suspension. I can go back to teaching when the new term starts."

"Well, that's good news, eh?" (She was pleased with the progress she was making on her Canadian accent.)

"I suppose so," he replied. Actually he had been looking forward to having the fall to work on the footnotes for his article on snake bites, with perhaps a few weeks in the northern woods to search for the Great White Moose. "And I am to have a new title. Abraham Lincoln Distinguished Professor of the American Civil War."

"*Distinguished* Professor! Awesome!" she exclaimed, and looked up at him admiringly.

"I suppose so," he repeated. The truth was, he had been remembering the beating he received his first day at Robinson-Fallis and was worried about what his colleagues would do when they learned Felicia Butterworth had decided to honour him with a chair.

"There is a problem," he went on. "She said I have to turn over the evidence I found about Lincoln. About his faking his own death and moving to Canada."

"But it's in those legal briefs, isn't it? The ones up north someplace?"

He nodded. "I explained that. But to tell you the truth, I don't think she was listening."

"Well, that's weird, eh."

"Weird, indeed."

"So what are you going to do?"

"I have no idea," he said, shaking his head. "None whatsoever."

She started to think. Reasoning was so much easier for her now than when they had first met. Funny that falling in love with someone of a most pedantic mind had proved the key to unlocking her own intellectual faculties.

"We'll just manufacture the evidence ourselves," she said at last.

He looked at her without comprehending.

"It'll be easy. You'll tell me what to say. I'll copy it out in Lincoln's handwriting."

"But—"

"No, really. Piece of cake. I learned forgery and counterfeiting at the CIA.

Even won a citation for producing a memorandum in Saddam Hussein's handwriting. Something about uranium in Niger. And it's not like you would be making anything up," she added, as if anticipating his objections. "Every bit of information we include will be absolutely true, based on what that trapper guy—"

"Slinger."

"Yeah, Slinger. Based on what Slinger told you."

Yale Templeton considered his options. Like most historians, he regarded his life's work—researching and writing about the past—as a sacred trust. To conspire in the manufacture of forged evidence would be, professionally speaking, an act of high treason. Still, the prospect of confessing to Felicia Butterworth that he was unable to provide her with the evidence she wanted literally made him shiver. He stared silently at the floor.

"I have an old friend from the Agency who can get me ink and paper like the kind Lincoln would have used," Bobbi Jo Jackson continued. "You'll just have to find me a sample of his handwriting. That shouldn't be too hard, should it?"

Yale Templeton looked up at her. "No, not too hard." And he went to his bookshelf, where he removed a slender volume published by the Library of Congress called *Long Remembered: Facsimiles of the Five Versions of the Gettysburg Address in the Handwriting of Abraham Lincoln.*

"Cool!" exclaimed Bobbi Jo Jackson, flipping through the pages. "Like I said. Piece of cake. Now all you have to do is tell me what to write."

Men have been known to abandon all caution for the love of a woman (or another man). They have fought duels, scaled mountains, ventured into wrathful seas. Some scholars believe it was love that led Vincent Van Gogh to cut off his ear and present it to a prostitute named Rachel. (Others claim it was a psychological disorder stemming from his relationship with his mother.) Yale Templeton may or may not have shared certain life experiences with Van Gogh, but he was hardly a man inclined to melodramatic gestures. Still, it tells us a great deal about the depth of his feeling for Bobbi Jo Jackson that, in the end and despite profound misgivings, he agreed to do what she proposed. (Although let it be noted here that he eased his conscience by making the following promise to himself: One day he would track down Slinger the Trapper, retrieve Lincoln's briefs, deliver them to Felicia Butterworth, and recover and destroy the forged evidence.)

LIII

The writing material arrived within hours of Bobbi Jo Jackson contacting her source in Washington: pencils, pens, a penknife, several bottles of ink, two pads of the bluish gray, wide-lined foolscap Lincoln preferred for writing formal documents, a dozen long, yellow government envelopes, and stationery of diverse quality, including the finest linen rag, some sheets even bearing the letterhead of the Executive Mansion. There was also a pasteboard, since Lincoln was known to write on his knees while travelling.

And it was fun, Yale Templeton found, forging evidence. Not as much fun, perhaps, as that first night he spent with Bobbi Jo Jackson at the motel out by the airport, but fun all the same. He had decided the document should be a letter to John Hay written by Lincoln himself just days before he left the town of Chapleau for the community in the northern wilderness where he would spend the last years of his life. He recognized that Lincoln probably would have used stationery purchased in Ontario. "But not necessarily," Bobbi Jo Jackson observed. "Anyway how likely is it that your President Butterworth will be able to tell the difference between Canadian and American paper?"

"Not very," Yale Templeton replied. "Not unless we write on a bag of Frito-Lay potato chips." It was the first time in his life he had ever attempted a joke.

Now you might suppose that he would find it impossibly challenging to

effect the writing style of Abraham Lincoln. After all, Lincoln's prose was
famously lean, economical. Yale Templeton's publications (if not his letters to
his mother) droned on and on and laboriously on. But despite his personal lack
of expressiveness—or perhaps as a result of it—he had an untapped talent for
mimicry. And so he knew almost instinctively how to go about capturing the
voice of the former president. It meant relying, for the most part, on simple
and disjunctive sentences and choosing words that had very precise meanings.
It meant, in addition, using strong rows of monosyllables to create moments
of dramatic tension. Finally it meant exploiting a variety of literary devices
that Lincoln liked to draw on: anaphora, alliteration, oxymoron, inversion.
He even misspelled the occasional word, just as Lincoln was prone to do. In
choosing his text, he followed the advice Bobbi Jo Jackson had given him:
He simply paraphrased what Slinger the Trapper had told him. But, feeling a
bit mischievous and experiencing a momentary (and quite uncharacteristic)
spark of inventiveness, he added a few details of his own. For example, that
Lincoln had once seen a white moose. He ended with a sentence eighty-two
words long, "exactly the length of the concluding sentence in the Gettysburg
Address," he noted with a satisfied smile.

Once he had a final draft of the letter, he turned it over to Bobbi Jo Jackson.
She scanned it quickly to get a sense of the rhythm and tone, then went to
her packet of writing materials to select a bottle of ink, several sheets of high
quality stationery (though without the Executive Mansion letterhead), and
three pens (which she sharpened quickly but adeptly with the penknife). He
had assumed that she would want to write at his desk and so had cleared
off all his notes, but instead she plunked herself down in the middle of the
living room floor, the pasteboard balanced on her knees. She set to writing
energetically, employing the powerful strokes, strong t-bars, and flexible
and uphill baselines that were distinctive features of Lincoln's script. She
worked in haste but throughout remained attentive to detail. And so each
lower-case *c* ended in a small curl, while the bottom loop of every *y* swung
to the right rather than the left. She also followed Lincoln in making her
(by which I mean Lincoln's) signature slightly larger than the script in the
body of the letter itself.

A remarkable job, Yale Templeton acknowledged when she was finished. It looked exactly—and he did mean *exactly*—like something written in Lincoln's hand. And she had produced it in a matter of hours.

"Now for the final touch," she announced. And with that, she went to the kitchen, returning moments later with some candles, oil, and matches. "This should do the trick," she said with a confident nod. "I mean, along with my eyeshadow and mascara, of course." Then she disappeared into the bathroom, re-emerging twenty minutes later holding the letter between her thumb and forefinger. The paper was now damp. It looked frayed, stained, and yellowed. It looked at least one hundred years old.

"So what do you think?" she asked. He did not reply, just stared in mute admiration.

All that remained was to deliver the letter. However, Yale Templeton could not bear the thought of meeting Felicia Butterworth face to face. Not again. Especially when the document he would be handing her would be a forgery. "No problemo," said Bobbi Jo Jackson. And late that night, she led him on a circuitous journey through the darker corners of the campus to the back of Graves Hall. After first making sure that no one was watching, she pulled a small crowbar from her jeans and pried open a basement window. Then, with Yale Templeton nervously leading the way, they slid cautiously along the corridors and up several flights of stairs to Felicia Butterworth's office. A rapid and artful deployment of the set of CIA-issue keys Bobbi Jo Jackson always carried with her, and they were inside. Together they gently laid the envelope containing the forged letter—it had "for President Butterworth" and "CONFIDENTIAL!" printed neatly across the front— on top of the stack of papers on her desk. Then they helped themselves to one of the many bags of Tostitos and Doritos on the sideboard, before slipping away into the night.

It had been an exhilarating experience for Yale Templeton. So exhilarating that he found it impossible to get to sleep. That night, and the night following as well.

LIV

Many kilometres across the sea, Yale Templeton's mother had also experienced moments of exhilaration in recent days, a result of her many conversations with the man she knew as Henry Hudson.

At the time of their first meeting, he had promised to return at regular intervals to keep her informed of his progress in mounting an expedition. And he had been as good as his word. Initially Richard Hakluyt the younger had made an effort to accompany him, if only to make sure he said "nothing as might alarme Her Majestie." But increasingly, with the passage of time, he had come on his own.

So far his attempts to raise a crew had been unsuccessful. Strange to say, none of the men who responded to his advertisements in the London newspapers were familiar with the kind of equipment used on the *Half Moon*. He hoped a trip to the public houses down by the docks in Southampton would produce better results.

The rest of what he had to report was much more promising. "Thanks to your generous benefactions," he told Yale Templeton's mother, "I have begun to acquire the necessary materials for constructing the ship: sturdy oak for the keels, lightweight pine for the topside planking, hemp for the rigging, and flax for the sails. Like all Dutch vessels it will be built according to the principles of the tangent arc system."

His reference to the Dutch, a nation she regarded with great suspicion, made her uneasy. She had assumed the ship would be in every respect English.

"But the Dutch ships were—I mean are—considerably faster," he explained. "Much better suited for travel on the open seas." Therefore better suited for getting him expeditiously across the ocean to the intrepid Y, he assumed he did not need to add. "Indeed, the design I am using has a variety of noteworthy features. If you will permit me ..." And unpacking a series of blueprints and spreading them out before her, he entered into a rather long-winded monologue on the particulars of the boat:

It would be seventy feet long with a beam of sixteen-and-a-half feet and the hold to the depth of eight feet; it would have a flat bottom with a shallow keel; the decks would be level, which meant they could be flooded in time of emergency, reducing the risk of explosion and fire, and meant, in addition, that all the gun ports would be in line, "allowing easy interchange of arms during battles"; the foremast, the fore-topmast, the mainmast and topmast would all be outfitted with square sails, the mizzenmast with a lateen sail, "that wondrous invention of the Arabs"; the bowsprit would carry a spritsail; the average speed would approach three-and-a-half knots.

He only once, swept up in a reverie of mizzenmasts and gunports, forgot himself and let slip an observation that threatened to betray his identity as a computer systems analyst from the twenty-first century. It was while describing his plans for the mainmast. It would be set at right angles to the keel, he had observed, close to the midsection of the ship. "Computer analysis indicates that the midsection was the centre of buoyancy and centre of gravity on all ocean-going Dutch vessels of the late sixteenth century." However, since Her Majesty had fallen asleep in the middle of his presentation, the remark went unnoticed.

No, it was not Henry Hudson's plans for constructing a replica of the *Half Moon* that left Yale Templeton's mother exhilarated. And it was not—not above all, anyway—his cheerful readiness to serenade her with madrigals. It was, rather, his unparalleled knowledge of English history. He had discovered early on that she was much more interested in the glorious past of the nation over which she imagined she ruled than in descriptions of zeniths, gunwales, orlop decks, and rabbets. In particular she was fascinated by stories about the monarchs who had, as she put it, "preceded her."

He had first told her about Boudicca, queen of the Iceni. (Better known to many as Boadicea). A fearless ruler, Boudicca organized massive resistance to the tyrannical Roman authorities, "and not far from this very spot." Moving her army at lightning speed across the countryside, she destroyed one Roman settlement after another, finally arriving at the city of Colchester, where the Emperor Claudius had, just years before, made a triumphal entry on an elephant.

("An elephant! How extraordinary!" exclaimed Yale Templeton's mother.)

Colchester stood as the pre-eminent symbol of Roman domination, with its forbidding temple and grandiose monuments sheltered behind massive stone walls. Yet Boudicca was undaunted. And inspired by her courage, her warriors took courage of their own. They battered the head off the statue of the emperor and hurled it into the river. Then they put torches to the buildings and burned the city to the ground.

Yale Templeton's mother was transfixed. And each time Henry Hudson came for a visit, she would ask him to tell her about some other royal personage. And so he did:

Arthur: The greatest of all English kings, whose coming had been foretold by the Welsh wizard Merlin. Arthur, who expelled the Saxons and subdued the Picts and the Irish. Who created a vast northern empire stretching from Scandinavia to Gaul and westward as far as Iceland. Who attracted the bravest and most gallant of knights to his castle at Caerleon-at-Usk. And who, with the lovely Guinevere at his side, presided over a court where one thousand ermine-clad noblemen assembled for spectacular pageants and tournaments, and for sumptuous feasting.

Richard the Lionheart: Intense blue eyes and a mane of golden hair. Invested at his coronation with golden sword and golden spurs as he stood beneath a golden canopy. A crusader for the Lord, and valiant and true. He captured Acre and crushed the fearsome Saladin at the battle of Arsuf. Taken prisoner on his journey back to England, he was held for ransom in Austria. In his absence his perfidious brother John declared him dead and laid claim to the throne. But thanks to the gallant efforts of Robin Hood and his band of merry men, Richard soon regained his freedom.

("I always loved that story," sighed Yale Templeton's mother.)

There was no limit to the vengeance Richard might have enacted on his return home, but instead he displayed that spirit of Christian charity for which he will ever be remembered. Grasping his trembling brother by the shoulders, he gave him the kiss of peace and said gently, "Think no more of it, John, you are only a child who has been led astray by evil councillors."

Eleanor of Castile: The beautiful wife of Edward I. So completely devoted to Edward that she accompanied him on his military campaigns. Once, when a would-be assassin stabbed him with a dagger dipped in venom, she sucked the poison from his wound. Their marriage was blessed with sixteen children. On Eleanor's death, Edward, in loving memory, arranged for a dozen majestic stone crosses to be erected along the route of her funeral procession from Lincolnshire to Westminster Abbey.

Edward III: Victor over the French at Crécy, but, like his grandfather Edward I, a man of most tender sensibilities. The tragic passing of his daughter Joan—who fell victim to the Black Death only weeks before she was to marry the Infante Pedro of Castile—was as a sword thrust to his heart. She has been "sent ahead to heaven," he said, "to reign among the choirs of virgins where she can intercede for our own offences before God." When Edward himself died, there was an outpouring of sorrow across the nation. Of his funeral, in which he was carried aloft on a bier borne by twenty-four knights dressed in black, the chronicler Froissart wrote, "To witness and hear the grief of the people, their sobs and lamentations on that day, would have rent anyone's heart."

Henry VII: Grandfather of Elizabeth. Founder of the Tudor dynasty upon his victory over the treacherous Richard III at Bosworth Field. Henry brought peace to the realm, imposed monarchical control over the nobility, reclaimed the Crown's feudal rights, and established financial stability. The grandeur of his vision was reflected in the magnificent chapel he built at Westminster Abbey, and in the tomb of gold (designed by the renowned Italian sculptor Pietro Torrigiano) in which his body now lies next to that of his beloved wife, the fair Elizabeth of York, angels at their heads, lions at their feet.

Henry Hudson recounted all this and much more on his visits to Yale Templeton's mother. She already knew the history of the English monarchy from books she had read as a young woman. But he had that rare capacity to make events of the distant past seem as if they had happened only yesterday. "One might almost believe that you were there yourself," she complimented him on one occasion.

On his most recent visit she had asked him, with some trepidation (not to mention great delicacy), to share what he knew about her mother, Anne Boleyn. "The things they told me when I was a child, they made her seem so horrible. But I think she must have been very beautiful."

"Very beautiful, yes. Very beautiful, indeed. With long dark hair and brown eyes. The King—your father—he loved her dearly. 'In heart, body, and will,' he once wrote. But she was more to him than a mere ornament. She helped him find the strength to save the kingdom from the perfidious clutches of the Pope and his minions. And so today the Church of England, with Your Majesty at its head, stands as a beacon of divine light to all peoples of the world."

She sighed. The weight of English history rested heavy on her shoulders. But it was inspiring to revisit the glorious past, no less inspiring than listening to the promise of the glorious future laid out for her by Richard Hakluyt the younger. In the vast northern wilderness where the brave Y. had chosen to cast his lot, England would realize its providential destiny. She sped Henry Hudson on his way with renewed urgency.

LV

It was several weeks before the Director of the CIA could begin to piece together how he had ended up in the wicker basket. Months later there were still large gaps in his memory.

It started shortly after his plane from Dallas touched down at Pearson airport in Toronto. Like most Americans he was shocked when Canadian immigration officials confiscated his assault rifle. Of course there was still his beloved Beretta packed away in his suitcase. But to avoid suspicion he had chosen to fly Air Canada, meaning his luggage had ended up in Moncton.

While he was standing in the terminal wondering what to do next, three of his fellow passengers sidled over to him. "From Alberta, right? Calgary, maybe?" they inquired with friendly grins. It was a reasonable guess, given that he was wearing a ten-gallon hat, a gift from the President on his last trip to the ranch. The three men were from Alberta themselves, and when they learned that the individual they were addressing was an American, they prostrated themselves before him and began to kiss his feet. "What a quaint custom," the Director of the CIA mused. Still, after ten minutes he thought he should be on his way. "Oh, but you must join us for dinner," one of the men insisted. And when he demurred, they told him that they had witnessed his treatment by immigration officials and had "the means to rectify the injustice." Since he was facing the daunting prospect of confronting Bobbi Jo Jackson alone (and now unarmed), he concluded that it was in his interests to accompany them.

They were staying, as it happened, at the very motel where Yale Templeton and Bobbi Jo Jackson had spent their first night together. Not that we should expect a similarly erotic result from the encounter the men had with the Director of the CIA, whatever the underlying origin of their lusting after things American. They were the founding members, they announced proudly, of a new political movement: the Alberta Idea. They had gone to Texas to observe first-hand a society unashamedly devoted to literal interpretation of the Bible and free enterprise. And the trip had been every bit as rewarding as they had hoped. They even got the chance to see Rush Limbaugh and five of the Dallas Cowboy Cheerleaders at the opening of a suburban mall.

The Director of the CIA was both surprised and impressed. He had not realized that such right-thinking people existed in Canada. And so began a love-in. Not literally, mind you. Not, as I said, with the erotic dimension of the rendezvous between Yale Templeton and Bobbi Jo Jackson. Not entirely, anyway. For one thing, no one burst into the room with a video camera. But the four men did find that they were bedfellows (as it were), sharing a common dream of a North America free of sin, free of gun laws, and most of all, free of taxes.

The men from Alberta pulled out a series of pamphlets to demonstrate how completely they identified with the American heartland—pamphlets on the folly of socialized medicine, on the evils of public television, on the corruption of organized labour, on the emasculating iniquity of feminism, on the blasphemy of gay marriage. Pamphlets with titles such as *How Government Handouts Destroy the Moral Fibre of the Poor*; *How Government Subsidies Strengthen the Moral Fibre of Multinational Corporations*; *Putting an End to Abortion: Because Life Is Sacred*; *Bringing Back Capital Punishment: Because Some Life Is Not All That Sacred*; *Immigrants: Speaking of Life That Is Not All That Sacred*; *Oil: The Myth of Global Warming*; *Evolution: A Perversion of the Godless*; *Oh, and In Case You Were Wondering, the Earth Is Flat*.

The Director of the CIA skimmed through all the pamphlets with great pleasure. To think that there was a political movement in Canada that so closely reflected his own vision. He asked the men from Alberta if they would be open to the prospect of annexation by the United States.

They looked at him with keen interest. "What would that mean exactly?"

"Well you would, of course, get to send representatives to Congress."

"And to the Senate?" one of the men asked.

"Yes, to the Senate as well."

"And how many senators would we have?"

"Two, the same as everyone else."

"And if the rest of Canada joins the United States, how many senators would Ontario have?"

"Why, two of course."

"Exactly the same, then. Not three or maybe four."

"Yes, exactly the same."

And the representatives of the Alberta Idea starting dancing around the room, whooping and hollering and high-fiving, before finally flinging themselves on the floor and kissing the feet of the Director of the CIA all over again.

The goal of Manifest Destiny was apparently much closer than anyone in Washington dared dream, the Director of the CIA said to himself. Maybe even closer than when Brian Mulroney was prime minister. "And imagine, I will have the privilege of breaking the news to the President."

But first, of course, he had a mission to complete. Without mentioning Yale Templeton by name, he explained that he was in Toronto to deal with someone who represented a profound threat to the United States.

"A terrorist, you mean," one of the men said.

Not the most apt description, perhaps, of the newly appointed Abraham Lincoln Distinguished Professor of the American Civil War, but ... "Yes," replied the Director of the CIA, "a terrorist." Which was why he needed to go well armed.

The men from Alberta agreed wholeheartedly. And opening up a trunk, they revealed a most wondrous cache of weapons. The Director of the CIA was beside himself with excitement. He took a few minutes to examine the firing mechanism on several of the handguns before selecting a Beretta (of course), a Glock, a derringer (with ankle holster), a Bowie knife, and, just to be on the safe side, a .300 Winchester Magnum.

"Whoa! Good choice with the rifle there, sir. You could bring down a moose with that."

Given his experience with immigration officials, he thought it best not to travel on public transit. Even taking a taxi posed risks. "The cab drivers in Toronto, they're all from Uganda or one of them other Middle Eastern countries," advised the member of the Alberta Idea responsible for immigration policy. So the Director of the CIA called up Avis and arranged for a rental van to be delivered to the entrance of the motel. It turned out a gun rack was unavailable. "We don't get much call for those in Toronto," the agent admitted. "Probably just as well," said one of the Albertans. "Better to keep the Winchester hidden." So the Director of the CIA slid the rifle under the back seat of the van, and after consulting a road map and making his goodbyes (allowing his new associates several more minutes for foot kissing), he was on his way.

The most sensible course, he decided, would be to park a couple of blocks from Yale Templeton's apartment and make his final approach on foot. It was night now, so he would have the advantage of darkness. Still, best to take evasive action. And he started to run snakily back and forth across the street, going from front yard to front yard crying "Serpentine! Serpentine!" (Standard CIA procedure ever since he had seen Peter Falk execute the manoeuvre in *The In-Laws*.) The result, however, was not quite as he had intended. When Mrs. Cordelia Devonshire-Hoskins saw a man weaving across the lawn of her stately mansion with a rifle slung over his shoulder, she did what she always did when the sanctity of Rosedale was threatened. Within seconds the Director of the CIA found himself pinned face first to the sidewalk by a team of police officers, a cocked revolver at his head and handcuffs severing the circulation to his wrists. It was a deeply humiliating experience, made worse by the fact he had to surrender all his new weapons.

The night he spent in the Don Jail was deeply humiliating as well, the only consolation being his cellmate, who was also an American. A Native American, in fact—direct descendant of the illustrious Penobscot chief Governor Neptune Lookalike. His own name was Henry David Thoreau Lookalike, and yes, he had been named after the famous author, "a close personal friend of my great-great-great-grandfather." For the next several hours he entertained the Director of the CIA with stories about Indian life and the world of American letters. As dawn approached he confided that "back on the reservation" he had an unpublished manuscript by Thoreau, "a penetrating exploration of the links between whale and moose" inspired by some ruminations passed down by Chief Neptune. He had long thought, he confessed, that he should make a gift of it "to someone like yourself who has an obvious appreciation for the role of Indians in the literary heritage of our great country." All he asked in return was a donation to the charitable foundation he had formed in support of Native poetry. He would even throw in a guide to fine dining in the vicinity of the Don Jail "at scarcely any charge." The Director of the CIA was deeply touched, so much so that he not only accepted the offer, but acceded to a request by his new acquaintance that they abide by a hallowed custom of the local Ojibwa population and seal their friendship by exchanging clothes.

Released the next morning on his own recognizance (since Canada allowed him the sorts of legal protection he conspired to deny foreigners in the United States), he started off in what he took to be the direction of Rosedale. Eventually he arrived at the corner of Church and Wellesley, where a crew was at work laying the foundation for a new branch of the YMCA. Nearby stood a policeman routing traffic away from the construction site. A good opportunity to get directions, the Director of the CIA thought.

Across the street Jerome Bakee was sitting at the bar of the Neuter Rooster. He had just started in on his fourth cosmopolitan when, looking up, he caught sight of a man in Native headdress and fringed imitation moosehide pants talking to a police officer and a construction worker. There was only one conclusion possible, at least for the corner of Church and Wellesley. "It's the Village People!" he shouted. And then he and everyone else in the bar poured out into the street.

Soon they were joined by clerks and customers from all the surrounding shops, and the Director of the CIA found himself, along with the police officer and the construction worker, hoisted into the air and passed along a sea of hands to a hastily assembled stage. The staff at the Neuter Rooster came running outside carrying a sound system, and suddenly Church Street was alive with the pulsating rhythm of "YMCA." Fortunately, the Director of the CIA was familiar with the song, having recently attended a bar mitzvah for a grandson of the chairman of the Federal Reserve Board. Inspired by the crowd, he put on a magnificent show. Even managed to fake his way through "In the Navy" and "Macho Man" before finishing with a twelve-minute dance solo drawing on his knowledge of Indian culture. (That is to say he shuffled across the stage shouting "Woo! Woo! Woo!" while whapping the palm of his hand against his mouth.)

All of which was carried live on the local evening news, and as a result, witnessed by Yale Templeton and Bobbi Jo Jackson. Not that they made a habit of watching the local news. But tonight, immediately afterward, the CBC was running a special edition of *The Nature of Things* called "The Moose, Our Misunderstood National Symbol."

"I wonder, do you think that dance is authentic?" said Yale Templeton, referring to the performance by the Director of the CIA. "I've never seen a First Nations chief do a back flip."

"Hard to tell," replied Bobbi Jo Jackson. "It is interesting, though. By the way would you mind if I moved the wicker basket for the old newspapers next to the front door? Just for a couple of days, I think."

Presumably at that point the fate of the Director of the CIA was, so to speak, sealed. After his terpsichorean improvisation at Church and Wellesley (followed by an evening of revelry at a private club in the neighbourhood), he tried to contact the representatives of the Alberta Idea. Alas, they had already checked out of their motel. He had promised the President that he would keep his mission secret, so he decided it best not to get in touch with anyone at the American Consulate. Instead he went to a costume store, where he purchased a mailman's uniform, a cap gun, and what the clerk told him was a mask of Henry Hudson. (Actually a mask of Leonid Brezhnev the store had been trying to unload since before the end of the Cold War. In his defence, the Director of the CIA *did* think the face looked familiar.)

A half hour later he was on the streets of Rosedale, though this time in disguise. Mindful of his disastrous experience just two days earlier, he decided to forego his Peter Falk imitation. Instead he strolled along as if he were simply another dedicated Canadian public servant going about his business. When he arrived at the apartment building where Yale Templeton lived, he discovered that the outside door was kept locked. Not wishing to arouse suspicion, he stood off to one side, making a pretence of sorting through some letters. When a tenant arrived burdened down with grocery bags, he tipped his cap and graciously offered to hold the door open for her. A few seconds later he was in the lobby. He had already ascertained that Yale Templeton lived on the second floor, in apartment B202. Locating the stairwell, he quickly ascended one flight and peeked out into the hall. To his relief, it was empty. Adjusting his mask, he made his way furtively past a nightstand and several potted plants, until he arrived at a door with a silver "B202" directly above a pair of miniature moose antlers. Instinctively wrapping his fingers around the handle of the cap gun in his pocket, he pushed the buzzer. At first all was silence. Then he heard the sound of a deadbolt being drawn back slowly, ever so slowly. The handle of the door began to turn and ...

Well, frankly, what happened next is so preposterous as to defy description. Suffice it to say, the Director of the CIA ended up inside a wicker basket surrounded by old editions of the *Globe and Mail* and *Toronto Star*. Because his arms were pinned next to his sides, he was prevented from getting to his Xanax. Smothering in his own panic, he passed out almost immediately. By the time he was removed from the basket and revived—this was several days later at the FedEx terminal in downtown Washington—his mind was a complete blank. As I noted previously, it would be several weeks before he could even begin to speak coherently about how he had ended up in the wicker basket. And he never did find out what happened to the original manuscript of *Fluke and Antler*.

LVI

Moose fight with others of their kind only in the rutting season.

SAMUEL MERRILL, *THE MOOSE BOOK*

S eptember has come upon the Great White Moose. It was some weeks ago that he began his trek from the Temagami district, and since then he has remained steadfast on course. He is headed for the Chapleau Crown Game Preserve, to fulfill his destiny. Or, as I phrased it earlier, his Manifest Destiny.

His direction has been north and west, over vast uninhabited (by humans) tracts of the Canadian Shield. Through forests and bogs, across rivers and lakes, along the edges of rocky outcroppings. From time to time his journey has brought him within a few kilometres of one of the isolated towns that fleck the northern wilderness—Shining Tree, Gogama, Milrod, Kukatush. But until today he has skirted all human settlements. By chance, though, rather than by design. He is moving without fear now— of humans but, more to the point, of the spectre whose memory until recently was a constant affliction. And so as he arrives late in the evening at the small settlement of Marshall's Revelation, he feels no impulse to make a detour. Quite the contrary, he ambles blithely ahead, straight down the middle of the main street.

Not that there is much for him to see: several homes, a drugstore, a diner, a grocery with a gas pump out front. The local headquarters for The Loyal Order of Moose distracts him momentarily, largely because of the magnificent set of antlers nailed above the front door. But it is only when he arrives at the appliance store that he comes to a full stop.

In the window is a television set inadvertently left on by a forgetful clerk. Looking out severely from the screen of the television (and fixing him with his eyes, so it must appear to the Great White Moose) is a man wearing a collar so large and seemingly so constricting that it awakens in the moose long dormant memories of the cumbersome halter his keeper used to put around his neck for certain ceremonial occasions among the Ojibwa. What he has chanced upon is that sanctified artifact of CBC television, Hockey Night in Canada. It is first intermission of a preseason contest between the Toronto Maple Leafs and Philadelphia Flyers. The man in the collar is an evangelical preacher who has just mounted his pulpit to deliver a blistering sermon devoted to his favourite subject, "The Holy Commandments of The Game." The Great White Moose regards him with ... what? Bewilderment? Curiosity? Alarm? Impossible to tell from his dispassionate expression.

"YOU KIDS OUT THERE," the preacher exhorts, "I'M GONNA SHOW YUH SUMPIN' HERE I NEVER NEVER EVER WANNA SEE ANY OF YOUSE DOIN'. LET'S RUN THAT CLIP." On the screen a Flyer defenceman skates up behind a centre on the Maple Leafs and hooks his feet out from under him. The Leaf crashes face first onto the ice, then lies there motionless, blood gushing from his nose.

"NOW, YUH SEE WHAT THAT THERE PHILLY DEFENCEMAN DID? I'M NOT GONNA MENTION WHERE HE COMES FROM, 'CAUSE YUH KNOW I CAN GET INTO TROUBLE FOR THAT KINDA THING." Then he picks up a Russian flag and waves it around his head. "BUT YOU KIDS, I WANT YUH TO UNDERSTAND, CHEAP SHOTS LIKE THAT, KNOCKIN'

SOMEONE DOWN FROM BEHIND, THAT'S NOT THE WAY TO PLAY THE GAME. NOT THE CANADIAN WAY."

And then a second film clip appears on the screen. A player on the Flyers (a left winger who scored a total of four goals the previous season while running up 312 minutes in penalties) and a player on the Maple Leafs (a right winger with five goals and 279 minutes in penalties) meet at the faceoff circle and start exchanging what appear to be pleasantries about their respective mothers. Then suddenly they drop their sticks and gloves and begin flailing away at each other with bare fists. Two minutes later they lie side by side on the ice, motionless, blood gushing from their noses.

"BEAUTY! YUH SEE THAT? FACE TO FACE! GOD LOVE 'EM! NOW THAT'S THE WAY *REAL* MEN PLAY HOCKEY!" chortled the preacher. "THAT'S THE *CANADIAN* WAY!"

There was no one else in Marshall's Revelation to witness the sermon on the television or to witness the Great White Moose witnessing it. The entire population of the village, young and old, male and female, had gone on a pilgrimage to Milrod to take in a hockey tournament involving twelve-year-olds from communities across the Far North of the province. Indeed, at the very moment when the left winger on the Flyers and the right winger on the Maple Leafs were preparing to knock each other senseless, the players on the team from Marshall's Revelation and their opponents were mobbed together at centre ice in the Milrod Arena, ritualistically acting out their own sacred claims to Canadian masculine identity.

The Great White Moose (before he was the Great White Moose) had now and then observed young Ojibwa children playing hockey on the frozen lakes near his home. So far as I am aware, however, on no occasion did he see a Native boy or girl hit another child in the face. But then, over the years, many discriminating observers have lamented the apparent inability of First Nations peoples to comprehend and assimilate the more edifying aspects of Canadian culture.

For himself, the Great White Moose had never had a taste for face-to-face combat, or indeed for combat of any kind. Those times when he encountered other male moose during his wanderings across Northern Ontario, and especially during the rutting season, he would tactfully reverse direction. Perhaps it was no more than an inevitable consequence of the fact that he had been neutered at birth. Certainly we can assume that the preacher in the oversized collar would have professed as much. But I am inclined to think that he was simply a gentle soul by nature, and that had he been born a human, he would have happily endorsed the traditional role Canadians like to imagine for themselves (at least away from hockey rinks) as the consummate peacekeepers of the world.

*And now for the exciting
conclusion!*

LVII

"And now for the exciting conclusion!" The speaker is Yale Templeton. It is September, the beginning of a new term, his introductory lecture in History 393. Ordinarily when meeting a class for the first time, he would distribute the syllabus, outline the course material, discuss required readings and written assignments, then dismiss the students without further comment. This time, however, staggered by the size of his audience, he feels moved to add an "exciting conclusion" to his lecture: He will show the students just how truly rewarding study of the American Civil War can be by offering two or three examples of the many thrilling details about the war that they can expect to learn over the coming weeks.

In previous years History 393 had been held in one of the smaller lecture halls in the Edifice Building. But the return of Yale Templeton to the classroom, whether because he had won a great victory in the battle for free speech in Canada, as some faculty and students would have it, or because he had been on a secret and apparently very dangerous mission for the university, as the administration now claimed, had seen enrolment in the course skyrocket. And so his lectures had been moved to the Lyceum, the only space on campus large enough to accommodate so many students: the fifteen hundred who had registered for the course, plus the additional five hundred who decided to take in the introductory lecture just to see if the newly designated Abraham Lincoln Distinguished Professor of the American Civil War might shed some light on his recent personal history or say something outrageous.

Not that all two thousand students still remained in the hall. As animated as he may have attempted to sound, Yale Templeton remained a remarkably monotonous speaker. And so there were a mere twelve hundred left in the Lyceum (and many fewer than that still awake) when he reached his "exciting conclusion": "You will learn many fascinating facts and statistics in this course. For example, how many of you are aware that pig iron production in the North went up 345 percent over the course of the war?" Not a single hand went up. Not even a hand belonging to the one student in class who might have been expected to know the statistic because he had heard it in the same course the previous spring—indeed, in the very same lecture where Professor Templeton presented his astonishing claim (fantasy, revelation) about the "supposed" assassination of Abraham Lincoln.

But then Joel did not have much of a memory for facts and statistics. And in any case, he had other things on his mind. Surveying the lecture hall, he saw more than six hundred ... no, make that seven hundred, women. Statuesque blondes, petite brunettes, fiery redheads. Women of a diverse array of physical types and ethnic backgrounds, each eminently desirable in her own way. True, many were unlikely to return for the second lecture. And their numbers could be expected to decline precipitously right up to the deadline for dropping courses without financial penalty. But Joel had long ago stopped troubling himself about practical realities where prospects for love were concerned.

LVIII

I t would overstate the case to suggest that Felicia Butterworth was surprised when she heard about the large enrolment for History 393. "A necessary, if unfortunate, consequence of the steps you had to take to deal with a difficult situation," as the Dean Responsible for Relations with the Mafia tactfully put it. Nor can it be said she was surprised that student militants and certain radical members of the faculty put their own interpretation on why she had honoured Yale Templeton with a chair. Still, she was simmering. The recent V-B Day (Victory Over Butterworth Day) that activists had organized on Regency Circle had been galling enough. (Although it was a small consolation that Frito-Lay reported unexpectedly high sales at the event. "Even revolutionaries love Doritos!" as the sign on one concession stand read.) But then a naked female student had locked herself in the Bell Mobility Tower. Felicia Butterworth still had "Solidarity Forever" ringing in her ears.

All the same, her management of the Templeton affair had, in the end, produced the desired outcome. The Vice-President for Manipulating the Media had issued a brief announcement to the press stating that, as a reward for his valuable service to the university, Yale Templeton was to become the first Abraham Lincoln Distinguished Professor of the American Civil War.

Those desiring further information were to direct their inquiries to the new Advisor to the President and CEO with Special Responsibility for Matters of Principle. And H. Avery Duck had done his part masterfully. He had provided every journalist who contacted him with a treatise outlining the ethical reasons why, in fact, the administration could *not* provide further information about the appointment. The preamble alone ran to 123 pages. The full text required three volumes, with two additional volumes for relevant supplementary material, including disquisitions by minor Scandinavian philosophers, haikus by Zen Buddhist masters, and scriptural commentary by Andalusian rabbinical scholars. As the Dean Responsible for Relations with the Mafia had suggested (not that H. Avery Duck needed any encouragement), he had created a new language, based on classical Greek, to convey the full enormity of the principles at stake. As an added touch he had cast his arguments in an obscure epic verse form. The result was exactly as the Dean Responsible for Relations with the Mafia had predicted: Most newspapers chose to bury the story of the Templeton appointment on a back page of the weekly Education Supplement. Television simply ignored it.

The other problem Felicia Butterworth had faced also resolved itself quite nicely, or so it seemed at the time. On her desk one morning she found an envelope containing a letter dated September 29, 1893, from Abraham Lincoln to John Hay. Initially she was confused. Had Yale Templeton not told her that the evidence he had found was contained in legal records? But never mind. The letter looked suitably old, authentic. Accordingly she had the Dean Responsible for Relations with the Mafia contact Vito, and Vito sent his nephews (or as the dean knew them, his godsons) to Toronto to take possession of the document.

What happened next can be described briefly. When Charles and Hugh, Vito's nephews, read the letter, they were stunned to discover that those crazy rumours about Lincoln—Lincoln, the most revered of all Americans after Jesus Christ—were apparently true. Here was the proof in Lincoln's own handwriting that he had faked his assassination so that he could move to Canada and live openly as a transvestite. "Think of the damage if this were to fall into the wrong hands, Uncle Vito," Hugh said. And so Vito took the only reasonable course. He put the document in the vault in his office for safekeeping. Put it in the vault for safekeeping, intending to offer it for sale on eBay. But then—mercifully, some might say—his short-term memory failed him (as it now so often did), and he forgot about the letter entirely. It remains in the vault to this day, awaiting discovery by some resourceful historian.

LIX

The President, of course, knew nothing about the letter. If he had—if he had believed that Vito had come into possession of the evidence Yale Templeton found—he would not have acted so rashly.

I am referring here to the decision he made at a meeting of his chief security officers in the private room in Walter Reed hospital where the Director of the CIA was recuperating. Not that the Director of the CIA was able to contribute to the conversation. He lay motionless in his bed, eyes riveted on the ceiling. Occasionally he would emit a deep gurgling sound.

The Assistant to the President for National Security Affairs arrived late, the afternoon matinee of *Peter Pan* at the Kennedy Center having run a few minutes over. He apologized to the President for appearing in his Captain Hook costume. "We have another show at seven, and I didn't think I would have time to change. You wouldn't believe how long it takes them to do my makeup." All present sympathized.

The President began the meeting by recounting the "unfortunate recent experiences" of the Director of the CIA, "as best as we have been able to reconstruct them." He then revealed what he had learned only hours earlier: that Felicia Butterworth had created an endowed chair for Yale Templeton.

"But it was only a few months ago that she suspended him," said the Director of the FBI. "Why honour him? Why now?"

"Good questions, Raymond. Very good questions. Here's how I see it. Butterworth built her reputation in the marketing department at Frito-Lay. When she took over as university president and CEO in Toronto, she initiated a very ambitious—and I am told spectacularly successful—fundraising campaign targeting corporate donors. I can only assume she has concluded that there is more money to be made by exploiting Templeton's notoriety than by keeping him silent. For all I know, next week we'll see him on television peddling Funyuns Onion-flavoured Rings."

"If you're right, Mr. President, then the Lincoln story is about to hit the front pages all over again," observed the Director of the FBI.

"My thinking exactly," replied the President. "We must act immediately."

"But what can we do?" asked the Executive Assistant to the Assistant Undersecretary of Transportation. "Everything we've tried has failed. I mean, just look ..." And he cast a pitiful glance at the figure lying in the bed.

The President shrugged. "What happened to the Director of the CIA, I can't say I'm surprised. Not entirely. The truth is, I put together a contingency plan back at the time of the break-in at the White House."

"You mean when you were hanging naked from the chandelier?" said the Executive Assistant to the Assistant Undersecretary of Transportation.

The President glowered at him. "I determined," he went on, speaking in sharp, measured tones, "that if the Director of the CIA was unable to complete his mission, I would go to Toronto and deal with Templeton myself. Really, I see no other choice."

"But Mr. President!" objected the Director of the FBI. "Think of the danger! Think of Bobbi Jo Jackson!"

"Ah yes, Bobbi Jo Jackson," sighed the President, who had in fact been thinking of scarcely anyone or anything else since the break-in. "Exactly my point. I am quite satisfied I am the only one who can make her ... uh ... see reason."

"I have to be honest with you, Mr. President," said the Assistant to the President for National Security Affairs, "the people of the United States will never stand for it. They will never let you put your life at risk."

"The people need never know," replied the President. "I will go in disguise."

"Go in disguise? Do you mean you're planning on facing Templeton and Bobbi Jo Jackson alone?" said the Director of the FBI.

"No, no," replied the President. "Of course not. Lowell here will go with me."

"What?!" cried the Executive Assistant to the Assistant Undersecretary of Transportation. "What?! Me?! *I'll* go with you?! But! ... But! ... "

Just then the Director of the CIA sat bolt upright in his bed. He grabbed a Beretta from under his pillow, directed it at the head of the Executive Assistant to the Assistant Undersecretary of Transportation, cried "Live Free or Die!" and then pulled the trigger. A little red flag popped out from the barrel of the gun. It had "Bang!" written in blue and white spangled letters on the side.

"It's good I had them modify that thing after the incident with the Puerto Rican orderly last week," said the President. The Director of the FBI and the Assistant to the President for National Security Affairs nodded in agreement, while the Executive Assistant to the Assistant Undersecretary of Transportation crumpled to a heap on the floor.

LX

For some years now when mail addressed to "Mrs. Templeton" arrived at the Tudor cottage in Saffron Walden, the occupant of the cottage would puzzle over the name, search her memory to no effect, then, typically, toss the envelope into the dustbin. Tradesmen in the locality had learned to deliver bills in person. They had learned as well that, if they wished to receive payment, it was advisable to drop to one knee, make a respectful bow, and refer to the occupant as "Your Majesty" or "Your Grace."

The letter that arrived for "Mrs. Templeton" on this particular day was quite unusual, however. For one thing it was addressed in the following way: "Mrs. Templeton, Mother of the Abraham Lincoln Distinguished Professor of the American Civil War." For another it had been sent from Canada, that distant northern land where her favourite courtier had gone to educate the natives in the benefits of gentle English governance. The postmark even had an image of that fearful Canadian beast, the moos or moosh. And so, suspecting that the security of the realm was at stake, the occupant of the cottage invoked her royal prerogative and opened the envelope addressed to a person she believed to be one of her subjects.

The letter inside, written by an overly zealous summer intern in the Office of the Fundraising Campaign at the university, was cryptic. Or rather it seemed cryptic to her. "You have no doubt learned by this time," it began, "that Yale Templeton has been accorded an unprecedented honour by the president and CEO of this renowned institution."

Indeed, she had learned no such thing. The new Abraham Lincoln Distinguished Professor of the American Civil War had declined to send his mother notification of his appointment. He had always resisted letting her know about his professional activities for fear that any reminder of his decision to devote his life's work to study of the United States would cause her distress. (Not to mention the fact that he still had no clue why Felicia Butterworth had decided to reward him with a prestigious chair.)

The letter continued: "The courageous actions taken by Professor Templeton in defence of his country speak for themselves. So does his scholarship, which has rightfully earned him a reputation as the 'foremost living authority on the American Civil War,' to quote the eminent historian St. Clair Russell Hill."

The letter then went on to suggest that, under the circumstances, Mrs. Templeton might think it proper to make a financial contribution to the university. Enclosed with the letter was a card outlining the various ways in which such a contribution could be made: By cheque. By "monthly deductions from your bank account." Or by VISA, Mastercard, or American Express (with spaces provided where the donor was to enter a "credit card no." and "date of expiry").

The letter and card were completely opaque to her. Even so, she found the language unsettling. And she immediately summoned Richard Hakluyt the younger to see if he could make sense of the documents.

Which he was unable to do, however, at least for the better part of the hour he spent brooding silently over them in her cottage. He scrutinized the envelope as well, especially the return address. But alas, the terms "Office of the Fundraising Campaign" and "Graves Hall" meant nothing to him. In the end he begged leave to take the documents back to the rectory at Wetheringsett. "Soe that I might have the opportunitie to review them at some length."

LXI

ale Templeton's mother was extremely surprised when Richard Hakluyt returned the very next morning. But, as he explained on his arrival, what he had discovered through a close reading of the letter and card meant that there was no time for delay.

"As Your Majestie her selfe didst notice, I hazarde, the letter speakes of a 'civil warre.' There is but a single possible conclusion. Hostilities have broken out among the Savages in Canada. Peradventure the French are responsible. Or, if the worst of our feares be realized, the Spaniardes and even the Portingales."

Yale Templeton's mother took a deep breath.

"There is more, Your Majestie. The letter acknowledges 'the courageous actions' that the intrepid Y. [or Yale Templeton, as Richard Hakluyt now knew him to be] has taken in defence of the realm ..."

"For which I will reward him most lavishly on his return," she reminded him.

"Ah, yes. Well, but ... " and here he dropped his eyes, "it is my most painefull dutie to informe thee that I beleve he is nowe a captive, held for ransom."

"For ransom!" exclaimed Yale Templeton's mother.

"I can conjure no other explanation wherefore the author of the communication hath asked for tribute."

Yale Templeton's mother fell quiet, pondering the news. Richard Hakluyt was quiet as well.

"At least," she said after some moments' reflection, "the request for tribute does allow us one comfort. Presumably our valiant wayfarer remains alive."

"But for how long?" Richard Hakluyt replied, revealing more concern than he intended.

"What are you suggesting?!" she said with alarm.

"The wordinge of the carde. Your Majestie will notice ..." and here he directed her attention to the phrase "date of expiry." He went on. "Quite clearly, unless the parties holding Y. receeve payment, they meane to put him to death. Howbeit only, I shoulde imagine, after first subjecting him to the very cruelest of tortures."

Yale Templeton's mother clutched her breast. Richard Hakluyt rushed to her side to keep her from falling, then helped ease her onto her throne.

"But what," she pleaded, "are their demands, exactly? How much tribute do they want? I see no figure mentioned. And why have they not provided a specific 'date of expiry'?"

Richard Hakluyt bowed his head in embarrassment. "I did pass the entier night asking my selfe those very same questions. Unhappily, I canst offer no answers. The very silence of the documents on these matters leads me to wonder whether the Savages responsible for the dastardly deede have any thought of releasing him once they have their handes on the ransom."

Shocking words. But as much as fear and despair gripped her heart, Yale Templeton's mother had that remarkable capacity, as the most beloved of monarchs do, to compose herself in times of crisis.

"Then we must act without delay," she ordered. "Notify Henry Hudson."

Richard Hakluyt smiled and bowed. "Verily, I did anticipate Your Majestie in this regarde. I have alreadie apprised him of the neede to mount his expedition posthaste."

And Yale Templeton's mother breathed a royal sigh of relief.

LXII

enry Hudson was, quite understandably, stunned when he received instructions to prepare to sail at once. He had barely acquired one-quarter of the materials needed to build a replica of the *Half Moon*. In fact, according to the schedule he had drafted—a schedule, incidentally, which the queen herself had approved—he was not to begin construction of the frame for another six weeks. And of the more than thirty potential crew members he had interviewed, not a single one had possessed the skills needed to man a sixteenth-century sailing vessel.

However, once he had time to reflect on the challenge he now faced, his attitude gybed 180 degrees (to use English nautical parlance). In his guise as Sebastian Higgs, twenty-first-century computer systems analyst from Bournemouth, he was well aware that solo voyages across the open seas were now commonplace. He even knew a stockbroker who had participated in a trans-oceanic race. "We have all the technology we need to virtually eliminate risk," he reassured himself. Indeed, as a computer systems analyst, he had access to the most advanced software dealing with weather forecasting and the monitoring of ocean currents. It would be possible for him to navigate the Atlantic alone.

But then a thought occurred to him. If he were simply to imitate the marine exploits of other men of his day, that would hardly serve the purpose of restoring his reputation fully and for all time. No, to gain the vindication he truly deserved, he would have to limit himself to equipment available during the Elizabethan Age. He would carry no radio on his journey, no radar, no computers. Nothing at all except an astrolabe. And the boat would have to be spare as well. A small craft, without even a cabin. Just large enough to hold salt cod and hard tack for a single person. (Although he decided to allow himself one anachronistic indulgence. He would bring along some limes to help ward off scurvy.)

His spirits renewed, he sent word to Richard Hakluyt the younger that he would set sail for Canada at dawn three days hence. "Withal it would be a great honour," he wrote, "if you and Her Majesty would come to the docks at Southampton to bid me Godspeed."

LXIII

Civilized man, seeking a foothold in the wilderness, begins by destroying the forests. He must have room for his cornfields, and for his village. Thus the moose, dependent on the forest for subsistence, retreats before the advancing axmen, with their guns and dogs—leaving civilized man to study the moose through the medium of a specimen stuffed by some upholsterer, perhaps, and displayed in a museum. As a result a large measure of mystery has always surrounded the moose ...

SAMUEL MERRILL, *THE MOOSE BOOK*

H ow to solve the mystery surrounding the Great White Moose? How, in particular, to interpret the forces that have led him to wander for so many disquieting years across the distant reaches of Northern Ontario only to bring him back at this moment to the Chapleau Crown Game Preserve, "the largest wildlife refuge in the world." I have previously alluded to his "Manifest Destiny." But what does that mean, exactly? Far too often humans use the term merely as a convenient (and none too subtle) justification for nakedly self-serving actions. Perhaps if we could penetrate the deeper meaning of communication between moose, we would find that they articulate a similar concept. Perhaps we would find that at times they also invoke it to excuse behaviour that is, on its face, inexcusable. But not the Great White Moose. Most assuredly not the Great White Moose.

But to return to my narrative: The stride of the Great White Moose is deliberate now and his course unwavering. He appears more at peace than at any time since the traumatic occasion of his resurrection. A result, you might think, of the fact that he has entered the legally protected shelter of a wildlife refuge. But personal experience long ago taught him that not even the most expansive of sanctuaries can provide security from Americans with their guns. In any case there seems little reason to believe that what has propelled him forward in recent weeks is a determination to secure his personal safety. Not when you consider that the path he is following leads directly to the cave of Slinger the Trapper. Why a moose with a very conspicuous instinct for self-preservation would risk confronting a man who has spent the better part of his more than seventy-five years on Earth circumventing attempts by Canadian authorities to preserve the northern forest as a safe haven for wildlife defies easy analysis. For the moment, his "Manifest Destiny" must remain obscure.

—— LXIV ——

I t had been some years since Yale Templeton's mother had stepped outside the little Tudor cottage and a much longer time since she had ventured beyond the town limits of Saffron Walden. Of course, in her imagination, she travelled widely and frequently. Why, wasn't it was only days ago that she had been to Tilbury to give an inspiring speech to the troops massed in wait for the despicable Armada? How she had revelled in Philip's humiliation! Just next week she would be going to Burghley House, ostensibly to consult with the Lord High Treasurer, but in reality to see his spectacular new gardens. Later there would be nostalgic trips to Hatfield House and Hampton Court. And she was already looking forward to the Christmas festivities at Whitehall Palace. Yes, her opportunities to relax amidst the splendours of Windsor Castle were increasingly few.

And so, when Richard Hakluyt the younger arrived at her door with a horse-drawn carriage to transport her to Southampton, her equilibrium (not, perhaps, the best term to describe her state of being) was unshaken. He had gone to the trouble to paint the royal coat of arms on the door, devoting particular attention to her motto, "Semper Eadem." Alas, while he had a talent for calligraphy, he was quite hopeless at representational art. Although the golden lion he produced could at least pass for a cat of some sort, his golden dragon looked like a beleaguered, elongated chicken. In the end he decided to cover his handiwork with a black cloth, "soe," as he told Her Majesty, "the Spaniardes and Portingales may not followe us to Henry Hudson and thereby gaine knowledge of his secrete mission." For the same reason he advised that they travel to Southampton alone, just the two of them. The presence of her usual attendants would only arouse suspicion.

On the journey south Yale Templeton's mother kept the curtains in the carriage drawn, again in the interests of security. From time to time, however, she peeked outside, and what she saw filled her with a mixture of pride and confusion. Pride because the neatly kept fields and hedges of the countryside, the bustling shops of the towns, and the dignified grandeur of city churches reminded her of the estimable character of the realm over which she was privileged to rule. Confusion because there was so much she did not recall ever having seen before. Carriages that moved without the aid of horses. Building facades with colourful images that danced and told stories. Even machines flying through the heavens. But then, why be surprised? she scolded herself. Here was just further evidence of the native ingenuity of the English people, her people.

When they arrived in Southampton, Richard Hakluyt misread the directions Henry Hudson had given him and they ended up at the Ocean Village Marina. Members of the Royal Southampton Yacht Club found it rather quaint to see an elderly woman of decidedly diminutive stature and wearing a crown descend from a horse-drawn carriage and negotiate her way among the slips, helped along by a middle-aged man who looked, quipped one observer, as if he were auditioning for the part of Sir Nicholas in *Love's Labour's Lost*.

After they had wandered about the docks for maybe twenty minutes, Richard Hakluyt realized his error and they set off in the direction of Town Quay. To the great satisfaction of Her Majesty, they passed signs along the way inviting travellers to the "Tudor Merchant's Hall" and the "Tudor House Museum." She was mystified by a series of flags announcing the "Odeon Multiplex Cinema." But what really arrested her attention was a large billboard that read, "While in Southampton, be sure to visit the Queen Elizabeth 2."

A few minutes later, as they neared Ocean Terminal, they passed another sign, which read:

QUEEN ELIZABETH 2
Hours of Viewing: 10 a.m. to 4 p.m.

Apparently their efforts to keep her trip a secret had failed. Not that the signs were entirely clear. Why *the* Queen Elizabeth? And why was the numeral 2 appended? Still, there obviously had been a breach of security. Which meant that the Spaniardes and Portingales were in all likelihood now aware that some major marine enterprise was in the offing. Why else would Her Majesty be making an unannounced trip to Southampton?

Richard Hakluyt suggested that, under the circumstances, it would be better to wait until sundown before continuing on to Town Quay. True, that would make it somewhat more difficult to find their way. But at least they would be able to operate under cover of darkness, away from the gaze of spies. As a result it was not until almost ten that they finally located Henry Hudson. He was sitting in a deck chair at the very far end of the outermost dock in the Town Quay Marina, where he had moored his sailboat "to avoid attracting attention."

The craft was a clinker-built dinghy constructed of sturdy spruce, eighteen feet long, with a single sail. It was stocked to the gunwales with salt cod, hard tack, limes, and barrels of water, enough to last a careful man for more than two months. On the stern, Henry Hudson had stencilled "*Discovery*." Richard Hakluyt was dismayed when he saw the boat. Whether or not it was seaworthy—and he had serious doubts—it hardly seemed capable of a trans-Atlantic crossing. But Yale Templeton's mother was enchanted. Of course, what she saw—what she *imagined* she saw—was not a dinghy but a stout-hulled bark, sixty-five feet in length. Her evident delight caused Henry Hudson to beam and Richard Hakluyt to keep his misgivings to himself.

The three of them spoke at length about the coming voyage. Henry Hudson thought that he would be able to reach Canada in five or perhaps six weeks, "assuming the winds are favourable." Of course, there would be the additional time required to determine the whereabouts of Y. and deal with his native captors. Her Majesty expressed concern that the Savages would become impatient, "having to wait such a lengthy time for their tribute." But Richard Hakluyt observed, reasonably enough, that the request for ransom had arrived for Mrs. Templeton ("whosoever that personage may be") only days earlier. "And Y. must surely have given the Savages cause to understand that ocean crossings must needes be of long duration."

Yale Templeton's mother had brought some of her most valuable pieces of jewellery, including several necklaces ("gifts from my loving father") and a "priceless golden tiara," to serve as a ransom. "But should the Savages turn treacherous"—by which she meant, should they accept the tribute yet refuse to release their hostage—"then you must take whatever steps are required to bring your mission to its desired conclusion." Henry Hudson pledged to Her Majesty that he would find a way to save the noble Y. "even should it cost me my own life."

In an effort to move the conversation in a more hopeful direction, Richard Hakluyt spoke of the "wondrous opportunitie" that the journey to Canada offered. "Forsooth," he said to Henry Hudson, "thou shalbe witness to the dawning of a new age in the historie of our faire Common weale." England, he prophesied—and here he was merely repeating what he had already told Her Majestie on numerous occasions—was about to come into possession of a great empire, rich beyond the lands of the hated Spanish.

Henry Hudson heartily concurred. "I am confident, Your Majesty, that I will not only be able to secure the release of Y. but help him take possession of that vast northern territory which promises to stand in the fullness of time as the brightest jewel in the crown of our glorious nation."

And then Yale Templeton's mother said what was surely the most astonishing thing of all the many astonishing things she had said since taking up residence at the Tudor cottage in Saffron Walden. She said: "I will go with you."

Henry Hudson and Richard Hakluyt the younger fell silent. They looked at each other in consternation. Surely Her Majesty was jesting. But no, she stumbled her way through the darkness back to the carriage, where she retrieved her small bag of personal belongings.

"Your Majesty," Henry Hudson remarked discreetly on her return, "do you think this wise?" He knew that, at a mere six stone, she was not likely to make a serious dent in his provisions. Still, her presence would almost certainly prove a distraction.

"I must most strongly proteste," said Richard Hakluyt, who now for the first time found the courage to risk offending her. "What you propose is farre, farre too dangerous. Be mindful, Your Majestie. You have responsibilities to your subjectes here, in our beloved England."

But while she graciously refrained from reproving him for his boldness, she allowed as she would hear no objections. "If, as you say, sir, England is about to enter a brilliant new age, and if the dawning of this age is to occur in Canada, then Canada is where I rightfully belong."

Her Majesty had spoken. There would be no more discussion. She spent the better part of the night writing letters to Lord Burghley and her other councillors, providing instructions for administration of the realm in her absence. Richard Hakluyt the younger had no choice but to promise that he would deliver the letters and do his best to see that her directions were carried out.

So it was that the following morning at dawn, Henry Hudson helped Yale Templeton's mother into the *Discovery* and the two of them set sail. By late afternoon they were far out to sea.

LXV

Yale Templeton would have been astonished had he heard his mother declare that she belonged in Canada. He would have been even more astonished if someone had told him that, at that moment, she was sitting on top of a crate of salt cod in a wooden dinghy somewhere off the southern coast of England. Sitting on top of a crate of salt cod in a wooden dinghy somewhere off the southern coast of England because she had joined an expedition to rescue him from "Savages." But then, as it happens, his own life was about to take quite an unexpected turn.

After delivering his fifth lecture of the term in History 393 (to an audience of fewer than 120 students, approximately half the total still enrolled in the course), he stopped by the History department office. In his mailbox he found a manila envelope addressed to "Professor Templeton, the Abraham Lincoln Distinguished Professor of the American Civil War." Enclosed was a letter written in a scrawling hand on a sheet of lined paper stained with splotches of whiskey. It read:

Professor,
On my trip to Hawk Junction last week, I happened to come across an old copy of the *Globe and Mail,* and what did I find on the back page

of the Education Supplement? Why, an article saying that you had been appointed the first Abraham Lincoln Distinguished Professor of the American Civil War! I could hardly believe my eyes. Abraham Lincoln Distinguished Professor. Now I have to admit, when you up and disappeared on me a few years back, I was mightily confused. I figured probably you'd just been pulling my leg about being a Lincoln expert. Probably you weren't even a real professor at all. The fact is, after so many years of living in the woods, I understand animals a lot better than I do people. I see now, though, that we probably just got our signals crossed about where to meet. So this must be the Good Lord's way of correcting our mistake. The article says, "Several months ago Professor Templeton became embroiled in controversy after he reportedly gave a lecture in which he claimed that President Abraham Lincoln had faked his own assassination so that he could come to Canada and live openly as a transvestite. That allegation is now widely believed to have been circulated by a disgruntled student." So I reckon you already have been doing your best to tell people the truth about Lincoln. Only I guess no one is willing to listen. What you need is the evidence. You need the legal briefs Lincoln left to my grandfather. So this is what I propose. I'll remain in my camp in the woods outside Hawk Junction for the next couple of weeks. Whenever it's convenient you come up here and check into the hotel. I'll look for you every day about noon. When we connect up, I'll take you out to my cave and you can examine the briefs. After that we'll figure out a way for getting them down to Toronto.

I'm closing in on eighty now. I don't know how many more years I have left to me. It's a great comfort to think that I will be able to carry out my grandfather's last wishes. The fact is, Professor, until I saw the article in the newspaper, I'd all but given up hope that the world would ever learn about the real Abraham Lincoln. Now I'm filled with joy. I'm very much looking forward to meeting up with you again.

With respect,

Slinger

On reading and then rereading the letter, Yale Templeton felt a chill. It was a chill of excitement, the excitement of knowing that he would soon have access to a most rare set of historical documents. It was a chill of anxiety, anxiety born of the fact that he had never completely erased from his memory the conversation between Curly and the cook at the diner in Hawk Junction. It was a chill of relief that he would now be able to acquire the evidence Felicia Butterworth wanted. And it was a chill of apprehension about what she would say or do when he confessed that the document he had given her some weeks earlier—the letter from Lincoln to John Hay—was in reality a forgery.

For her part, Bobbi Jo Jackson had a much less complicated reaction to the communication from Slinger. "Awesome!" she exclaimed. "When do we leave?"

He had not actually worked out that particular detail yet. He had classes every Monday, Wednesday, and Friday. Even if Section 9, Paragraph 7 of the collective agreement had not mandated a reprimand for any professor who skipped a class "without just cause," he still would have been disinclined to cancel a lecture. It was, as far as he was concerned, a question of duty. Not, as you might think, his duty to his students. Rather, his duty to the participants in the Civil War. How could he possibly leave out a single fact or statistic without committing an injustice against some or other of those soldiers and civilians whose lives had been tightly intertwined with his own for so many years?

"Not to worry," said Bobbi Jo Jackson. "We'll leave after your lecture Friday morning. It's over at ten, right? I can have us in Hawk Junction by late afternoon. We'll meet up with Slinger the next day, get the briefs, and be back home Sunday night. You won't miss any classes."

"I'm afraid to say," Yale Templeton replied, "that is somewhat unrealistic. Slinger keeps the briefs in the cave where he lives, deep in the woods. As I recall, he told me that it would take perhaps a week to get there from Hawk Junction."

She thought for a moment. "Then I tell you what. We'll drive up Friday and see him Saturday. You can introduce us and then catch the bus back to Toronto. I'll go with Slinger to the cave, get the briefs, and have them back here in a couple of weeks. No problem, really. I love canoe trips. He travels by canoe, right? I don't know whether I ever told you about it, but the CIA sent me on a whitewater rafting course down in Costa Rica one winter. It was really cool, especially after the volcano erupted."

So it was settled. They would leave following his lecture Friday morning. But first, Yale Templeton decided, there was something he would have to do. Something he would keep secret from Bobbi Jo Jackson. That something was this: He would write a note to Felicia Butterworth explaining that the document he had given her a few weeks earlier had been a forgery. He wanted to apologize for that, the note would say. The truth was, her insistence that he turn over the evidence he had uncovered about Lincoln—turn it over without delay—had led him to an act of desperation. But now he had the means to rectify his misdeed. The individual who had the legal records proving that Lincoln had faked his assassination and moved to Canada had contacted him by mail. "I will be leaving immediately after my lecture on Friday to meet with him." He added as a postscript that Felicia Butterworth need not worry: He was cognizant of his teaching obligations under the collective agreement and would not miss any of his scheduled classes.

All that remained for him was to deliver the note. He was disinclined to give it to her directly. That, after all, was the reason for putting his thoughts into writing, so that he could avoid dealing with her in person. The best thing, he reasoned, would be to leave the note on her desk, just as he had left the forgery on her desk. And he would not do it until late Thursday. That way, by the time she got around to reading the note, he would be in the middle of his Friday lecture, or maybe, if luck was on his side, already on his way north.

Thursday night he followed the same circuitous route through the darker corners of the campus to the back of Graves Hall that he and Bobbi Jo Jackson had taken several weeks earlier. He accessed the building through a basement window with a crowbar, and used the set of CIA-issue keys to open the door to Felicia Butterworth's office. ("I need your keys to get into the History department," he had told Bobbi Jo Jackson. "I accidentally locked my own keys in a carrel at the library.") Once inside, he lay the envelope containing the note—it had "for President Butterworth" and "CONFIDENTIAL!" printed neatly across the front—gently on top of the stack of papers on her desk. Then he slipped away into the night. He fairly flew all the way home, he was so elated. It was not just that he had unburdened himself of his deep feelings of guilt over participating in the forging of a historical document. There was the thrill of knowing that he had planned and carried out a guerrilla operation, and entirely on his own. "I was just like one of Quantrill's raiders," he said proudly to Bobbi Jo Jackson when he arrived home and confessed what he had done. She smiled the kind of smile that could temporarily make him forget about the proper punctuation for footnotes.

—— LXVI ——

The shriek carried along the corridors of Graves Hall, all the way down into the basement, and up to the roof. Deans, vice-presidents, the registrar, administrative staff, everyone went running for cover. Only the Dean Responsible for Relations with the Mafia remained calm. He walked directly to the room where the shriek had originated, the Office of the President and CEO.

Felicia Butterworth was slumped in her chair, staring at a piece of paper. Her face was ghostly, reminiscent of the ghostliness of the Great White Moose at the moment of his resurrection. Or perhaps, to make an arguably more appropriate comparison (since, like Elizabeth I, she had flaming red hair), reminiscent of the chalky whiteness Elizabeth used to apply to her face to reveal her inner purity. Not that the whiteness of Felicia Butterworth's face betokened purity, inner or otherwise. It was a product of fright, the kind of fright that the Dean Responsible for Relations with the Mafia had never previously seen on her face through all their years together.

She held the piece of paper out to him. It was, as you probably have guessed, the note that Yale Templeton had left for her.

The dean read the note and shook his head. "So the letter was a forgery," was his only comment.

"A forgery," Felicia Butterworth repeated, her voice now drained of all emotion. "I'm a dead man."

They stood there, the two of them, staring at the note without exchanging a word. There was nothing to be said, really. The situation in which she now found herself was painfully apparent to both of them: A powerful mafia don had ordered her to get the evidence Yale Templeton had uncovered about Abraham Lincoln. Furthermore, the Don apparently had close ties with the White House. And what had she given him? (Or, perhaps, given *them*, the Don and the President both.) Why, a forgery! A piece of sheer historical fabrication! How long would it be before the Don ... before the President! ... discovered the truth?

It was the dean who broke the silence. "This may not be the catastrophe it appears to be," he said, making an effort to sound reassuring.

She did not respond, just exhaled deeply, blowing out her cheeks.

"Well," he continued, "it's been some time now since the Don sent his godsons to collect the letter, right?"

"Yes, more than a month."

"And you haven't heard anything from Chicago to suggest there's a problem?"

"I haven't heard anything at all."

"Okay, then let's assume the Don doesn't know the letter is forged."

She shrugged.

"That means we have time."

"Time for what?"

"Time to get our hands on the real evidence. Look, Templeton says ..." He handed the note back to her. "He says he's going to meet with the man who has the records we need. 'Legal records,' he says. He'll be meeting with him today, it sounds like. If we get possession of the records, you may be able to convince the Don to forget about the phony letter. Hell, if we're lucky, the letter says pretty much the same thing as the legal records. In that case the Don may never even *realize* the letter is phony."

The colour began to return to her face. "So you're saying I should tell Templeton, 'You get me the real evidence this time or else!!'" And she picked up two bags of Doritos and slammed them together, resorting to her favourite method of showing that she meant business.

"No! No! No threats! That's why he gave you the forgery. He panicked."

She sagged. "So what do you suggest?"

"I say we follow him."

"Follow him?"

"After his lecture. We follow him to the meeting. Then we deal directly with his contact. Hey, we can offer a lot more for the records than Templeton can. Or if necessary"—and here he took the brass knuckles out of his pocket and polished them against his sleeve—"we use a less negotiable form of persuasion."

Felicia Butterworth smiled. "As usual, Bugsy, your advice is impeccable. I knew there was a reason I keep you around."

The dean averted his eyes in embarrassment. "What we need to know," he said, still looking away, "is when Templeton gives his lecture."

Felicia Butterworth hit the intercom. "Dolores," she called. But her secretary was nowhere to be found. Or rather, she was to be found in a broom closet, where she was still in hiding. So the Dean Responsible for Relations with the Mafia went into her office and located the course calendar himself. As it turned out, all lectures for History 393, The American Civil War, were between nine and ten in the morning.

"What time is it now?" asked Felicia Butterworth, starting to turn pale again.

The dean looked at his watch. "Exactly 9:48," he replied.

"Then we may already be too late," she said, pushing past him.

"I doubt it," the dean replied coolly. "Templeton lectures right next door and I'm parked out front."

—— LXVII ——

The dean's watch must have been running slow because by the time they got outside, students were already filing out of the Lyceum. Or perhaps, excited by the prospect of seeing the legal briefs, Yale Templeton had rushed through his lecture. Then again it was not uncommon for students to leave his classes early. In any case, Felicia Butterworth and the dean concealed themselves in the shadows of Graves Hall to watch and wait.

It was just after ten when he emerged. But then he did something that they could hardly have anticipated. He got into a waiting car, a black Toyota Corolla driven by a blonde in sunglasses (who reminded the dean of Marilyn Monroe, only better looking). "Hurry!" the dean shouted to Felicia Butterworth, and he raced across Regency Circle toward his El Dorado. Just then, however, a silver Mercedes convertible swung wildly out from behind the Lyceum, slammed into the dean, sending him cartwheeling across the pavement, and raced off in what appeared to be pursuit of the Toyota. Witnesses would testify that the driver was cleverly disguised as a faceless bureaucrat. Next to him was a very handsome if somewhat masculine-looking woman who had been a touch heavy-handed with her makeup. She was wearing a chic, perfectly tailored purple cocktail dress and had a pink boa around her neck, which flapped seductively in the wind.

Felicia Butterworth ran over to the dean and knelt down beside him. His legs were pointing in four directions and his eyes had glazed over. Groans struggled up from somewhere deep in his chest. She snatched the keys out of his hand and flew toward the El Dorado. She grabbed the first student she saw and cried, "Can you drive this thing?!" The benumbed student nodded mechanically. She shoved him behind the steering wheel, then flung herself across him headfirst into the passenger seat. "Follow those cars!" she screamed. And as he turned the key in the ignition, Joel fell hopelessly, unreservedly, abjectly in love.

LXVIII

Like all mammals, moose are fond of salt.

SAMUEL MERRILL, *THE MOOSE BOOK*

B ut now we must turn our attention from the three cars careening through the streets of Toronto and step back into history. Just about a week back, mind you. By the sort of extraordinary coincidence that usually happens only in third-rate novels, the Great White Moose arrived at the cave of Slinger the Trapper just minutes after Slinger had set off on that fateful trip to Hawk Junction where he would learn that Yale Templeton had been appointed the Abraham Lincoln Distinguished Professor of the American Civil War.

It is Manifest Destiny that has brought the Great White Moose to this secluded corner of the Canadian wilderness. Of course, whether or not his destiny was in fact "manifest" to the moose himself might be open to debate. Who among us can claim true insight into the trajectory of his or her own life? So often what seems manifest (to the individual, to a generation, to a nation, to an age) is shown, with the passage of time, to have been mere delusion. That, I would respectfully submit, is why historians have always been a necessity. To expose the fantasies of the past. Not that Yale Templeton thought himself in the business of exposing fantasies. Nor, perhaps, do I mean to suggest that we should consider his existence a "necessity." But even the incremental compiling of seemingly trivial bits of information (with properly annotated footnotes) has its value. Or so, at least, goes the theory.

In any event, that the Great White Moose has arrived at the cave of Slinger the Trapper is a fact beyond dispute, whatever meaning the Great White Moose himself may attribute to it. He seems curiously undisturbed by evidence of recent human activity: water dripping off the charred logs of an extinguished campfire; the smell of roasted duck. Still, he is suitably cautious. He hesitates at the opening in the rock face and peers inside. The cave extends some distance back but is neither wide nor high. The single kerosene lamp Slinger keeps on hand is unlit, and so everything is shrouded in darkness. Just as well, because the trappings of the cave are hardly of a sort to encourage feelings of security in the moose or, indeed, any woodland creature. On the ground lies a large black bearskin, faded and torn from years of use as a rug. One wall of the cave is festooned with animal pelts—beaver mostly, but also deer and rabbits. No moosehides, though. Not currently. And no antlers, either. A small consolation for the Great White Moose, perhaps. But on a second wall, directly opposite, metal traps of different sizes and shapes are arrayed. Most are mottled with dried blood. So are the winter coat and snowshoes hanging on pegs nearby.

Slinger had chiselled four pine shelves into the granite at the far end of the cave. Here he kept a variety of canned goods for those days when he was disinclined or unable to go in search of fresh game. The truth is, as he admitted reluctantly to himself, he no longer had the energy or the enthusiasm for those extended hunting trips that had dominated his earlier years. As he did not admit to himself, he had also developed a taste for Chef Boyardee products, in particular Beefaroni, which he liberally spiced with garlic powder, Tabasco, and Worcestershire sauce. On the top shelf he kept several jars of Strub's kosher dill pickles. Old dills, not the newer ones, which he complained lacked bite. He had the cook at the diner in Hawk Junction order them in specially for him from Pancer's Delicatessen in Toronto.

The only items of furniture in the cave were a table and chair, which he had crafted out of cedar. He of course took most of his cooking utensils with him on his journeys, but near the table sat a large, empty pot. Next to the pot was a barrel filled with water. However, his principal source of liquid sustenance was (as you might have guessed) whiskey, many bottles of which—some filled, more than a few half-consumed—could be found in two cases pushed up against the wall where the pelts were hanging. (The remaining cases he stored in a root cellar outside.) There were empties as well, most lying on their sides close to the pile of twigs, maple leaves, and moss that served as his bed on those winter nights when storms raged and it was too dangerous to sleep outside.

I said there were only two items of furniture, the table and chair. That actually is a bit misleading. There was, of course, a cedar chest, more than fifty years old. It sat at the back of the cave, just below the shelves. There was a lock on the chest, although if the Great White Moose had been able to see in the dark and somehow overcome his colour-blindness, he would have noticed that it was thickly encrusted with rust.

"The moose's superiority in his sense of smell and hearing," Samuel Merrill writes, "much more than offsets his deficiency of vision." There were no sounds, so the Great White Moose effectively had to rely on his nose to navigate the cave. One smell overwhelmed all others: the bouquet of whiskey, which the moose found ... well ... intoxicating. But eventually (even as he was growing somewhat light-headed) he detected a faint fragrance of moss. And to quote Samuel Merrill yet again, "moss and lichen too are on his menu." The moose started toward what he assumed would be a delightful lunch. Who knows, perhaps at that moment he began to suspect that his Manifest Destiny was nothing more than to enjoy a carefully harvested and arranged helping of moss. However, as he moved forward, he stepped on one of the empty bottles of whiskey. The glass shattered, and while he suffered no injury, the noise startled him. Jumping backward, he bumped into the wall where the traps were suspended, knocking several loose. The largest one, when it hit the ground, snapped violently shut, sending a jagged reverberation bouncing back and forth off the walls and ceiling.

Unnerved, the Great White Moose started to shamble toward the faint light at the entrance to the cave. However, he caught a hoof on the large pot, lost his balance, and collapsed onto the chair and table. He jerked himself up and bolted forward, but stumbled into the barrel of water. Swivelling sideways now, he stumbled again, landing heavily on the cases of whiskey. This time the shattering glass left him with cuts and scratches.

You might expect that here he would surrender to panic. But, drawing on the internal resources he had somehow developed over the previous few months, he collected himself and, like a Civil War general who has discovered his adversary holds an impregnable position, prudently halted his advance. The farthest recesses of the cave offered the best hope for safety—or so it seemed to the Great White Moose at the time—and he started a strategic retreat. He had to rely largely on instinct now. Still, he managed to reach the very back of the cave without further misadventure. Or I should say, *almost* reach the very back of the cave. His last step turned out to be an unfortunate one, since his hoof came crashing down through the top of the cedar chest. As he struggled to free himself, the rusted lock tore loose, and the old wood split apart, laying bare the priceless legal records that the chest had sheltered for more than half a century.

And then, from directly above him, the Great White Moose heard a strange sound. He stopped thrashing about and stood perfectly still to listen. A jar of Strub's pickles had tipped over on its side and was rolling along the top shelf. And because Slinger had been careless when he put the jar away (an inevitable consequence of his choice of accompanying beverage when he ate pickles), the lid was loose. By the time the jar dropped over the end of the shelf, the lid had fallen aside, leaving the contents to spill onto the head of the moose. Pickles bounced off his nose. Brine followed, rolling across his lips.

Now moose, like all mammals, are fond of salt. As the Great White Moose stood there licking his lips, his disquiet began first to subside and then to give way to epicurean delight. He bent over, picked up a pickle, and sampled it. It was tangy, refreshing. He finished it, ate another, and then another.

And when all the pickles were gone, he continued to gorge himself, though now on the brine-saturated records at his feet. Which is why it is possible to say with some authority that, in addition to moss and lichens, in addition to the twigs, leaves, and bark of a variety of maples, in addition to willow, birch, alder, poplar, mountain ash, and witch hazel, in addition to the stems, roots, and pads of water lilies, and in addition to young spruces and ground hemlock and the leaves and twigs of other coniferous plants, moose like to dine on legal briefs. Or at least legal briefs that are well over one hundred years old and have been soaked in pickle brine.

The question of whether moose can experience a sense of guilt is intriguing but currently unresolved. Even if the answer is yes, we might well wonder whether the Great White Moose would have felt guilty about consuming—consuming in its entirety by the time he was done—a set of documents whose immeasurable historical significance was of interest only to a species he had long ago learned to mistrust. But then again, how else are we to account for the surging pain he began to feel in the pit of his stomach only minutes after finishing his meal?

─── LXIX ───

B ut now we must return to the car chase. You can visualize it by recalling
the famous chase scene from *Bullitt*: Steve McQueen in his Ford Mustang
GT careering through Russian Hill in San Francisco, pursued by and
pursuing the bad guys in their Dodge Charger, both cars reaching speeds
better than 120 miles per hour, both cars becoming airborne on Taylor
Street. Not that downtown Toronto looks much like San Francisco. I mean,
apart from maybe Spadina over by Casa Loma, the few hills would hardly
inconvenience a small child on a tricycle. In any case, Yale Templeton, Bobbi
Jo Jackson, and their pursuers have long ago escaped the city boundaries.
Still, the scene from *Bullitt* does conjure up the vehicular gymnastics, the
extreme danger, the riveting tension, and as we shall see, the spectacular
climax now being played out in the vastness of Northern Ontario.

Of course, in *Bullitt*, professional stuntmen performed the more dangerous
manoeuvres. Only Bobbi Jo Jackson among our three drivers has the skill
and experience to handle a car over difficult terrain at speeds three, four, or
five times the legal limits. Joel and the Executive Assistant to the Assistant
Undersecretary of Transportation have taken turns careening off street signs,
parked cars, fire hydrants, trees, utility poles, and each other. And then there
is the carnage the two of them have left behind. Only my regard for your

tender sensibilities, dear reader, prevents me from providing the truly gory details: the awful, and it must be said, needless, sacrifice of life, both human and porcupine.

You might suppose that the El Dorado, with Joel behind the wheel, would have been demolished in the chase. But in fact it has survived relatively unscathed. We can attribute that principally to the foresight of the Dean Responsible for Relations with the Mafia, who equipped all his vehicles with bulletproof glass, heavy-gauge reinforced steel, and special torsion bars and shocks. Still, how are we to explain Joel's ability to stay in visual contact with Yale Templeton and the Corolla or, when he loses sight of them, to find them again? Is it the overpowering love he feels for the woman barking out commands in the seat next to him? Is it maybe fear of the very same woman? Can we ever really separate the two emotions, fear and love?

And what about the Executive Assistant to the Assistant Undersecretary of Transportation? Is he driven by love as well? By fear? The Mercedes, unlike the El Dorado, suffers massive damage: The windshield is shattered, the grille, trunk, and doors crumpled like used aluminum foil. Two days later the rear bumper will be found at a construction site in Toronto near where the old Downsview Air Force base used to be. Three days later the convertible top will be found hanging, next to the pink boa, from the branches of a birch tree along an ATV trail. "Good thing the agent talked us into taking out collision insurance," commented the Executive Assistant to the Assistant Undersecretary of Transportation after broadsiding a tractor-trailer. But the President made no reply, busy as he was touching up his lipstick at the time.

Not that either love or fear alone can entirely explain how it was that Joel and the Executive Assistant to the Assistant Undersecretary of Transportation were able to keep pace, more or less, with the Corolla. Fortune played a role as well. When Bobbi Jo Jackson had cut across the construction site in Downsview—one of several unsuccessful diversionary tactics she attempted before heading out of Toronto—her front wheel kicked up a spike, which drilled a small puncture into her gas tank. After that she had to keep down her speed to conserve fuel. Even so, she was able to elude her pursuers long enough to pull off the highway and improvise a plug for the leak out of her thong and kazoo. But moments after she returned to the road, there they were again, in her rear-view mirror. Later on she was able to elude them for a second time. But now she was running low on gas. And when she stopped to fill up at a small convenience store just off the highway near Espanola (not far, as it happens, from the Ojibwa reserve where the Great White Moose spent the first, untroubled years of his life), the El Dorado and Mercedes shot past her. That gave her the opportunity to slip back a few kilometres and detour along an old logging road. But somehow, near Elliot Lake, Joel and the Executive Assistant to the Assistant Undersecretary of Transportation picked up her trail again. The chase resumed, continuing right through Sault Ste. Marie and on up the eastern shore of Lake Superior.

Which is where we find them now:

Swerving through a trailer park, where Joel and the Executive Assistant to the Assistant Undersecretary of Transportation flatten the shower stalls and slam into half a dozen mobile homes.

On to a garbage dump, where Joel and the Executive Assistant to the Assistant Undersecretary of Transportation plough into a pyramid of discarded car parts, sending more than a dozen tires bouncing across the ground and onto the highway. One manages to find its way into the back seat of the Mercedes.

Across the carefully manicured lawn and tennis court of a holiday resort (where remnants of the net end up entangled on the aerial of the Mercedes), and then down to the shore of Lake Superior, where Joel and the Executive Assistant to the Assistant Undersecretary of Transportation send tourists bouncing across the beach and onto the highway.

It is at this point, amidst all the mayhem, that Bobbi Jo Jackson decides her best hope for escape is sheer speed. Normally, of course, the Corolla would be no match for a Mercedes and customized Cadillac. However, she made some adjustments to the engine after she picked up the car from the rental agency. The Corolla—for some reason she always asked for a Corolla—is capable of travelling much faster than the maximum 180 kilometres per hour indicated on the speedometer. She swings back onto the highway and slashes past a convoy of truck drivers, who stare at her in amazement. Her wheels seem to barely touch the asphalt. The way ahead looks clear.

For more than half an hour she is able to run flat out. Then the highway starts to climb. A steep climb. On the right are trees and outcroppings of Canadian Shield granite. On the left is the awesome panorama of Lake Superior. Up and up the Corolla goes, higher and higher. Eventually the highway curves around a bend and then straightens out along a stretch that skirts the edge of a cliff. There is a lookout here where tourists can pull over and enjoy the spectacular view. Not that a man and woman travelling at speeds upwards of 280 kilometres an hour are likely to take advantage of that particular opportunity. But at least they appear to have escaped their pursuers. Bobbi Jo Jackson smiles as she virtually rises out of her seat to put full weight onto the accelerator. It takes her completely by surprise when Yale Templeton shouts, "Stop!!!"

LXX

The creature was every bit as majestic as Yale Templeton had imagined. Well, as majestic as a moose can be while rolling around in a wallow. A wallow, I might add, that included the last undigested bits of Lincoln's briefs. Which presumably explains why the Great White Moose was so obviously filled with happiness.

The wallow was in a clearing off to the right, elevated just a little above the highway. But after he stepped out of the car, Yale Templeton did not move toward the moose. Nor did he even bother to put on his orange balaclava or reach for his kazoo. He simply stood by the side of the road watching in mute admiration. The Great White Moose, if he noticed Yale Templeton at all, was evidently not the least bit concerned.

Meanwhile, Bobbi Jo Jackson had sprinted back down the road and into the woods just a little past the bend. She found the decaying trunk of a tree that had been uprooted in a storm and dragged it out onto the highway. Then she ran back into the woods and rolled first one and then a second boulder out next to the tree trunk. "That should do it," she said to herself, slapping her hands together. Then she scrambled back to the car and gathered up the jars of currant jelly, strawberry, raspberry, and apricot jam, honey, hot fudge, and marshmallow sauce (not to mention the litre-sized bottle of Mazola oil) that she had packed for the trip, that she packed for all their trips. She carried the containers down the highway and dumped them out in front of her makeshift barricade. Then she grabbed two flares from the glove compartment and concealed herself behind a large white pine.

It was not long before the El Dorado came hurtling around the bend. She took aim with one of the flares and fired it directly at the windshield. "Christ!" shrieked Felicia Butterworth, as flames scorched the glass. The car started to plane through the Mazola oil, honey, preserves, and sauces. It caromed off one of the boulders, spun backwards, then slid sideways across the highway toward the edge of the cliff. "Hit the brakes! Hit the brakes!" screamed Felicia Butterworth. But Joel was remembering advice his father had given him some years earlier. "My boy," his father had said, "if your car ever spins out of control on a slippery road, do *not* apply the brakes. Remain calm and turn your wheels in the direction of the skid." Since Joel always made it a practice to ignore advice his parents gave him, he did as Felicia Butterworth ordered and slammed on the brakes. The El Dorado shuddered to a stop centimetres from the cliff, flipped up on its rear bumper, bounced backward across the highway, then finally came to a violent halt in a stand of fir trees. Car, driver, and passenger were all left upside down, the latter two seemingly as inanimate as the former; although, on a more positive note, at least they remained in compliance with the provision of the *Ontario Highway Traffic Act* requiring use of seatbelts at all times.

Only seconds later the Mercedes also shot around the curve. Once again Bobbi Jo Jackson fired off a flare. Unlike Felicia Butterworth, the President did not panic, mainly because at that moment he was bent over painting Primal Chic polish on his toenails. "Damn!" he yelled, as the car started to slide and nail polish splashed up on the ruffled hem of his dress. As if in imitation of the El Dorado, the Mercedes planed through the Mazola oil and preserves and sauces, caromed off one of the boulders, spun backwards, then slid sideways across the highway toward the edge of the cliff. At that instance the Executive Assistant to the Assistant Undersecretary of Transportation remembered advice *his* father had given him many years earlier. "My boy," his father had said, "if your car ever spins out of control on a slippery road, do *not* apply the brakes. Remain calm and turn your wheels in the direction of the skid." Being a dutiful son, the Executive Assistant to the Assistant Undersecretary of Transportation had always done exactly as his parents had instructed. And so he allowed the car to continue spiralling. The Mercedes responded by executing a complete revolution and then coming to a standstill. However, its wheels continued to spin furiously, spitting up hot fudge and currant jelly and marshmallow sauce and Mazola oil. You might almost have thought it was taking a moment to consider its options. But then, as if bowing to the inevitable, it suddenly gripped the asphalt and rocketed ahead. Rocketed ahead straight over the precipice. Straight over the precipice, carrying its passenger and driver out into that oblivion to which, depending on your point of view, Divine Providence or the laws of physics so deservedly consigned them.

Or perhaps not.

LXXI

O r perhaps not. Some weeks after the magnificent state funeral for the President, carried live on satellite TV around the world, the *National Enquirer* ran a special edition with the following headline emblazoned across the front page: "PRESIDENT ALIVE AND WELL IN CANADA!"

The accompanying article, based on the testimony of an "eyewitness," claimed that the President had not been killed in a car accident, as the White House had reported, but had faked his own death so that he could escape to Canada and realize his childhood dream of living as a transvestite. If that sounded strangely familiar, it was hardly a coincidence. The President had gone, the article said, to take up residence in the very same community of expatriate Americans that Abraham Lincoln had helped to establish in the wilderness of Northern Ontario more than a century before.

Apparently in the first years of its existence the community had served solely as a refuge for transvestites. But Lincoln came to conceive of it as "a grand experiment in freedom." Not freedom the way so many of his fellow countrymen had come to define it, as mere license to pursue material advantage without restraint. Rather, freedom as an alternative to the vacuousness of everyday life. Freedom of imagination. Freedom to choose a personal identity unconstrained by conventions of race, ethnicity, religion, or even sex.

346 Michael Wayne

Of course, Lincoln was above all else a practical man. He recognized that, to create an environment in which imagination could soar, it would be necessary to adopt a social contract based on a realistic assessment of the human condition. In order to ensure that no person had to devote himself or herself exclusively to the necessary but mundane task of securing sustenance, the settlement would be a true commonwealth: a society in which material goods and the demands of labour would be equitably shared. Decision-making would be democratic, but approval of initiatives affecting the community as a whole would require consensus. In this Lincoln was drawing on the wisdom of the local Native population.

Of course, it would be forbidden for one individual to exercise dominion over another. To Lincoln, slavery was the inevitable result of all systems of hierarchy. Mutually agreed upon fantasies were the only exceptions he was prepared to allow. So, to use one of his favourite examples, if a woman (or man, for that matter) adopted the identity of the Queen of England, that would be perfectly acceptable, provided she made no attempt to prevent those she thought of as her subjects from pursuing their own personally satisfying forms of self-imagining. In terms of religion, individuals were free to practice whatever rituals they wished in their own homes but not to preach or proselytize. So-called sacred texts, Lincoln believed, were best understood as products of the human imagination, no less, no more. All who joined the community were expected to concern themselves with the here and now, not the hereafter, which he regarded as unknown and unknowable.

During the years that Lincoln remained alive, members of the community worked hard to turn his dream into a reality. But after his death, some of those who had been especially close to him became disheartened and returned to the United States. Left behind was a core group of only about a dozen settlers, bolstered from time to time by an unexpected arrival who had heard rumours about the "experiment in freedom." The most notable and surprising newcomer was President William McKinley, who, like Lincoln, staged his own assassination to cover his flight to Canada. However, during the early part of the twentieth century the population slowly dwindled, until by the 1930s there were only three men left and no women.

The rejuvenation of the community can be traced to 1935, when the famed humorist Will Rogers, in the wake of reports that he had been killed in a plane crash, slipped into Canada, and with the help of an Ojibwa guide, located what remained of the settlement. He set about to revive Lincoln's dream, a task made easier the following year when Amelia Earhart arrived and began airlifting in more disaffected Americans. Among her passengers were many well-known figures, including George Gershwin and Bessie Smith in 1937, and the brilliant blues guitarist Robert Johnson, a year later. Smith and Johnson had heard about Earhart's "underground airline" through a grapevine tracing back to the days before the Civil War, when slaves from the Old South had escaped to freedom in Canada West.

F. Scott Fitzgerald and Nathanael West reached the settlement together in 1940. They established a literary society, founded a small publishing house, and later collaborated on a novel based on life among the settlers, which painted a decidedly more optimistic view of human relations than either *The Great Gatsby* or *Day of the Locust*. Only a few years later the first professional athletes appeared, Lou Gehrig and Josh Gibson. The two renowned sluggers organized a softball league as well as a summer camp for children, both of which continue to this day. Glenn Miller arrived in late 1944, and during the following years took some of the burden for air transportation off the appreciative Earhart. Miller also brought his own mellow version of jazz to the community. Bebop followed in the person of Charlie Parker, who was of course attracted by the promise of artistic freedom. Parker recruited the young trumpet player Clifford Brown as well as Billie Holiday and the saxophonist Lester Young. Holiday and Young started up a small café, where they delighted patrons for many years with their haunting duets. It was just a two-minute stroll through the woods from the scaled-down version of Ryman Auditorium where Hank Williams performed.

The same possibilities for freedom of expression that were attractive to Charlie Parker proved a lure for Jackson Pollock. He produced a dramatic series of murals for the concert hall, which opened in 1958. Buddy Holly, Richie Valens, and "The Big Bopper" performed there the following February. However, probably no one had a greater impact during the decade of the

1950s than James Dean. Working with Carole Lombard, he revived the drama society that had provided so many pleasurable hours for Abraham Lincoln. Among the more notable productions Dean and Lombard mounted were the Shakespearean comedy *As You Like It*, and *Porgy and Bess*, which George Gershwin adapted for a Canadian wilderness setting. Dean also directed performances of the two operas and three musical comedies that Gershwin wrote after his move to Ontario.

It was, however, the decade of the 1960s when local culture blossomed most spectacularly. Sylvia Plath came and Flannery O'Connor. Ernest Hemingway and Jack Kerouac. Patsy Cline and Jim Reeves. Otis Redding and Sam Cooke. Dinah Washington. Judy Garland. Lenny Bruce. Marilyn Monroe arrived in 1962. Together she and James Dean set up the first film company. John Kennedy followed her a year later and Bobby Kennedy five years after that. But no one had a greater impact on the settlement than Malcolm X and Martin Luther King, Jr. United in their disillusionment with the American dream and united as well in their commitment to the principles on which the community was founded, they agreed to give up preaching, took up residence together, and led a series of educational seminars devoted to exploring how the meaning and exercise of freedom had evolved over the course of human history.

Since the 1960s notable Americans have continued to find their way to the settlement. Diane Arbus. Richard Brautigan. Anne Sexton. Robert MacArthur. Arthur Ashe. "Pistol Pete" Maravich. John Belushi. Natalie Wood. Bobby Darin. Duane Allman. Mama Cass. Marvin Gaye. Alvin Ailey, Jimmy Hoffa. Abbie Hoffman. More recent arrivals include Tupac Shakur and the Notorious B.I.G., John Kennedy, Jr., reunited at last with his father and uncle, Paul Wellstone, Hunter S. Thompson, Stephen Jay Gould, and now, finally, the President.

Today the community covers almost ten square kilometres. The cabins, numbering more than one hundred, are all modest in size but vary widely in conception. Some few are square and rough-hewn, like so many cottages across the Canadian north. Others are vibrant with colour and unique in design, distinguished by sweeping curves and odd angles. The very fine concert hall, with the Pollock murals, still survives, and in addition there is a theatre, a community centre, a hospital, a baseball field, and basketball and tennis courts. The favourite winter sport is, of course, hockey—non-contact hockey. Each December, when the lake freezes over, a delegation of young men and women takes on the task of sawing wooden planks and building a rink. And with the arrival of a caterer from San Francisco fifteen years ago, there is now a very fine restaurant serving a variety of traditional American dishes, ranging from Boston clam chowder to hamburgers to gumbo to barbecue to, of course, apple pie. The specialty of the house, however, is another dessert, a Lady Baltimore cake. Each year the caterer bakes a gigantic version in the shape of a moose for the annual Canada Day celebration.

Human nature being what it is, minor conflicts arise from time to time. Overall, however, the community is doing well. Material goods are by and large equitably distributed. And while there are occasional complaints that some or other resident might, say, contribute more to keeping the grounds clean, work seems to get done without anyone having to take on an undue burden. The settlement introduced universal health care long before the rest of Canada. But most noteworthy of all, given Lincoln's vision of human emancipation, each person is free to craft his or her own identity, and to change identities whenever and as often as he or she wishes. Race carries no public meaning in the community, nor, for that matter, do ethnicity, religion, or sex. You are who, or what, you imagine yourself to be.

This extraordinary level of freedom has produced an exceptional sense of closeness among residents. Everyone comes together to commemorate Lincoln's birthday as well as festivals marking important moments in the history of the settlement, and also for Canadian public holidays. Births are celebrated by all; deaths mourned by all. Each morning the caterer and a rotating crew of volunteers serve a communal breakfast—during the summer months on the shores of the lake, and during the rest of the year in the community centre. And once a week, at twilight, everyone gathers at a clearing in the woods to hear storytellers weave magic tales, to roast marshmallows over the campfire and make s'mores, and as the flames flicker low, to listen to Elvis sing "Imagine," accompanied by Jimi on guitar, with Janis, Jim, Kurt, and John Lennon himself providing backup vocals and Michael doing the moonwalk.

LXXII

A small item on a back page of the same special edition of the *National Enquirer* revealed that Felicia Butterworth had vanished under mysterious circumstances. Apparently also gone, under no less mysterious circumstances, was over half the three-billion-dollar university endowment fund. The Dean Responsible for Relations with the Mafia was said to be helping police with their inquiries.

In a 453-page press release, written in a language invented specifically for the occasion, Acting University President and CEO H. Avery Duck reaffirmed the commitment of the institution to "the very highest of ethical standards." Accordingly, as the first act of his administration, he distributed a 77-page memorandum to all cafeteria staff outlining the issues of principle to be addressed when considering which condiments to make available to students at dinner time.

─── LXXIII ───

S tand on Telegraph Hill in St. John's and look out to sea. Can you see a small boat, a clinker-built dinghy with a single sail? There would be a crew of two, a man in his thirties and a diminutive woman of advanced age. The woman is likely wearing a crown.

No, I can't see them either. But don't lose heart. The English never do. They are a resolute, tenacious people. Dauntless and self-assured. Utterly confident in the superiority of their culture and possessed of a quiet faith in their ability to prevail against all odds, no matter how seemingly hopeless. Remember, it was these very qualities that allowed them to acquire the greatest empire the world has ever seen. Of course, it is the same qualities that explain why they *lost* the greatest empire the world has ever seen. But this would hardly seem to be a good time to dwell on negative thoughts.

───── LXXIV ─────

W ho is that sitting on the floor, writing furiously, a pasteboard balanced on her knees? Why, it's Bobbi Jo Jackson! Scattered around her are sheets of bluish gray, wide-lined foolscap, much like the kind of paper Lincoln used. She has only been at work for a few days, yet the floor is already covered with hundreds of pages in her distinctive shorthand script. What we have here are the beginnings of her acclaimed work, *Manifest Deception: The American Plot to Take Over Canada*. By the time she has finished, she will not only have demonstrated beyond the shadow of a doubt that the White House was, and remains, deeply implicated in separatist activities in Quebec, but she will also have explored in unprecedented depth the history of American designs on Canadian land and resources.

Eventually her desire to understand the origins of American expansionism will take her back into the colonial period, and that in turn will lead to her second great project: English attitudes toward the colonization of Canada. Of necessity she will spend much of her time exploring records from the age of Elizabeth I. Among her most valuable sources will be *The Principal Navigations, Voyages, and Discoveries of the English Nation made by sea or over land to the most remote and farthest distant quarters of the earth, at any time within the compass of these 1500 yeares* by Richard Hakluyt the younger. After a trip to London to examine the records of the

Colonial Office, she and Yale Templeton will visit the quaint old Tudor cottage in Saffron Walden, then bicycle to Cambridge, where they will wander hand in hand along the backs and punt down the river to Grantchester for cream teas.

For her third work, she will revisit the history of French Canada. She will discover that the romantic stories woven by René Purelaine and his brother, while not without grains of truth, hardly do justice to the complexity of the Canadian past. Here she will begin to develop her groundbreaking insights into the delicate interplay between material interest and the stories historical actors tell themselves about their own intentions and the workings of fate.

There will be further volumes as well. On the Portuguese fisherman who made their way to the Grand Banks off Newfoundland during the fifteenth century, before the famous voyages of Cabot and Cartier. On the Vikings and their settlement at L'Anse aux Meadows. But most notably, on First Nations peoples. Relying heavily on oral histories gathered in interviews with Native elders (here her extraordinary linguistic abilities will prove invaluable), she will produce a series of award-winning studies ranging from a radical reassessment of how and when Canada was originally settled to a sensitive interpretation of contemporary Ojibwa culture.

Between writing books she will turn out scholarly articles for the Canadian Historical Association on various immigrant groups: Scotch-Irish, Germans, Italians, Jews, Greeks, Ukrainians, Jamaicans, Chinese, Vietnamese, Somalis, many more. And when she is done, she will draw on her years of wide-ranging research to produce what will become her most celebrated work, *Imagining Canada*, in which she will explore in great subtlety and depth how the Canadian landscape effectively served as a vast untreated canvas on which so many different people painted so many inspiring dreams. It hardly matters, she will conclude, that the dreams invariably turned out to be hopelessly naive.

After that there will be just one more story for her to tell, the history of the small settlement Abraham Lincoln helped found. "But you don't have enough evidence," Yale Templeton will protest. "All we know is what Slinger the Trapper told us. Think how paltry your footnotes will be." (Her footnotes, let it be noted, were always beyond reproach.) And so she will put her story in the form of a work of fiction, a novel. And in a whimsical moment, she will decide to call the novel *Lincoln's Briefs*. Needless to say, Yale Templeton will not get the play on words.

═══ LXXV ═══

B ut now it is time to say goodbye to that selfsame Yale Templeton. The question is: How best to go about it? I had thought, perhaps, to contrive to get him entangled in hemp rope and strapped to the back of the Great White Moose. That way the two of them could spend eternity together, shambling through the vast forests of the Canadian North. However, as you no doubt have noticed, I am already more than a little indebted to Herman Melville. One more borrowed allusion and you might charge me with plagiarism.

Had I decided to write a satire, I might have sent Yale Templeton off to Turkey to consult with a dervish, and then brought him home to cultivate his garden (if he had a garden). That was how Voltaire bid farewell to Candide. Or perhaps I could have had him, in the manner of Don Quixote, recognize the folly of his obsession (for the Great White Moose) and die a broken man. I might even have arranged to have a poignant epitaph engraved on his tombstone.

We live, however, in perilous times. More perilous, I have to believe, than the times in which Cervantes lived, in which Voltaire lived. Too perilous for satire it seems. An author today has an obligation to portray the institutions of our society with all the seriousness they deserve. Which I have endeavoured to do.

But to return to the problem at hand: How to take our leave of Yale Templeton? Love and history dominated his life, so arguably the sensible course would be to seek guidance from a work built upon the same themes. For reasons that will become clear momentarily, my choice is *Der Zauberberg* by Thomas Mann, *The Magic Mountain*. For those unfamiliar with the novel, let me briefly summarize the story line:

The central character, Hans Castorp, journeys from his home in Hamburg to the Swiss Alps to visit a cousin who is a patient at a small hospital, or sanatorium. While there he develops what appear to be the symptoms of tuberculosis and decides to stay at the hospital for treatment. Even though it is never entirely clear whether he has actually contracted the disease, he stays and stays and stays. By the end of the novel he has been atop the "magic mountain" for seven years. The better part of Mann's narrative is devoted to exploring the relationships Hans Castorp forms with the other residents at the hospital, both patients and staff.

There are a number of obvious parallels between the experiences of Hans Castorp and Yale Templeton:

Throughout *The Magic Mountain*, Hans Castorp remains confined, by personal choice, to the vicinity of the hospital. With the exception of one short trip to Chicago and another to Je-me-souviens, Quebec, Yale Templeton remains confined, by personal choice, to the province of Ontario.

Hans Castorp meets two men—Herr Settembrini, an Italian humanist and champion of scientific rationalism, and Naphta, a Jew turned Jesuit, pessimist, mystic, and proponent of terrorism—who command his attention and influence his understanding of European history. Yale Templeton meets two men—Slinger the Trapper and Louis Montcalm—who similarly command his attention and influence his understanding of North American history.

Hans Castorp falls in love with an exotic Russian beauty named Clavdia Chauchat. Yale Templeton falls in love with a stunning American blonde, Bobbi Jo Jackson.

But more than anything else, what links the two characters is their personalities. In the very first sentence of the very first chapter of *The Magic Mountain* we learn that Hans Castorp is "ein einfacher jungen Mensch": "an unassuming young man." Is there a more apt description for Yale Templeton? Elsewhere I have referred to him as a man "more acted upon than acting." It means much the same thing.

However, my point is not just that Hans Castorp and Yale Templeton are alike in being unremarkable men. It is that they are unremarkable men who live in extraordinary times. *The Magic Mountain* takes place during the years leading up to World War I. Yale Templeton is a contemporary of ours: yours and mine. He inhabits the same troubled world as we do.

In the final scene of *The Magic Mountain*, Mann leaves Hans Castorp wandering across the countryside, his fate uncertain. That seems eminently sensible to me. History can have no definitive end, and Hans Castorp is a child of history. Yale Templeton is a child of history, too. Let us leave him wandering as well. Wandering across the ancient landscape of the Canadian Shield.

Of course, the contexts Thomas Mann and I have created are not exactly identical. The countryside in which Hans Castorp finds himself is an unnamed battlefield in a horrific war, the deadliest the world had yet witnessed. Bombs are exploding all around him. He has to climb across the mud-spattered, blood-spattered bodies of other conscripts, fallen friends. His own prospects seem hardly more promising. "Deine Aussichten sind schlecht," Mann tells him.

And Yale Templeton? Well, despite what you may have heard, there is only minor danger involved in tracking a domesticated moose that has been painted white. And when he tires of his wandering, he can always return to his beloved facts and statistics about boot sizes and casualties and his equally beloved footnotes. He can return as well to the prestige that must inevitably attach to the first Abraham Lincoln Distinguished Professor of the American Civil War. (There is already talk that the university will commission a portrait of him by Phil Richards.) Then too, waiting for him is a woman who reminds people of Marilyn Monroe, but is even better looking. And brilliant, as it turns out. Chances are that he will be all right.

―――――――――――――――
―――――――――――――――

*Meanwhile, somewhere in
Toronto ...*

LXXVI

Meanwhile, somewhere in Toronto, Joel was in love.